THE

SNOW

BIRCH

Books by John Mantley

The 27th Day

The Snow Birch

THE

SNOW

BIRCH

JOHN
MANTLEY

E. P. Dutton & Co., Inc.

NEW YORK · 1958

**Library of Congress Catalog Card
Number: 58-7817**

AMERICAN BOOK–STRATFORD PRESS, INC.
NEW YORK

THE

SNOW

BIRCH

1

He was a small man built like a slender wedge, with broad shoulders, no hips, and a shock of unruly black hair. His eyes too were dark and his smile slow and rare and infectious. Ireland lay thick on his tongue and thicker in the fierce determination which burned in his eyes. He arrived in the north country with little more than the clothes he wore on his back. He found a hard but beautiful land of lakes and islands and white-plumed rivers, where the pointed noses of pine and fir nuzzled a wind-swept sky, and the black earth was broken by the gnarled knees of granite rock. A fierce, lonely land where men lived by the whistling thunk of a double-bitted ax and the cruel clang of a steel trap snapping shut on valuable fur.

At first, he knew nothing about pelts or timber and when, after the first snows, he tried to walk on the unwieldy snow-shoes, he floundered helplessly like a wounded antelope. The trappers and loggers shook their heads. They wondered what had brought him to Canada and he explained soberly that he had come to make his fortune. They laughed at him until they saw his eyes and they asked curiously how long he thought it would take. He replied with stubborn conviction that it must not take more than two years. He would trap in the winter and he would work the logging camps in the summer. They saw that he meant it. They warned him of the dangers of northern winters; of temperatures that plummeted to thirty and forty below; of the madness that sometimes overtook a man, alone and snowbound in the wilderness; of the knowledge a man needed of where and how to set his traps to make it pay well. And he listened and nodded gravely for he was not a fool. He asked a multitude of questions and he wrote down everything he was ever told in a little black book and pored over it by the light of a coal-oil lamp while other men slept. He haunted the trading posts until he knew the quality and value of furs as well as any man in the area, and because his persistence could not be denied, they taught him how to handle a dog team and how to pelt and stretch a skin and to set traps. Within a month, he spent the last of his little store of cash for supplies and disappeared.

Men offered long odds that he would never be seen again and were closer to the truth than they knew. In spite of his black book he got frostbitten and he almost died. He was mauled by a wolverine which had been caught in one of his traps. He was snowbound for three weeks, and for three days he hung on the verge of madness. He came back in the spring hollow-cheeked and wide-eyed walking like a man in a dream. But he came back with one of the largest fur packs in the province of Ontario. Men looked at him in awe. They told him nothing in the world was worth the punishment he was giving himself. They told him, too, that a man who now weighed little more than a hundred pounds would never get a job at a lumber camp where endurance and muscle power were at a premium. But the foreman of the third company he tried was a man who knew men. He looked at Tom Sharron's eyes instead of his wasted body and he took him on. Sharron swung an ax. Sometimes he was too tired to eat and for the first two weeks his hands were like raw meat. He never complained. When the lumberjacks saw the handle of his ax slippery with blood, they tried to do his work for him but he only thrust them aside and set his lips and went on driving himself. And in the privacy of his bunk in the logging camp he would pore over the picture of a girl. A lovely girl with

8

wide-set eyes and a proud head and he would stare at his torn hands and pray softly that they would heal soon. For the girl in the picture was young and she was beautiful and she would not wait forever.

He did not even have her word that she would wait at all. But he had a feeling and he never went against his feelings. He had met her at a picnic and from the first moment their eyes had met, he had felt a singing under his heart and a lightness in his head. They had said very little. There had been so little time. But their hands had touched and their eyes had looked deep. He had said finally and bluntly, "Are you spoken for, Mary Maureen?" And she had blushed and shaken the wealth of blue-black hair from her ivory skin, and the soft lilting voice of her said, "I am and I'm not. I've given an answer to no one. Would yourself be thinkin' about it?" And he had nodded gravely and said, "I would, but I've nothin' to offer." She had smiled then, the even white teeth sparkling in the sun, and she'd said, "There's those that have much and those that have little, but I've yet to meet the man that had nothin'."

He'd turned his hands over and looked at them and he'd held them up and said, "I've these and a great burnin' inside of me. And I've heard that in Canada a man with a will can make much with little. But there's the question of time."

She nodded. "There is that. But I'll be startin' to teach the graders again come autumn. . . . I'm thinkin' it'll go quickly."

"Would you believe a man if he said he loved you with his whole heart after just these few moments?"

She'd tossed her head then— Ah, the arch of that lovely neck! And she'd said with the gentle laughter deep in her black eyes, "I've learned not to trust the lot of you. There's no lengths you'd not be going to to turn a young girl's head." But she softened then and said, "Yet there's something in

9

you, Tom Sharron, that makes me think you'd not just be makin' conversation."

They had parted shortly after. He had gone to Dublin for a passport and then to the steamship offices. He worked his way to Montreal aboard a cattle boat and he worked his way to this logging camp and to three thousand and seventeen dollars in a year and he'd written once. Her reply was dog-eared and almost unreadable now, but he could quote every word by heart. She'd not said she was waiting but she was not taken either. Another year. Just one more year, and he could offer her less than she deserved but a good deal more than the nothing he had when he left. It was a nervous, comforting thought.

The next year was not quite as good because he found he couldn't wait through another winter, and he came out of the wood early with half a pack. But still he cleared twenty-one hundred dollars. He put most of his money in a bank in Montreal and he bought traveler's checks with the rest and he went back to Ireland. It was April and the crocuses were in bloom. He met her at the school. He was waiting in the doorway after she dismissed her class. When she saw him, she put a hand to her throat and bit her lip, then she brushed at her eye as if there might be something in it and she said, "So it's yourself that's back at last."

For the first time, seeing her standing there, the sun streaming through the window behind her and catching the lights in her hair after he'd dreamed so long, he couldn't speak. There was a great lump of something in his throat and that wild singing under his heart again. He just stood and looked and swallowed like a schoolboy till she came to him and took his arm.

They walked in silence. Out of the village and over the stiles and across the fields and up to the hilltop where the valley was green and soft below and the village all made of toy houses. Still at the end he couldn't believe it was real; that she was there on his arm, the softness of her close to him, the scent of her making him lightheaded and choking him up till he didn't trust himself to speak. They sat down on a fallen tree and after a while, because he couldn't think of anything to say, he took out his bankbook and his traveler's checks and laid them in her lap. But she didn't look at them. She looked at him instead and her eyes were deep-tender and soft for she saw how thin he was and the long scar on his cheek that the wolverine had made and how the two years had put lines in his face and shadows under his eyes. And she said, so soft he could hardly hear, "It's a great gift you've brought to the likes of me." He understood when she closed the books and the checks and handed them back to him, still without looking at either. And something had broken inside him. The lump came up from his throat and into his eyes and the sob tore itself out of him and she held his shoulders while he cried, the tears streaming from her own eyes, for she knew now she'd found a man she'd follow to the ends of the earth.

He told her about the land he'd found; about the green forests and the granite cliffs and the rich black soil and the lakes and the islands, and the loneliness and the glory. She'd said just two words, "Show me." He looked at her and he said, "But you'll have to be agreein' to marry me first." Her smile came back. The one with the sparkle of laughter deep down in it, and she said, "I did that the moment I first laid eyes on you. If it's the sayin' of the words you're thinkin' about, then let's get on with it."

And the words were said. The rich, sonorous words, "To love, honor and obey until death do you part." And he kissed her for the first time. He thought she was the loveliest bride the world had ever known, and there were few who could have proved him wrong. The white lace looked whiter than ever against the blue-black hair and the color in her cheeks was more vivid than the orange blossoms in her arms, and her eyes had a happiness that surpasses understanding. They fled out through a shower of rice and shoes and embraces and good wishes and went straight to the ship.

One month later they stood on another hilltop. In front of them, the broad evergreen hills swept away to the horizon, rich and green under cloud mountains marching across a wind-swept sky. In the valley, sun glinted on the surface of a lake bluer than any lake should ever be. The air swirled into their lungs, heavy with the scent of pine and wild flowers. Mary Sharron stood enraptured, trembling inwardly at the grandeur of it.

Tom raised a finger and pointed below where a small clearing among the close-packed firs was sparsely studded with miniature evergreens not more than two feet high. Among the new trees, daisies and buttercups made a carpet of white and gold. "There," he said, "there, where the big trees are gone."

Mary nodded, her eyes bright. "Yes, there."

He put his arm around her shoulders and drew her close. "I'd not want you to stay for my sake alone. It's not too late to change your mind. I want you to be sure it's what you want."

Mary stared for a long time. Then she turned to her husband. "It's all I want."

"It'll not be an easy life. In the winter, we'll likely be snowbound for weeks at a time and the temperature will go down to forty below zero."

She let her eyes run out to the horizon where the massed pines stood at attention, and she laughed, a bright infectious bubble of sound. "Well, we'll not lack for the means of keepin' ourselves warm."

"You'll have to cook over a wood stove. There'll be no plumbin', no conveniences of any kind."

"Are you tryin' to discourage me?"

He smiled again, the slow rare smile that brought the crinkles into the corners of his eyes. "You know better than that, darlin'."

"And haven't you been sayin' some shameful and outrageous things about my figure when your manhood was upon you?"

He blushed furiously while her eyes twinkled. "You're a brazen hussy for bringin' up the likes of that in the broad light of day," he said.

"Are you denyin' it now?"

"I'm denyin' nothin' a-tall, but I fail to see what it's got to do with whether or not you'd want to stay."

"I was only thinkin' that since you seem to be so taken with what the Good Lord has been pleased to give me, that livin' the way you describe it, there'd be little chance of me runnin' to fat after a few months."

He laughed outright and swept her into his arms. "Sure an' it's the truth you're speakin'. I never thought of it. An' now that you've put me in mind of. . . ."

"Tom Sharron, stop it! Have you no shame at all? What if someone came by?"

He grinned again. "Here? In the heart of this wilderness? It's one of the advantages that, in my modesty, I forgot to mention."

"You've no modesty a-tall, man, none at all." But her arms were tight against him as she spoke and her breath warm and quick against his cheek. He bore her back on the soft moss and her hair was a dark cloud against the waxen petals of the flowers. And the desire rose in him like dark fire and poured around her and into her and through her. The scent of the pine needles and the rich black earth was in their nostrils, and above them the white birches and the evergreens rustled in concert to their whispered urgencies. And something of all this entered into Mary Sharron along with the seeds of life.

13

For of this moment, a child was born. A child who was to know at once a great understanding and a great loneliness. For there was in him the spirit of the wilderness.

He was born with a full head of hair that was as black as midnight. He had his mother's dark eyes and his father's small-boned, almost delicate face.

Mary bore him in the enormous four-poster bed they had brought with them from Ireland. There was no doctor, for Robbie Sharron came into the world at six minutes past midnight on Christmas day, when the snow was piled to the level of the windows around the new farmhouse. Tom heard the child's first cry as he ran between the great cauldron of water bubbling on the kitchen stove and the books on midwifery lying open on the dining room table. He came and took the red squalling bundle and tied off the umbilical cord as the books had said. And he washed his son and wrapped him in soft flannel and put him in Mary's arms. He looked at the little pinched face, the mottled skin and the tightly shut eyes and he knew why he was a man and why it had had to be this woman above all others. And he had the beginnings of an understanding of many things he had not known before. Later, after she had slept, they unwrapped the baby together and went over him from the top of his head to his miniature toes and they found him perfect. And they held to each other and they looked at him again. Outside, the wind swept the snow against the panes and somewhere, far off, a wolf howled his loneliness to the night, but inside the room the fire crackled warm and secure, and Robbie Sharron nuzzled frantically at his mother's breast, gulping and gasping and sucking so that they heard the milk splash in his stomach with every mouthful, and they looked at each other in wonder and delight as parents have done since the dawn of time. This they had wrought together.

Abruptly, Mary cried out softly. "Oh! Lord save us!"

"Darlin', what is it?"

"It's nothin'. It's just he's so strong, he hurts!"

"It's a wonder he's not destroyin' you entirely. He's no control a-tall."

"He's starvin', the poor little thing."

"Are they all like that?"

"Like what?"

"I mean, do they clutch at you with their little hands and gulp so you can hear it splashin' in their insides like a fountain?"

"They do. But there's few that have the strength of this one."

"I'll not argue about that. I put my finger in his hand an' he come near to squeezin' it clean off."

"He looks like you."

"He don't look like much of anythin', if you'd have the truth of it, but just the fact of him puts a catch to your throat."

She adjusted the blanket tenderly. "He's beautiful. I'll not have you sayin' otherwise."

"Do they all have hair like that?"

"Certainly not. It's a rare thing for a child to be born with hair you can comb, and it so black, too."

"He's got shoulders like a stevedore. Why do you suppose he doesn't open his eyes?"

"He's only a few hours old. Will you give him time?"

"But I'd like to know the color."

"They're blue."

"And how do you know?"

"Here, look."

"Look out now! You'll hurt him! Saints preserve us, they're bluer than forget-me-nots! Will they stay like that, do you think?"

15

"I'm not sure, but I think they're always blue at the first."

"And when do they change then?"

"After the first few months."

"The wonder of it! Why has he stopped eatin'?"

"He's had enough."

"He's awful still. Are you sure he's all right?"

"Don't you see he's almost asleep? Here, put him in his cradle."

"Me? But I don't dare. He might come apart in me hands!"

"I've seen you handle a newborn lamb. There's little gentler than your hands. Take him."

"Mary, I . . ."

"Take him!"

Gingerly, he lifted his son, his brow creased with anxiety, and he crossed the room as if he were treading among eggs. He laid him gently in the cradle and covered him. When he turned back, his wife was asleep.

He stood for a long time watching her. The spread of her dark hair on the pillow, the soft curve of her lips a little pale now from what she had been through, the swell of her full breasts beneath the coverlet. And he turned and looked at the cradle which had been empty and waiting all these breathless months and where the new little life now slept quietly, the hiccoughs gone. And he bent down and kissed his wife tenderly on her forehead and this was the real beginning.

2

The rabbit had its long pink ears laid back flat against its body. Its eyes were bright with pain. The haunches trembled slightly and another tiny, naked, gluey bundle was deposited on the straw. The rabbit lay panting for a few seconds and then turned her head to examine her litter. Six of them were of a size, but the seventh was smaller than any of the others. After a minute the doe licked them clean. She struggled a little on the straw and the blind mouselike offsprings sensed that food was near. Drunkenly, they floundered and fumbled for her teats, blindly planting their feet on each others' heads and stomachs, forcing their brothers away from the source of food. After a while six of them were feeding gluttonously, but the seventh and smallest was not strong enough to squeeze his way in. He wriggled pitifully on the straw.

Outside the cage a boy perched precariously on the edge of an old egg crate, his chin cupped in his hands, watching. He was a small child burnt to the color of dark mahogany by the summer sun. His feet were bare and he had a pair of faded denim overalls pulled over his naked shoulders. The grubby hand resting against the cheek showed half a dozen minor cuts and scratches, but the fingers themselves were long and well formed. He had a shock of unruly black hair, one lock of which had fallen unnoticed across his forehead, and above the big dark eyes the black brows were drawn together in an expression of concern. After a moment he opened the cage and lifted one of the normal babies away from the mother. He set the smaller one in its place. The little one flung its head back and forth frantically, then found the teat and began to nurse. Robbie Sharron settled himself in satisfaction but, even as he watched, the rabbit he had pulled away began to struggle back. There was a soundless but ruthless battle and the smaller one was more deprived of what should have been his birthright. Robbie frowned impatiently and replaced him again. Again he was butted away. Robbie shook his head then pulled the crate closer to the cage. One by one he pulled the larger nurslings away from the mother and set the weakest one in their places. When they finally stopped feeding, the little one had had a little more than the rest.

Satisfied, Robbie shut the door of the cage, put one bare foot against the frame and pushed. The crate on which he was sitting began to tilt backwards at a perilous angle. He pushed harder. The crate overbalanced. There was a moment of breathless falling then he tumbled into a pile of straw on the floor of the barn. He lay there blowing the chaff from his face by directing jets of air from his mouth with his lower lip. In the rafters above him half a dozen mourning doves were waddling importantly around each other making gurgling noises like air bubbles in a water pipe. Robbie cooed at them, then abruptly pulled himself up from the straw and went out of the barn scuffing his feet in the soft dust of the yard. Outside the door the bear cub saw him, made a helter-skelter run in his direction, fell over his chain and ended up in a ball of dust and fur. Robbie laughed, unclipped his collar and cuddled him. The cub wriggled ecstatically and tried to lick his ear. Robbie buried his face in the cub's fur and brought it away smudged with dust and a piece of straw dangling from his hair. "Be quiet now will you?" he said. "I want to see your paw." The cub wriggled even more rapturously while Robbie snickered. "Will you give over for a minute, you crazy thing?" He finally got the paw in his hand and looked at it carefully. The infection where the porcupine quills had been drawn was almost gone. He set the cub down and clipped him to his chain again.

Tom Sharron came out to the back porch. He said, "Top of the mornin' to you, lad."

Robbie looked up from his preoccupation with the bear and grinned. "The rabbit has had her babies!"

"Has she now?"

"Yes. One of them was that puny I had to help him nurse. He'd have died for sure if I hadn't been there."

His seven-year-old face was suddenly grave. "Father, it's not fair at all. The littlest ones need it the most."

"There's no denyin' that, Robbie, but it's nature's way."

Robbie frowned. "But he might turn out to be prettier than all the rest, or smarter maybe."

"He might."

"Well, I'll not be lettin' him die."

Tom nodded helplessly. "I'm sure of that."

"Do you know I saw Lightnin' this mornin', Father?"

"You mean the fawn with the blaze on his forehead? The one you had for so long here at the house?"

"Yes, sir. Just at sunup it was. I was there at the door to the barn and Lightnin' came out and stood at the edge of the wood right there where the dead pine rises above the rest. He looked straight at me, Father. Do you suppose he remembers he once lived here?"

"I don't know, lad. It's been more than two years since you set him free. But then again there's no tellin' with the dumb creatures. I'm glad he's all right."

" 'Tis strange to remember he was once a wee thing suckin' the milk from my fingers. Can I go to the beaver dam?"

Tom smiled at the abruptness of the transition. "Are you finished with your chores then?"

Robbie picked up a wood chip with his bare toes and drew

19

an uneven circle in the dust next to a tuft of bruised grass. "Well, I . . . I'm *almost* finished."

"Almost, is it? And what have you left undone?"

"Well, you see what with the rabbits and all, I'm afraid I didn't quite finish the choppin'."

Tom took out his pipe and glanced toward the woods. The evergreens sparkled in the bright sun and the tall lean birches were like white beckoning fingers. It bid fair to be the warmest day of the year. In an hour or two the heat would begin to swim off the corrugated roof of the root shed. It must be hard for a lad to be cutting wood on a morning like this when the world was spread out before him waiting. "All right, lad, off with you."

Robbie's face creased with delight. He was off running practically before the words were out of his father's mouth. He ducked through the rail fence and started across the potato field running with that peculiar intense gait of the very young.

Tom watched him till he disappeared into the woods and then turned and went back into the kitchen. Mary had her hands deep in flour and she looked up brushing the hair back from her brow with her forearm. "Is it over then?"

"What?"

"Why the birth, man. Did you not know your son was up before dawn to make sure it went all right?"

"It's over. He saved the life of a puny one." He shook his head ruefully. "I'm not sure but I think we now have forty-five rabbits. We'll be up to our ears in fur come autumn."

"Did you speak to him about it?"

Tom rubbed a hand across his chin sheepishly, "Well now, I meant to, lass, but I—well I just couldn't get it out of me."

Mary sighed. "Sure for a great lout of a thing like yourself you've not the courage of a mouse where the lad's concerned." But her eyes were soft.

"Where is he now?"

"Off to the woods like the divil himself was after him."

"Can you tell me now what he does when he's out there all alone?"

Tom grinned. "Why he talks to the bears, girl. Did you not know that?"

"You're out of your head, Tom Sharron!"

"I'm only goin' by what he says."

"Do you not realize that nine-tenths of what he says is make-believe?"

"Well, I thought so myself for a while but now I'm not so sure." He pulled his nose thoughtfully. "Do you mind the time last week when he was late for supper and I went lookin' for him?"

"I do. You were gone a terrible time too if I remember right."

"Well, it was a fine evenin'. The air was warm and soft without a breath o' wind but there was a gentle stirrin' all around like the earth itself was breathin' softly. And when I got among the trees I couldn't bring myself to start cryin' out after the boy in a great bawlin' voice. It would've been like hollerin' in a holy place. So I just went on walkin' softly and I came upon himself quite by accident. He was sittin' at the foot of a great fir tree just off the deer run, all scrunched up and as quiet as a little mouse, his big eyes watchin' everythin'. And I got a strange feelin' inside me and I thought how odd it was for himself, so full of runnin' and leapin' and hurlin' himself about most of the time, to be sittin' there like he was carved from the livin' stone and not so much as blinkin' an eyelash. So I stood there just watchin' an' not wantin' to disturb him."

"But what was there to see?"

"Nothin'. Nothin' a-tall that I could discover though I watched till my eyes ached from the tryin'. I thought I'd been quiet, mind, and I was well behind so he could not have seen me, but after a bit he turned and looked straight at me. His eyes were sparklin' with divilment and he says gentle like, 'Sure and they'll not come out, Father, with you makin' all that noise!' Noise is it! I tell you for part of the time I don't think I was even breathin'."

Mary laughed. "Well, what was it he was expectin'?"

"Why the partridges, girl, and the rabbits and sometimes a fox or a deer. He sits downwind of them so they don't smell him and he sits so still they don't hear him and they come out of their burrows and they bustle about the weeds payin' him no more heed than as if he were a part of the tree."

"I wonder if it could be true. Has he told you about the beaver?"

"He has. He swears by St. Patrick himself he's seen the beavers buildin' their dams and lookin' after their young. Now you know yourself there's scarce a man in this whole country's seen this. They set up sentries, an' when anythin' comes near the ones that're set to watch slap their great flat tails on the black water and a man's lucky to get within a quarter of a mile of their colony without their disappearin' entirely. I've lugged canoes over more of their crazy dams than I like to remember but I've yet to see a beaver except in a trap. If it's true he's seen 'em it's uncanny."

"Well, true or not he'll be comin' to little harm watchin' the beaver. It's the bear I'm worried about, or is it pullin' my leg you were about that?"

"Well, I was sort of. It was only yesterday he told me and I couldn't help laughin'. He said he was watchin' one of the otters have dinner. You know how they take clams out of the water and eat them on rocks in the middle of the stream. And along comes this bear—lookin' to catch himself a trout in the shallows, I suppose—and he gets to within about five feet of the lad before he sees him."

"Saints preserve us!"

"All there is between Robbie and the bear is a wild rasp-berry bush. Well, the bear looks at the lad over the top of the bush and he cocks his head on one side and sort of grunts in surprise and Robbie, not to be outdone mind you, grunts right back."

"Oh, Tom, Tom! The lad is mad!"

"Well, they go on like this, gruntin' back and forth, until I guess the bear gets tired of the conversation and ambles off. Accordin' to the lad the fur around the creature's mouth was all stained with the juice o' wild berries and he had a big patch of burs stuck right on the tip of one ear. Do you know what he called it?"

"What, man?"

"Droll!"

"Droll?"

"Droll. That's his own word for it and one he learned from you, no doubt. It looked so droll, mind you, it was all he could do to keep from laughin' right in the creature's face."

"And do you believe this, man?"

"I tell you, I don't know. One moment I think it's all the greatest nonsense I ever heard, and the next I begin to wonder. All I do know is that the last thing I'd call several hundred pounds of wild animal five feet away from me is 'droll.' But that's what your son insists he was. And friendly for all that."

"Tom, you've got to speak to him."

"About talkin' to bears?"

"Stop that nonsense, now. Do you think we ought to forbid him to go into the woods alone?"

"Oh, I don't think we can do that. He's been let run free too long. He wouldn't understand."

"But if it's the truth he's tellin' then he's flirtin' with death every moment of the day."

"Well, I did *talk* to him about bein' careful."

"And what did he say?"

23

"He said he was never anythin' else. He pointed out that the animals don't hurt him a-tall. And I had to admit it was the truth. He's never got so much as a scratch from one of them."

"He does seem to have a way with the creatures, there's no denyin' that. Do you mind the time he brought home the marten with a broken leg and neither of us could get near it?"

"I'll not forget that soon. And that's another thing. Could you not explain to him, without hurtin' his feelin's, that we've not time to be nursin' all them sick animals he brings home to us. It's a movin' thing the way he can't stand to see them suffer and all, but the house is a menagerie. I feel like Jehovah to the wilderness."

"Tom Sharron, that's blasphemy! And who was it who brought home that bear cub and set it down right in the middle of my clean kitchen table?"

"Well, what was I to do? Let the poor thing limp around full of porcupine quills for the wolves to get?"

"And do you think your son feels any different about the creatures he wants to help?"

"Oh, there's no use talkin'. I might as well complain to the wind. Would you give us a kiss?"

"I would not after the blasphemy you've just been utterin' Be off with you now. Have you nothin' atall to do this mornin'?"

Tom pulled himself to his feet and sighed. " 'Tis slaves to our women we are, all of us . . . it's a pitiful thing to see."

"Pitiful, is it? 'Tis lucky you are to have a fine strappin' woman like myself to do the work while you loaf around complainin' because we have to feed a few helpless creatures that are too weak to look after themselves."

He seized her round the waist and buried his head in her neck. "You're right about one thing. You're a fine figure of a woman."

24

She struggled, "Will you stop that? Can't you see I'm covered with flour?"

"Am I made of steel that I can watch you with fire in your eyes and breast heavin' and not lay hands on you? Ah, 'tis a terrible temptation y'are for a weak thing like myself."

"I'm married into a house of crazy people! I've a son that talks to wild bears and a husband who's daft entirely. Don't you see I've work to do?"

He released her. "All right. But is there some little thing I could do this mornin' to show you how much I love you?"

"You could get us some venison, that's what you could do. We'll be havin' the last of it for supper."

He shook his head dubiously. "I've not seen a sign of deer about the place for nearly a month. Three times I've been out and three times I've come back with my hands empty."

Mary's eyes got the glint of laughter. "Well, if you make as much noise in the woods as Robbie says, it's no wonder you don't get near the creatures."

"Near them! I tell you there's not a sign of them."

"It'll do no harm to try again. And take the boy with you this time. He's that eager to go he's about to burst."

"So, that's it, is it? Don't you know he'll be under my feet every inch of the way?"

"That's as may be, but I'll not be surprised if he shows you where they've been hidin' themselves."

"It's nonsense you're talkin' but I suppose I'll have no peace from the pair of you till you've had your will of me. I'll take him come mornin'. It's too late this day. And I hope the both of you will leave off pesterin' me."

She leaned over and kissed him lightly. "It's a terrible life we lead you, I know. Now away with you so I can finish here or there'll be no bread for supper."

3

Robbie was standing in a small glade in the woods, a green garter snake coiled up his bare arm. He was watching the way the little red tongue forked in and out of the mouth and the dry sinuous body writhed and twisted in fluid movement around his wrist. From a nearby tree, a gray squirrel scolded him raucously. He looked up laughing and let the snake go. He began to coax the squirrel, holding out his arm. The little animal ran nervously halfway down the tree, stopped, stared, and then fled behind the trunk. A second later it edged into sight, tail flicking alertly. Robbie coaxed it again. It flitted down the tree, across the ground and halfway up his pants leg. He slowly put his hand in his pocket and took out an acorn. The squirrel scrambled the rest of the way in a hurry. Once squatted on Robbie's wrist, it seemed to lose most of its fright. It held the nut in its tiny forepaws and turned it over and over with scrupulous dexterity, then split the shell with its sharp white teeth. It crunched the meat, its plump jaws quivering with delight.

Robbie began to walk through the woods. The squirrel stayed on his hand. When it had finished the nut, it ran down to the pocket of Robbie's overalls and stuck its head inside. It found another nut and emerged holding it in its mouth. Robbie laughed again. "You're nothin' more than a thief, is all!" he told it darkly. The squirrel cocked its head on one side and examined Robbie with its bright birdlike eyes, then leapt to a nearby branch and flicked out of sight.

The forest was thickening now. The great trunks of pine

and fir reared themselves around him, walling him in, dwarfing his tiny figure as he followed the narrow deer trail. If he looked up, he could see patches of bright June sky through the sharp spears of the pines and here and there shafts of sunlight filtered through to the forest floor, bathing the lush green ferns, the black rotting windfalls, the creamy fungus oysters and the curlings of white birch in a haze of pale gold. Off to his left, he heard the crash of saplings followed by the muffled snuffling of a bear. Ahead of him, a porcupine waddled solemnly across the trail. Beneath his bare feet, the path was moist and cool to the touch and he moved as confidently as a man might move through a long familiar room. Each tree and fern was at once unique and familiar to him. He saw, in passing, the outcropping of gray granite where only last week he had come upon a red fox, its jaws scarlet with blood, holding a partridge between its paws. Rusty spots were still on the stone. There was the tree beneath which he had crouched last autumn, his heart hammering in awe and wonder, as he watched two great moose in clashing conflict. Here, the rings of white fungus where he had cut his name last summer. If you looked very close, you could still see the faint outline of the big R.

He searched the moist earth for signs of deer but there were none. For some reason the deer had stopped using this run. They now came to water from the far side of the stream, ranging back up toward Thunder Rock and around to the east corner of the lake, but there were bear tracks, followed by the prints of two small cubs. Here at the edge of the run, the cubs had scuffled and rolled in the brush not more than ten minutes earlier for the fern fronds were fresh-crushed and a drop of white sap oozed out of the broken stem of a milkweed. A rabbit bolted out of the undergrowth to his left, lanced across the path and flung a handful of bright red stump rot onto the path with its flying feet. Robbie grinned. "Sure an' that's one rabbit you've missed, Mr. Fox," he crowed happily. A bluejay chattered noisily and then a whole covey of partridge rustled away without taking flight.

Abruptly the forest began to thin and he saw the bright glint of sun on water. The ground led him gently down to the stream and he stepped out of the shadow of the trees into the open. After the soft gloom of the forest, he had to squint against the glare, and the small patch of white sand was hot against the soles of his feet. Ahead of him, a shiver of minnows flashed across the sand bar and was gone. He stuck his feet in the water, worked his toes into the sand and stood stock-still. After a second, the minnows came back. They'd already forgotten that they'd been frightened. They cruised aimlessly round his legs and out over the edge of the deeper water where the sand bar fell away. The hot sun felt good on his bare head and shoulders. It bounced off the ripples in the water and exploded against the face of the granite cliff a few yards upstream. From the branch of a tree anchored precariously halfway up the face of the outcropping, a kingfisher plummeted down, knifed into the stream, then hurtled upward, bearing a small trout in its beak. The trout wriggled loose and began to fall back toward the water. The fisher banked steeply, dived, caught the fish a split second before it struck, then wheeled and raced its reflection down stream, a white and cobalt blur against the dark green of the trees. Robbie was sure the bird had dropped the fish purposely just for the thrill of that swift banking turn and dive to recapture it.

A big dark shadow drifted slowly into view along the edge of the bar—a rainbow trout! Robbie watched it. It floated lazily under the bank to his left where the water was shadowed by a big willow bush. Robbie eased himself down on the grass and withdrew his legs from the water until he was lying full length on the bank with his head and shoulders over the stream. The big trout was an undulating shadow at the bottom of the pool, its gill covers moving lazily, sending up tiny puffs of white sand. Robbie slid one hand into the water so slowly there wasn't a ripple. Inch by inch, he moved the hand down until it was directly behind the fish. Once the tail twitched sharply and the fish tensed for flight, but a second later it relaxed again. The hand in position, Robbie began to move it slowly back and forth in almost imperceptible movement. The trout spun around lazily. It looked curiously at this new underwater plant. It swam over to it and then lay still. Robbie moved his finger a fraction of an inch and touched the fish's side. The fish didn't move. It stayed where it was, its gills still moving rhythmically while Robbie gently moved his fingers back and forth along its scales. After a second or two, it swam groggily away as if a little drunk from this new experience. Robbie laughed. The Frenchman Dubois had taught him that trick. It had been very hard learning to do it. It took tremendous patience and he had failed more times than he could remember, but now he knew how. He could do it almost every time.

He flung himself on his back and expertly pulled the top section of a piece of grass out of its stalk. He chewed it till the sap ran fresh and cool on his tongue, then wound the pale green end around his finger. He looked at the water. The minnows were back—a black swarm on the bar. He got to his feet cautiously, leaped off the bank and landed with a splash in the shallow water. The minnows scattered like bright steel needles, and down the bank he heard the plop of frogs diving for the shelter of the bottom.

He decided there was still time enough for the beaver dam before lunch and began to wade downstream toward the lake. The water rose over his ankles and made his legs ache with the cold, but it was warming rapidly. Less than a week ago, it had been so icy he couldn't stand it. He turned over a brown stone and caught a big crawfish, getting his fingers pinched for his trouble. When he dropped it, it swam backwards with abrupt flicking motions and disappeared under the same stone from which he had dislodged it. Robbie shook his head at its perversity. You'd think having been caught under that stone it would look for a safer place to hide. He stopped to watch a pair of turtles basking in the sun and almost stepped on a bullfrog as big as a dinner plate. The frog was squatting on a lily pad and was too lazy to move. Robbie had to prod him twice before he gave a weak garumph and plopped into the water. Even then he didn't dive. He just lay there floating on the surface. Robbie prodded him gently again and he swam lethargically toward the shore. "You're goin' to get yourself eaten like that!" Robbie told him prophetically.

As he approached the beaver dam, he began to move as slowly as he could, pushing his legs through the water rather than lifting them so that not even the smallest droplet falling from one of his feet would break the normal rhythm of the stream. It didn't work. It had never worked. Before he reached the bend behind which the dam was hidden, he heard the sharp smack! of a flat tail on the water. He hurled himself forward, splashing wildly downstream, but he was too late. In the seconds it took him to reach the point where he could see the dam, the colony had been deserted. Or so it seemed. The water lay calm and unruffled in the sun. To one side a tree was half gnawed through and the ground around it littered with white wood chips but there was no sign of a beaver. He stood there breathing heavily and shivering a little from the cold water he had splashed on his bare skin. Only once had he succeeded in surprising the beavers at their work. That time he had come by land, inching his way cautiously through the thick underbrush until he could peer through the saplings at the brink of the pond. It had taken him almost two hours. Since then he had watched them hundreds of times, but always by walking boldly in and then waiting patiently till they got over their fright and emerged.

He stood there drinking in the scene before him. This was his secret place. His favorite haunt in all the forest. In the spring, when the stream was high with melting snows, it backed up here so that no trees grew below the high water line. But now, when the waters had receded, the shelving banks were lush with green grasses and a blaze of wild flowers. Their bright yellows, scarlets and rich purples were brazen against the glossy green of the pines and spruce. The sun blazed down and dazzled off the black water and, along the eastern edges of the pond, it made a pattern of spidery gold where it filtered through the trees. Beyond the high water mark, the trees themselves were massed, thick and dark, with great green ferns thrusting out from their roots and carpets of rich cool moss climbing to the trunks themselves. On the hottest days you had only to go a few steps into those thick shadows to feel the moist air touching your skin with a million cool fragrant fingers. At the far end of the pond, the beavers had built their dam, and on quiet days like this, the air was alive with the constant gentle murmur of waters whispering over the spill.

Where Robbie stood on the bar at the entrance to the pond, the water was clear as crystal rippling over the white sand but where it shelved away, it was a rich amber shading into jet black in the deeper pools. All the northern lakes and rivers were like this for they were all soft water fed by rain and melting snows. Wherever they were deep or still, centuries of decomposing leaves and vegetation had dyed them black as ink. If you swam underwater and looked up to the surface when the sun was strong, you could see the millions of dark specks, like motes of dust in a sunbeam, that gave the water its color.

Robbie moved forward slowly and the icy water moved

31

up to his calves and then to his knees. He shivered half in delight and half at the daring of an idea which was forming in the back of his mind. He had never swum this early before! It was really much too cold but. . . . He moved forward another step. The sand on the steep incline gave a little beneath his feet and he gasped audibly as the water touched his groin. That's where it was the worst. The next worse place was when it came up inch by inch around your middle and brought the goose pimples out all over your arms. He gritted his teeth and moved forward another foot. The sun was hot on his face and shoulders but the lower half of his body was numb. It was madness to go any farther. And all at once he knew he was going to swim. He *had* to swim! He could do it just by throwing himself forward, but somehow he knew that was not the way it had to be done. He had to get in slowly, step by step. He moved forward another pace and the water came up swiftly, making him gasp again. His teeth began to chatter and he was standing on tiptoe. He had his arms held high above his head. The water reached his neck. He took a deep breath, ducked his head under and then flung himself forward, arms flailing wildly. The shock tore the air from his lungs and left him panting for breath. His whole body was numb with the icy pain of it. When he put his face down the cold made his temples ache. He took another deep breath and began to swim across the pond toward the dam. He kept saying aloud, "Oh, oh, oh!" And then abruptly, when he was halfway across, his body got used to it. The cold became a tingling delight. He reached the dam, somersaulted, splashed ecstatically, then turned and swam back, picturing the beavers crouching in their huts beneath the surface, wondering what the wild commotion was above their heads. When he got to the shallows and stood upright, he laughed aloud in sheer delight. He'd done it! He'd been swimming the first week in June! He waded to the shore and flung himself down on the warm grass. His teeth began to chatter again and the goose pimples on his skinny arms made the black hairs stand almost straight, but he was filled with a delicious excitement. He had done a secret and daring thing and he was proud. He rolled over on his back, savoring the knowledge of his triumph. He hadn't even jumped in as he might have done to get it over quickly. He had walked in slowly, step by step, unflinchingly . . . well, almost unflinchingly. And he'd swum clear across the pond and back. He shivered as the warm sun drove the ice from his veins. He was warming now but the overalls were cold and clammy. He stood up and stripped them off and hung them on a branch of a tree. Where they had covered his skinny frame, the flesh was white as milk. He examined the sharp demarcation where white met dark, then stretched out again on the grass at the base of a rough old pine. Just above his head, an extrusion of gum had formed a bubble of bright gold. He touched it. It was warm from the sun and soft. Through the tough dry film of skin, he could feel the liquid gum oozing thick and viscous beneath his fingers. He took a stick and broke the membrane. A bright golden teardrop fell out of the wound and dropped on a curl of birch bark. He put his nose to it and let the pine scent tickle his nostrils. If he touched it, the gum would turn black on his skin and not even his mother's soap would get it off.

He rolled over on his other side and lay perfectly still watching the sun on the water. The surface broke and a black head appeared and the beaver swam swiftly toward the bank a few yards away from Robbie. It cut the water smoothly, leaving a widening V-shaped wake and a little bubbly swirl right behind its head. It reached the shore, hesitated, then waddled out toward the half-gnawed tree. When it began to work on the wood, other heads appeared all over the pond. In no time at all, the little glade was a hive of activity. The beavers knew Robbie was there. He was in plain sight. But they were so used to him by now that as long as he kept perfectly still, they ignored him. If he so much as changed position, everything would stop. All the black heads would swivel toward him and they would wait tensely for his next movement. If he got up, half a dozen tails would slap the water and they would disappear. He couldn't exactly call them friends because he had never touched one of them and they never came closer to him than a few feet, but they tolerated him—something few trappers could have been brought to believe. Robbie watched them in fascination. It never ceased to amaze him how they could manipulate branches several times their own size by using the leverage of the current, or how they packed the mud down on the dam using their tails like the flat side of a spade. They felled full-sized trees by sheer stubborn persistence, but they never knew where they were going to fall and he had seen them running frantically first one way and then the other as the tree began to topple.

He was almost dry now and he suddenly felt ravenously hungry. He glanced up at the sun. It had to be almost lunch time, but the overalls were still dripping. He couldn't go home soaking wet. His mother would have his hide for swimming so early. His stomach growled and he remembered the bowl of green apples he'd seen on the table that morning. He just bet his mother had made an apple pie for lunch. His mouth watered. He closed his eyes. He saw the green apple skins curling from beneath the blade of her paring knife; he visualized the white segments as they dropped from her slender fingers into the porcelain saucepan. He followed the pie into the oven and saw it come out, hot and steaming with the bits of apple nestled deep down in a golden crust and dripping with a rich honey syrup. It had been a hideous mistake to go swimming. Why was it he always thought of the consequences of something when it was too late? If he were late for lunch he might not be allowed to have any pie, and what was worse,

34

he might not be allowed on the front porch after supper. It was the severest punishment he knew, for those moments just after supper were the most precious in his whole day.

Right after the evening meal, his father would push his chair back from the table, glance across at his son and say, "Well, Robbie?" with that questioning note in his voice and the smile behind his eyes. And Robbie would run and get the whittling sticks and he and his father would go out to the front porch and sit down side by side on the steps. After a while, Tom Sharron would look slowly at Robbie and wink one eye and Robbie would wink back and then, surreptitiously, because Mary Sharron had told them both quite firmly it was not the gentlemanly thing to do, they would let out two—sometimes three—notches on their belts because each knew that the other was about to burst. After that Tom Sharron would heave a great sigh of relief and he and Robbie would begin trimming down the whittling sticks with smooth easy strokes. It was a wonderful experience to watch the clean white wood curling ahead of the knife and to see the smooth silky grain change as the knife bit deeper into its heart while the pile of white shavings grew at their feet. He could imagine the feel of the knife right now; the hilt of it hard against the heel of his hand and the touch of the rough bark in his other palm. They were good feelings, as familiar to him as the big blue veins which stood out on his father's wrist and forearm or the little laugh crinkles at the corners of his eyes.

Sometimes they talked while they whittled but mostly, they just sat in silence listening to Mary Sharron singing in the kitchen, and smiling grown-up smiles at the happy banging of pots from the inside. Afterwards, she would come out and join them. She would stare at them a moment as if in disapproval, and then she would say: "And what do you two men think you're doin' out here all by yourselves? And were you born in a barn, the both of you? Look at those shavin's all over my front steps!" Robbie would look at his father and bubble with laughter inside because he knew it was all right. They would start brushing away the shavings in mock terror while Mary Sharron tapped her foot impatiently. And when the step was clear, she would sit beside them, and sometimes she would put her arm around Robbie and sing the songs of Ireland in a soft clear voice that put a lump under your heart.

It was the same every night while it was warm enough to sit outside, and it never lost its charm; the soft warm smell of the summer night, the swooping of bats and swallows in the half light, the far-off cry of a loon, the crimson sky behind the hill and the dark silhouettes of the pine trees limned against the horizon, and sometimes when he was allowed to stay up very late, the northern lights would crackle through the evening silences before rushing up the sky.

But mostly, just at the moment when the sun sank behind the western hill, his father would lay a calloused hand against the back of Robbie's neck in the awkward gesture of affection the boy had grown to love and Robbie would get up and kiss his mother good night and go in to bed. Often before he went to sleep, he would hear the gentle murmur of their voices from the porch, and sometimes his mother would go on singing quietly long after dark.

Robbie could not know it as he lay there on the bank of the beaver pond in the bright morning sun, but ever afterwards the sound of a woman's voice in the summer dusk could move him almost to tears, filling him with a strange longing he could not quite understand. All he knew at the moment was that if he were late for lunch, he might be deprived of all this. He jumped up and felt the overalls. All over the pond tails smacked the water and beavers scuttled for the water in confusion. The overalls were still damp but a few white spots had begun to appear on the bib. He pulled them on over his warm skin, shuddering at the clammy touch.

It was worse than getting into the water, but with luck they might be dry by the time he got home. From far off came the faint sound of a dinner triangle. Robbie hurdled a fallen log and began to run.

He broke out of the forest, vaulted the fence to the potato field and sprinted toward the house. He arrived gasping at the porch and flung open the screen door. His father and mother were already at the table. He swallowed. "Am I late? I ran all the way."

Mary looked at him, the shadow of a smile touching her lips. "Well, I'm glad you told us you'd been runnin'. We'd not have known it otherwise."

Robbie grinned sheepishly. "Am I in time then?"

Tom motioned to a chair. "Sit down, lad. We've not said grace."

Robbie bounced into his seat and bowed his head. He could smell the apple pie and his stomach was squirming like a thing alive.

Tom Sharron said, "Dear Lord, we want to thank You this day and in this hour for the plenty with which You have blessed our table. For this Thy bounty we are truly grateful. Amen!"

Robbie flung up his head. "Are we havin' pie, Mother?"

Mary smiled. "Now how did you know that, young man?"

"I smelled it and I saw the apples on the table before I left this mornin'."

"Did you now?" She heaped his father's plate with stew from the great tureen and Robbie's eyes followed the plate like a starving animal's.

Tom grinned. "Mother, I think we'd best serve the lad first. I've a feelin' he'll not last till you get his plate ready."

"Tom Sharron, you take that plate back! How am I to teach the boy manners if you spoil him all the time?"

Robbie looked from one to the other. During the discussion, his own plate was not getting filled. "Mother, please!"

"All right, all right, here you are." She filled his dish and passed it. Robbie bent his head and took a great mouthful. It was nectar!

"Take your time, young man! You're not goin' to a fire." She rumpled his hair fondly and froze.

He raised his head sharply. "Yes, ma'am?"

"What's happened to your hair?"

"My hair?" He put a hand up to his head and got a cold empty feeling in the pit of his stomach that had nothing to do with hunger. His hair was wet! He swallowed. "Well . . . I . . ."

"Have you been swimmin', young man?"

Tom hid a grin behind his hand. "Oh I hardly think the lad would have been swimmin' this early, Mother. The water's that cold only an otter could stand it."

"Then would you mind tellin' me, Tom Sharron, how his hair got all wet?"

"Well now, he maybe slipped and fell. Is that it, Robbie?"

Robbie looked at his father gratefully. "Well I . . . I . . . did sort of stumble in the shallows."

Mary put her hands on her hips. "In the shallows, is it? And did you go in head first when you stumbled?"

"No, ma'am."

"Then you were swimmin'?"

He dropped his head. "Yes, ma'am."

"I thought so. Is it mad you are? And the water that cold you could get a cramp and go down before you could even cry out."

"But I wasn't swimmin' in the lake, Mother, only at the beaver dam. It's only a little pond," he concluded desperately.

Mary sighed and shook her head.

"Nobody told me not to, Mother!"

"But you knew it wasn't right just the same, did you not?"

38

"Yes, ma'am. But somethin' got into me. I just *had* to."

"But how could you stand it when it was that cold?"

"Well I don't exactly know but it was because of the cold I had to do it."

Mary spread her hands and looked directly at Tom. "And you know where he gets that from now, don't you?"

Tom grinned. "I do. An' I also know where he gets his nasty little sense of humor and his habits of pokin' into things that don't concern him a-tall."

Mary smiled in spite of herself. "All right all right."

"Will you give over now and let the lad eat his dinner?" Tom said. "It's nothin' so terrible he's done after all."

Mary shook her head. "You're impossible, both of you. You stick together like leeches. But mind you, young man, I'll not have you swimmin' again till the water is warm."

Robbie felt the cold spot dissolving slowly. It was all right after all. "Yes, ma'am," he said.

"Now eat before it gets cold and when you've finished your father has somethin' to tell you."

Tom raised his eyes questioningly. Behind Robbie's head, Mary set her lips in exasperation, then put her hands above her head and wiggled them in an imitation of rabbit's ears. Robbie, having missed his mother's pantomime, turned from one parent to the other in bewilderment.

"What is it, Father?"

Mary said, "Can you not finish your dinner first?"

"But I can listen just as well when I eat, Mother."

Tom took a deep draught of tea and cleared his throat. "Well now, I'll tell you, Robbie . . . you see . . ." He glanced at Mary beseechingly, but she folded her arms and waited. A sudden gleam came into Tom's eyes. "Well, it's like this, Robbie. Your mother says we're about out of venison and she's been after me to take you on the hunt tomorrow."

Over Robbie's gasp of delight, Mary exploded. "Tom Shar-

39

ron, it's a disgrace as a parent, you are! You tell that boy about the rabbits and be quick about it."

Robbie felt a start of anxiety. "What about the rabbits, Father?"

Tom rubbed one hand across his chin. "Well son, it's like this . . . your mother and I bought those rabbits to raise for food, lad, and . . ."

Robbie's face was suffused with alarm. "You're not goin' to kill them!"

Mary reached out and put a hand on his arm. "Now now, Robbie. Don't be jumpin' to conclusions."

Robbie refused to be placated. "What is it, Father? Tell me."

Tom shifted uncomfortably in his chair. "Well, lad, it's just that we started with three of the lovely little creatures an' now we've forty-five. By the end of the summer, we'll have over a hundred. What are we goin' to do with them all?"

Robbie swallowed. "We could build more cages."

"We could, son, but they'd soon fill them too. There'll be no end to their breedin'. Now you won't let us kill them, so what's to be done?"

Robbie chewed his lip in an agony of indecision. "Could we not let them go?" he ventured finally.

Tom shook his head. "I don't think that would be the right thing to do. They've grown up here in captivity. They're not like the bear cub and the fawns you had, and all the other animals you've brought back from the woods. They've no protective coloration and they'd not know how to look after themselves if you turned them loose. They'd all be dead from the foxes and the weasels in a day or two."

"I don't want them killed!" Robbie said desperately.

Mary put a hand on his arm again. "Robbie, we've no intention of killin' them. But will you let your father take them to town and sell them?"

40

Robbie stared blankly at his mother. "Take them to town? What would happen to them then?"

Mary took a deep breath and smiled bravely. "Well, I think perhaps we might find some other little boys to buy them. Boys who have never owned a rabbit before."

Robbie's eyes brightened. "They'd not be hurt then, would they?"

"I wouldn't think so. And you can keep two or three of them, so long as they're all males or all females, so there'll not be another forty of them come spring."

Robbie nodded vigorously. "Yes. That's fine. As long as they're all right. But what about the huntin'?" His eyes, now that he knew the rabbits were safe, were shining with excitement. "Is it true, Father? Are we really goin'?"

Tom smiled. "We are. You've been at me for a long time an' now your mother's pesterin' me too, I've no choice but to take you."

Robbie leaped from his chair and flung himself around the room. "Whee! I'm goin' huntin'! Glory hallelujah! Can I take the wooden gun you carved for me?"

"I don't see why not."

Robbie sat back down and finished his dinner, but so full of excitement was he that even the apple pie was an anticlimax.

When he'd left the table, Mary shook her head and smiled. "I dearly love to see him like that, with his eyes sparklin' an' the laughter bubblin' out of him like a young freshet."

"I hope he won't be too disappointed if we find nothin' on the morrow."

"It won't matter a bit, Tom. It's the thoughts of goin' out with you on a man's business that's put the fire in his head."

"I'm glad he took the business of the rabbits so well."

"So am I. But it's little help, you were," she said tartly. "If I'd left it to you, he'd never have been told."

41

"It's just that I can't bear to hurt the lad. He's so innocent-like about everythin', an' there's a pure goodness in him when it comes to the things he loves. It scalds the heart out of me to take his pets away from him."

"An' do you think I don't have the same feelin's? It's not a thing that either of us has much stomach for, Saints preserve us! But all the same I think we're wrong, the both of us, to be lyin' to him."

"It's only to save hurtin' him, lass."

"I know, I know, but I've a great fear in me that the time'll come when he'll have to know the truth and then all the fairy tales we've been preachin' to him in the past will only make it harder for him. We'd have been better off to kill the rabbits like we planned, no matter how he felt."

Tom drew his eyebrows together and squinted out at her shrewdly. "An' would you have had the nerve to do it, even once, knowin' the way he feels?"

"Oh stop it! You know I wouldn't, but I still say that we're doin' him a great injustice, the both of us. It's us that's needin' the courage to face the facts, not him."

Tom Sharron wiped a sleeve across his perspiring forehead and sighed. They had been out since dawn without seeing a sign of a deer. The sun was high now and Tom's shirt was stuck to his back, sodden with perspiration. More than anything else, he wanted a cool dewy glass of cider. He laid his rifle in the fork of a windfall and eased himself down on a stump. Robbie glanced at him anxiously. When Tom had come into the kitchen at daybreak, he'd found the boy sitting expectantly at the table, fully dressed. Getting breakfast into him had been a major chore. From the moment they left the house, Robbie had ranged back and forth in front of his father like an overanxious bird dog, carrying his wooden rifle at the ready and freezing into comic attitudes of alertness at every sound.

Tom raised his head and met the boy's eyes. "I'm sorry, Robbie."

"Aren't we going to hunt any more, sir?"

"Oh I don't think it's much use a-tall, Robbie. I don't think there's a deer within a hundred miles of this place."

Robbie dropped his eyes and scuffed uneasily at the black loam with one bare foot. "But you told Mother that we'd not come back until we found one."

"Did I now? Well, I may have said somethin' of the sort, but it was more in the way of wishful thinkin' than anythin' else. It was before I realized there was such a terrible dearth of game."

Robbie wet his lips. "Are we goin' home then, Father?"

"Unless you've a better suggestion. Your mother's set her heart on us gettin' a buck this mornin', but we've been searchin' for more than three hours."

"Couldn't we try just a little longer?"

Tom looked at Robbie and pulled his nose thoughtfully. The boy had his head down and appeared to be intensely preoccupied with an ants' nest at the base of the stump, but a slow line of color was creeping up the back of his neck—a sure sign that he had done something not entirely commendable.

"I know how you feel, lad, but there's work to be done at the farm. We can't spend a whole day chasin' a will-o'-the-wisp."

Robbie sucked in his lower lip, glanced at the sun, picked at a scab on his shoulder and thrust the tip of his big toe under a convenient rock. Finally he said, "No, sir."

Tom would have bet a good deal that this involved something more than just returning to the house. He tried again. "Is there somethin' you'd like to say, son?"

43

Robbie raised his eyes and stared into space a good foot above his father's head. He said in a very small voice, "I know where they are, sir."

Tom started visibly. "What's that?"

"I know where the deer are."

"Is it pullin' my leg, you are?"

"No, sir."

"You're standin' there, lad, and tellin' me you've let us tramp for three hours and all the time you knew we were lookin' in the wrong places?"

"Yes, sir."

Tom let the idea sink in for a moment and then, in spite of himself, he began to chuckle. "Well, in the name of all the fairies on the burnin' hill, would you mind tellin' your thickheaded father *why*?"

"I thought if I said where they were right off, you'd go there and shoot one and the hunt'd be over in no time a-tall."

Tom stared blankly.

"You've never taken me before and I . . . well, I wanted for it to last. We *might* have found a deer in this part."

Tom had recovered enough to speak. "But you don't really think so?"

"No, sir."

"And all that castin' about for signs and pretendin' you'd found one and the losin' it was all make-believe?"

Robbie nodded silently, head down.

"Would you tell me now where they are?"

"They're at the ford above the beaver dam."

"The ford! But in the name of all that's holy, that's less than a mile from the house!"

"That's why."

Tom scrubbed his chin ruefully with the back of his hand and grinned. "Will they still be there, do you think?"

44

"Not all of them. There's seven, you see. But one of them comes later than the rest."

"A buck?"

"Yes, sir, but he's small."

"All the better. We can't keep meat for long in this weather, even in the cellar. And how do you know about them?"

"I see them there every day. But mostly they come earlier—just after dawn."

Tom nodded in ironic amusement. "Naturally."

"Sometimes they come back again in the afternoon, and always at sunset."

"Tell me somethin', lad. Does your mother know that you have this wealth of information?"

"Yes, sir."

"I kind of thought she might. I'm in the middle of a conspiracy. Off with you now, and if we don't find that buck, me lad, you'll be in trouble. You and your mother both. Away with you!"

Robbie grinned delightedly. He seized his wooden rifle and started away at such a pace that Tom had to run to keep up with him.

They found the deer exactly where Robbie had said they would. The buck was just leaving the ford when they caught sight of him, but he was too far away for a clean shot and as they tried to make their way closer, the buck moved off upstream.

Tom sighed in relief. "Well, that's that!"

There wasn't a hope of trailing the buck through the country into which he had disappeared. The trees were so thick he could be a dozen feet away and not be seen. Tom sighed and hefted his rifle philosophically. "It was a good try, Robbie. Now we'd better get on home."

Robbie looked at his father in consternation. "But aren't we goin' to shoot him?"

"But he's gone, lad! Nobody could find him in that jungle."

"I can."

"Is it mad you are?"

"No, sir. I can find him. I know I can. Please, sir!"

Tom shook his head haplessly. "All right. The mornin's about done anyway. We'll have one more try, if you're that set on it."

Robbie led the way upstream and into the closely packed trees. It was immediately apparent to Tom that the boy was not trying to follow the deer. Instead he was making a wide circle that would bring them out ahead of the animal. The ludicrous game he had played after they left the house and tramped fruitlessly through the forest west of the house was forgotten. The boy was moving purposefully now, silent as an animal, with every sense alert. Watching him, Tom was struck by the fact that a stranger, coming upon him like this, could well have taken him for a spirit of the woods. His shock of unruly black hair growing low on his neck, his big dark eyes and his small intense features made him look precisely like one of the "little people" the Irish so dearly loved and were always professing to see. Only the tattered overalls which had been stitched and restitched at the knees, until Mary Sharron had just given up hope, betrayed the fact that he had any other home. And the nature of the place into which Robbie had led them added to the illusion. Tom had never been in a forest as dense as this. Great trees pressed close upon them, thick and immensely tall, so that a man walked on the forest floor far below their lowest branches in a vault of thin green silence. The air was damp and difficult to breathe, heavy with the scent of resin and decay. The light was a smoky blue, shading to purple in the darker shadows. Thick moss grew halfway up the mottled trunks and rolled away under foot, softening the outlines of the granite upthrusts and the eerie shapes of ancient windfalls. Tiny depressions cupped distillations of clear water and made a soft sucking sound when you moved your feet. Giant ferns grew lush in the hollows, and scarlet and ocher fungus made bright blotches of color at the bases of the trees. Nothing moved. Except for the muffled squelching of their feet in the damp moss, the silence was absolute. There was no sign of life. It was a place to put a spell on a man's tongue and strange thoughts in his mind. A place where the spirit closed upon itself and longed for the hot sun and a patch of open sky.

They had scarcely got fairly into this section when Robbie stopped and waited for his father to catch up. His small oval face was grave and his eyes darkly secret. He said in a husky whisper, "Follow me close now, Father. We've got to take a special way through here."

Tom restrained a smile with an effort. He nodded somberly. "I'll not forget. Lead on."

Robbie bobbed his head and started away again. They moved in single file for several minutes and again Tom was astonished at how sure the boy seemed of his direction. He never hesitated. He seemed to know exactly where he was going and yet one part of this forest was so like another that it would be easy to lose even an experienced woodsman in the green and empty catacomb. They went on in silence for another ten minutes. Then, ahead of him, Tom saw Robbie skirting the edge of an open space in the heavy growth of trees. It comprised a kind of shallow basin carpeted with the inevitable moss and then rose sharply at the farther side to a ridge about fourteen feet high. Along the rim of this ridge the trees reared themselves like black sentinels spreading their boughs high above the basin as if to conceal it but on the slope itself the only growth was one gnarled, twisted hemlock.

Robbie avoided the open altogether and toiled up the slope

hugging the border of trees on the left where the pitch was steeper and more difficult. Halfway up he stopped and looked back as his father broke into the clearing. Tom was tired. He assessed the angle up which Robbie was climbing and shook his head. He had promised the boy to follow close but it was much easier to cut straight across the open and the far slope looked easier to scale. He took one step and a stick landed at his feet. He looked up. Robbie was motioning him frantically to go back. He frowned, shook his head, and pointed ahead of him. He took another step and Robbie shouted, "Father, don't!" He scrambled quickly back down the slope. He said impatiently, "Father, I told you to follow me *carefully!*"

Tom sighed. "Robbie, don't you think this has gone far enough? I don't mind goin' after the deer but I don't see any reason why I should follow you over the most difficult trail you can find."

Robbie seized his wooden rifle by the barrel and straining forward he prodded the mossy skin of the basin a few feet ahead of them. The moss tore like rotten cloth revealing a thick black slime. An instant later the surface bulged upwards in a series of small ominous bubbles. The bubbles burst releasing a heavy fetid stench. Robbie straightened up. He said, "It's a quagmire, Father."

Tom swallowed and unconsciously moved back a step. His footprints filled slowly with a viscous black liquid. He shook his head. He said, "There's little need to tell me that now. You should have told me before we came into this place. And how is it that you said nothin' before?"

Robbie squirmed. "Well, sir, I did tell you to follow close—we had to be careful. I—I thought if I told you more you might not want to come."

"You were right. And what's got into you prowlin' about in a place as dangerous as this?"

"It's not dangerous, Father, as long as you're careful."

48

"Not dangerous! It's a miracle you were not sucked down at once the first time you came here."

"No, it isn't, Father. I was careful as could be. You see I knew there had to be some kind of danger 'cause the animals never come here. I was lookin' to see what it was that kept them away."

"They've more sense than my son and that's plain to see." He turned and surveyed the towering trees, the blotches of fungus and the unnatural growth of ferns. He said, "And are there more of these deathtraps around?"

"Lots. But this is the only big one I know of. You see the rains run down off the slope there and collect here in the basin. I think that's how it must have started."

"Do you now? Well, I don't want you comin' here ever again, lad, careful or not. And I think you'd better lead us back out at once."

"Please, sir! Don't make us go back now. It's only a short way till we're out of it. It's much easier to go ahead than to go back. And I'm sure the deer will be there."

"And what makes you so sure?"

"Well, sir, they circle up here often. I've followed them. I think because they don't expect danger from this side and they only have to watch one direction at a time."

Tom sighed again. "All right, if you're sure we're almost through then go ahead—but watch your step."

Robbie's face brightened. "There's no danger at all, Father, if you'll just follow me close."

Tom threw a rueful look at his footprints now filled with the black ooze. "Don't worry about that!"

Robbie turned away and together they toiled up the slope at the side of the glade with Tom taking care to stay directly behind the boy. Minutes later the trees began to thin and shafts of sunlight lanced through the tracery of boughs. The ground grew firmer under foot. Robbie stopped and glanced back, his eyes bright with excitement. He made a sign that they must move as cautiously as possible. Tom nodded and followed again as the boy cut sharply to his right into an area where the bush once more had its normal look and where the ground was more difficult to traverse because the underbrush was thick and dry. Tom did his best to move quietly but he shook his head in dismay. Robbie moved like a wraith, his bare feet picking their way among the dry twigs and sear bunches of grass as if each toe had an eye of its own. They went on for about a hundred yards and Robbie suddenly held up his hand and then pointed ahead. Tom strained his eyes but he could see nothing that remotely resembled a deer. He shook his head. Robbie slid back until he was directly in front of his father and extended his arm again. He was so tense, his fingers were shaking. On the air, he slowly traced the outline of a stag. Tom started.

The deer was there all right, but so beautifully camouflaged against the green sapling and the russet brown brush dappled with sunlight that you had to trace his outline with your eyes to make sure you saw him. Tom felt his heart begin to hammer in a familiar manner. He nodded and cautiously began to raise the rifle.

Beneath his father's upraised arm, Robbie was beside himself. The blood was pounding in his ears and his mouth had gone dry as a bone. It seemed to take an interminable time before his father got the rifle to his shoulder and drew a sight along the blue-black barrel. Then time seemed to come to a standstill. Robbie saw the rest of the action in a slow, exaggerated motion: the closing of the left eyelid as his father sighted, the deep breath which he drew and held, the gradual, inexorable constriction of the trigger finger. Then, suddenly, the rifle slammed hard. A bluejay screamed. A partridge exploded out of the ferns, its wings flashing in terror. The buck leaped high into the air, made a twisting leap and crashed to the ground.

Robbie screeched with delight. "You got him!" "Father, you got him!" He leaped forward, crashing wildly through the ferns, hurdling fallen logs and smashing aside the branches in his way.

His father shouted, "Be careful, Robbie!"

But Robbie didn't hear. Still burning with the terrible excitement of the kill, he lunged through the circle of trees and stood panting at the side of the deer.

The animal was not dead. The instant Tom fired, the deer, sensing danger, had spun toward him. The soft-nosed bullet aimed for the heart had struck, instead, at the base of the neck ripping through the jugular and shattering the backbone. It had emerged almost opposite the point where it had entered, tearing a great gaping hole in the animal's flesh. The deer's leap at the moment of impact had turned him end for end leaving the wound fully exposed. Now with the crippled animal still alive the heart was pumping frantically driving torrents of blood into the severed jugular. The blood exploded from the wound in a red fountain drenching the deer's golden coat and dyeing the earth and leaves a darkening scarlet. The splintering of the backbone had paralyzed the deer's body but its enormous wet-brown eyes rolled toward Robbie. They held him with a kind of hypnotic horror while his nostrils filled with the sick sweet smell of blood and the gluttonous buzzing of the flies thundered in his ears. Already it seemed like an eternity since he had reached the deer's side and still the wound gushed crimson. Robbie's temples pounded with an unknown terror; his eyes bulged from their sockets. And still he could not turn his head away. And then as he watched, the huge eyes began to glaze. It seemed to Robbie that in those last moments they pierced him with pathetic and helpless accusation. The liquid pain swimming in their depths changed

51

to frozen horror. The great body quivered once and was still. The eyes now were two blank ugly pools of jelly. Only seconds ago they had been aware of sun and shadow, leaf and stone. A fly lit and crawled slowly across one gelid eyeball and Robbie threw up. He threw up all over the blank, pitiful eyes and the vomit made a sickening pattern in the blood driving the flies into a droning frenzy. As from a great distance, Robbie heard his father moving through the brush and his voice saying, "Well done, Robbie. If you'd not seen him, we'd have missed him for sure!" The hot sting of tears was in Robbie's eyes. A choking sob tore itself out of his throat. He turned and ran. He ran blindly, unknowingly, and Tom Sharron hadn't a hope of catching him.

When Robbie stopped, it was only because he could run no farther. His limbs were trembling and his breath came in great convulsive sobs. And then he was sick again. He kept on being sick long after his stomach had emptied itself.

All he could see before him were the buck's glazing eyes and the blood turning black where it oozed from the hole in his neck. After a while there was a noise in the brush and he heard his father calling. He turned and crawled into the undergrowth. His father passed quite close to him, his face white and strained. Robbie bit his lips and hugged his knees to his chest. His mouth felt sour and the smell of his own retching hung thick and close about him. After a while his father disappeared. The sounds of his movement faded away. Robbie came out of his hiding place. He stood up. His head felt fuzzy and his eyes and throat ached. He walked for a long time, his face wooden—his movements slow as if only his legs were alive. Once from far off he heard his father calling and he stopped and listened but the voice was very far away and it wasn't repeated. He came to the shore of a lake. Beneath his feet a duck swam out from a crevice in the granite shoreline followed by nine miniature replicas of herself. Any other time he would have thrown a stick near her, to watch her plane over the water in a splashing frenzy with her brood windmilling behind her. Today he didn't even see them.

He looked up. It was past noon and great gray clouds were piling like shadowed snowdrifts against the wall of sky. The sun was bright and hot. It dazzled off the lake and hurt his eyes. It burnt his shoulders and his arms and his face. But it didn't warm him inside. He skirted a hedge of shrubbery and slid down the steep side of the outcropping to where the water met the earth at its base. His feet squelched and the black mud oozed coldly between his toes. He waded out into the water. When it was up to his armpits he let himself fall forward face down. He hung there till he had to raise his head and breathe. He began to swim slowly out into the lake. Fifty yards from shore he stopped stroking and let himself hang face down again. He opened his eyes under water. Near the surface it was the color of pine tree gum with little black specks in it like motes of dust in a sunbeam and a few feet below it turned purple and then black.

If only he had the courage! He stopped moving his arms and let himself sink. The water closed over his head and he went down slowly, keeping his eyes open. The amber color changed into the purple and then to the black he had seen from above. He closed his eyes. He let the air bubble out of his lungs feeling the pressure building up around his chest. His downward motion stopped and he moved his hands, pushing himself deeper. The pressure increased. The blood thundered in his ears. If he could only wait a little more, go just a little deeper it would be done. The pain in his chest became excruciating. He opened his eyes. There was nothing but blackness around him—the impenetrable darkness of death. He had only to open his mouth now and it would be over. He raised his head. Far, far above him there was a dim amber glow where the sun drenched the surface. He couldn't see the sky or the trees or the rocks. He would never see the sun again. Suddenly the panic in him broke. He pumped his legs and flailed frantically with his arms, clawing for the surface. His eyes were bulging from their sockets, his lungs bursting. For one hideous moment he knew he was drowning, then his head broke the surface. He gasped so frantically for air that he swallowed a mouthful of water and choked and gasped as he floundered. There was terror in him now and he looked around for the land. There was an island closer than the shore he had left. He swam toward it and pulled himself out on the strip of granite beach. He lay there trembling for a long while, then struggled erect and moved into the pines. There was a little glade in the center of the island and a kind of cave in the rocks. He flung himself down on the grass in front of the cave.

No one would ever find him here. Even if he died they would never find him. Maybe in a hundred years someone would camp on this island—a fur trapper or a fisherman and they would find his bones moldering in the grass and they would wonder what had happened. Would they be able to tell they were a boy's bones, he wondered. Or would they think some grownup had died? He wished he had had the courage to open his mouth under water. Then it would all be over. It was better to die when you hated your own father and yourself even more. He buried his head in his arms and sobbed. He was close to exhaustion and the sobbing emptied him. The sun warmed him. He slept. The sun moved across the sky and then was covered by the clouds. Thunder rolled and the rain came down suddenly drenching the earth. It awakened Robbie. He looked up into a sky that was almost black and the raindrops were icy against his skin.

The retching and the tears and that first terrible run had wrung every drop of moisture from his body and his skin was hot and dry. He shivered and crawled under the rock but he couldn't stop himself from shaking. He sat there with his knees pulled to his chest while the light faded and the rain lashed the earth to the sky with long gray ribbons. When it was over Robbie stared out from under the rock in the clearing that was almost black. A dismal world where the forlorn dripping of water made a cold pattern on the silence. Overhead the sky was a deep violet color but it was black in the east. In a few minutes it would be dark. Robbie's teeth began to chatter. He felt lightheaded and feverish. Silver spots swam before his eyes and he blinked and shook his head. The movement made him giddy. He got to his feet unsteadily and walked down to the water. He stepped in and the water burnt his ankles like fire. His teeth began to chatter again. He forced himself into the water. He swam lethargically. It took forever to reach the shore line. When he got out of the water he stumbled into the trees and started unsteadily toward the farm.

The moonlight slanted through the bedroom window and lay like liquid mercury along the ridges of the counterpane. It made strange patterns of silver and shadow in the darkened room, constantly changing form and shape as Tom Sharron twisted in a futile effort to sleep. Twice, Mary saw him rise and heard him cautiously enter Robbie's room. Both times he was gone a long time. When he came back the second time, Mary sat up in bed. Her loosened hair fell about her shoulders in a dark halo. In the soft luminous light, the oval of her face was extraordinarily beautiful. She put a hand on her husband's arm.

"Tom, you've got to get some sleep."

Against the window, his face was a dark blur. He didn't speak, but she heard the shuddering sigh which followed her words. Mary caught her breath, then threw back the covers and slid across the bed until she could touch him. He felt her

55

breasts warm against his back and she put her arms around him, pressing her cheek against the side of his face.

She said gently, "Tom, you must stop this."

He pulled away from her, setting his bare feet on the cold floor and staring out of the window. He sat silent for a long while, then he said thickly, "You don't know what it was like. Right up to the moment he saw the deer, he was so excited and so happy." He shook his head helplessly. "How could I know what it would do to him? How could I know?"

"We should never have let him go. We should have guessed that he couldn't bear to see anything killed."

"But he knew we were going to shoot the deer!"

"He didn't realize. At his age death is only a word. It has no significance a-tall."

"He's seen dead animals before."

"He's not watched one die . . . not one he helped to kill. That must have magnified everything in his eyes. Then, too, you remember he had that fawn Lightnin', the one with the blaze on its forehead, for almost a year. That would have made it worse."

"Will he be all right, do you think?"

"Of course he will. It's been a shock, that's all."

Tom shook his head again. "The way he looked when he came home. Like he was dyin' with the black horror of it inside him. And himself the happiest boy that ever was. It's enough to scald the heart out of a man."

"Will you listen to me now? It had to happen some time. Let's thank the good Lord that it happened now when we're here to comfort him and look after him."

"And how am I to face him, come mornin'? What am I to say?"

"You'll say the truth as soft as you can. That you take no joy in killin' and there are few that do. But it's a part of livin', like bein' born and growin' up and dyin' when your time is on you. It's not somethin' you can make out doesn't exist by turnin' your face away. You'll know what to say when you must."

She put her arms around him and held him tightly, rubbing her face against the stubble of his cheek. She got him to sleep at last, but she lay there wide-eyed and deeply troubled. Once she dozed and awoke to find him pressed close against her, his head in the hollow of her shoulder and one muscular arm thrown across her breasts. She bit her lips and absently stroked his hair as he slept. She hadn't found him so since the week prior to Robbie's birth. She had known then that he was more anxious than she. They had both professed confidence that Robbie would be born without complications, but inwardly both had been worried. Snowbound and miles from a doctor, it had not been an easy thing to face the birth of a child. And then, in spite of their concern, it had been an easy, natural delivery. The good fortune which had surrounded them since their first meeting had showed no sign of lapsing. Life had been almost too perfect. Something had to go wrong. The tragedy was that this could have been avoided because they should have known! Only yesterday they had seen the pain flare in his eyes when he thought the rabbits were going to be hurt.

Since the time he began to walk, he had appointed himself the personal healer and guardian of every wounded or broken thing which came within his reach. He'd brought home with equal solicitude a blind partridge or a maimed and vicious marten, lisping, "Fix it, Mother . . . it's hurted." And she had "fixed it" when she could. Sometimes it had been easy: put a splint on a broken leg; bathe a gash that a lethal tooth or claw had laid open to the bone. But there had been other times when she looked at the hapless burdens her son laid so trustingly at her feet and had asked for a miracle. And somehow, perhaps because of her son's blind faith in her, the mira-

57

cles had nearly always come. But she could see even now the anguish in his little pinched face, the helpless concern in his eyes, when, despite her best efforts, one of his little charges died.

What must he have felt when he saw a great beautiful creature like a deer with the lifeblood pumping out of it before his eyes? She sighed deeply. What wise man was it had said: "It was always in the obvious places that parents failed their children?" She had spoken bravely enough to Tom when he asked: "What am I to say to him?" But what, after all, was there to say? Would words be able to heal a wound opened by the nature of life itself? Would it help a child, whose self-appointed task had been the preservation of life, to know that Man was the greatest destroyer of all? That his food, his clothing, and most of his worldly goods were bought at the expense of the helpless creatures to whom Robbie had given his heart? Would the brutal truth of all this lessen the final tragedy of death in the eyes of a small boy? The irony was that he had been in the middle of it since he was born but only yesterday had he seen clearly what it meant. He had gone out to kill with his eyes sparkling with excitement. He had come home shaken to the core of his little being, walking in the rubble of his dream. And they had done this to him. They'd let him walk into it with his eyes open, helpless. And now while he was still naked and defenseless, his heart bleeding inside him, they had to twist the knife in the wound. They had to tell him: it's true, all of it. This is life. This is what goes on all the time. And you have to learn to accept it, because though your strength is the strength of thousands, you can't prevail against it. You can only die a little inside with the knowing. Finally, she slept.

Both of them were awake before dawn. They dressed in heavy silence, ears cocked for a sound from Robbie's room. They went into the kitchen and tried to find things to do.

When they heard him stirring, their eyes met. It was Mary who saw what they were doing. She forced a smile.

"Is it a wake we're at, the both of us? Are we tryin' to destroy him entirely, draggin' ourselves around like black shadows in the valley of disaster? It's a black enough mornin' the boy'll be facin' this day without our addin' to his troubles with long faces and dismal thoughts."

Tom straightened. "You're right as usual, lass. But I'd give a lot more than I own to have it over."

She came to him and kissed him lightly.

"Listen to him! The man that has faced a wolverine with his bare hands and a knife only, tremblin' like an aspen leaf in the wind at facin' a small boy!"

He shook his head. "I'd face the wolverine and a dozen of his brothers every day of my life for the next ten years could I but be over those few minutes."

"Will you show me what you're made of and smile?"

"I will, I will. Hush now. Here he comes."

Robbie appeared in the doorway. He was still pale. He stood on the threshold of the kitchen, his eyes downcast.

"Ah, there you are, Robbie," Mary said lightly. She came and led him to the table.

Tom looked across at him and shifted self-consciously. "Now then, lad, do you think you could manage some eggs this mornin'?"

Robbie shook his head and his voice was almost inaudible. "No thank you, sir."

Tom looked up at Mary supplicatingly. She said, "You'll have to eat somethin', lad. You've got to keep your strength up."

"Yes, ma'am."

"That's better." She went to the stove, slid two eggs onto a plate and brought it back to the table. Robbie lifted his fork dutifully and put it to his mouth. He chewed and then gagged,

59

trying to force the food down his throat. Mary bit her lip and put a hand on his arm. "Never mind, son. If you can't, you can't."

Robbie felt the tears welling up in his eyes. Suddenly, he flung himself out of his chair and into his mother's arms, sobbing brokenly. Mary held him tightly, stroking his hair. "There, there, lad! It's all right now, it's all right. Don't cry, lad, don't."

Through the sobs, his voice came chokingly. "Mother, it's that sorry I am for what I've done."

"Robbie, you've no call to be sorry. It's your father and I that are askin' your pardon. There's nothin' you've done that's wrong. Nothin' at all, lad." She gazed helplessly at Tom while Robbie's little frame shook in her arms. She put a hand under his chin and raised the tearstained face. "Look at me. Now listen to what I'm sayin'. There's no blame belongin' to you a-tall for what happened yesterday. There's nothin' you've done that's wrong. Do you understand that now?"

He nodded.

"Now then, dry your eyes and sit down." She urged him gently off her lap and back to his seat. "It's a man's world you'll be facin' from now on and I think it's only fair that you face it with a man's privileges. Will you take that glass of milk away, Father, and bring the lad a cup. I'm thinkin' a drop of coffee might do him a world of good."

Mary poured the cup Tom brought half full of coffee, filled it the rest of the way with milk, then added two large spoonfuls of sugar. "There now. Try that."

Robbie scrubbed his eyes with the back of his hand and looked at the coffee. It was the first time in his life he had ever been allowed coffee. Even under the circumstances, it was too great a privilege to ignore. He took the cup gingerly and raised it to his lips.

"Careful now, it's hot!"

"Yes, ma'am." He sipped it and straightened a little in his chair. He set the cup back down in an exact imitation of his father. Mary felt a catch in her throat.

"Do you like it?"

Robbie's voice was still unsteady. "Yes, ma'am."

"Good. Now then, Robbie. We've no wish to upset you, but after what happened yesterday, there're some things that have got to be explained. I'm thinkin' we made a great mistake in not takin' them up sooner. Will you listen while your father tries to make it clear to you."

A wild stab of anxiety hit Robbie. He got a cold, empty feeling in the pit of his stomach and he clutched his spoon desperately as if it were the only solid object in the room. He didn't exactly know what was wrong with him, but despite his mother's words, he knew he had done something unforgivable. He had failed his first big test of manhood. Not even the coffee sitting before him could deceive him about that. A man didn't get sick at the sight of blood. A man didn't run away from death. There was something wrong with him. And the terrible thing was he didn't want to be any different. He didn't want to kill things. He didn't want to watch them die. It wasn't right. No one, not even his father, would ever convince him of that. He stared desperately at a crack in the kitchen table, wishing he could crawl into it and be hidden from his parents' sight. If only he could die right now. Right this minute, so he wouldn't have to go on thinking about what had happened and what was going to happen as long as he lived.

Tom Sharron saw his son's knuckles whiten about the handle of the spoon and looked at his wife beseechingly. Mary bit her lip. She wanted to put her arms around her son and tell him he'd never have to hear another word about killing as long as he lived. But she couldn't do that. The longer this wound was left open, the more dangerous it would get. Better

61

to close it even if some of the poison was left inside than to let it fester.

"Go ahead, Tom."

Tom pushed away his untouched plate. "Robbie, I'm not much of a man at explainin' things but I'll do the best I can. Will you hear me?"

Robbie nodded again without raising his head.

"I don't quite know how to say what I mean, but I remember when I was little, I had a slingshot and I got tired of just shootin' at trees and stones and things, and there was this little bird sittin' on top of a bush, singin' he was fit to burst his lungs. I took me slingshot and I didn't think a-tall. I was all excited like you were yesterday and I flung the stone and I hit it. And all of a sudden, the singin' stopped and the poor little thing fell down all limp and lifeless. I ran over to it and I was that proud, mind you, that I'd hit it the first time and all, and I picked it up and held it in me hand. Its little soft body was still warm. And I knew that I'd done a terrible thing. It had been singin' its heart out from the sheer joy of bein' alive, and just to satisfy a foolish fancy, I'd taken away its life. And the awful thing was that nobody could ever give that life back. It was gone forever. Somethin' that God had put into the world for everyone to love and enjoy, I'd taken away. And I felt sick, just like you did yesterday, and I cried for a long time. Since then, I've never killed any livin' thing without a good reason. For years, it took all the strength I had to kill anything a-tall, even when I had the best reason in the world. Now there are men who like to kill. They hunt for the fun of it. I've even heard it said that it's man's instinct to hunt and to kill, for that's the way he kept himself alive when he didn't know how to grow things for food. But I've never had that feelin' in myself and I don't think you ever will either. But I've had to face the truth, as you've got to face it, that killin'—terrible as it seems to you now—is part of the pattern of existence. As much a part as . . . well, eatin' or plowin' or pumpin' water. It's part of the pattern God made when He created the world. The foxes kill the partridges and the wolves kill the deer, because if they didn't, they'd die themselves. You know that. You've seen it happen in the forest time and again." Robbie looked up for the first time, his eyes haggard.

He said, "But the animals kill because they *have* to. We don't!"

Tom took a deep breath. "Robbie, I'd give the world and all that's in it just to be able to tell you you've said the truth. But it's not so, son. If it weren't in part for the furs I trap in the winter, we'd not have this roof over our heads and you'd not have clothes to protect you from the cold when the ice is on the land. Your shoes are made of leather. Do you not see that an animal had to be killed before those shoes could be made? And then there's the question of food. A man can't live on vegetables alone. I've heard that some have done it, but I can't believe they've the strength to do a man's work. Man must have meat to live. And clothes to wear, and money to buy things he needs for himself and his family. Now whether he kills himself or buys the things that are made from what another man has killed makes little difference for all that I can see. Would you have me refusin' your mother, who I love with all me heart, the necessaries of life because I'd not take the pelt of a beaver or a mink? Don't you see that God makes the creatures breed and multiply because He knows that some must die for others to live? And when you come to see this, the killin' of an animal is not so terrible as it seems at first."

Robbie sat with his head down, the words swimming through his mind. He was old enough to see the truth of his father's words, but deep within was a hard core of rebellion. No matter what his father said, it was wrong for a man to kill! Nothing would ever make him believe otherwise. But it

63

was useless to argue. He had no words to make them see. He swallowed painfully and raised his head.

"Yes, sir. May I go outside?"

"Of course, lad, if you'd like to."

Robbie slipped from his place and walked slowly out of the kitchen door. After that first sip, he had not touched the coffee of manhood.

Tom glanced at Mary. "I said it all wrong, didn't I?"

She reached across the table and pressed his hand reassuringly. "No man could have said it better. But it's a hard truth for him to understand. It'll take time for him to accept it."

"Will he ever, do you think?"

"Faith and I don't know. Is it so important, then? So long as he faces the truth . . ."

"I don't know either. I only know I'd tear the heart out of myself and cast it in the dust if I could draw the sorrow from him." He turned and stared out the screen door at the fresh bright morning. "It is a strange thing," he said, "how the sun can be shinin' and the birds singin' and the world flowerin' with promise, and a little child can be carryin' a bit of darkness in his soul. He'll be lonely now. The world has changed for him in the past few hours." He pulled himself to his feet and went out.

Mary sat staring at the door. Then, she looked down at her son's first cup of coffee. She thought how she had waited for the moment when she would see the pride in his eyes when she set it before him. And that was another little thing she had lost. She bit her lip furiously, but the tears came in spite of it and she put her apron to her face. Mary Mother of God, they should have known!

4

Robbie sat scrunched up at the base of an ancient pine. Overhead the branches sighed and twenty feet away a porcupine rustled in a thicket. Robbie didn't hear them. He had his forehead squeezed tight between his fists while he stared unseeingly into the distance. His mind was churning with the things his father had said. They were all true. Life was a continuous circle of death and killing. The trout ate the minnows —the hawk swooped on the mouse—half a dozen animals fed on their smaller neighbors. He had seen these things happen. He had seen the red fox lunge out of a thicket and sink his deadly little fangs into the neck of a rabbit. He heard the rabbit scream like a baby in the instant before its death—the only time in its life it ever made a sound. And he had felt only a deep pity for the rabbit that it had not been more watchful. And he'd never hated the fox because it had killed. Why then should it be so much more terrible when a man killed? Why should the deer's great brown eyes, bright with terror, still be staring at him? Why should the buzzing of the flies still sound in his ears or the sight of the deer's bright blood still be in his eyes? He'd seen dead animals before. Lots of them. He'd even seen them die. But not close up like that . . . not with the knowledge that he had been responsible.

It was all terribly confusing. He couldn't sort out the conflict of emotions raging in him. One moment he would be hating his father and the next he'd be hating himself even more. And there was no way to make his parents understand. He rubbed his fists into his eyes. To his left a fox drifted through the undergrowth and scented the covey of partridge. He began to stalk. Robbie flung a pine cone at him. The fox bolted away—a rusty blur in the undergrowth. Robbie felt better. He stood up and started sadly for home.

For almost a fortnight the atmosphere around the farm was a little strained. Whenever a chicken or a pig had to be killed Robbie managed to be absent and on those evenings he had little appetite. Mary didn't press him and Tom pretended not to notice. Gradually things returned to normal. The shooting of the deer was not mentioned and Robbie never again asked to accompany his father when the latter was carrying a rifle. If Tom was bitterly disappointed he never let it be known. The incident was outwardly forgotten but each member of the family bore its scar.

Robbie continued to roam the woods and to make them a part of himself. He did not realize that he was storing memories for the future. He could not foresee that he was never to feel anything so delicious as the hard slippery surface of the dried pine needles beneath his bare feet, nor to smell anything so clean and pure as the scent which rose from the forest floor after a rain. Nor had he any way of knowing that the almost daily trips he took to Needle Rock down by the lake before day broke were to remain in his memory as some of the most perfect moments of his life. Almost every morning, after bringing in the wood and drawing the water from the well, he would slip the latch on the gate and be off down the road before the sun rose, feeling the moist, dew-laden dust heavy between his toes. Then he would cut across the cow field and think how tough his feet had become since the spring when the tender soles quivered at the touch of those same thistles he was now deliberately squashing beneath his feet. And very soon he would be at the edge of the forest surrounding the lake. It was a matter of moments to slip through the misty trees, slide down the pine needles of the slope, and come at last to the clump of spruce surrounding a big white birch from which he had decided he was going to make himself a birchbark canoe as soon as he was a little bigger. He would slip through a hole in the maze of underbrush beneath the trees, scramble up the steep, stone face beyond, and be poised on the topmost pinnacle of a big granite block. It was weird and wonderful.

In back of him, almost level with his face, were the still, silent tops of the trees beneath which he had made his way a few moments before, but in front of him was nothingness. A great void with white swirling mist and wispy tendrils of fog that ran out over the rock and curled themselves around his legs. Beneath that white blanket was the lake, but just at dawn the water was always hidden. Even the farther shore which was only a half mile away was swallowed up in mist, so he felt as if he were standing on the edge of the world.

He would wait patiently until the precise moment when the first rays of the rising sun had begun to add a golden tint to the top layers of mist, then he would raise his hands solemnly, stretch them out before him, and the miracle would begin. Inch by inch, the shimmering mantle would begin to rise from the lake, revealing at first only the still, black surface of the water; and then, as the field of vision widened, the little circular tracks where the water bugs made their merry-go-round, or the bigger ripples where the trout rose to inspect the morning. And then, slowly, the far side of the lake would begin to appear. At first it was only the rocks at the edge and then the fallen logs and broken branches, lying half in and half out of the water as if frozen in black marble. Finally, just about the time he could see halfway up the trunks of the nearest trees, the vague outline of the whole farther shore would be visible; and suddenly, so quickly that he was never quite prepared for it, all of the mist would be gone and there would stand the lake and the opposite forests and all the rocks and the strip of white beach smiling at you in the bright morning sunlight and daring you to pretend it hadn't been there at all a few minutes before.

Robbie made the pilgrimage almost every morning. It was his favorite enjoyment next to the front porch sitting after dinner. But along about the beginning of August, the mist on the lake became progressively thinner, until one morning when he arrived just before dawn, he found the water lying below him dark and quiet and somehow ominous without its customary covering. He ran home in a fever of excitement.

He burst into the kitchen, gasping for breath: "Father . . . Father, there's no mist on the lake!"

Tom Sharron, frowning, turned from his breakfast table to look at him. "Are you sure, lad?"

"I'm sure, sir. I ran all the way to tell you . . ."

Tom laid his pipe on the table and looked at Mary. He said quietly, "It's worse than we thought, then."

Mary knitted her brows anxiously and Robbie looked from one of his parents to the other in bewilderment.

"Father, why is the mist not there any more?"

"There's no moisture in the air, son. Have you not noticed how dry it is in the brush?"

"I have. Even the animals make a lot of noise moving around. But it'll be all right when it rains."

Tom picked up his pipe and sucked it somberly. "*If* it rains, son. If not, I'm afraid that we may be in for trouble."

"What kind, sir?"

Tom frowned. "Fire, lad." He glanced at Mary. "Has there not been a fire since he was born?"

She shook her head. "Not really. There was one in the next valley when he was a few months old. Do you not remember there was that farm that burned?"

"Ah yes. Now I do. But none that he's ever seen." He turned back to Robbie. "Fire is the greatest danger we face

68

here, son. It can strike faster than lightnin' and burn like a comet's tail. There's little a man can do if it gets a good start and has a bit of a wind to help it."

"Would the animals get burned?"

"I'm afraid they would. Those that don't get out in time. They'd fare better, most of them, did the fire not put them in a panic. I've seen them run straight into the flames when they might have got clean away if they'd only looked about them a little."

Robbie's eyes were wide as Tom continued: "I want you to stay close to the house from now on. Keep your eyes open and the first time you see a wisp of smoke, you run and tell me as fast as you can."

Robbie nodded gravely. "Yes, sir." He went out.

Mary passed her forearm over her brow. "Lord save us, it's hot, and it not nine o'clock yet."

Tom lit his pipe, dropped a little metal cover over the bowl and broke the match in his finger. "It'll be hotter."

"Will there really be fire, do you think?"

"Unless we get rain soon, I'm sure of it. The only question is how soon and how big."

They did not get rain. Each morning the sun staggered into the sky, roary-eyed and merciless, and each evening it plummeted out of sight trailing flaming promises for the morrow. The atmosphere became almost unbearable. The only cool places were the ice house, the preserve cellar, and the lake. But even the lake looked hot. It lay like a piece of polished blue glass in the center of the scorched earth; while the heat waves swam off its surface and hurt your eyes if you looked directly at them. The birds stopped trying to sing in the parched air. The dogs lay in the shadow of the house with their tongues lolling out. Even the fish would not bite.

Between the glaring white furrows of the fields and the ach-ing blue of the sky, nothing moved except the heat waves. The whole universe seemed to be waiting; tense, expectant and parched. In the forest, the wild creatures were more nervous than Robbie had ever seen them. A sound, which a few weeks before, would merely have frozen them into sharp attention, now sent them crashing wildly away without rhyme or reason, and the harried looks on his parents' faces told Robbie of their growing anxiety. The fire watchers climbed their towers, red-eyed and exhausted from days of watching and waiting, and still nothing happened.

And so the days went by and the crackling in the underbrush grew louder and the whispering heat swam over the land like a great undulating sickness, and the sun seared its way through the parched air out of a sky that was as blue and hard and brittle as a china plate; and the only sound in the universe seemed to be the droning of the beetles against the screens.

And at last it came. At eleven o'clock of a Sunday morning, about the middle of August, a thin white wisp of smoke rose straight up into the motionless air from behind the hill to the northeast. Almost at the same moment, the signal from the fire tower winked out the message which struck terror into the northland. Fire!

Within forty seconds of the alarm, Tom Sharron was off on the mare to answer the summons for help, but within forty minutes, the entire sky beyond the hill was blotted out by white smoke. Men poured in by the dozens, from an area covering over two hundred square miles, and passed the wild creatures coming out. Deer, bear, moose, quail, partridge, loon and porcupine fled in abject terror, while man in a tenth of their numbers rushed to meet his oldest and most terrible enemy face to face.

Late that first afternoon, Robbie went with his mother to the fire lines carrying food and coffee to the men. As they approached the fire area, the air was choked with dust and smoke, and so hot it seared their nostrils as they breathed. From the crest of the hill where his mother insisted he remain, the whole valley appeared to be enveloped in flames and smoke. He watched the fire roaring from tree to tree in a kind of insensate frenzy while great livid tongues licked at the sky, detonating volatile gases high in the air with a thunderous roar and a blinding flash. He saw giant firs go up in one single puff, like a torch, with a sudden, excruciating whooooooooom! of agony, and then continue to burn while sparks sucked on by the fire's wind ignited trees, three and four removed. He saw as well as heard trunks, that had taken a century to mature, go crashing down with a sound like exploding dynamite, tearing flaming gashes in the lesser trees and sending up great clouds of sparks and smoke. All the time beneath the sudden explosions of sound and the booming death screams of the spruces and firs was a steady, insistent crackling as of a thousand small rifles being fired at one time. He saw men staggering out of the smoke and ash, their hair and eyebrows singed by ground fires and their blackened faces covered by handkerchiefs to keep out the smoke, their clothes full of holes where hot sparks had fallen and burnt through before they were extinguished; men, red-eyed from the acrid smoke, tottering from exhaustion, rubbing goose grease on raw hands and seared faces, gulping mouthfuls of food and swallows of coffee; then returning once more to the uneven battle against the flames.

It was terrible and frightening, and at home that night, lying naked on his bed, his sheets soaked with perspiration, Robbie slept fitfully and dreamed of a great dragon made of fire whose cavernous mouth, belching flame and smoke, swallowed everything in its path, cutting a great, livid swath through forest, hayfields, barns and houses; and in front of it, Robbie was running frantically, feeling it coming closer and closer until he woke up shouting to find his mother shaking him and telling him everything was all right.

The fire raged for three days. Days in which exhausted men, eating when they could and risking their lives when necessary, fought it to a standstill. But victory was not achieved without sacrifice. One life was lost in the struggle. Tom Sharron did not come back.

5

In later years Robbie had only a very hazy idea of the period following his father's death. He remembered the vision of his mother sitting very still in her customary chair. In the vision she had a very white face and a very black dress and she stared straight ahead into nothingness. When he spoke to her she didn't seem to hear him. He remembered becoming very hungry and going out to the garden and pulling up raw carrots to eat because he was afraid to disturb her.

And later, after the people had come in black clothes—the men with their hats in their hands and the women with damp handkerchiefs, he remembered his mother going about the daily tasks of cooking and milking with expressionless face and dead eyes. Only these things remained. All the little incidental things and the big things, if there were any, disappeared.

He was too young to suffer the full impact of his father's death but some of the laughter went out of his eyes and the bright bubble of wonder through which he had looked at the world before the death of the deer lost a little more of its sheen. He could not shake off the conviction that he had something to do with the series of mishaps which had culminated in the fire. In his young mind they were somehow related. There was no one to tell him that the relationship he envisioned did not exist; that he had invented it because he wanted to punish himself for disappointing his father. His mother, in other circumstances, would have understood, but not now. Now he was alone. And a terrible thing kept happening. The woods drew him like a magnet and sometimes in the cool shadows and zebra sunlight beneath the pines he would find himself whistling or laughing out loud at the ridiculous antics of an otter, exactly as he had before his father's death, and then he would remember and feel guiltier than ever.

He felt most wretched after supper when he had been accustomed to sit out on the front porch with his father whittling on white pine sticks and feeling so full of dinner that he had to let out two or three notches on his belt. Now when he went out alone, all the good feeling was gone. He missed the sound of his mother singing happily in the kitchen and even the banging of pots seemed somehow subdued. As he sat alone in the gathering dusk, he kept looking around for that familiar face with the deep lines that ran from the nose down around the mouth and the little laugh crinkles at the corners of the eyes. It just didn't seem possible that it would never be there again.

He remembered his father's long, strong fingers with the black soil imbedded beneath the scarred nails and the black hairs bristling out of the back of those muscular forearms and he felt a strange sense of incompleteness. He missed that safe, contented feeling which his father's presence had given him and whereas he had always felt quite grownup as the white shavings of his whittling stick fell beside those of his father's, he now somehow felt very small and very alone.

Sometimes his mother would come out and sit beside him and although she tried very hard to talk to him, she couldn't quite seem to say the right things; and once when he looked at her in a rather confused way, she turned and ran into the house, holding her apron to her face. Robbie went in after her and found her crying. She was lying face down on the crazy quilt, her body convulsed with grief.

Robbie had never seen his mother cry before, and he didn't

know what to do. He tried to talk to her but she wouldn't answer him. She looked so small and defeated and unhappy lying there on the bed that he felt a great lump rising in his own throat and before he had time to check them, the tears came and he was crying too, but silently, not like his mother, and he felt very ashamed and went out to the yard. With the tears still running down his cheeks, he worked the pump handle until the clear, cold water gushed out of the spout. Then he took a cupful of it and brought it in to his mother. By the time he reached her, he had subdued his own tears, but he couldn't bring himself to ask her to take the cup of water. He just stood there beside the bed, feeling choked and bewildered, holding the cup out in a fruitless gesture of childish understanding toward her back. Finally he took the cup back to the kitchen, and because he couldn't think of anything else to do, he went out on the porch and sat down. He could still hear his mother sobbing. The sobs went on steadily for a long time. They went up to a terrible pitch and the tremendous outpouring of dammed-up emotion caught at Robbie's heart until he had to squeeze his fists together to keep his own tears from starting again. It was quite dark before the sobbing stopped altogether.

Later still, his mother came out on the porch. In the bright moonlight he could see that her face was swollen and her eyes were red, but something had gone out of them. She sat down on the steps beside him and put her arms around him silently and held him so tightly and so close that his elbow got squashed in his chest and it hurt. When she finally released him, new tears hung in her eyes, but she was smiling for the first time. It was a funny, wistful sort of smile but it was enough for Robbie to know that something good had happened. He didn't quite know what, but he felt that his mother's crying had something to do with it.

After that night, things were a great deal better, but it soon became apparent that something would have to be done to keep the farm going. Robbie worked harder than he ever had before. There was not even time for the woods or the beaver dam. But in spite of all his efforts and his mother's, the work piled up. The neighbors helped as much as possible, but the nearest farm was Jed Clawson's four miles down the road and Jed had his own work to do.

Mary took Robbie to town and they made inquiries to find out if they could hire anyone to help, but all the men were working the logging camps. Hired hands were an almost unknown luxury in the wilderness. The reason was simple. A man who wanted to farm could hack his own home out of the wilderness. The land was free for the taking. The materials for building, if he couldn't afford lumber, could be cut anywhere he wanted to swing an ax.

Mary and Robbie came home silent and preoccupied. After dinner, Robbie sat with heavy-lidded eyes under the light of the coal-oil lamp watching his mother slowly transforming a ball of wool into a pair of stockings. Just before going to bed, he said tentatively, "Mother what are we going to do?"

She looked up at him helplessly, and put the knitting aside. "I don't know, darlin'. I don't know." She looked so close to tears that he came to her and hugged her and she held him very tight for a long, long time, then told him in a thick voice to go to bed.

After she had tucked him in and listened to his prayers, she went to her own bedroom, but it was hours before she was able to sleep. She lay on the bed wide-eyed and wakeful and for the first time in days managed, by a desperate and sustained effort, not to cry. She knew that somehow she had to get control of herself. Life had to go on. She had Robbie to think of and the farm that Tom had worked so hard to build for both of them. Giving way to the futile and exhausting grief which had racked her continually since she realized Tom was gone only made her task more difficult. Yet controlling her emotions was desperately difficult. Her love for Tom Sharron had been so deep and the fabrics of their lives so closely interwoven that with his death a part of her being had been wrenched away, leaving an emptiness that she knew could never again be filled. Even now it seemed impossible that she would never see him again. Half a dozen times a day she would look out through the screen door, and expect to see him striding across the fields or splashing under the pump before coming in to meals. And then she would realize that he wasn't there, and would not be there, ever again. And the pain would lance through her and she would feel her throat constricting and her eyes filling with hot tears and she would squeeze them tight shut and pray. "Mary, Mother of God, teach me how to live without him!" She would walk through the house, and try as she would to put it out of her mind, she found herself thinking: He sat in this chair, he trimmed this lamp, he was reading this book. Here is the page he turned down to mark his place. And she would find herself leaning faintly against the table while the agony of anguish and loneliness flushed over her again.

The nighttimes were the worst of all. In the darkness, she would lie there, defenseless as the flood of memories surged through her, for in this bed he had loved her, his dear hands and his strong body had roused and satisfied her desire. Sometimes she had wakened and watched him as he slept and thanked God for the fact of him; for what he was and what he had given her.

And now it was over and she had to go on alone. Many women would have left the farm, would have torn themselves away from everything that made them remember. But to Mary, it represented everything she loved. It had been the work of his hands, the achievement of his toil. Like Robbie it was a thing they had wrought together. She had to find a way to save it. But how? A woman and a small boy could not hope to carry the burden which had only just been managed by the combined efforts of all three of them when Tom had been alive. And where were they to get help? She debated the wisdom of sending an ad to the papers in Toronto and Montreal, and then she fell asleep.

She was wakened just after dawn by the sound of an ax from the barnyard. She shook her head in dismay. Robbie was out working without even a mouthful of food! She pulled on her robe and hurried out of her bedroom. She bumped into Robbie in his nightgown in the living room. They stared at each other in surprise and then wordlessly rushed to the back door.

In the back yard, a huge man with a dirty bandage on his right arm, was methodically splitting wood. Mary pushed open the screen door. She said uncertainly, "Good morning?"

The man turned. He had a big head with stiff blond hair that was cut raggedly at the base of his neck. The face was stolid with high cheekbones and a big blunt nose, the chin square and stubborn with a deep cleft so that although he was clean-shaven, the cleft held a little trench of blond beard the razor had not been able to reach. The eyes were stone gray and dark and they burned at Mary with a restless, resentful fire that almost made her catch her breath. She had seen the man once or twice before in Pineville. A grim, taciturn giant who spoke to no one. There was a story connected with him. She'd heard it when she first came here eight years ago, but now it eluded her. She wet her lips. "It's Mr. Carter, is it not?"

The man flipped the heavy ax and caught it halfway toward the bit. "Yeah," he said. "I heard you lost your man."

Mary closed her eyes and put her hand against the doorjamb. "Yes."

78

"He done me a favor once. They said in town you was lookin' for help."

For the first time, she noticed the battered suitcase on the stump behind him. "Were you thinkin' of stayin' permanently?"

He tucked the ax under his arm, spat on his hands and rubbed them together. "That's what you wanted, ain't it?"

She bit her lip. "Why, yes. I suppose so."

"Well, I'm here." He hooked another stump toward him and split it expertly with three clean strokes. She waited for a moment, but he continued to split the wood without looking at her again. She shut the door slowly. She needed help and she needed it badly, but there was something about the man in the yard that frightened her. What was it she had heard about him?

She dressed hurriedly and made an enormous breakfast for the first time since Tom's death. Bacon and eggs, wheatcakes, hot biscuits and wild strawberry jam. When she called the man, he came in and sat and ate silently, his eyes on his plate. When he had finished, he mopped his plate with a whole biscuit and stuffed it into his mouth. Mary cleared her throat, then said a little stiffly, "If you're intendin' to stay, we'd better talk about your salary."

He shrugged. "It ain't important."

"But it is. How . . . much would you be gettin' at the loggin' camp?"

"Eighty a month and board."

"I'll give you ninety, then."

He shook his head. "I like farmin'. I hate loggin'. You got no call to pay me more because you need me."

The curtness of his tone had a way of making everything he said sound like a challenge. She said, "Well, I don't know what to say except that we're grateful, Mr. Carter."

"My name's Fred. I was pokin' around before you was up.

79

I seen a room off the end of the barn. All right if I put my stuff in there?"

"Yes, of course."

He pushed his chair back, crossed to the door and turned. He chewed at the edge of his lip a moment, then said, "I'm sorry about your man. I liked him." He turned and went out before she could reply. She took a deep breath.

Robbie looked at her with large solemn eyes. After a second, he said, "Is he goin' to take Father's place?"

She reached across the table and patted his hand. "There's nobody could do that, Robbie. But we do need him. Now, help me with these dishes. We're goin' for a ride."

"Where?"

"Over to see the Clawsons."

Robbie frowned and looked out through the screen door to where Fred was still chopping wood. He said abruptly, "I don't like him."

"Robbie, you mustn't say things like that. We've no right to pass judgment on the man till we know him better."

"But he looks like he's always mad at somethin'."

"I'm sure it's just his way. Finish dryin' the dishes now or we'll not get out of here before noon."

When the dishes were done, she opened the kitchen door and asked Fred if he would hitch the mare. He nodded and went off to the barn. When she came out a few minutes later, the horse and buggy were waiting. Fred was finishing the wood. He didn't offer to help her into the buggy. She got into the seat and turned, hesitating. Should she tell him what ought to be done? She decided against it. He would probably know as well as she. She drove off without saying good-by because Fred never raised his head to look after them.

Later as they turned into the gate of the Clawson farm, a dog came yapping at Midnight's heels and the horse shied. Mary said, "Now stop that, you silly creature!" The dog barked even louder and slashed at Midnight's foreleg. The horse reared. Robbie leaped down from the seat. He held out his hand to the dog and said, "Come, Bessy! Here girl!" Immediately the dog stopped worrying the horse and began to wag her tail. She came up to Robbie and put her wet muzzle in his hand. He rubbed her head. Jed Clawson came out of the barn and waved to Mary. She drove on up and stopped, leaving Robbie at the gate.

Jed was a small, twisted, wiry man with rust-red hair and enormous freckles. He handed her out of the buggy and looked down the drive to where Robbie was frolicking with Bessy and shook his head. "That boy of yours sure has got a way with animals. That there dog is mean. She won't even let my own kids near her. Lookit the way she takes to Robbie!" Mary smiled. Robbie's effect on animals was a commonplace with her. Before she could reply, Bedelia Clawson sailed out of the house.

"Mary! Mary Sharron! Why, land sakes, you're a sight for sore eyes!" She embraced Mary and kissed her on the cheek. She was a plump woman with graying brown hair and small bright eyes over which she wore gold-rimmed spectacles. She was an inveterate gossip and a shameless busybody, but she had a heart as big as a pumpkin and nothing was too much trouble for those she regarded as friends. She drew Mary toward the house with Jed in her wake. "Come in and have a cup of tea. We've been meanin' to get over to see you again this week but the corn had to be got in and we just couldn't seem to get away."

Robbie came bouncing up. Jed rumpled his hair. "Howdy, Robbie."

"Good mornin', Mr. Clawson. Could I play with Pete and Billy?"

"Course you can, son, but I don't rightly know where you'd find 'em. Down by the creek, maybe."

"I'll find 'em!" Robbie ran off, and Mary called after him. "Don't be too long, Robbie. We can't stay . . ."

Bedelia bridled. "You can't! I was hopin' you'd come for lunch."

"No. Thank you, Bedelia, there's too much to be done."

Bedelia led the way into the kitchen and put the teapot on. Jed sat down at the table and lit his pipe. He said shrewdly, "Your help showed up yet?"

Mary looked at him in surprise. "You knew about it?"

"I was in Pineville yesterday. Meant to come over last night and tell you he was comin', but the cow looked like she was gonna drop a calf and I didn't dare leave. Figured he wouldn't show up for a day or two. He must of walked out last night."

"Yes, he arrived this mornin'. He was choppin' wood when we got up."

Jed nodded. "He's a worker, all right."

Bedelia set the cups on the table and plumped herself down in a chair. "Well, I still say that Fred Carter's no kind of a man to be workin' out there alone with a woman and a child."

Mary frowned. "Why, Bedelia?"

"Land sakes, girl, don't you know about him?"

"No. That's what I came about. I remember hearin' somethin' when I first came to Pineville, but I've entirely forgotten now."

"Well, it's not likely you'd remember. It all happened before Tom brought you here. He was around for the last of it, though."

Jed said, "It was near ten years ago. Will you hold it against the man for the rest of his life?"

Mary looked from one to the other. "What happened?"

Bedelia's eyes glistened. "Well, I hardly know where to begin, there's so much to tell."

Jed snorted derisively.

"Hush, Jed. This is serious now."

82

"Oh, it's serious, all right," Jed said. "An' if it ain't, you'll make it that way."

"Are you going to let me tell her or not?"

He waved his pipe. "Tell away!"

"Well, he come here first about ten or twelve years back. He had a younger brother with him. Least he said it was his brother, though, I swear, the boy didn't look a thing like Fred. He was thin and kinda delicate-looking with a weak chin and soft hands, but this Fred looked after him like he was somethin' special. He worked the loggin' camps in the summer and trapped come winter, just like Tom. But from the first, he had nothin' but trouble. Jed says it was just bad luck, but I say it was God's punishment on him."

Jed snorted with impatience this time. "For *what*, in Heaven's name?"

"Nobody knows for what," she said primly, "but a man sows what he reaps, mark my words!"

"I ain't done much but mark 'em for twenty-one years," Jed said satirically.

Bedelia threw him an impatient look, but the story was too good to interrupt. "Well, everything he ever touched seemed to be trouble. Second year he bought himself four milkin' cows and they all got some kind of disease and had to be shot. Then his brother got into some trouble with a married woman. It was a terrible scandal. Her name was Winifred Stoke and we all thought she was such a nice person!"

"Maw, there ain't no reason to go into names."

"Why, for Heaven's sake, Jed, the woman's been gone all this time. Mary don't even know her. Next year a hailstorm wiped out his crops and never touched another farm in the whole countryside. We all began to feel sorry for him until . . . well, I can hardly bring myself to say it."

Jed blew out a great cloud of smoke. "Ain't a whole team

83

o' mules could keep you from it. You or any woman hereabouts."

"Jed Clawson, why don't you go out and finish your hayin'?"

"Not on your life. I'm stayin' here to see the man gets justice done him. Git on with it."

Bedelia sighed in exasperation but continued. "Well, 'long about the fourth year, Fred started lookin' around for a wife. Now you know as well as me that there aren't many unmarried women up here except the kind that follow the loggin' camps. Well, wouldn't you know Fred gets to seein' a lot of one of these hussies. She wasn't more than eighteen at the most. I declare, it's a disgrace and the law ought to do somethin' about it!"

"She was an eyeful," Jed interjected, "with green eyes and long red hair. . . ."

"And she'd been with half the men in the territory," Bedelia finished icily.

"Nobody's denyin' that. But give the man his due. She was pretty and she turned out a lot better than any of you give her credit for."

"She was still a loose woman!"

Mary brushed a hand across her forehead impatiently. "What happened, Bedelia?"

Bedelia took a breath. "Well, what didn't happen is more like it. Fred Carter married this . . . this creature. Then the three of them, Fred, his brother and the girl lived together out on his farm. It was just disgraceful! Oh, I've got to admit that it worked out better than anyone expected," she added reluctantly, "but nobody knows how it would have come out eventually!"

"Damn it, woman, you got no right to say that!" Jed exploded angrily. "The truth is you women was just dyin' for her to start rollin' her eyes at some logger and for Fred to do murder over it so's you could say 'I told you so!'"

84

"Jed Claw—"

"Don't you 'Jed Clawson' me! If you're goin' to crucify the man, then do it with all the facts!" Jed turned heatedly to Mary. "The truth is, Mary, the girl made him a good wife but the country folk cut 'em both dead from the moment they got hitched."

"Well, what on earth did you expect?" Bedelia demanded righteously. "Even his own brother kicked up a terrible fuss."

"It don't appear to me like that kid had any call to throw stones," Jed said sourly. "Matter of fact, Mary, 'bout the only person that would have anythin' to do with 'em was your husband. He had dinner with 'em once or twice that I know of, and when he met 'em on the street, he'd raise his hat to the girl like she was a real lady. It was somethin' to see the way that child came alive when he talked to her. Fred Carter never said nothin', but you could see he was pleased, too, and he deserves a lot more credit than 'Beddy' here or anyone else wants to give 'im. Nobody ever had the courage to say nothin' out loud, o' course, but they made their feelin's plain enough. There was lots of times when Carter coulda caused trouble, but he never did. What makes the womenfolk mad is, in spite of everythin', it worked out fine. For more'n a year, everythin' came out right for him. It even seemed like he might've licked his jinx. Folks began sayin' that maybe the girl'd brought him luck. Then the summer before Tom brought you back here it happened."

Bedelia said, "I thought I was tellin' this story."

"Well, you wasn't tellin' it to suit me," Jed said stubbornly, "an' I'm gonna finish. You kin give her your own version afterwards."

Bedelia set her mouth angrily, but Jed ignored her. He said, "It was a fire. It started about two miles from Carter's homestead just before dawn. There was a stiff wind blowin' an' it was on 'em before they knew it. Now nobody knows exactly what happened, because when it was over, Carter was a changed man and he wouldn't never talk about it, but he was out of his head for a spell and what, with his babbling, and what they found when they got to the farm later, they put together a pretty clear picture. They musta woke up when the fire was only a short distance away. Fred got the horse out of the barn and was tryin' to hitch it up in the yard. The wife and brother was inside tryin' to save a few valuables. The fire was comin' on like an avalanche. The smoke must have panicked the horse 'cause it went wild. It kicked Fred, knockin' him down and breakin' three of his ribs. Then it bolted, draggin' the cart over him and breakin' both his legs to boot. Only reason it didn't get clear away is it got the wagon wheel stuck behind the gatepost and couldn't tear it loose. Fred lay there in the dust callin' out to his wife and brother, but he was hurt so bad he couldn't make nobody hear. He tried to crawl over to the house and only succeeded in pushin' the stump of one of them broken ribs right through the wall of his chest. He was bleedin' like a stuck pig. After a while, the boy come runnin' out. He saw the fire roarin' down on him and he saw his brother lyin' there with the blood spurtin' out and he jist froze—stood there lookin' at that blood like he was mesmerized. Doc McLeod says that's what Fred kept moanin' about later. How the kid stared at the blood. Finally, what with the fire an' all, I guess the boy just went berserk. He cut out, leavin' the girl in the house and his brother there in the yard, and he got into the buggy. Somehow he got the wheel loose from the gate and went tearin' off. Only the horse bolted the wrong way, like animals often do, and took him straight into the fire. Fred saw it happen and then the fire got to the house. When this happened, the girl tried to run out. She got as far as the back door with a book of weddin' pictures in one hand and a suitcase in the other, before the fire caught her. It got her hair first and then

86

her clothes. In a couple of seconds, she was a human torch. Fred had to lie there and watch her burn to death in front of his eyes."

Mary put a hand to her temples. "Mary, Mother of God!" she said softly.

Jed went suddenly white. He had completely forgotten that less than a month ago Mary's husband had died in the fire. He stammered awkwardly, "Mary . . . I . . . I'm sorry. I didn't think. I . . ."

"No, no. Go on. How was it he wasn't burned?"

"You're sure . . . ?"

"Please, Jed."

"Well, he *was* burned. Bad enough to keep him in the hospital for months. There was some talk that they even did plastic surgery on him. But, you see, he wasn't right close to the house. He was in the open yard and there was a big water tank on stilts. The fire got to the tank and burned out the stilts and dumped a coupla hundred gallons of water practically on top of him. The whole barnyard was soaked when they found him. He'd been there for about ten hours. Nobody can figger how he lived through it."

"And after all that, he came back?"

"Yep. Nobody can figger that either. Did he come back because he's just so damn stubborn that he can't be licked till he's dead? Or did he come back 'cause he just ain't got no place else to go? I'd give a lot to know, but he ain't the kind of man you'd care to ask personal questions of now. Once, maybe, but not now. Ever since that fire, he's gone around like a human powder keg with the fuse sputterin' in his eyes. Nobody gets in his way."

"Has he caused trouble?"

"Not that I know of. But nobody's give him cause, either."

Mary shook her head unbelievingly. "It's a frightening story. And he was burned out again last month?"

"Yep. He's runnin' true to form. 'Ceptin' I never would've expected him to let himself out as a hired hand. Don't seem like him, somehow."

Mary heard Fred's words: "Your husband done me a favor once." She knew now what the favor had been. It occurred to her that Fred Carter had more quality than people gave him credit for. She was glad that Jed instead of Bedelia had told the story. She moistened her lips and brushed the dark hair back from her face. The story had harrowed her, coming so close on Tom's death, but she felt a deep helpless sympathy for Fred Carter. They had both lost something irreplaceable to fire. It didn't matter what the girl had been. He had loved her and she had died. She understood now the deep resentment in his eyes, the grim mask of his face. He was a man who'd been beaten to his knees so often that he had nothing left but defiance. She wished she knew more about him. She said, "Do you know anything about his life before he came here?"

Bedelia shook her head. "He was always a strange one. Not like he is now, of course, but he didn't make friends easy and he never talked about himself. I tell you, I wouldn't want him around. There's no tellin' what a man like that might do."

Mary smiled wanly. "Oh, I think you're exaggeratin', Bedelia. And anyway, I've no choice in the matter. I've got to have help and there's no place else to get it."

Bedelia looked hurt. "Well, you know your own business best, but if it was me—"

"Well, it ain't you," Jed said. "Git the girl some more tea. That's cold."

Bedelia was instantly all contrition. "Oh, gracious me! Jed upsets me so sometimes I just don't know what I'm doin'. Here." She poured out a fresh cup for Mary and refreshed her own. Mary sipped it gratefully.

Robbie burst into the room. "Are we ready, Mother?"

88

She smiled. "Yes, I think we are, Robbie. Did you have a good play with Pete and Billy?"

He dropped his eyes. "Yes, ma'am."

She inclined her head and looked at him closely. She suspected there might have been a little trouble, but she decided not to make an issue of it. Somehow Robbie and the Clawson children never seemed to get on very well together. She finished her tea, kissed Bedelia and let Jed help her into the buggy. Robbie walked by the horse's head to keep the dog away till they got outside the gate.

On the way home, she went over Fred Carter's story. He might not be the best possible person for the job, but she felt a good deal better about him than she had this morning. Her only concern now was: was he a good farmer?

6

Mary's concern was groundless. Fred turned out to be not only an excellent farmer but a tireless worker. He seemed to derive the greatest satisfaction from jobs which taxed him to the utmost. He shouldered the awkward sacks of potatoes as though they were feather pillows, and at the woodpile, the ax, powered by his big shoulders, bit through the pine logs as if they were paper. He was a grim, taciturn, cryptic man who never smiled and who went about his work as if the next hour might bring another of the tragedies which had stalked him most of his life. He was impossible to like or to get close to. And yet, for Mary and Robbie alike, he exercised a strange fascination. For Mary, the fascination was in the man himself and what he had been through. What kind of a man, in a straight-laced community like the northern settlers' would have the courage to marry a prostitute and still hold his head high as Carter had apparently done? And, like Jed, she wondered what perverse psychological quirk had brought him back to the scene of repeated disasters. Surely the north could hold nothing but the bitterest memories for him. Then there was that point about Tom's having befriended them in the face of everyone's opposition. It was not unlike him, of course, but there was something frightening in it as if all this had been preordained. She remembered now that Tom had refused to talk about him much and she realized why. He had been prepared to accept the censure of the settlers himself, but he wouldn't risk her reputation. He'd spoken to Carter once or twice in Pineville but he had never introduced the man to Mary. And now a month after his death, a kind thing Tom had done before their marriage had brought her help when it was needed most. She felt sure Fred had come to repay a debt he felt he owed. He had said, "He done me a favor once" as if that were all the explanation that was needed.

Robbie, on the other hand, was fascinated by the physical man. He began by disliking him intensely because he resented the fact that Fred did everything around the farm as well and sometimes better than his father. And somehow to Robbie this seemed like sacrilege. Yet as the weeks passed, his resentment melted slowly. He began to develop a grudging interest. The boy had had almost no opportunity for meeting strangers and Fred's very bigness was in itself exciting to the imagination of a seven-year-old. Once when the wagon wheel had to be fixed, Fred had lifted the chassis with one shoulder and wrenched the wheel off without even using a jack. Another time Robbie saw him straighten the tines on a garden fork with his bare hands. He began to follow Fred around and, as his shyness evaporated, he sometimes handed Fred a spade or a nail when it was needed.

Fred accepted these overtures in silence until Robbie began to supplement them with advice and suggestions as to how things ought to be done. The suggestions he offered were invariably highly complicated but Tom and Mary had made it a point to listen because they believed in encouraging the boy to think for himself. Afterward they would explain patiently why the way they were doing things was more feasible. It was a kind of a game at the conclusion of which Robbie would nod with childish gravity while his parents exchanged amused glances over his head. Unfortunately the kind of patience required for all this had not been built into Fred Carter, nor was he equipped to cope with the dialectic behind it. He told Robbie gruffly to keep out of his way. Robbie, deeply hurt, complied. He had never been rebuffed before and he didn't understand. He had only wanted to help and now Fred didn't want him around.

For his part, Fred hadn't wanted to hurt the child, but Robbie's being around all the time when he was working made him uneasy. He had never been around children and he didn't understand them. He had had no real childhood of his own. Such games as were played in the slum where he grew up had always been denied him because he was too big to play with boys his own age and too clumsy and inexperienced to play with those his own size. He had learned in the streets the lessons of loneliness. He learned at home the catechism of rejection. His father had been a huge rock of a man who fought in the ring under the name of Tiger Lane. The Tiger had terrible power in his hand and this, coupled with a reckless courage, had moved sports writers to hail him as the greatest heavyweight potential since Jess Williard. And then with the championship of the world practically his, he had been stricken with a disease which had left his bones as brittle as glass. It had been the beginning of the end. Against everyone's advice he had fought once more—a disaster which had put him in the hospital for months and left him penniless and partly crippled. His roaring good spirits had turned to brooding melancholy. He lived in his scrapbooks and in the local bars where for free drinks he refought his days of glory. Had he been a lesser fighter or one who had not so nearly reached his pinnacle, he might have survived. But there were too many who knew him. Too many who came to see the poor hulk who would have been champion, dancing on brittle legs in front of an imaginary opponent. At home he would stare in drunken bitterness at his son's strong young bones as if he saw in them a mockery of his own misery.

Fred had been almost five when the Tiger fought his last fight . . . aware in a vague, childish way that his father was a great man. He had adored the genial giant who taught him to double his little hands into fists—how to crouch and weave and block punches with his forearms—and then allowed the child to pummel him unmercifully while he roared in mock terror. It had been a good beginning but the man who came back from the hospital walking with the aid of canes was a stranger. The child moved in fear of him waiting for a return of the ready smile, the booming laughter. They never came. And when the boy, in a pitiful attempt to resurrect what he had lost, hurled himself on his father one evening, fists flying as of old, the man flung him aside and lurched to his feet trembling with anger.

Even at five, Fred knew better than to turn to his mother. Darlene Carter was a vain, somewhat stupid woman with a full figure and bleached blond hair. She had married into a world of excitement, steadily growing purses and high adventure. She could not now reconcile herself to a cold-water flat and the alcoholic shell of a man who could have bought her the world. She had never wanted the child. He was an unfortunate accident. After the Tiger's defeat, she cried constantly and, when the Tiger began spending his evenings in the bars, she began to spend hers elsewhere. The defections, unfortunately, produced another "accident." The bitter wrangling about this child went on until the Tiger, stung, into a desperate bid for money, had taken part in an attempted holdup and was sent to the state penitentiary for ten years.

Thereafter, Fred had almost no supervision whatsoever. In the beginning he roamed the streets and even the bigger boys soon learned to leave him alone, for in a fight he was the Tiger in miniature. But later he got interested in the scrapbooks which littered the flat. He read the glowing accounts of his father's courage. He began to forget the drunkenness, the brutality and the shame of the two years between his father's last fight and his imprisonment. He began to build the man in the image of the newspapers and his own memory. He decided that when his father returned, things would be different. He, Fred, would work and bring enough money home so that his father would never again be driven to theft to support his family. He got a job in a grocery store by day and he set pins in a bowling alley at night. It was an eighteen-hour day that established in the youngster a pattern of industry he was never able to break. But it left him no time to develop a facility for getting on with other people. His size embarrassed him and to cover his shyness he developed a deliberate belligerence which kept people at a distance.

And the money piled up. By the time his father returned, Fred was fourteen and already only a half inch short of six feet. The Tiger was thinner, paler, and more helpless than ever. He had spent much of the seven years, to which his sentence had been reduced, in the prison hospital. When Fred offered him the money he had saved the Tiger wept, clutching the boy fiercely, mumbling incoherent endearments and promises to start anew. But the promises were never kept. The corrosion of self-pity and helplessness had eaten too deeply. Within a week, the Tiger began to drink the money away. Time and time again he was jailed for drunkenness. Fighting now for the mere symbol of the only love he had known, Fred had paid his father's fines and dragged him home only to find him gone again when he returned from work in the evening. The deeper the Tiger sank, the more the sight of his strapping son seemed to depress him. He began to goad the boy and, when thoroughly drunk, tried to beat him. Fred, knowing how weak his father was, dared not strike back. Gradually the last flicker even of pity died. Fred closed himself up and took the abuse till he could take it no more. Then he ran away. He took with him the boy whom he now knew was not his father's son because the boy pleaded so earnestly to go. Billy was a thin, sickly child with a constantly running nose and it wasn't till much later that the emptiness of Fred's own life drove him to a fondness for the boy. Billy couldn't work and couldn't fight. He was wholly dependent and this realization brought Fred a sense of responsibility which he fashioned into a reason for existence. Not until he married did he find anything else which might justify the struggle. He had never tried to examine his feelings for the girl. She had loved him and looked after him and he had been important to her. It had been enough. It hadn't mattered what she had been. She had altered, if only slightly, the complexion of his existence. And then it had all been destroyed.

Not only the marriage, but in those moments of frightful insight during the fire, he had seen that the boy hadn't been a reason for living after all. He'd been a cheat and a liar and, worst of all, a coward. He'd left the girl and his brother to die when he might have saved all of them. Fred didn't know why he had come back to the north, but he had. He'd built another house and tilled more land but his heart hadn't been in it, and it had not meant much when his labor had gone up in smoke a second time. Then he had heard about Tom Sharron. The only man who had treated him and Millie like human beings. He hadn't tried to analyze his feelings, but the Sharron farm had drawn him like a magnet. He hadn't counted on the boy's presence and he'd forgotten the woman was so pretty, but in the long run it didn't matter. He didn't want any more attachments. He didn't want any more responsibilities. He wanted only to be left alone to do what he knew how to do best—run a farm. Thus when Robbie made his attempts at friendship, Fred rebuffed him coldly. He just didn't want to be bothered.

It was the wrong way to go about getting rid of Robbie. The boy had a natural desire to be liked and Fred's surliness, after Robbie recovered from the original rejection, only served as a kind of challenge. He no longer tried to approach Fred directly but he began studying him from a distance. Fred had a funny way of hitching up his trousers with his elbows before tackling a job, and quite without realizing it, Robbie began to emulate this trait as he had emulated so many of his father's.

Mary saw and was troubled. She knew there had to be a model for Robbie's development, and sympathetic as she felt toward the hired man, she didn't want the model to be Fred Carter. It wasn't his fault, of course, but among other things he ate like a pig, using his hands whenever possible, picking his teeth with his fingernails and shoveling food into his mouth with a knife. It was an unhealthy example for Robbie, whom she had tried so hard to bring up properly. Under normal circumstances, she would have served the hired man separately, but since he was in a sense a neighbor and had volunteered his services for less than he could have received if he had wanted to make the most of his position, she felt obligated to treat him almost as one of the family. She couldn't presume to correct his manners, but about two weeks after Fred's arrival the point came when something had to be done. The meal was almost over and Fred was sopping up the gravy from his plate with a piece of bread. Robbie watched him for a second and suddenly broke a piece off his own bread and began to imitate him. Mary bit her lip and took a deep breath.

"Robbie," she said quietly, "there's plenty more if you're still hungry. There's no necessity to scrape your plate like that." She felt herself blush as Fred looked up at her. She had one frightful moment when she just knew Robbie was going to say, "But Fred does it like that." Mercifully, he didn't. She heard him mutter, "Yes, ma'am," and he excused himself from the table. Fred turned to watch him go. Then he looked down at his own plate. He dropped the piece of gravy-soaked bread and the blood mounted slowly to his face. He pushed his chair back and went out.

A little before suppertime he came into the kitchen. He rubbed a hand across his mouth and he said, "I got some patchin' to do on the fence. I'd like to finish before it gets dark. Could I eat later?"

He was offering her the opportunity she sought, but suddenly she knew she couldn't accept it. She said, "Of course, Fred. We'll wait till you're ready, then."

"Ain't no call for you and the boy to wait. I'll git somethin' later."

She felt achingly sorry for him. "All right, Fred."

He came in some time after they had eaten and she served him. She sat at the table to keep him company and he dropped his knife twice. The second time, his face got red as fire and he said angrily, "Ain't you got nothin' to do?"

She knew what caused it. She even knew he wasn't to blame, but the sharpness of his tone broke something inside her. No man had ever spoken to her like that in her life. She stood up, her eyes blazing. "It's sorry I am, Mr. Carter, that I've been a bother to you. In the future, you can eat by yourself and I hope you enjoy it!" She turned and swept out of the room.

She'd no sooner left than she knew she had been wrong. She felt ashamed, and a few minutes later she went back to the kitchen to apologize. The room was empty, the food untouched. She gnawed at the corner of her lip worriedly, then went to the medicine cabinet and took out some ointment and bandages.

She went out to the barn and knocked on the door. He opened it. It was a small door and his big frame almost filled it. With the lamplight behind him, she could not see his face. She said, "I . . . I thought I ought to change the bandage on that arm. It's awfully dirty."

97

"It's awright."

"But I feel responsible. It should be changed regularly. Please?"

He hesitated and then stepped back. "Come on in."

She came in. Tom had used the room occasionally when the sow was about to farrow or the mare to foal, but she had forgotten how small and bare it really was. A piece of old sacking hung over the single window. There was a narrow cot with sagging springs, a few hooks for clothes, a rickety table and a battered wooden chair. She looked around her contritely.

"I'm afraid we'll have to do something about this room for you."

He shrugged. "It's okay. I'll need some insulation come winter is all."

"We'll talk about it later." She motioned toward the bed. "Sit down."

He let himself down and she pulled up the single chair and took the big hand in her lap. He didn't say anything. As she unwrapped the bandage, she said, "Did you do this fightin' the fire?"

"Yep."

He was not easy to talk to. She finished unwrapping the arm and looked. It had been a bad burn but it had healed beautifully except for one point near the elbow where the skin was still raw and oozing. A portion of the gauze had stuck ⁺o the skin around it. She pulled it loose as gently as she could but it must have hurt more than a little. He didn't flinch and she looked up. He was staring at her and he looked away quickly, the muscles along his jaw bunching angrily. But in that brief glance she had seen something strange. For the first time, his eyes had not had that bitter defiant look. They had looked bewildered and, for some strange reason,

98

a little frightened. She finished wrapping the wound and stood up.

"There. That should be fine in a few days, I'm thinkin'."

He nodded, still without looking at her.

"Fred . . . I . . . I'm sorry for what I said. It was the Irish in me, I imagine. I hope you'll not take it seriously."

He shrugged. "It don't matter. Could I have my meals out here?"

She bit her lip and hesitated. "You could not. I've enough work to do as it is without servin' you separately. You'll be eatin' with us as usual and that's the end of it!" She turned and went out.

Fred watched her go, a strange mixture of emotions written on his somber face. He had never known a woman like her before. He didn't know how to act and he didn't know what to say. Her presence disturbed him. It made him alternately angry and uneasy. He didn't know how to cope with her. He found himself thinking of the soft sheen of her hair in the lamplight and he wished abruptly that he had not come to the Sharron farm.

Mary went back to the house and put the remainder of the dressing in the cupboard. She felt mildly pleased she had resolved the eating problem successfully without further hurting Fred's feelings, but something even more disturbing had taken possession of her. Once during the moment when she had been bandaging Fred's arm, she had become acutely conscious of the fact that she was a woman and he was a man and that they were sitting together in a small room four miles from the nearest human habitation. It was a situation she would gladly have foregone but one over which she had no control. Once, a few days earlier when she had been taking down the weekly wash, she had turned to find him staring at her. He had looked away quickly, but the incident had both

99

frightened and angered her. It did not cross her mind that the situation might be even more difficult for Fred. She was still a young woman and her present unhappiness did not detract from her beauty. Her body was still the body of a young girl; her bosom full and firm and her waist small. Women had been known to say her hips were a trifle too wide but no man had ever thought so. Her complexion was rich and soft and her eyes had lost none of their dark luster. It would have been strange if all this had made no impression on him.

But in her present state, Mary would not have been able to accept this if someone had explained it to her. Since her marriage to Tom Sharron just after her eighteenth birthday a little more than eight years had passed. Eight years which had taken her away from her teaching duties in Ireland to this hard young country she had grown to love. They had been rich years. Years of watching a frame house grow into a home—a forest into a farm—and a dream into a life. And because making a home in the wilderness was an arduous task, she had ceased to think of herself as she really was—a young and lovely woman—and had been happy devoting all her time and attention to the urgent business of living. If she thought of herself at all, it had been in terms of a wife and mother. And then, with that look in the barnyard and her feeling tonight, she had been shocked into the realization that she was no longer a woman protected by the sanctity and security of the marriage bonds but a woman still four years short of thirty without a husband. It was not a comforting thought.

She went to bed determined to watch Fred's behavior scrupulously and, at the slightest sign of familiarity, to put him in his place.

The opportunity never came. At breakfast the following

morning, he ate slowly, one eye on her and one on his plate. He didn't mimic anything she did, but at lunch time she noticed he spread his napkin on his lap instead of tucking it under his chin and only once did he use his knife for the purpose of putting food into his mouth.

7

The breath of frost came into the air. The leaves of all but
the evergreens were splashed with great masses of flaming
color. The juniper bushes were bright with scarlet berries and
the ground was awash with swirling eddies of violent hues
as the fallen leaves flowed over the land in yellow and black
and hectic red. Robbie thought it was as if the rainbow had
suddenly been shattered into a million fragments and the
ragged pieces poured over the countryside. He took to sliding
down the slopes of the forest ravine on the dead leaves which
were even more slippery than the pine needles and built great
heaps of them in the hollows. Then he would run as fast as
his legs would carry him, leap off the rise, land with a great
rustling splash in their midst and lie there laughing while the
bright little parachutes that had exploded out of the pile
drifted down on top of him. He liked the dry, pungent smell
of the leaves and the feel of their sharp smoothness against
his skin.

The waters of the lakes became too cold for swimming
and made his arms ache when he tried to tickle the trout.
The mornings saw the grass and stubbled fields covered with
layers of hoar frost and the air was alive with the honking of
geese in perfect formation winging their way south.

The grapes had ripened in the arbor behind the porch and
the house was heavy with the smell of grape jam and crab-
apple jelly. There were potatoes to be stored and apples to be
packed and turnips to be waxed and the million and one
other chores which meant the end of bare feet and swimming,

of quiet hours in the sun or lazy afternoons in the cool, green shade of the forest.

Fred installed a small potbellied stove in his room and began breaking out skis, toboggans, snowshoes and the big sleigh, so that he could check and repair them whenever he had a spare moment.

And abruptly, with a suddenness that, in spite of their urgent preparation caught them unprepared, winter was upon the land. Robbie went to bed one night and when he arose the next morning, the fields and roads were gone. There were little toboggan slides in the corners of the windows against the frames, while outside the snow was still falling in big, soft, silent flakes. In the barnyard, the golden wood chips and the brown straw, the bruised grass and the bare dust spots had disappeared. In their place, a clean, white, shimmering coat was unmarred except for one set of big footprints where Fred had made his way to the house for breakfast.

At the breakfast table a few minutes later, Robbie, in an uncontrollable itch to be outside, gulped his food shamelessly until he caught his mother looking at him in a reproving manner. At which point he suddenly acquired a very intense interest in the tablecloth and a considerably lower rate of transition between his mouth and his plate. Mary watched him with a shadow of a smile turning the corners of her mouth, then turned to Fred.

"Fred, do you think this snow is going to continue?"

Fred folded his napkin and laid it on the table beside his plate. "Kinda hard to say. Might. What's on your mind?"

"I was thinkin' that we need supplies badly. I hadn't counted on the snow comin' so soon. How deep is it?"

"Two, three inches, maybe. But if it keeps up like this, we'll have over a foot by dark."

"Would you have time to go down to the village and get what supplies we need today?"

"Well, yeah . . . I suppose so."

"What do you mean, 'you suppose so?' Have you somethin' more important to do?"

"Well, not exactly. I was figgerin' on puttin' up that tar paper on the inside of my room today. Now that the cold weather's here, it's hard to keep that place warm without insulation." He rubbed the stubble of his chin thoughtfully. " 'Course we oughta git some supplies, cause if this keeps up, the mare won't be able to pull the cart."

"And that'll mean you'll have to go down to the village on snowshoes with the toboggan?"

"Yep." He straightened up decisively. "I better go today and leave the room till tomorrow."

"No," Mary said. "That's not fair. I'll not have you freezin' to death because I didn't tell you sooner we'd be needin' supplies. Robbie and I will go. As soon as you've finished breakfast, you'd better hitch Midnight to the sleigh."

Fred's customarily dark face got darker. "Look, I don't *have* to do the room today. I can go to the village. You stay here."

It was the angry tone, the same sharp, provocative attack which had set Mary's teeth on edge so many times before.

"We'll manage!" she said angrily.

Robbie, watching tensely for the outcome, saw the knots of hard muscle leap into prominence on Fred's jaw. If Fred won the argument, it meant that Robbie would not be asked to go, whereas his mother had already said she would take him. For a moment, Fred looked as if he would explode, then he said, "Okay. I'll hitch up the wagon."

Robbie's eyes were as big as saucers. "Mother, are we really goin' to the village?"

Mary Sharron looked troubled. She had allowed her annoyance at Fred to override her better judgment. Unless there was a storm, the trip wasn't dangerous, but it might be definitely unpleasant. Fred was perfectly right, and what was more, she knew it. Taking the horse and sleigh into the village in this weather was no job for a woman. If it continued to snow, it was going to need a strong hand on the reins and maybe a stronger pair of arms to get the sleigh out of the ditch on the way back. But her pride would not permit her to tell Fred that she had decided not to go. She would just have to be extra careful and get back as soon as possible. She looked at Robbie and could have bitten off her tongue for saying that she would take him with her. He would cause her no trouble, but to take him along would be to add a further responsibility. She wanted to tell him he couldn't go, but she didn't know how. She had always made it a point to keep her promises to him.

"Robbie," she said, "maybe I'd better be goin' alone. Maybe you ought to stay here and help Fred. There's a great deal to be done."

Robbie knew better than to coax. But his look of painful entreaty was more than she could bear. She weakened a little.

"But, Robbie, it may be late when we come back."

It was the wrong thing to say. Robbie straightened up. Here was a challenge he could meet. He thrust his lower lip out purposefully and made his voice as deep as he could: "Father said when he was away, I was to look after you."

Mary felt a lump come into her throat. One dark lock of hair was falling over his forehead and he had set his jaw in a faithful imitation of his father. Mary could see Tom Sharron in every line of his face and every attitude of his body.

"All right," she said, "run and get your things," knowing she had made two mistakes in the space of a few minutes.

Fred watched them out the gate, his face even grimmer than usual. It was crazy for a woman to be goin' out in this weather. Plain damn foolishness. Only she was so pigheaded stubborn nobody could tell her! You just had to get a little sharp with her and them black eyes would start blazin' and you might just as well give up. It was his fault too. He should never have let her know he intended fixin' the room today. If it hadn't been for that. . . . Well, what was the matter with him? It wasn't his business. He wasn't her keeper. If she wouldn't listen, it wasn't his fault. He kicked angrily at the gatepost and, blowing on his hands, went back up to the house.

8

Mary Sharron found the going easier than she had anticipated. Midnight was not having much difficulty in finding her footing in the snow and seemed only a little nervous. Robbie, on the other hand, was having the time of his life. He was sticking his tongue out as far as possible trying to catch the big, soft flakes which sifted down around them and dissolved in his mouth with a sharp tingle. Mary watched him and laughed. The snow was falling less heavily now and with the increased visibility, she could afford to relax a little. Robbie looked so absurd with his head thrust forward and his red tongue going every which way to catch the falling flakes. He grinned up at her, his eyes shining with excitement.

"Try it, Mother—it's fun!"

She laughed again. "I certainly will not. I don't intend to have my tongue frozen."

"Oh, Mother," he said, "you don't understand at all. It's not cold. It's just funny. It makes your tongue tickle."

"It's mad you are. I've always known it." But she stuck her tongue out to please him.

When their tongues began to ache from the unusual exercise, they sang Christmas carols and hymns and folk songs as the miles slipped behind them. And all the while, the snow fell soundlessly and steadily and purposefully.

It was almost thirteen miles to Pineville and it was noon before they arrived. Robbie had been to the village before with his father, so it was not new to him, but he never failed to be impressed by the sight of the streets lined on either side with stores and houses for a distance that was as long as their potato field.

The big general store for which they were headed had a false front which made it appear two stories high, and in Robbie's young life this was the ultimate in architectural development. He looked upon Mr. Campbell, the proprietor, as a very unusual being, not only because he owned a store two stories high but also because he had an automobile that was sometimes parked in the narrow alleyway beside the store.

There were two Ford cars with chains in front of the general store and half a dozen rigs and horses. They tied Midnight to the hitching post, entered the store and were greeted by almost everyone for whom Campbell's was the closest source of supply. Their numbers gave Mary a little nudge of unease, because it meant a long wait before Mr. Campbell and his wife could get around to filling her order. Obviously, they had all been caught unprepared by the unexpected snow and, like Mary, had determined to get their winter supplies before drifted roads made the trip impossible except by ski, snowshoe or dog sled. There was nothing to do but wait. Had someone offered to let Mary take their place in line, she would have had to refuse. It was an unwritten law that the first come was first served, for the snow worked an equal hardship on all of them and many of them had farther to go than Mary. Someone brought up a chair and she joined the group seated around the stove whose great potbelly showed streaks of orange fire.

To Robbie, the delay was better than a birthday present. He was in his element. He had been inside the store on only three occasions and each time it had been for such a brief period that it had only served to whet his curiosity. But now he had an opportunity which he had prayed for more often than he could remember, for Campbell's general store was a world in itself, completely different from anything he had ever experienced. It was more wonderful in its provocation than the Pandora's box his mother had so often told him about. He was to see many stores in later years, stores with marble floors and uniformed attendants who dispensed expensive goods illuminated by indirect lights from under polished glass counters, but none of them, in Robbie's mind, could ever hope to equal the sheer beauty, the profound magnificence of Campbell's General Store and Feed Emporium.

The first thing that struck him was the smell. It was a challenge to his imagination, an irresistible provocation to his insatiable curiosity. Twenty years later, when Campbell's store had been burned to the ground, never to be rebuilt, the smell of its interior would still linger in Robbie's nostrils and the mere remembrance would send a shiver of delight through him.

The smell that pervades a true country store is unique. There is nothing quite like it in this world and little hope that there will be anything to compare with it in the next. It is a redolence whose intoxication can only partly be described. There is the sharp, spicy tang of dried ginger, the exotic incense of black tea and the heavy fragrance of ground coffee from the battered red grinder on the back shelf. There is the mouth-watering smell of licorice, jelly beans and the scrambled assortment of marshmallow balls, jawbreakers and maple sugar cubes in the glass case beneath the counter. There is the pungent, pervasive odor of great circular cheeses piled layer on layer in the back room; the dark mysterious effluvium of rolled tar paper; the earthy emanation of seeds and grain; the dry redolence of soda crackers, the sweet pungence of molasses, the musk of saddle soap and harness leather, corduroy and packed wool, and a thousand other odors just as piquant and as tantalizing, but whose source cannot be identified and whose essence escapes description. But it is these indefinable perfumes mingling with the rest and spiced with the overall odor of dust and wood smoke that make a Canadian country store the source of one sublime, provocative, intoxicating aroma so unique that once sensed, it cannot be forgotten.

But it was not the smell alone which was exciting about Campbell's store. It was so full that the only open space inside its walls was the circular area bounded by upturned empty boxes around the stove. Elsewhere, it was a man-made jungle.

Within its confines, you could buy anything from a live goldfish to a dozen bear traps, but only Mr. Campbell could have found either of them for you. It was all a man could do to thread his way through the standing sheaves of hoes, pitchforks, bags of feed, masses of harness leather, bundles of shingles, rolls of tar paper, and the great coils of hempen rope. The tables were piled high with sweaters, levis, corduroys, axes, boxes of nails, masses of tools; and it was only by burrowing through layer after layer of miscellaneous articles that you could get any idea of what the table originally supported. There you might find anything from several gross of flypaper rolls or a few boxes of hairpins to a half dozen pair of high-button shoes. And yet, Mr. Campbell, as if by some divine instinct, could find you a calico dress pattern as easily as he could locate a barrel of flour.

The customers had long since given up trying to find things for themselves. They sat patiently on their cracker barrels, exchanging ideas about weather and traps and waited for Mr. Campbell to serve them.

The delay, to Robbie, was a long standing dream come true. Never before had he had a chance to peer into all the dark corners of the store, to climb up on boxes and orange crates, to penetrate the mysterious dusty darkness back from the edges of the shelves, which was all he could see from the floor. Never before had he had time to lean perilously over the top of a half empty barrel with never an idea, until his eyes cleared the rim, what wondrous commodity would be stored in its depths. And never before had he had a chance to follow his nose to the source of all the delicious and mysterious odors which mingled in the air. Now that the chance had come, he made the most of it. He pursued his explorations until his hair was white with flour, his fingers sticky with molasses and his mouth one large black smear from the long licorice whip Mary had bought him. Mr. Campbell, who had seen other little boys do the same thing, watched and smiled and shook his head when Mary asked him, in pantomime, if he wanted Robbie to stop.

It was almost three o'clock when Mary's turn at the counter finally came, and it was closer to four when the last bag of flour was loaded aboard the cart. Her heart skipped a beat when she stepped outside the door. The snow was perceptibly deeper, the air had a bite to it, and the big silent flakes were being hurried along by the first signs of a rising wind. Mr. Campbell cast a dubious eye at the gray overcast as he came around to unhitch Midnight.

"Think ye'll be able to make it all right, Mary?"

"Oh, I think so. Thank you, Ian."

"There's a wind risin'. It may blow up real nasty before ye get back."

"There's little to do but try."

"Well, I don't know about that now. There's no real danger, of course. If it were a man now, I'd say go ahead. But if ye should go into the ditch, ye could no lift them sacks of flour out to lighten the cart. Why don't you and Robbie stay here for the night? We could put ye up with no trouble at all. Be mighty glad to have ye."

"It's more than kind of you, Ian, but we've got to get back. There's the hired man, you know, and if we're not home by dark, he might spend half the night lookin' for us. We'll go along now while Midnight can still be of some use to us."

"All right, Mary. Ye know best what you've got to do, but we'd be mighty glad to have ye. 'Course if you're set on goin', ye'd better get started. Looks to me like the sooner ye get there, the better."

"Thank you, Ian. We'll be on our way now."

Mary flipped the reins and clucked to Midnight, who started up none too willingly. For the first few miles, it wasn't bad. There was no doubt about it that the wind was increasing and the temperature was going down rapidly, but several other carts had preceded them this far along the road and the tracks were not yet drifted over, so that Midnight picked her way without too much difficulty. Eventually, however, tracks of the Clawson cart turned off. Ahead of them was a flat unbroken sheet of whiteness. The tracks they themselves had made that morning were completely obliterated. Still, there was no need for immediate worry. Midnight could find the road as long as it was possible to see the trees on either side, and if the storm got no worse, they would make the farm without trouble. She urged Midnight on, but the horse was not to be hurried. She picked her way carefully, cautiously and, it seemed to Mary, with maddening slowness.

It was beginning to grow dark and, for the first time, Mary began to feel the heavy, insidious cold sliding under her thick coat. She could smell the coming of the storm. There was a brittle tension in the air, and the sharp cold pulled her nostrils together with each indrawn breath. She drew her collar higher as her ears began to tingle unpleasantly. She knew the signs. There was going to be one of those vicious preseason storms, as rigorous as any the winter would see, and it wasn't far away.

She wondered if she should turn back. The road leading to the Clawson farm where the last cart had turned off could not be more than a mile or two behind them. And then, even as she was considering, the storm broke. The first blast of wind struck with such force it nearly knocked them from their seats. It tore the breath from their mouths and left them gasping. Even with their heads hunched deep into their shoulders and their eyes narrowed to tiny slits, it was hopeless to try to penetrate the storm.

Ahead of them was a swirling, menacing vortex of flying snow. It was madness to go on. She jerked on the reins to turn Midnight and the horse started around, but the pivoting back wheels piled snow high above their hub caps and could be made to turn no farther. She stifled the sudden start of panic that flashed in her and hauled on the reins to pull Midnight around the other way. The mare shied and then, as Mary insisted, pulled reluctantly around to the right. A few steps and her footing disappeared. She floundered for a few seconds in the soft snow and then regained the road, panting, her nostrils flaring and her eyes dilated with fright. Nothing could induce her to turn again.

It took a moment for Mary to accept the truth. They went forward or they froze where they were. She shouted at Midnight and the horse threw her weight against the traces. The heavily laden cart went forward about a foot and stopped. Midnight had been able to keep it moving when it had a little momentum, but she was obviously going to have trouble starting it from a stationary position in the deepening snow. Mary shouted to the mare again and slapped the lines against her flanks. Again the mare surged forward a foot or two, slipped awkwardly, and recovered to stand once more, trembling and frightened.

Mary bit her lip and ran a hand over her face, into which the biting granules of snow were driving with painful force. Her head ached from the intense cold pressing against her temples. Her nose was running and there was excruciating pain now in her ears and cheeks. Her fingers were numb. That terrible sense of futility which affects anyone who has faced a blizzard began to gnaw at her, but again she fought it down.

113

She looked at Robbie. He had his face hunched so far into his shoulders you could see only part of his face. His nose, too, was running and his face was raw. She had to shout to make herself heard over the shrieking of the wind.

"Robbie, we'll have to get down and help Midnight."

Robbie nodded. He scrambled out of the cart and in a moment he and Mary, at the horse's head, tried to lead her out of the drift. Even in the short time they had been stuck, the snow had almost drifted over their tracks behind and, as they watched, they could see it piling up against the wheels. It was a frightening sensation—as if those marks in the snow, which were being obliterated as they watched, were their last link with the rest of the world.

Midnight tried valiantly and the cart began to move slowly, and then stopped. Robbie ran up to the cart, lifted the seat board, and produced a shovel. He cleared a lane in front of each wheel for a distance of five or six feet, and then shouted, "Get in, Mother. Try again!"

Mary climbed into the cart and snapped the reins against the horse's flanks as hard as she could. This time Midnight managed to keep the cart going, but only with great difficulty. She was pulling so hard she was slipping and sliding with each step. Every time the cart slowed, Mary thought how strange it was that the most important thing in the world could turn out to be the steady movement of four wagon wheels.

Robbie, back in the cart, huddled beside his mother. He wound his muffler about his face to keep out the piercing wind. It was almost dark. For about half an hour, Midnight tried valiantly to keep going, but as darkness fell, she became more and more unsure of her footing. Twice she slipped off the road, only managing to recover before all was lost; but eventually, what Mary had been dreading happened.

The mare got completely off the road and plunged into a drifted hole up to her belly. She floundered helplessly in the traces. There was only one thing to do. Mary climbed out of the buggy and began to unhitch the horse. To do this, she had to take off her gloves and before she'd finished, the wind and the incredible cold had driven all feelings from her fingers. It communicated itself to her entire body. It seemed to flow up her arms and along her veins like water, while the snow sought out and found every cranny and crevice of her clothing.

Robbie was faring no better, but between them they managed to unbuckle the harness and get Midnight back on the road. Mary took one look at the cart and knew it was there to stay. The horse was still trembling from fright and cold. It was dark now and the wind showed no signs of dropping. It came to her abruptly that there was little chance of her getting out of this, but there was still hope for Robbie. They had to be within a mile or two of the farm.

She put her mouth close to her son's ear and shouted over the wild moaning of the wind. "Robbie, I want you to get on Midnight and see if she will take you home. Get Fred to bring the sleigh out here after me. All he's got to do is follow the road and he'll find me. Do you understand?"

Robbie shook his head in refusal.

"Darlin', please do as I tell you," Mary shouted. "The horse can't carry both of us in this snow."

He set his jaw and shouted back. "I won't leave you."

Mary saw it was useless. She knew she couldn't go far in the snow with her long skirts, but she had to try. "All right, darlin'. Let's go together."

It had been Mary's hope that Midnight would lead them home, but from the first it was apparent that Midnight was not going to lead them anywhere. She stood stock-still in front of the cart and wouldn't move except to turn her withers to the wind. Nothing would induce her to move. There was no alternative but to leave her.

They started off down the road hand in hand, bent almost double, fighting for each step, and each with an arm raised to their forehead to protect their faces from the lashing fury of the snow. Mary's full skirt caught the wind like a parachute and made each step an agony of effort. Twice she fell, and with Robbie's help struggled to her feet. But after the first few minutes, she knew it was useless. The pain in her fingers and feet was excruciating—the blood pounded in her temples —the air seared her lungs with frozen fire. When she collapsed for the third time, she motioned weakly for Robbie to go on without her. He knelt down and tried to lift her but he was not strong enough even to raise her to a sitting position. He shook her frantically, the tears running down his face, the wind tearing the breath from his mouth when he tried to make her hear. Finally he realized it was useless. He stood up.

He understood about the cold as he understood about the forest. If he couldn't get his mother home quickly, she would die here in the snow. He took off his own coat and wrapped it around her huddled figure. The wind slashed at his shirt and leggings and ripped the scarf from around his neck. It disappeared in the white swirl the instant it left him. He stood looking down at his mother for one second, and then forsaking the road which rambled all over the countryside before it reached the farm, he turned and did what appeared to be an insane thing. He plunged headlong into the mass of trees bordering the road.

Beneath the branches, the wind was less violent but the snow clawed at his feet and beat against his body. He stumbled on hidden stumps and rocks, and where they tore his shins and his hands, the blood froze. He staggered drunkenly against invisible trunks and floundered through drifts that were waist high. After a while, his breath came in great sobbing gasps as it had on one other terrible run not so long ago. Each time he fell, he got up a little more slowly, but he kept going. Through it all, one thing remained constant—his direction. He ran straight. Straight as the finger of God through the icy darkness. He could not even see the trees directly ahead of him but he never deviated from his course. No human should have been able to find the way in the darkness let alone in the teeth of a raging blizzard, but Robbie found it. He almost stunned himself when he ran into the fence surrounding the farm.

He pulled himself to his feet, struggled through the wooden rails, floundered across the open area to the barn and flung open the door to Fred's room. There was blood on his left leg and on both hands. He was hatless, coatless, covered with snow.

Fred took one look at him and reached for his coat and snowshoes. "How long ago did you leave her?"

Robbie gasped, "Don't know . . . I ran . . ."

"Git in the house an' fix those cuts. I'll find her." He had his feet in the big snowshoes and started for the door.

Robbie flung himself forward. "No . . . no . . . she'll die if you go by the road . . . too long."

Fred pushed the boy aside wordlessly, snatched the long toboggan from the wall of the barn and stepped out into the wind. Robbie rushed after him, caught at his legs, and Fred fell. He got up cursing. "What's the matter with you?"

Robbie was crying again. "It's too far by the road!"

Fred set his jaw. "And how else can I reach her?"

"I told you. I'll take you. There!" He pointed into the fury of snow where the forest began beyond the potato field.

Fred looked at Robbie as if he were truly insane. "You're crazy! Nobody could find their way through that!"

"I can."

"And maybe you can tell me how'd I get the toboggan through the undergrowth. Git in the house. I tell you, I'll find her!"

117

"I want to go!"

"You'd never make it! Git in the house like you're told."
He reached out and slapped Robbie full in the face. It was the
first time in his life Robbie had ever been struck in the face.
It stunned him enough to make him realize that Fred was
right. Even if he could find his way back through the woods,
they could never get the toboggan through the trees. He
turned and went into the house.

Fred started down the drive, flinging the big ovals of netted
gut outwards and forwards with the awkward rolling motion
of the experienced shoer. They took him across the snow
with remarkable speed. But sustaining that initial speed was
something else. The effort required to move quickly on snowshoes is not only exhausting but dangerous. Suck too much of
that frozen air into overworked lungs and you get lung frost.
It kills quickly and painfully. Fred kept his head well down
in his furs, breathing into the space between his parka and his
underclothing where his body heat warmed the air a little.
By the time he reached the cart, his legs were trembling with
the effort.

There was no sign of Mary. The cart itself was half full of
snow. It looked as if it might have been there for hours. He
tried to pierce the snowswept darkness with narrowed eyes,
but the storm lantern showed him a marble wall. He left the
toboggan by the cart and began making widening circles in
the snow. After five minutes, his left snowshoe landed on a
soft mound and sank deeper than a shoe should. He scraped
away the drifted snow and found Robbie's parka. Beneath
it was the dark bundle he sought.

Mary was asleep, her senses already lulled into a peaceful
numbness by the cold. He slapped her hard, then took off his
mittens and pinched her cruelly. She stirred and opened her
eyes. He kept slapping her till her white face got scarlet from
the blows. Her eyes were glazed, but she was awake.

118

He flung her onto the toboggan and started back. Every few yards he had to stop and go back and slap her again, shake her violently till she opened her eyes. He would never have made it back to the farm if the wind had not begun to drop. When that happened, he covered more distance between his stops. By the time he got back, his head was swimming and his heart thundering against his ribs.

He carried her into the house, dumped her on the bed, ripped off her outer clothing and pulled the blankets over her. He piled wood on the bedroom stove till the roaring crackling fire flung the heat out in waves. He ransacked the kitchen cupboard until he found some cherry brandy and, jerking her roughly into a sitting position, forced it down her throat.

She choked and gagged, but he kept on pounding her on the back and pouring the liquid into her. It ran out of her mouth and onto the blankets and her underclothes, but she got some of it. He slapped her again till her head rocked and the angry weals stood out on her face. She moaned and opened her eyes. He rubbed her hands and feet. He went into the kitchen and made steaming black coffee from the big pot he had put on the stove before Robbie found him. He got almost two cups of that into her and more brandy before he was satisfied. The color began to come back. Her body grew warmer as the circulation increased. She moaned and he began to relax. Only then did he remember Robbie.

He found the boy face down on his own bed. He took off all the boy's clothes and rubbed him with a rough towel till his flesh was red. He gave him the last of the brandy and some coffee, put crude bandages on his cuts and thrust him into bed with his mother.

He watched until both of them were sleeping normally, then sank down on the chesterfield. The jellylike quivering of his insides began to abate. He put his feet up and sighed. He was asleep almost before the sigh escaped his lips.

He awoke about an hour later and put more wood in the stove. Mary and Robbie still slept. He sat down on the side of the bed and looked at them. Mary's dark hair made a soft halo on the pillow. Her skin was creamy white and soft except for where his fingers had left the ugly red splotches and, over the faint purple of her closed eyelids, the dark brows arched gracefully. Her lips were slightly parted and beginning to regain their color. He sat studying her face, memorizing the curve of the cheek and mouth, the way the hair swept back from the temples. Cautiously, he put out a hand and touched her hair. She stirred and he jerked the hand back as if it had been burned. He went out into the kitchen.

The storm had almost blown itself out. He decided he had better go and see about the horse and supplies. The thought of making the trip again was not pleasant, but if the mare froze to death, things would be even more difficult.

By the time he had put on his boots and coat and stepped out into the darkness, the wind had almost died. He made his way down the road slowly, his head pulled deep into his furs. He found the mare and began to lead her back.

The mare's floundering went almost unnoticed. Fred's face was preoccupied. He was not even aware of how long the journey took.

9

Mary awoke to the insistent thrust of a bony knee in the small of her back. She pushed back the covers and twisted to find Robbie curled beside her. There was a crude bandage wound awkwardly around one knee and a crust of dried blood on the upturned palm of one hand, but he slept peacefully and his breathing was deep and regular. She exhaled slowly in grateful relief and brushed a tousled lock back from Robbie's forehead. He was nude except for the rumpled bath towel in which Fred had wrapped him and which was now twisted around his ankle and she realized with a slight start of embarrassment that she herself had been sleeping in her underclothes. She pulled the covers over her and lay back on the pillow trying to remember what had happened.

At first she could recall nothing but the gradual numbness which had overtaken her in the snow after Robbie left; but as her mind awakened, she began to recollect disjointed fragments of the trip home. Fred had put her on a toboggan and he had slapped her to make her wake up. She put a hand to her face and found it tender and slightly swollen. It was a miracle she was still alive. She wondered what time it was. The room was dim, but a bright ruler of sunshine showed at the bottom of the window blind. She heard a footfall in the dining room outside her door and felt her heartbeat quicken in sudden renewed embarrassment. It wasn't going to be easy to face Fred this morning in view of what happened. Had she not been both rude and headstrong, all of this might have been avoided.

The door opened and Fred crossed to the window and raised the blind. Sunshine flooded the room. Robbie awakened and rubbed his eyes. Mary pushed herself up on one elbow. Fred stood with his back to the window. He looked drawn as if he had been up most of the night. She felt a surge of contrition. She said tentatively, "Good mornin', Fred."

The stone-gray eyes swept from her to Robbie and back again. He said, "You all right?"

She nodded self-consciously and looked at Robbie. "Yes, I think so. Robbie?"

Robbie grinned sleepily and rubbed his eyes. "Yes, ma'am."

She waited for some response from Fred and when none came, moistened her lips. "I'm afraid we both owe you a great deal, Fred." He made a sound that was half snort and half grunt and strode out of the room. She heard the rattle of dishes and cutlery and a second later, he came back in bearing a huge breakfast tray which he set on the bed. Mary looked at the tray in astonishment and then could scarcely restrain a smile. The coffee was several shades blacker than ink and the eggs looked as though they might have been run through a mangle. She said, "Fred, this was awfully kind of you, but it wasn't necessary. We're perfectly all right, really."

He scowled. "The porridge is lumpy, but I ain't much of a hand at cookin'."

She looked up at him again. The grim mask of his face had not altered. The familiar resentment still burned in his eyes. And yet there was something terribly stable about him at this moment, and not for the first time she felt a disquieting electricity in his physical presence.

She said gently, "I'm sure it'll be fine, Fred. Thank you."

He went out closing the door without a word. Robbie plunged into the porridge but Mary shook her head in dismay. The things Fred did never seemed to coincide with the way he did them. It was almost as if he were at war not only with the world, but with himself. She sighed and applied herself to the food. After the first mouthful, she looked at Robbie and they both giggled. The porridge was indeed lumpy.

Later in the day, both Robbie and Mary were up and about and within a short time the near tragedy of the storm was almost forgotten, but it had at least one fortuitous aftermath. Fred was as curt as ever, but the vindication of his judgment in regard to the storm seemed to have made him a trifle more tolerant. He allowed Robbie to help him cut the summer supply of ice from the frozen lake. And Robbie, who had had a long talk with his mother about Fred, worked so earnestly and so quietly that Fred began to let him help with other things. Fred did not notice that Robbie never happened to be present when the time came for the rounds of the traps or the skinning of animals and he developed a kind of gruff tolerance for the boy which by Fred's standards almost amounted to affection. For Robbie there was neither the warmth or the understanding in his relationship with Fred that there had been with his father, but the substitute was a great deal better than no relationship at all.

The winter flowed on into Christmas. Fred surprised both the Sharrons by producing a pair of handmade snowshoes for Robbie and a battery radio for Mary which he had bought from a mail-order catalogue. And in spite of the brusque, almost belligerent manner in which he tossed them under the Christmas tree, Mary was touched.

By Easter Sunday, snow was still on the ground but there were signs that spring was not far off. Fred prepared the gear for tapping the maple trees and just as winter had descended upon them unexpectedly, so spring slipped into the countryside one night early in May and lay smiling upon the land. For weeks thereafter the air was heavy with the scent of life's rebirth. The tender green shoots began to nudge their way

123

out of the wet black earth and robins began tugging unwilling angleworms out of the soft ground of the farmyard.

The season wore on and Robbie came in from the forest, his arms loaded with trilliums for the kitchen table. The last vestige of ice disappeared from the rivers and lakes. The world, rid for a few more months of the iron grip of winter, took a deep breath of the spring air and proceeded to clothe itself in perfume and pastels. Robbie renewed his acquaintance with the beavers and the chipmunks and longed for the time when he could leave off his heavy clothing and slip along the deer runs in overalls and bare feet.

When the dirt roads had dried sufficiently to make them passable, Jed Clawson drove over to the Sharron farm to say that there was a crate waiting for Fred in Brownsville. Robbie's eyes opened wide and even Mary found it difficult to restrain her curiosity. The arrival of any kind of a package was a matter of more than passing interest.

Fred said, with typical curtness, "Why didn't you bring it out with you?"

"Would have," said Jed, "but you gotta sign for it."

"Oh."

Robbie couldn't restrain himself any further. "What is it, Fred?"

Mary frowned. "Robbie!"

Robbie looked down, abashed. He said, "Well, he doesn't have to tell me if he doesn't want to."

"Indeed he doesn't, and I hope he won't after that rudeness."

To her disappointment, Fred did not rise to the bait. He said, "If I get started now, I should be back before dark."

Robbie helped hitch the horse, praying every moment that Fred would soften and allow him to go along, but the invitation wasn't forthcoming. He was forced to watch the man drive out the gate alone.

124

Fred went through Pineville without stopping. He returned late in the afternoon with a large wooden crate. He stopped in front of the general store and half a dozen people came out on the front porch including Mr. and Mrs. Campbell and Bedelia Clawson.

Somebody said, "What you got there, Fred . . . one of them newfangled potato peelers?"

Fred colored. "Ain't you got nothin' better to do?"

The man grinned. "Nope." Since the news of Fred's rescue of the Sharrons had got about, Fred was no longer a pariah and the country folk had learned to take his gruff manner for granted. The man glanced around at the other settlers. "We heard you had a good-sized thingamabob settin' around in Brownsville. Been waitin' half the day to see what it is."

Mr. Campbell grinned too. "Somethin' we can do for you, Fred?"

Fred twisted uncomfortably on the wagon seat. He hadn't counted on half the territory being present. "I got somethin' here I don't know how to work. Thought maybe you'd know."

Mr. Campbell scrubbed his chin with his hand. "I cannae rightly say, man, until you tell me what 'tis."

Fred took a breath. "It's a phonograph."

A low murmur of interest went over the group. Bedelia glanced at Mrs. Campbell and the two women exchanged knowing looks.

Bedelia said archly, "Land sakes, Fred, I didn't know you was interested in music?"

"I ain't. But the woman out there says she likes it and the kid ought to get to know about it. The batteries is always runnin' down on the radio."

Mr. Campbell went into the store and came back with a crowbar. "Well, let's open her up and have a look."

Half a dozen pairs of hands assisted in the prying open of the crate. The machine was eased out of the box and onto

125

the floor of the wagon. It sat there with its rich wood gleaming in the late afternoon sun. Somebody found the crank arm and inserted it.

Bedelia said, "Why, it's just beautiful, Fred. Mary will have a fit, she'll be so pleased."

Mr. Campbell said, "Where's the records?"

His wife drew out a cardboard package taped to the side of the crate. "Here they are."

"Let's hope they're not broken."

Fred watched as the box was opened and the shiny black records emerged.

Mr. Campbell read: "Beethoven, Mawzart."

Bedelia said, "Land sakes, Ian, it's not *Bee*thoven, it's *Bay*thoven and Mosart."

Mr. Campbell scowled. "Well, now who in the world is supposed to know that? Here's some more . . . Waggoner," he said heavily.

"*Wau*gner!"

"Here then, you read them," he said impatiently. He handed Bedelia the records. She took them with a lordly air. "Waugner," she said proudly, "Waugner—Lizzut . . ." Mrs. Campbell tapped her on the arm and whispered in her ear. Bedelia hesitated, then shook her head firmly. "No, Fern, I'm sure it's Lizzut—France Lizzut! You never pronounce them the way they look." She turned another record. "Oh, here's one I know very well: excerpts from *Carmen*. Toreador da-da-da-da-da! It's all about a bullfight." The men looked at one another and nodded approvingly. "And the last one is Puseeni *Madame Butterfly*. That's another opera."

"And what's that one about?" Mr. Campbell demanded.

"Well, land sakes, it's a . . . a . . . it's about a woman who dreams she's a butterfly."

Again the bystanders nodded sagely. All except Mrs. Campbell, who didn't know for sure what Madame Butterfly was but she had a strong suspicion it had something to do with water lilies.

Bedelia turned to Fred. "Why, I think you've done wonderfully, Fred. How did you know what to order?"

Fred shrugged. "I just copied out the catalogue numbers. How do you make it go?"

Almost everyone knew the answer to that. They found the package of needles and cranked the handle. Bedelia selected her favorite. They set the record on the turntable and lowered the needle with elaborate care. The rich vibrant overture to *Carmen* filled the clearing. It was a strange tableau. A glossy phonograph on the back of a sun-bleached wagon. A group of rough settlers in levis and homespun standing in the soft white dust of the street and hemmed in by a wall of burnished evergreens, listening raptly. When it was over, there was a chorus of approval. Someone said, "Come on, Fred, play the rest of them," but Fred shook his head.

"I got to git goin' or it'll be dark before I can make it back to the farm."

Reluctantly, they helped him set the phonograph back in the crate, reminded him how to insert the needles and told him not to worry because Mary was sure to know how to run it. They watched him go off across the bridge and into the trees.

Bedelia and Fern Campbell stayed together in the street as the rest of the people climbed into their rigs and drove off. When they were alone, Bedelia said eagerly, "It's just like we said."

Fern nodded. "He's practically a different man. Do you think he's really taken with her?"

"Mercy sakes, of *course* he is! Why else would he buy her a phonograph? Christmas time, it was a radio. And didn't he save her life? Why, it's as plain as the nose on your face."

"What about Mary?"

Bedelia frowned dramatically. "Well, now, there's the hitch. She's still so upset about Tom that I don't think she's given a thought to her position."

"You can't blame her. He was a fine man. When I think what it'd be like without Ian I get cold chills all through me."

"Land sakes, woman, we all feel the same way! But after all, it's been almost a year now. She can't go on livin' alone with that man out there and him worshipin' her the way he does. It's just not right."

"But what if she doesn't want him?"

"She will. We've just got to give her a bit more time. He's not at all bad looking when he stops scowling," she said thoughtfully.

"But what about that other thing?"

"Oh, that's all water under the bridge. It was over ten years ago. He's a changed man. You don't see him flyin' after those shameless hussies now, do you?"

"Nooo, but still. Would you take him?"

"Lan a-goshen, how do I know? A woman can't tell a thing like that till she's confronted with it. But I say in spite of everything, it would be a good match."

"Even if she doesn't love him?"

"Well, supposin' she doesn't. What's she going to do?"

Fern sighed. "You're right. But somehow it does seem a bit unfair. . . ."

As Fred drove through the gate of the farm Robbie burst around the corner of the house and ran up the drive beside the horse.

"Did you get it, Fred?"

Fred nodded and got out of the wagon. He dragged the big crate to the tailboard and lifted it off. "You take the mare into the barn," he said to Robbie.

The delay was exasperating. Robbie tingled to know what was in the box but he did as he was told, then tore back to the house. Fred had set the crate down in the middle of the room. Mary stood by watching with unabashed curiosity. It was obvious that it was something for the house, or Fred would not have brought it inside. He pulled off the lid and lifted out the rich mahogany box. Mary gasped.

"Fred, what is it?"

He raised the top of the player and revealed the turntable. Mary's eyes grew wide with delight. She bit her lip.

"Oh, Fred!"

At the intensity of her delight, he felt the blood rush to his cheeks. Mary looked up and stared at him. The blush deepened to scarlet.

"I hope it's what you wanted," he said.

"It's exactly what I wanted. But, Fred, you shouldn't have done this. It's much too expensive!"

"You said the kid needs to learn about music."

Her heart turned over inside her. There was something terribly touching about this uncouth giant, but along with it there was also something a little disturbing. She was aware that he no longer looked at her impersonally, and these gifts, kind as they were, put her under an obligation she would rather have foregone. And yet she couldn't refuse them without hurting his feelings, particularly when she remembered how often and how terribly he had been hurt in the past. She could only stand there trying to thank him with words and failing hopelessly to warn him that he must not expect more of her than she was prepared to give.

He said, "There's some records. Bedelia says two of 'em are operas. One's about a bullfight."

"*Carmen?* Oh wonderful!" She found the records and began to look through them. "Oh, Fred! Look, Robbie! Beethoven, Mozart, Franz Liszt . . . Bizet's *Carmen* and Puccini's *Madame Butterfly!*"

Fred shifted. "Is that the way you pronounce them names?"

129

Mary smiled. "Why, yes. Why?"

Fred shrugged and the glint of something that might have been amusement came into his eyes. "I kinda figgered Bedelia was overreachin' herself."

Mary laughed. "Did she tell you what to get, then?"

"No. I copied the numbers out of the catalogue, but I stopped in the village on the way back from Brownsville, so I'd be sure to know how it worked and if I got the right things. Bedelia said they was all right." He pointed to the one in Mary's hand. "That one there's about a woman who dreams she's a butterfly."

"Madame Butterfly?"

"Yeah."

Mary restrained a smile. "Fred, it's a lovely present. You couldn't have gotten anything we wanted more. Now Robbie can see that there was something more to European history than just war and politics. What do you say to that, young man?"

Robbie's eyes glowed. "Yes, ma'am."

"And have you nothin' to say to Fred?"

Robbie said, "Thank you, Fred. Thank you very much." He meant it with all his heart.

There were few evenings thereafter when the deep chorus of the frogs or the plaintive cries of the night birds in the vicinity of the Sharron farm were not stilled at least briefly by the magic thunder of the *Eroica* or the haunting sweetness of Mozart's *Magic Flute*.

10

Fred forked the last great pile of hay onto the wagon and leaned his pitchfork against the load. The sweat rolled off his naked back in streams and he wiped his forearm across his eyes and then dug into his pocket for a package of Bull Durham.

It was one of those days when the air was so clear and bright you could almost see it. The sky was a polished blue bowl resting on the circle of hills. Beyond the clearing the maples were green gold against the velvet of the pines, and in the distance the heat waves swam off the roof of the smoke house and shimmered up from the dust of the barnyard. Fred rolled the cigarette slowly, feeling his muscles relax and the sweat cooling his skin as it dried. He looked around him in satisfaction. The land looked good and the summer's harvest had been even better than he had expected.

On top of the wagon, Robbie spread the forkful of hay and then slid to the ground. He watched gravely as Fred licked the cigarette paper, twisted the end expertly, and then hitched his trousers with his elbows and reached for a match. He lit the match on the steel rim of the wagon wheel and broke it carefully after lighting the cigarette. Unexpectedly, he looked down and flicked the match at Robbie. Robbie ducked and grinned in surprise. Coming erect, he automatically hitched his trousers with his elbows as Fred had done a moment earlier.

Fred pulled on the cigarette and blew the smoke out slowly. He watched it float away and then glanced at Robbie again, noticing the hard little boy muscles that were coming into Robbie's arms and shoulders. He reached out and caught Robbie's upper arm in one big calloused palm.

"You gitten some meat on you, boy," he said.

Robbie grinned again, shyly. It was the first time Fred had ever touched him in a friendly way or said anything that might be construed as approval. He scratched at the straw with one bare foot, slid his toes under a little hutch of dry grass and kicked it into the air. The chaff floated straight down in the quiet air.

Fred took a deep drag on his cigarette and frowned a little. Finally, he said, "You ever been to a carnival, kid?"

Robbie said, "What's a carnival?"

Fred scratched the back of his head with a thumbnail and pursed his lips. "Well, it's a kind o' city made outta tents. You pay money to git into it an' then they got fat women and sword swallowers and guys that eat fire."

Robbie's eyes grew wide. "Eat fire?"

"They light bulrushes and things like that and then they put 'em out in their mouths."

"Sure an' it must burn them somethin' terrible!"

"Don't seem to. A man figgers to cut his throat swallowin' them swords, too, but they don't never seem to do it somehow. I reckon people keep on watchin' 'cause they know someday they might."

"Why do they?"

"Why do they what?"

"Eat fire and swallow swords."

Fred shrugged. "Why to make money, I guess. People pay to see 'em do it."

"Is the fat lady as fat as Mrs. Clawson?"

Fred spat. "Hell, she ain't fat. These women are big. Make four of old Mrs. Clawson."

"What else is there?"

"Well, there's games, see. You get to throw baseballs at milk bottles and if you knock the milk bottles down you get a prize."

Robbie scratched his head, thoughtfully. He was interested but confused. "But is it not a great waste of milk?"

"They ain't real bottles," Fred said, impatiently, "they're made of wood or somethin'."

Robbie nodded. He still wasn't clear on the whole principle but he wisely decided not to pursue it further. "What else is there?"

Fred thought for a moment. "There's pink lemonade."

Robbie's eyes lighted like magic. "*Pink* lemonade?"

"Yep, and they got a thing called a merry-go-round."

"What's a merry-go-round?"

"It's a thing that goes round with horses on it."

"Real horses?"

"No, not real horses. Wood ones. They go up and down on a pole."

"Why?"

Fred flung his cigarette down and ground it, angrily. "How the hell do I know why! 'Cause kids like to ride on 'em that's why."

"Did you ever ride on them then?"

"No, I ain't. Now let's get this load up to the barn."

"Yes, sir." Robbie climbed into the seat and watched Fred follow. He was dying to ask more questions but he held his tongue. Fred always got impatient if you talked too much. This morning was the longest conversation they'd ever had. But the vision of a man who ate fire and a woman four times as fat as Mrs. Clawson and pink lemonade stayed inside him. It germinated. A city of tents had enormous possibilities.

When the haying was finished he ran to the house and leaned over the cutting board where Mary was paring vegetables for lunch. His damp hair was hanging in his eyes and the sweat on his upper lip had caught a fine film of dust from the hay. His shoulders were streaked with dirt where the perspiration had run in rivulets down his skin. Mary shook her head helplessly. "Saints preserve us, lad, you can get yourself dirtier than any child that ever lived."

"We've been hayin', Mother."

"You don't say. And what do you want in my kitchen?"

Robbie shoved the dark hair back from his eyes. "Can a man eat fire now?"

"Of course he can't, silly. Whatever put that in your head?"

"Fred says he can. He says a man can swallow swords, too, and that there's a woman fatter than Mrs. Clawson . . . four times fatter maybe."

Mary kept a straight face with difficulty. "Robbie, Mrs. Clawson's not fat. You're not to talk like that. It's very rude, son."

"Yes, ma'am. But what about the man who eats fire?"

"Well, in circuses there are people who swallow swords and the like of that, but they only do it because it's not natural. Do you see what I mean?"

"I do not."

Mary sighed. "Well, in a circus men do strange things just because they know that other men can't. People will pay money to see something that they don't believe can be done."

"Is a circus like a carnival?"

"In a way. A carnival is smaller, is all. And why all this talk about fire-eaters and carnivals?"

"Fred told me." Mary put down the paring knife in surprise.

"Did he now? That doesn't seem like him a-tall."

Robbie frowned, gravely. "I didn't think so myself, but he said a lot this mornin'. He says there's a merry-go-round and pink lemonade and a place where you try to break milk bottles for prizes."

Mary turned away with a strange look on her face. She was realizing for the first time how really isolated they were. In the city a child Robbie's age would know all about such things and here he was struggling just to comprehend what it meant. She said, "Sit down here, Robbie, and I'll tell you all I know."

She told him and as he began to grasp the meaning of her words his eyes got wider and wider. His mouth fell open in slightly ludicrous astonishment. Spun sugar on sticks, dogs that rode horseback, carrousels, shooting gallerys, bands in colored uniforms, candied apples, wheels that took you right up into the sky. Why it was a whole world made just for having fun! He thought he would rather see a carnival than anything else he could think of. He went out of the kitchen with a strangely rapt look on his face and watching him Mary felt a little catch at her heart.

That night after supper, Fred pushed his chair back from the table and instead of going out to the barn as was his custom, he scratched his neck self-consciously and then turned to Mary. "There's somethin' I'd like to speak to you about."

"Of course, Fred, what is it?"

"The hayin's almost finished. Come the week end there's nothin' particular got to be done."

She waited expectantly.

"There's a carnival comin' to Brownsville."

You could almost hear the sound of Robbie's eyelids snapping upwards. He could hardly believe he had heard correctly. He held his breath while his mother looked at him in amusement. "So that's what all the talk was about this mornin'?"

"I didn't know about the carnival, Mother. Cross my heart, I didn't."

"Is it thinkin' of goin' you were, Fred?"

"Well, it ain't so much me but the boy here. He ain't never been to a fair. I figger it's somethin' a kid's got a right to. I

seen the poster when I was in Brownsville gettin' the phonograph."

Mary frowned. "You'd like to take Robbie to the fair
then?"

Fred took a breath and twisted in his chair. "Well, it ain't
only Robbie. I figgered maybe you'd like to go, too. You ain't
been out since I been here."

"Well, I don't know, Fred." Inwardly she was more than
pleased at the thought that Robbie might see the fair but
she was also a little disturbed by the implications of her going to the carnival with Fred. It meant that their relationship
would have to undergo a change which she was not sure she
wanted. On the other hand, she could hardly refuse. It was unexpectedly thoughtful of him to think of Robbie and it was
natural enough for her to go along. While she hesitated, Robbie said, "Oh, please, Mother. Just this once. I've never been
at all."

Mary sighed. "Well, darlin', I see no reason why we
shouldn't go except that Brownsville is thirty miles away and
it would be a terrible trip by buggy."

"Oh, Mommy, we could do it now. You know we could."

Fred said, "If that's all that's worryin' you, there's no problem. Jed's kids have got the measles an' he ain't goin'. He says
he'll lend us the Ford for the day. It ain't more'n an hour by
car."

Robbie began to tingle all over. He felt that any second he
might just explode right out of his body. A fair and a ride
in an automobile all in one day! It was almost too much to get
his imagination around. He'd never ridden in an automobile.
Once his father had asked Mr. Campbell to give Robbie a
ride but when they got in, Mr. Campbell hadn't been able to
get the car started. The frustration had been with Robbie ever
since. And here, if his mother would only consent, was another
chance. He squirmed on his chair in an agony of suspense.

136

Watching him, Mary, even if she had wanted to refuse would have been helpless.

"Well, Fred," she said, "it seems we've no choice but to accept your invitation with thanks!"

"Whoops! We're goin' to the fair—we're goin' to the fair!" Robbie lunged out of his chair and, spreading his arms like an airplane, zoomed around the kitchen. He dived at his mother and she fended him off, laughing, "Go on with you now. Is it gone crazy you are?"

When Fred left, Robbie threw his arms around his mother and hugged her till she lost her breath. "Go on with you," she said again. "I suppose we won't be gettin' a lick of work out of you for the next few days."

While Robbie was assuring his mother with all the fervor at his command that he would be a veritable avalanche of destruction as far as the work was concerned, Fred made his way to the barn. He sat down on the bunk in his room.

He was remembering the way she looked when she smiled; the way her brows pulled together when she was worried or perplexed, and the way her breast swelled above the gingham apron. The thoughts made his heart hammer and put a strange whispering emptiness in the pit of his stomach. There was a curious ache growing inside him. One which he didn't understand.

11

Mary set the picnic basket on the grass and sank down beneath the big maple tree. Her face was flushed and her eyes shining. "Gracious," she said, laughingly, "I've not been so exhausted since I had all four of the terrible Hennessys in one class."

Fred lowered himself to the grass beside her. He said, "He's a handful all right."

"He's havin' that good a time, it tires me out just to watch him."

"He ain't missin' anythin', that's for sure."

"Where is he now?"

"On them airplane swings."

"Again?"

"He likes 'em."

"Did you tell him where we'd be?"

"Yep. But I don't think he'll be wantin' any lunch."

"Oh, I'm so afraid he'll be sick."

"A kid's entitled to get sick at his first carnival."

She smiled then. "Were you?"

"I never seen one 'til I was growed."

"And why not?"

Fred shrugged. "There was never nobody to take us."

"Never?"

"Well, once my paw set out to bring us to a circus. Me and my brother Billy. We never got there."

"Why?"

"He met some of his cronies on the street and told us to

wait outside till he had a beer. We waited for three hours. When he came out he was drunk and he didn't have no money left. Billy cried all the way home. That's the closest we ever got."

"But that's terrible."

He dropped his eyes. "It was a long time ago."

She studied him for a moment as he pulled at the grass between his feet. He had on a stiff collar which was rapidly wilting around the edges. The sleeves of his shiny blue serge suit were too short, and the material stretched perilously tight across his big shoulders. She could see the outlines of the muscles through the cloth. His stiff blond hair was dutifully combed but it stuck up at the back around the cowlick like a peacock's tail. He had cut himself twice while shaving and his neck was red from the unaccustomed pressure of the hard collar. In spite of everything, he looked ruthlessly scrubbed and even the scarred and broken fingernails had somehow been cleaned. He had made a tremendous effort. She suddenly felt a surge of tenderness for him. He was not a stupid man and had his background and opportunities been different, there was no telling what he might have become. As it was, he was a misfit. And, if the portions of his life she knew about were any criterion, he had been badgered by misfortune since the day he was born. It was little wonder he had not developed an engaging personality. And there was nothing anyone could do for him. That was the real tragedy. Perhaps that was what made her uneasy sometimes. That and a sense of something in him which was unresolved and a little frightening.

Today was the first day she hadn't felt it. The first time that his eyes had lost a little of their resentfulness. He had actually been fun. He had won all sorts of prizes at the games and the Ford was full of teddy bears and plaster statues he had pressed on her and Robbie. He had taken no liberties except for putting an arm around her once on the ferris wheel. She

139

had been expecting something of the sort and had been prepared to resent it. But somehow she hadn't. The day wouldn't permit. The bright sun, the gay colors, the laughing faces, the shrieks of mock terror, and the raucous bellowing of the calliope, had woven a kind of enchantment. It had made her a little lightheaded so that her heart had even beat a trifle faster when Fred held her. And then Robbie had been in transports of excitement and that, too, had been irresistible and infectious. She had not been so happy or had so much fun since Tom died. And for the first time, the thought of him did not hurt the way it had and she realized that at last she had struggled up that first long step back to sanity.

She pulled her damp hair away from the nape of her neck and lay back on the grass. The shaded turf was cool against her. Above, through the thick leaves of the maple, there were tiny patches of blue and little balls of cotton cloud. Down by the lake a boy shouted, "Dad! Dad, I've got a whopper. Quick!" She smiled and closed her eyes. After a moment or two, she heard Fred say, "Here he comes." She opened her eyes and looked. He pointed behind her. She sat up and followed the direction of his finger. Robbie was wandering through the trees with a large pink cotton candy on a paper cone clutched in his hand. Every so often he would stop and examine a group of picnickers and if they laughed his face would crease in a smile, then he would bury it in the big ball of fluff and pull it away with patches of sugar stuck all over his mouth. His hair was tousled and his face was dirty. He had his shoes tied by their laces and hung around his neck. When he saw them he came over and stood there grinning rapturously.

Mary said, "Saints preserve us, Robbie, not more sweets!"

The shameless grin widened. To her knowledge, he had had five glasses of pink lemonade, three candy apples, four hot dogs, two bags of peanuts, a box of cracker jack, and an uncounted number of candy flosses like the one he was carrying. He stuck out his tongue and retrieved a bit of sugar stuck at the side of his mouth.

Mary shook her head. "Would you mind tellin' me why you had to take off your shoes?"

"They hurt."

"But, Robbie, you can't be . . . oh, why not. If they're uncomfortable, there's no reason in the world for you to be wearin' them."

Robbie took the shoes from around his neck and dumped them beneath the tree. "Can I go on the merry-go-round?"

"But you've been on it half a dozen times already."

He shook his head. "Only twice. I've been on the airplane swings more."

"But, Robbie, don't you get sick goin' round and round like that?"

He shook his head. "I like it."

She smiled. "All right then. I don't suppose you'll be wantin' any lunch." For just a second she thought he looked a bit green but he rallied bravely.

"No, thank you." He pursed his lips, sucked in a last blob of half melted sugar from the paper cone, then put the dirty fingers in his mouth and licked them, rapturously.

Mary said, "Robbie! Do you not see those fingers are covered with dirt?"

"Yes, ma'am." But his eyes were devilish. "You've got to eat a peck o' dirt before you die!"

"Well, you've had more than your share this day alone. Now be off with you and don't get lost."

"No, ma'am." He turned and went off, skipping first on one foot and then the other. Mary shook her head again.

"Faith and I don't know what I'm goin' to do with him."

Fred ran a finger round his wilted collar and stared after

141

Robbie thoughtfully. After a moment he said, "I ain't never seen a kid that happy before."

The tone of his voice brought Mary's head up. He was still following Robbie's dwindling figure with grave absorption. She understood abruptly why Fred had insisted on buying Robbie everything he wanted, and why he had stubbornly refused to let her give the child any of her own money. She bent her head and opened the picnic basket. She took out a sandwich and held it toward Fred. "Are you hungry?"

"What?"

She smiled. "I said, are you hungry?"

"Oh, thanks." He took the sandwich and the greater part of it disappeared in one enormous bite. "How old is he?"

"Why, I thought you knew. He's eight."

"He ain't very big for eight, is he?"

There it was again. The cryptic, almost brutal, observation. It wasn't the words. Anyone else could have said them and they would have been a simple statement of fact. When Fred said them it made her hackles rise so that even in her present mood she had to force herself not to make an angry retort. She took a breath.

"He's always been small," she said.

"Yeah." He stared at her a second. "You was a school-teacher."

It was a statement more than a question but she nodded. "Yes, in Ireland."

"What did you teach?"

"Oh, most everythin'. Readin', writin', arithmetic, geography, history."

He swallowed the last of the sandwich and she saw his Adam's apple bob as it went down. "I left in the third grade."

"And why did you do that?"

"They put my paw in jail. I kept gettin' into fights with the

142

kids. They called him a jailbird. It was true but it made me mad. Billy couldn't fight. He just used to cry."

"Didn't your mother mind you leavin' school?"

"She didn't seem to care. We ran away after a while."

"And how old were you then?"

"Fourteen or fifteen, I guess."

"What did you do then?"

"I worked."

"Where?"

"On a railroad gang."

"At fifteen?"

"I was big for my age. I told 'em I was seventeen. Don't know as they believed me, but they give me a man's wages. It was better than livin' at home."

"You've never seen your parents since?"

"Nope. Billy got sick once and he wanted his maw. I took him back."

"They must have been glad to see you."

"They was gone—both of 'em. Nobody knew where."

"How terrible!"

He broke a stick in his fingers and tossed the fragments away. "It was a long time ago," he said again. "Don't do no good cryin' about it now. Can I have another sandwich?"

"Sorry. Of course, you can." She held out the basket and then poured tea from the thermos. He took the cup and looked at her. "You havin' a good time?"

She smiled. "I'd not have missed it for the world. I feel like I'm nineteen all over again."

He nodded, soberly. "That's good. You look different."

She laughed. "How?"

He scratched his head. "I don't know. I guess maybe you look nineteen."

She laughed again, the bright bubble of sound he hadn't heard in all the months he'd been on the farm. "Well, now, if you've had enough I think we could straighten up here. The time's passin' and I'd like to see the midgets 'fore we go."

He took the basket and helped her to her feet. They went off through the trees. In the distance, Lily Cartwright from Pineville nudged her husband. "Harry, look!"

Harry, lying on his back with an arm thrown across his eyes, grunted. "What is it?"

"Look, silly, quick!"

He raised up on one elbow. "What?"

"There." She pointed through the trees in the picnic grounds.

He shrugged. "I don't see nothin'," he said, irritably.

"You're impossible. It's Mary Sharron!"

"What about it?"

"Why, she's with her hired man—that Fred Carter. He had his arm around her a moment ago and she was smiling at him."

"Oh, for the love of Mike!"

She thrust out her lower lip. "Well, maybe you don't think that's anything but after all they're livin' together alone out there on her farm."

"So what?"

"So it's very interesting that's all."

Harry laid back on the grass in his original position. "Why don't you women keep your noses out of other people's affairs?" After a few seconds he went back to sleep but his wife continued to stare avidly after the dwindling figures of Mary and Fred. She could hardly wait to get back to Pineville to spread the news.

They stayed at the carnival until after dark so Robbie could watch the lights come on. Except for one gloomy afternoon in Brownsville when the light of the sawmill had burned briefly before closing time, Robbie had never seen electric lights. He gasped as the city of tents exploded into a splendor

144

past imagining. Every booth, every platform, shimmered and glowed. The lights climbed guy wires, winked under taut canvas, gleamed on the gaudy banners. From the open tent fronts rivers of warm radiance poured onto the creamy wood chips of the midway and high, high up, the red, green and yellow lights of the ferris wheel moved in a perfect arc against the darkening sky. As if the change had infected them, too, the barkers shouted more loudly, the calliope clanged and wheezed in delight, men laughed and women shrieked. Robbie was stabbed through with the wonder of it. Beyond the tents, the outlines of trees and hills turned themselves into dark silhouettes; the shadows marched in across the road and parking lot but the lights were orange fireflies among the maples of the picnic ground and the carnival was an island of pleasure in the night. Robbie was speechless. They pulled him away slowly, while his eyes devoured and memorized the scene. He climbed wordlessly into the back seat of the Ford, stared till the last light on the topmost pinnacle of the ferris wheel was obscured by a hill and still he did not move. He stayed where he was, his eyes glued to the spot where the light had disappeared.

When they got home they found him asleep in the back seat. He had a tiny smile tucked around the corners of his mouth and he slept so soundly that Fred carried him into his room and put him to bed without awakening him.

Mary brewed coffee and she and Fred sat on opposite sides of the table in the kitchen. For the first time in the day they were both a little self-conscious. Except for that moment in the barn more than a year ago it was the first time they had been alone together as a man and a woman. They were both conscious of the fact that during the day their relationship had changed but away from the gaiety and excitement of the carnival they didn't quite know how to take one another.

Mary poured the coffee and then broke the silence. "Fred,

I don't know how to thank you for today. I don't think I've ever seen Robbie so happy."

Fred shrugged a little awkwardly. "Yeah. He seemed to get a kick out of it."

"Seemed! He loved every minute of it. He'll be talkin' about it for weeks. It's nice for him to have a good time like that. Especially since there aren't any other children for him to play with."

There was a long silence. Finally, Fred said, bluntly, "I'm glad *you* had a good time."

"Oh, I did! It was wonderful. It was fine of you to take us both."

He fiddled with his teaspoon for a moment. "You should get out like that more often," he said roughly. "It would do you good." He looked across the table at her. She was looking down at the moment and her face was a little drawn from the strain of the day. It had the effect of making her look very appealing and helpless. Fred wet his lips and felt the desire rise up in him. As if she had sensed it, she looked up and met his eye. For a second, their eyes locked and held; and then Fred picked up his cup, drained it, and took out the spoon.

He got to his feet. "Well, I better get the milkin' done. Good night."

"Good night, Fred." She stretched out her hand and he took it. "Thank you again. You have been very kind."

Her hand felt very soft in his. He held it for a moment and then let it go. "Good night," he said again, and went out the kitchen door into the night.

Mary stood looking after him for a long time.

12

For three weeks after the carnival, the country folk had a field day speculating on the relationship between Mary Sharron and her hired man. Mary went to town twice and found herself alternately angered and amused at the general air of expectation, the knowing looks and the thinly veiled questions as to how she had enjoyed herself. The gossip came as no particular surprise. Knowing the north country she had been expecting something of the sort and, at home, she resolutely put it out of her mind. However, within a week of her last visit to town, two incidents occurred which brought the gossip into somewhat sharper focus.

In a sense the incidents were related and they began late in the morning when she and Fred were packing apples outside the barn. They had been working for perhaps half an hour when Robbie pushed open the gate and hurried up the drive. He had almost reached the concealment of the house when Fred glanced up and saw him an instant before he disappeared from view.

Mary, following Fred's frown, said, "What is it, Fred?"

"Robbie."

"I don't see him."

"He just disappeared behind the house."

"Are you sure? He's been at the Clawson's all morning."

" 'Course I'm sure. Looked to me like he was hopin' we wouldn't see him."

Mary knitted her brow. "That's strange. It's not like him

a-tall." She glanced at Fred again and then raised her voice and called, "Robbie! Robbie!!"

"You want me to go get him?"

"No, he'll come. Robbie!"

There was a long pause, then Robbie appeared at the corner of the house. He came toward them slowly, head down, feet dragging in the dust of the driveway. Instantly Mary dropped the basket of apples and made a lunge in his direction. Fred's big hand flicked out, snapping her to a halt. "Leave him alone."

"But there's somethin' wrong!"

"He ain't a baby. Let's find out what it is, before you go jumpin' to conclusions."

Mary shook the restraining hand off, angrily, but waited while Robbie came forward. He stopped about thirty feet away.

She swallowed the lump in her throat and tried to make her voice sound normal. "Robbie, what is it? What's the matter?"

Robbie drew a circle in the dust with one bare foot and shook his head, refusing to look up. "Robbie, come over here." Again the death march began. He moved his feet as if each one was made of lead. Finally, he stood almost in front of her. His shirt was torn, his hair full of dust, and his fists were tightly clenched. "Robbie, look at me."

He raised his head. His nose was bleeding, one eye was swelling visibly and his lip was cut. Mary gave a choked cry and opened her arms. "Darlin'!"

Again Fred's hand bit into her arm hard. "For the love of Mike, woman, *leave him be!* Can't you see he don't want to be mollycoddled?" Fred was right. At Mary's cry, Robbie had winced and when she opened her arms to him, he had actually backed up. She bit her lip, trying to keep herself under control. He looked so frightful!

148

As if he had read her thoughts, Fred chuckled. "Git a hold of yourself, woman. He ain't hurt. He's just messed up a little." He took a step toward Robbie and squatted down. He eyed the nose and the bleeding lip critically. "Been in a fight, huh?"

Mary caught her breath. Fred said, "Look, you might as well get used to this. He's a boy. It may be the first fight he's been in, but as sure as hell it won't be the last." Mary felt her temper flaring. With an effort, she forced herself to say nothing. Fred looked at Robbie. "How'd it happen?"

Robbie swallowed painfully. "They were shooting at the cat with their air rifle."

"Who?"

"Pete and Billy."

"The Clawson kids?"

Robbie nodded. "I told them it wasn't right, but they just laughed at me."

"Then what?"

"They shot some more and . . . and . . ."

"And you tried to stop them?"

"Yes."

Fred glanced up at Mary. "Looks like it was his fault all right."

Mary exploded. "*His* fault! Because he tried to keep a dumb animal from being hurt?"

Fred snorted. "It wasn't none of his business. He's got no call to interfere with what the Clawsons do or don't do."

"Perhaps you'd like it better if Robbie had let them kill the cat?"

"Don't appear to me as if he'd stopped 'em one way or another. Did you?"

Robbie shook his head miserably.

"I thought not. All he did was get himself beat up. Guess

149

I'll have to teach him how to take care of himself. Which one was it?"

Robbie hung his head again. "Both of them."

Fred snorted. "Both of 'em? Well, at least, you don't do things by halves. You go on with your mother. She'll put some venison on that eye."

Robbie turned and started toward the kitchen door and Mary followed without a word. In the kitchen, as she bathed the battered face, Robbie looked at her. "Mommy, was it wrong like Fred said, to try and stop them from hurtin' the cat?"

"No, darlin', that is . . ." She stopped, torn between the truth and the thought that if she condoned his behavior, he'd probably get into more fights defending his convictions. "No, you were right, Robbie, except that you should try to persuade them without resortin' to violence."

"But I *did* try, Mommy!"

Mary sighed, "Yes." There was no answer to that. There never would be an answer to that. There hadn't been in the whole history of mankind. She put a final cold compress on his nose, gave him a pat on the head, and sent him out to play. After he had gone, she sat down at the table and put her head in her hands.

Fred was right, of course. He had handled the situation the way only a man could. She did not agree with his reasoning about Robbie's position in the argument, but he had kept her from making a fool of herself in Robbie's eyes. Furthermore, he was right when he said Robbie had to be shown how to take care of himself. The world was hard. One had to learn to fight, physically as well as morally, and the former, a woman couldn't teach a man child. She sighed and stood up. As she went out the door, Bedelia Clawson drove her buggy into the gate. Her round, chubby face was wreathed in an anxious frown.

150

She scrambled out of the rig and came toward Mary. "Mary, Mary, I'm so terribly sorry. I just got the truth out of Pete and Billy. They had a fight with Robbie."

"I know, Bedelia."

"Is he all right? I mean, they didn't hurt him?"

"Not really. He had a bloodied nose and a black eye. Nothing serious."

"Oh, Mary . . . I'm simply mortified. I really don't know what we're going to do with those boys. They're holy terrors, both of them. And they're so much bigger than Robbie."

Mary forced a smile she was far from feeling. "It's all right, Bedelia, really it is. Boys will be boys, you know. Come and have a cup of tea."

"Well, if you're sure it's all right?"

"Don't be silly, Bedelia, come in."

"Thank you. I can't tell you how upset I've been. I'll see that Jed laces them both when he comes in."

Mary thought it might help if Bedelia did a little lacing herself, but she didn't say so. She brewed the tea listening with half an ear while Bedelia chattered on, inconsequentially, about one thing and another. It wasn't until Mary was filling the cups that Bedelia fell abruptly silent. Mary glanced up in surprise in time to see her friend's eyes filling with a kind of nervous anticipation and her lips pursing to an expression of exaggerated concern. Mary sighed inwardly. What she had just witnessed was an infallible sign that Bedelia was about to plunge into something that was none of her business. She stirred some sugar into her tea and waited. Bedelia glanced around melodramatically as if there might be an eavesdropper behind the kitchen stove, then leaned across the table and spoke in a confidential whisper. "Mary, I hadn't intended to say a word about this, but now that I'm here. . . ."

"Yes?"

"Well, land sakes', child, it's no business of mine . . . it's just that I think you ought to know for your own good."

"Know what, Bedelia?"

"I hardly know how to say it . . . after all, we are friends . . . and I, for one, know that there's not a word of truth in . . . Oh, landa goshen, I just don't know whether I dare!"

"What is it, Bedelia?"

"Well, the truth is, Mary . . . there's talk in the village."

"About Fred and me?"

Bedelia's jaw dropped in astonishment. "You mean you know?"

"I've known for some time."

"Well, gracious, child, aren't you upset?"

"Not really . . . it was bound to happen."

Bedelia shook her head. This was not going at all as she had expected. She said, "Well, after all, Mary, you really can't blame them in a way. It's as plain as the nose on your face that the man is wild about you and after all, he did kiss you on the ferris wheel."

"Bedelia, how dare you!"

Bedelia got scarlet. "Well, I . . . I'm only repeating what I heard."

"Well, you heard wrong! For your information, Fred Carter has never kissed me in his life."

Bedelia was seriously flustered. "Well, now, you see it's just like I thought. I knew it was all talk from the first."

Mary put her head in her hands and laughed helplessly. "Oh, Bedelia!"

"Mary, what's the matter? Are you all right?"

Mary raised her head. "Yes, I'm all right."

"If I'd known it would upset you so I'd never have breathed a word of it."

"Of course you wouldn't."

"I only said what I did to warn you. I did it for your own good."

"Yes, I know."

"I know there's nothing between you and Fred and you know it but there are *some* people who have nothin' better to do than imagine things. The trouble is that even though it's all in their minds, a person can't pretend it doesn't exist."

"Now tell me, Bedelia, what would you do if you were in my position?"

"Gracious, I don't know! You can't very well get rid of Carter. You need him so. And you can't just go on as you are. . . ."

"That only leaves one alternative, doesn't it?"

"Oh, Mary, we all know how you felt about Tom. But he's been gone for over a year, child. You've got yourself to think of and Robbie, and the farm. And you can't deny the man's in love with you?"

"Is he?"

"You know he is. And he has improved so much since he's been around you. Why, I just bet that after another year or two you'll have made him over so nobody would even recognize him."

"Supposing he doesn't want to be made over."

"Of course he will. Look at the way he's changed already. And he's not unattractive when he stops scowling."

"Then you suggest I marry Fred?"

"Well, it's not for me to say, Mary, but everyone thinks that. . . ."

"I understand, Bedelia."

Bedelia held her breath. "Then you will marry him?"

Mary smiled helplessly. "I don't know, Bedelia, he hasn't asked me."

Mary's first impulse on Bedelia's departure was to treat the whole episode as she had the gossip in the village, but later that evening she found herself beginning to consider the implications of Bedelia's visit more seriously. At the moment Bedelia was only repeating gossip. She knew that. There was little to talk about in the north and any kind of relationship between unmarried people was bound to excite more than passing interest. But the more she thought, the more she began to realize that gossip, however erroneous it might be, was something that could not be ignored indefinitely. The people of the north had a very strict moral code. In deference to her grief and their own respect for Tom Sharron, they had held the code in abeyance for a reasonable period in the knowledge that the farm had to be kept up and a man was needed for that purpose. But, as Bedelia had pointed out, more than a year had passed since Tom's death and the time was approaching when she must take stock of her position. It would not do in this sparsely populated land to alienate the few good friends she had by ignoring convention. It seemed probable that after this flurry of knowing and vicarious excitement had passed, tongues would begin to wag in deadly earnest. She wiped the last plate thoughtfully, then hung up her apron and went out to the front porch. Robbie was squatting on the top step and he looked up at her and smiled as she sat down in the big rocker. His eye had now turned a beautiful purple black and she winced as he thoughtfully prodded the swollen flesh over the cheekbone.

She said, "Does it hurt?"

He turned to her again. "Not much, but it feels funny . . . like it was bigger than my head."

She managed to smile. "It almost is."

"Fred says it will be gone in a few days."

She sat back in her chair and stared out at the sky for a few moments. Then she said, "You like Fred, don't you, Robbie?"

Robbie frowned. It was a bad time to ask him for the remark Fred had made about the cat was still fresh in his memory. He wanted to say he hated Fred but he was essentially an honest child and if he hated Fred, then he also hated the Clawson kids and all the hunters and trappers who didn't mind killing or maiming animals in their traps . . . even his own father. He weighed Fred's remark about the cat against the carnival and the phonograph and the snowshoes and the man's sheer bigness and he said, "I guess I like him all right."

"Would you like it if he stayed here forever?"

"Is he not goin' to?"

"Well, I don't know. It's just somethin' to think about. He's only working here you know."

"I'd not like for him to go away. He gives us such nice things—like the phonograph."

Mary smiled. "Is that the only reason you want him to stay with us?"

Robbie pondered gravely, "He can bend fork tines in his hands."

"Can he now?"

"He can that and lift the wagon without a jack."

"Robbie, . . . Supposin' . . . supposin' Fred were to be your father. Would you like that?"

"My father's dead."

"Well, I don't mean your real father. I mean sort of another father."

"How could he be that now?"

Mary sighed. "Well now that your father isn't with us any more, I'm what's called a widow. If I ever married again, my new husband would be your stepfather."

"Are you going to marry Fred, then?"

"Well, I wouldn't say I'm going to marry *anyone*. I was only thinkin' about the possibility."

He put his hand on his chin and considered it. Finally he said, "Couldn't we just go on as we are?"

155

"I'm afraid not—not for much longer, anyway."

"Why not?"

"Well, I can't explain, lad. You'd not understand. You will someday."

"Do you want to marry Fred?"

She hesitated. "I haven't given it much thought until just now." She put an arm around him. "But I won't marry anyone unless you want it."

Robbie put his chin in his hand. "Would it make much difference—if you married Fred, I mean?"

"Not really. He'd have to sleep in the house instead of the barn, that's about all."

Robbie considered gravely. It didn't seem like a very big change. "All right, marry him."

Mary laughed. "Now wait a minute. Let's not be losin' our heads. I'm not the least bit sure I want to get married, but even if I did, I'd have to wait for the man to ask me first."

"Why couldn't you ask him?"

She laughed again. "That's another thing that may be a little difficult for you to understand. Women don't ask men to marry them. They have to be asked."

"Why?"

"Well, I don't know exactly. It's just the way things are. So you mustn't say anything to Fred or anyone else."

"All right."

"And if I decide not to, you won't mind too much, will you?"

He shook his head.

And so the first barrier was removed. Fred had not been consulted, but then few men ever are.

13

A few days after Bedelia's visit, Fred went over to the Clawson farm to help lay a new flooring in the barn loft. Jed hadn't asked for his help, but Fred had seen Jed buying the new lumber in Pineville and had not forgotten that Jed had loaned him his car and refused to accept anything for the favor.

They finished the work along about late afternoon and Jed, grateful for the assistance in a job which was backbreaking for one man but relatively easy for two, opened a bottle to celebrate. A half hour later, neither of them was fully sober. Jed had always had a secret and somewhat guilty admiration for Fred because the man was everything that he himself was not. Jed was a small man, Fred was a giant. Jed's past had been open and uneventful, Fred's had been mysterious and fraught with crisis and danger. Jed had spent his life with a simple, gossipy country girl while Fred had married a sexy young prostitute. Jed had always wondered how a prostitute made love and what she said to her man when they were in bed together. Years ago when he was making love to Beddy regularly and listening to her girlish squeals of ecstasy, he would try to imagine what Fred's wife would be like if she were flexing her loins beneath him,—what lewd, lascivious things she might be whispering in his ear. What tricks to excite a man did she know that would horrify Beddy if they were even suggested to her. Standing next to a man who knew the answers to all these questions gave Jed a peculiar feeling of pride and envy. He felt expansive and convivial. They were standing on the new planking of the loft leaning against the safety bar

157

of the open haying door. Above the low-lying hill, the top of the Sharron house was just visible with a streamer of silver smoke glued to the top of the chimney. Jed took a long pull at the half empty bottle and handed it to Fred. "Seems like Mary's started the vittles already." Fred grunted and tipped the bottle to his lips.

"She cook good?"

Fred wiped his mouth with the back of his hand and passed the bottle back. "Best I ever et."

"Better'n Millie, huh?"

"Millie couldn't cook worth a damn."

Jed took a deep breath but he didn't have the nerve. He had a suspicion Fred wouldn't tell him anyway. He said, instead, "She's quite a woman, Mary. Prettier'n a young doe. Always figgered she was too good for this country. We all thought she'd pull out after Tom was killed, but we was wrong."

"She ain't the kind that gives up."

"Seems like she'd of had to if you hadn't come along. Sure was nice of you to take her to the fair."

"I figgered the kid'd get a kick out of it."

"Her too. She must be real lonely."

"Lonely?"

"A woman's been married long as she has gits kinda forgotten when her husband ain't around to take her places."

There was a long silence while Fred considered this remark. He pulled a splinter out of the safety bar and broke it in his fingers. After a while he said, "You figger she'll ever git married again?"

Jed pursed his lips. He thought about the conversation Bedelia had had with Mary and he said, "Seems like she pretty near has to, don't it?"

"Why?"

"She's still young and purty. Twon't do for her to keep you on too long. Folks'll begin to talk."

Fred's head snapped up. A dangerous look came into his eyes. "You heard anybody say anythin' against her?"

"No, I ain't," Jed said quickly. "Leastways, not yet . . ."

"I'll kill the man says a word against her. Don't they know she's a lady?"

"'Course they do. But that ain't gonna stop 'em from talkin'. They ain't got much else to do hereabouts."

Fred's face went tight. His eyes smoldered. He knew only too well how people talked. If their tongues drove him from the Sharron farm, he'd make them sorry for it. He reached out and gripped Jed's arm with a force that made Jed wince. He said slowly, "You tell me the truth. They started talkin' already, ain't they?"

Jed turned a trifle white, realizing he'd gone too far. "Well, I did hear a few things, nothin' serious, mind, but I think folks figger . . . since you took her to the carnival an' all. . . ."

Fred released Jed abruptly and turned to stare stonily out over the fields. Jed rubbed his bruised arm and wet his lips. Despite his concern at the way the conversation had gone, he felt a little sorry for the big man. Bedelia had said Fred was in love with Mary. He took a long swig from the bottle and the added warmth gave him courage. He said, "Listen, it ain't none of my business, but if you want to stay on, why don't you marry her yourself?"

Fred straightened slowly and looked at Jed. "What!"

"I said if you want to stay on, why don't you marry her yourself?"

"You crazy?"

"What's so crazy about it?"

"She wouldn't have nobody like me!"

"She went to the carnival with you."

"She went because the kid hadn't ever seen one. She'll do anything for that kid."

Jed took another stiff belt. He was warming to his subject even though his tongue was a little thick. "Awright, tell me this. If she don't marry you, what she gonna do?"

"How do you mean?"

"Listen, Fred. Whether you like it or not, sooner or later, the talkers are gonna git to her. When that happens, she's gotta do one of two things . . . let you go or marry you. She got no other choice. If she lets you go, where's she gonna git help? You know yourself it can't be had. Besides, that kid needs a father. You tell me, you got any good hard reason for thinkin' she won't marry you?"

Fred's craggy face furrowed into a look of acute bewilderment. He stood for so long without moving that Jed began to feel uncomfortable; then without a word, Fred turned on his heel, crossed to the trap door and swung down the ladder out of sight. A minute later he drove the rig out of the barn and went out the gate without looking back.

Halfway to the Sharron farm, he pulled the mare off the road and let her crop the grass while he sat in the seat of the buggy nervously twisting and untwisting the end of the buggy whip. He was there for a full hour before he again pulled the horse onto the road and headed for home.

When he got back he avoided Mary until she called him for dinner; then he sat at the table without taking his eyes from the plate. When he had finished he went straight out to the barn.

Mary washed the dishes thoughtfully and put Robbie to bed. She was sure Fred had heard something at the Clawson farm and she thought she knew what that something was. She came out of Robbie's room and began to put the dishes away. She dropped a plate and when she bent to retrieve the fragments she saw that her fingers were shaking. Annoyed, she tried to shake off her nervousness.

She went out on the front porch and sat down on the rocker. Her intuition told her that the decision about Fred was going to be thrust upon her a lot sooner than she had expected. He was not a man to ponder decisions. If, as she suspected, he had heard something he could be expected to appear almost momentarily. She wondered if he knew he was in love with her and how it was a woman always sensed something like that immediately.

She let her mind run over the incident in which Robbie had come home from the Clawson's, cut and bleeding, and the way Fred had handled it. He had handled the situation as Tom might have done, if he were alive, and as she herself never could. In other respects, she knew she was capable but when it came to questions of Robbie's welfare, her emotions became so involved she was not to be trusted. He had actually winced when she had blurted out that saccharine "Oh darling." It was hard to remember he was no longer a baby. He was growing up. He'd be nine come Christmas. He needed a man's hand in his upbringing. She marshaled all the other reasons she had for accepting Fred's proposal, if and when it came. They were impressive. A marriage with Fred would insure that the farm grew and flourished and provide Robbie with money for an education when he got older. It would protect her against the censure of her neighbors; it would ease the burden of responsibility she had been carrying since Tom's death, not only of Robbie's upbringing and education, but also of the running of the farm itself. Against this, she could only offer the argument that Fred was crude and uneducated, but even this was softened somewhat by the fact that he was generous, honest, industrious and competent. Those were the facts.

Why, then, did she keep avoiding the logical conclusion

they dictated? Because she was still in love with Tom Sharron? Because she had, in spite of every effort, shackled herself to his memory? She doubted that. He held a place in her heart which no one could ever fill and the memory of him, on occasions, could still drench her with anguish but she had learned to live without him; and, since that day at the carnival, she sensed a steady change in her attitude toward Fred. Little things like a tendency to tidy her hair when he was about and a certain quickening of her pulses when she caught him looking at her. And this in itself was a great change, for it no longer annoyed her and more than once she had experienced an unexpected wave of tenderness toward him. If only he weren't so coarse . . . so lacking in the little courtesies which she'd always found so irresistible in men. If only he would smile and display some semblance of humor. Perhaps it was this, more than anything else, that filled her with vague anxiety at the thought of binding herself to him for life.

She got no farther for there was a footstep at the side of the house. Fred came around the corner and stood in the shadow of the porch. She could feel his eyes fixed on her. She felt a renewed wave of nervousness and she said without turning, "Good evenin', Fred."

There was a lengthy pause and then he said, "Evenin'." He came up the side steps and sat down with his back to her and stared off toward the darkening hills. He said nothing but she sensed the struggle in him. There was a fluttering now in the pit of her stomach and her palms were moist. It was ridiculous for her to carry on like this, and still she couldn't help it. In the distance a loon laughed hysterically. A bat wheeled through the dusk. On the crest of the hill to the west, two pine trees, towering above their neighbors in black silhouette thrust ragged spears into the belly of the night. The last of the day's light in a suffusion of pale blood flowed into the horizon. Fred said, "There's talk."

She moistened her lips and tried to keep her voice easy. "Talk?"

"About us. They're sayin' . . . they're sayin' you can't keep me on here much longer."

"Yes . . . I've heard."

"Is it true?"

"I . . . I don't know, Fred."

Suddenly he slammed his fists together. "They got no right! . . . *They got no goddam right!*"

The naked desperation in his voice made her want to put her arms around him and comfort him as she would a child. He took his fists apart and studied his hands. Then he said, "They're sayin' the kid needs a father."

This time she found her voice. "I suppose they're right."

"I s'pose a kid needs somebody . . . a man, I mean."

"Yes."

"You think he likes me?"

"I'm sure he does."

The next was hard, very hard, but he got it out in a rush. "I was wonderin' if maybe you shared the kid's feelin's."

She took a breath, "Well, I do Fred." And then because she had to say something else— "You've been very kind to Robbie and me." She was crucifying him and she knew it and she couldn't help it.

Fred tried again. He sensed that everything was wrong and yet this had seemed all right when he rehearsed it in the barn. Now it sounded terrible. His voice was uneven and hollow. He set his teeth, girded his loins, and tried again. "I can run a farm . . . I can run a farm better'n anybody in this country . . . this place needs somebody that knows how to run it."

Mary said nothing. She knew it was coming and she was trying desperately to compose herself.

Fred waited for a reply and when none came he braced himself and in a burst of frustration, hurled the words at her. "Look, why don't we get married?"

The words tore through Mary's thoughts. Here it was. There was no more time for evasion. He had asked her point-blank. She had to reply. Her heart was beating so loudly she was sure he could hear it. She opened her mouth to say yes, and the words would not come. She stood up. She realized that for some unfathomable and stupid reason she was on the verge of tears. "I'm sorry, Fred," she gasped. "I can't!" She turned and ran into the house.

Fred stood up, the dreadful finality of the words hammering in his brain. *She had refused him!* He turned and strode off the porch, his face black, his pulses pounding. *She had refused him!* Then all Jed's talk had been so much drunken slop. She never had any intention of marrying him! He'd made a fool of himself. Now he had botched the whole business! He hadn't even told her he loved her. It had been about as romantic as a crap game and as exciting as weeding turnips. He ripped open the door to the barn. He felt like he wanted to kill somebody. He tried the door to his room and it stuck. With a sudden release of pent-up viciousness, he slammed his huge fist through the panel. It splintered into a thousand pieces. The blood ran off his torn knuckles. He looked at them unseeingly and then smashed his hand again and again into the panel until only the splintered framework remained. He flung open the door, cursing and ripping up the mattress of his bed. He uncorked a bottle and held it to his lips till it was more than half empty. The hot liquid burned his throat and stomach. His eyes were wild as he tilted the bottle again, emptied it, and then with one violent movement hurled it through the window into the dark. The sound of smashing glass exploded into the silence of the night. He stood stock-still, looking at the shattered pane, a little trickle of liquor running down his mouth, and then flung himself on the bed. He lay there for a long while. The raw liquor seared his stomach and made his head swim. The drunker he got, the clearer the pattern became. She'd made a fool of him! They'd all made a fool of him. They had set their stinking trap and he had walked into it and now they could laugh at him. A half hour passed while he goaded himself on his stupidity and his failure. All the other failures of his life presented themselves. Father, brother, wife, homestead. They marched across his memory searing him with bitter irons. Everything he had worked for, everything he had ever wanted, had been ripped away from him or turned to ashes in his mouth. He had accepted all that, but suddenly he knew he wasn't going to accept any more. He wanted this woman more than anything he'd ever wanted in his life, and the resolution born of liquor and a lifetime of frustration crystallized. He pushed himself to his feet. He was thoroughly drunk. Refuse him would she? Well, she was right over in that house and if he couldn't have her one way, he'd damn well have her another. He started out of the room, weaving on his feet.

Mary's tears had not come. Away from Fred, her fears had evaporated. She lay on the bed in her room in an agony of confusion. Why hadn't she been able to say yes? It was the only logical thing to do and the only possible thing to do and then, when he had asked her, she had behaved like a silly, frightened school girl.

"Get a hold of yourself," she said aloud. "Act like a normal human being. Are you going to jeopardize Robbie's future, the farm, and your own reputation in the community, because he isn't a knight in shining armor? Or are you going to behave like a grown-up, sensible woman and accept an offer of marriage which will solve all your problems?" There was but one answer. She determined she would put an end to this nonsense right here and now. She would go out and apologize to Fred and accept his proposal.

165

She left the house as Fred was stumbling through the darkness toward the door of the barn. Her eyes were unaccustomed to the dark after the lamplight in the house and she had to pick her way carefully across the yard. She didn't see Fred until she came upon him at the doorway to the barn. The surprise of seeing him so unexpectedly, startled her. His face was in deep shadow and he made no effort to move. He had seen her coming in the moonlight and the surprise had momentarily stopped him. He stood steadying himself against a beam just inside the doorway, savoring the moment. She was beautiful as she stood there trying to pierce the darkness and see his face. The waves in her hair were holding cupfuls of molten moonlight and her mouth looked black and inviting. Fred ran his tongue over his dry lips and was shifting his weight to reach for her, when she spoke.

"Fred, I'm sorry for the way I behaved. I want to marry you, and I will whenever you like."

There was such a long pause that Mary wondered if he had heard. Then without saying anything, he reached out and pulled her roughly into his embrace; for a brief second before his mouth crushed down on hers, she caught the acrid odor of cheap liquor. She was suddenly aware that his whole body was trembling. Then he released her, and without a word, stalked off into the darkness. Mary put a hand up to her bruised lips and went back into the house, her senses reeling and her mind in a turmoil; and Fred, by the light of the lamp, repaired the door and window of his room.

14

Robbie sat on the back steps of the town hall and shivered. He had come out without his coat and the night was cold. Within a few days there would probably be snow but Robbie was not thinking about that. He was atremble with something he didn't understand. The sounds of the party came faintly to his ears through the closed doors behind him and from the windows along the side of the hall the light spilled out on the dead grass and frost-wilted weeds. Above him, the stars were cold crystal in the black sky, but he didn't see them. He saw his mother kissing Fred Carter and heard her promising to love and obey him, and he felt again the sudden stabbing wrench at his insides, that he had known when it happened. It was all wrong! It wasn't the way his mother had said it would be at all. She hadn't told him marriage meant this. She had said the only difference would be that Fred Carter would sleep in the house instead of the barn. He was the hired man. Why should she obey him now when he had always obeyed her before. And why should she love him? She oughtn't to love anybody but his real father and himself. It wasn't fair! He knew he'd agreed but now that it had happened, he'd changed his mind. It just didn't seem right that Fred could be the hired man one day and his father the next, and all of it just because there was a party and the saying of a few words. When it came right down to it, a father was something you were born with and if he died then that should be the end of it. There could be friends afterwards and neighbors and hired men but not any more fathers.

Also, there was something else he hadn't thought about before. He had sprung Fred's traps last year but if Fred was his father it wouldn't be right to spring them any more, would it? And with Fred living in the house he might discover Robbie's secret. The thing that only his mother and father had known. If they hadn't understood how would Fred feel? He put his head in his hands. He shivered again. He was beginning to feel really cold but he didn't want to go back inside. People kept patting him on the head with strange, knowing looks, and saying, "Well, Robbie, how does it feel to have a new father?" And he didn't know how to answer them. There was everything in the world to eat inside—candy and cake and jelly and hot bread and pumpkin pie, but for the first time in his memory he didn't feel like sweets. He just wished it hadn't happened—any of it. He wished that he could wake up tomorrow and his mother would still be his mother and not Fred Carter's wife. He sat there watching the big orange moon creep above the trees until the door opened behind him. His mother stood on the threshold. She said, "Robbie! I've been lookin' everywhere for you. What on earth are you doing out here?"

Robbie bit his lip. "It was too hot inside."

"But, darlin', you'll catch your death of cold out here without a coat. Please come in!"

"I don't want to!"

She started. It was the first time she had heard that note of rebellion in his voice. She stared for a second, then went back inside and took two coats from the checkroom table. She pulled one over her own shoulders and then stepped outside and closed the door. She put the oversized jacket around Robbie and sat down on the steps beside him.

"What is it, Robbie?"

"It's nothin' a-tall!" His voice was husky and distant.

She took his chin in her hands and pulled his face to hers.

168

"Robbie!" His eyes were full of tears. She caught her breath. "Oh, Robbie, what is it?"

He swallowed. "You kissed him."

She frowned anxiously. "But, of course I did, darlin', it's part of the ceremony."

"You didn't tell me."

"Well, I suppose I didn't. I just took it for granted that you knew but—"

"You said you'd love him and obey him." The desolation in his voice stunned her. She felt her throat thickening.

"Robbie, I thought you *wanted* me to marry Fred. You said you *liked* him."

"Will you have to kiss him again?"

Very suddenly she felt a little sick. "Yes, I will."

"Often?"

"As often as he wants me to." In her own ears her voice sounded hollow and empty.

"And obey him?"

"Robbie, he is my husband now," she said, desperately. "In the eyes of God and man I'm bound to him."

He could see his mother was about to cry and he knew he had done it. Everyone inside had been laughing and wishing her happiness and he had hurt her. She wanted him to be happy about what she had done. Everything always worked out wrong somehow. He said, bravely, "I . . . I guess it's all right. I couldn't get near you there were so many people."

She pulled him into her arms. "Oh, darlin'," she said, "and you were the only one I really wanted near me."

There was a pause, then his voice half muffled because she was holding him so tight said, chokingly, "More than Fred?"

She released him and held him away from her, looking at him quizzically, then suddenly the fear went out of her eyes. She gave a little broken sound and then pulled his head against her bosom and she began to laugh and cry at the same time.

169

"Oh yes, darlin', of course! More than anyone else in the whole world. Oh, you frightened me so. Robbie, you mustn't be jealous of Fred."

"Jealous?"

"I mean, you must never think that because he's my husband I love him more than you. I could never love anyone as much as I love you. You've got to remember that always. Nothing has changed really. I've got a new husband and you have a new father, that's all. It doesn't make any difference between us."

"Do I have to call him father?"

"Perhaps not. What would you like to call him?"

"Fred?"

"No, I don't think that would be quite polite now. What about sir?"

"Yes, ma'am," he said, obediently.

She held him at arm's length again studying his grave, pinched little face. "Robbie, it's all right, isn't it?"

Robbie told his first big lie. "Yes, Mother, it's all right."

She dabbed at her eyes with her handkerchief. "Well, then, we'd better get back inside. Fred'll be wonderin' what happened to us."

He hesitated. "Couldn't we stay out a little longer?"

She glanced toward the closed door, uncertainly. "Well, I don't know, Robbie. . . ."

"Please, Mother! We could walk down to the road and back, is all."

"But why?"

"I just want to, that's all."

She didn't know what to do. She shouldn't go off now. It wasn't right, but it wasn't right for Robbie, either. He needed reassurance now—at this moment. He had to know that he was not being pushed out of her life; that he was as important to her as the party and Fred and the people inside.

170

She smiled. "All right, but just down to the bridge and back."
He took her hand and they walked off together.

Inside the hall, Fred stood at the cider bowl. His face was
flushed. A sea of smiling faces and bright go-to-meetin'
clothes surged around him. A solid roar of voices and laughter
filled the room and at the far end of the hall somebody was
tuning a fiddle. Vast quantities of food and cider were being
passed from hand to hand. People he scarcely knew were
crowding in to him, pumping his hand and offering congratu-
lations. His head swam. Mary had been gone a long time and
he wished she'd come back. He didn't know how to take this
sudden popularity, so when the men thumped him on the
back and made rough jokes he only looked around for Mary
and nodded self-consciously and drank furiously. The men,
who had never seen him drink before watched the process
with awe.

Fred was not aware of how much he had drunk. He was still
numb with the attempt to absorb what had happened to him.
After his violent anger and his wild determination to take her
by force, Mary's acceptance had stunned him. He hadn't been
able to get the fingers of his mind around the fact. He had
alternated between the conviction that it was all a monstrous
joke and cold sweats at the thought of how close he had come
to ruining everything. Right up to the moment she had knelt
beside him and murmured "I do" he had been tense and un-
certain. He had heard her voice with a strange feeling of disbelief and absorbed her presence in a kind of waking dream.
Only now—now when the fermented apple juice was coursing
through his veins and burning the tensions out of his taut
nerves was he able to absorb the fact that it had really happened. He was married again. And to a woman he had never
even dared to hope for. The most beautiful woman he had
ever known. She was his! And he had a farm again. A farm
of his own and he was a respected member of the community.

Women who had turned their heads aside when he passed ten years ago were now wishing him well. Men who had been reluctant to speak to him were wringing his hand. All this within a few days of the time when he had almost damned himself forever. All this because a little over a year ago he had come to the Sharron farm to pay a debt. He began to push his way through the crowd looking for Mary. He couldn't find her but she had to be somewhere. He felt a sudden irresistible impulse to shout aloud. He stood in the middle of the floor, and flung his arms wide. "Anybody seen my wife?" The men laughed and the women tittered. He spun slowly, searching the room, weaving a little.

"Mary Carter, come out!"

"Here I am!" The voice came from the back door. Mary was coming into the hall with Robbie beside her. She came up to him and tried to kiss him on the cheek but the cider and the excitement had gone to his head. He swept her off the floor and into his arms and planted a resounding kiss on her mouth. She struggled to free herself feeling the hot flush of embarrassment redden her cheeks.

"Fred, please!"

The note in her voice sobered him a little. He set her on her feet, suddenly aware that he had made a mistake. "I'm . . . I'm sorry," he muttered.

There was an edge of ice in her smile, "It's all right, really it is. But don't you think it's about time we were gettin' home?"

He looked around in disappointment. "But they're just startin' the dance."

She said, "I'm sorry, Fred, but it's quite late and there is Robbie, you know."

He looked back at her for a second, his eyes abnormally bright. "Oh, yeah, Robbie." He swayed, then held up his hands and the room fell quiet. He said, "Ladies and gents, with your kind permission me and Mary—me and Mrs. Carter are now goin' home. We thank you fer comin' to the weddin'." Everyone applauded, lustily. He turned to her, solemnly, "Okay?"

"Fine. Shall we go then?" She steered him toward the door, followed by the whole hall of people. Half a dozen pairs of hands helped them into the carriage. Mary looked around. "Where's Robbie?"

"Here I am."

She turned to see him sitting scrunched up in the back. She felt another twinge of uneasiness and forced it aside.

"Well, don't be sittin' back there alone, lad. Come up here in the front with us."

Robbie climbed in front, wordlessly. Fred clucked to the horses and they started off. There was a chorus of good-bys, somebody threw a handful of rice, and one or two of the more inebriated males made a few suggestive remarks only to be shushed by their women. Within seconds, they were crossing the bridge and the hall was blocked from view by the trees. The sounds of revelry faded and shortly thereafter there was only the clip clop of Midnight's hooves, the eerie familiar chorus of crickets and the garumphing of the bull frogs in the silence. The full moon was now high and shed enough light so that the road was a gray ribbon winding ahead of them into the night. She could not help thinking how different this was from a warm June afternoon over ten years ago when she had left the little stone church in her Irish village wearing a white bridal gown and carrying a bouquet of real orange blossoms. The pupils of her school had made an aisle through which she and Tom had run in a deluge of rice and confetti. She quickly put the thought away from her.

Fred put his arm around her and somewhat thickly began to sing *Shine On Harvest Moon*. His booming off-key baritone stilled the frogs and sent the echoes flying in the rocks and

173

trees. Mary turned to Robbie. He had his eyes closed. He was pretending to be asleep. He pretended so hard that after a while he actually did go to sleep. He was awakened once sometime later when Mary moved suddenly and he heard her say, "Please! You'll waken Robbie!" As he slid off to sleep again, he heard Fred muttering something indistinguishable.

It was midnight by the time they drew up in the barnyard. Robbie was still asleep and Fred helped Mary out of the carriage. "You go on in," he said, "I'll bring the kid in after I've unhitched the mare." Mary went into the house without a word. She was burning with the memory of Fred's advances on the way home. His awkward fumbling with Robbie sleeping on her shoulder had revived all her old fears. Getting ready for bed her fingers were trembling.

In the barn, Fred stabled the horse. Mary's nearness in the carriage had aroused him and the cold air had made him drunker. He pictured her in the bedroom getting out of her clothes. He saw the whiteness of her breasts, imagined her slipping between the sheets waiting for him. Oddly he found courage deserting him. He found a bottle in the tackroom and took several long swallows. By the time he had replaced the bottle and hung up the harness he was beginning to weave unsteadily. He picked up Robbie and carried him toward the house.

Mary heard him open the kitchen door and go through the living room to Robbie's bedroom. She clutched the covers fiercely and closed her eyes. "Dear God," she whispered, "please help me through this night. Help me never to let him know how I feel." A chair overturned with a crash in the next room. Oh God, she thought, he's drunk, terribly drunk! She remembered how his hard lips had bruised hers that night at the door of the barn and how his iron fingers had left dark bruises on her waist and shoulders. She pulled the covers tighter around her as if they offered protection. For the first time, she realized how little she really knew about him. He was drunk tonight and he had been drunk the night she accepted his proposal. Had he been drinking all the time without her knowing? Suddenly, she was afraid. She heard his footsteps coming back. The door of her bedroom swung open. After a moment, she opened her eyes. He had not moved. He stood on the threshold, his big frame filling the doorway. He was swaying slightly. She closed her eyes. The tears forced themselves out from beneath the tightly closed lids and Fred Carter shut the door behind him.

15

Fred awakened. He opened his eyes but the light seared like acid and he shut them tight again. His head throbbed and his tongue was thick. He lay still for a few seconds then slid his feet over the edge of the bed and put them against the cold floor. The shock helped a little. He tried opening his eyes again but the light still hurt. He got up and fumbled his way toward the washstand. It wasn't where it should have been but he found it somehow and poured some water from the china pitcher into the washbowl. He sloshed the water over his neck and shoulders. The water was warm! He straightened up abruptly and opened his eyes wide. On the washstand were his toothbrush and shaving things, but the washstand wasn't familiar. He spun around. The big four-poster bed, the curtained windows! He put his hands to his head and groaned. Christ! Christ Almighty! He stumbled back to the bed and sat down, running his hands through his hair. There was a sound from outside the bedroom door and he started as though he had been struck. When the noise wasn't repeated he got up and locked the door and stood, leaning against it.

His mind churned painfully, trying to follow the sequence of yesterday. He remembered everything up to the wedding ceremony and the party, but then it began to get hazy. She'd left him alone with all those people. He couldn't remember why, but he'd been nervy and uncomfortable. He'd begun to pour the cider into him. The ride home was vague but he'd stabled the horse, he thought, and carried the kid in to bed. His consciousness stumbled, then, at what it uncovered and he swore again beneath his breath. He'd finished it off with the remains of that rotgut in the barn! After that everything was a blank. God knows what he had said or done! In his condition he'd probably stumbled into her room and taken her as he would one of the women in a house. If he had, he'd smashed everything before it began. She'd never understand. She'd never forgive him. And you couldn't blame her. He slammed his fists together in helpless fury at his own stupidity. Why had he gotten drunk? *Why?* The answer came slowly to his fogged brain. Because he was scared, that's why. And out of fear he'd done the very thing that was bound to open him like a clam and show the full picture of what he was and had always been.

He remembered how it had been with his first wife. She'd taken him drunk before their marriage but the only fight they'd ever had afterwards was when he'd come home blind with drink and dragged her into the bedroom. The thoughts of how Mary would react made his skin crawl. He went to the window and looked out. It was a gray dismal day. The clouds were dark and foreboding and the stubbled fields were covered with hoar frost. His throat felt rough and dry. He turned from the window and drank from the pitcher. He spat most of it out. He'd forgotten it had been heated. He needed a cup of coffee badly, but he couldn't bring himself to go out of the room and face her. He looked in the mirror. His eyes were bloodshot and his hair tousled. He needed a shave badly. He cleaned his teeth, shaved, and combed his hair. He went to the door and unlocked it, still he couldn't go out. He paced back and forth a couple of times. It didn't help. He couldn't stay here all day. He took a deep breath and went out to the kitchen. He stopped on the threshold. She had her back to him. She straightened as she heard him clear his throat, but she didn't turn. He took a deep breath. He said earnestly, "I . . . I'm sorry—I didn't mean to get drunk." She didn't turn. He felt sick and ashamed and angry all at once. "You got to believe me," he said, desperately, "I wouldn't hurt you for nothin' in the world. I don't know what I done or what I said but if it'll make you feel better I'll go back to sleepin' in the barn!"

She turned then and his mouth fell open in shock. There was no trace of anger on her face. There was even a tinge of sympathy in her eyes. She said, "You don't deserve to be told this. But the truth of it all is, you said nothin' and you did nothin'." He looked at her blankly and she smiled. "You don't remember?"

He shook his head.

"Nothin' a-tall," she prodded.

He dropped his eyes. "I remember comin' home. I stabled the horse and carried the kid into bed and . . ."

"And I'm thinkin' you must have had somethin' to drink in the barn?"

He nodded. "I don't know why."

"It was that that did it then?"

"Did what?"

"You fell asleep before you finished undressin' yourself. It's a time I had gettin' the pajamas on a great hulk like yourself." She watched him in consternation. He had not moved but something was happening to his face. It was like a china plate cracking slowly. It was not quite a smile but the closest he had ever come to it. The expression stuck like it was painted on.

He said, finally, "Can I have some coffee?"

"You can that. It's been waitin' these two hours."

He came to the table and sat. He was feeling like a man who had been reprieved when they had already put the noose around his neck and taken a strain on the rope. She brought the coffee and he waved away the cream. He took an enormous swallow of the scalding beverage. "I didn't mean to get drunk.

I was all right till you left, then I guess I got nervous. I didn't know how to talk to all them people."

She sat opposite him. "It was my fault. I shouldn't have left you for so long."

"Why did you?"

"I had to find Robbie. He'd disappeared."

"What for?"

She frowned. "Well, I think the truth of it was he was jealous."

"Jealous! Of who?"

"Of you. He saw you kiss me, and well . . . I think the whole ceremony was somethin' of a shock to him. He thought I wouldn't love him any more."

"The kid's crazy!"

A shadow went over her face, then she said, "Fred, he's only eight. He doesn't know any better."

"Yeah, I guess you're right."

"He'll be all right when he gets used to it. Drink your coffee before it gets cold."

He picked up the cup and looked at it curiously. "Where did this come from?"

"It's a little weddin' present, is all."

He put the cup down and looked at her. "You got it for me?"

"Don't you like it then?"

He grew red. He said, uneasily, "I didn't get nothin' for you. I was supposed to, wasn't I?"

"It doesn't matter. You've brought me enough presents. The phonograph and the radio."

He said doggedly. "I shoulda got you somethin'." He swore under his breath and then stood up. "I better get at the milkin'. What time is it?"

"Almost eight."

"Eight! Why didn't you wake me?"

179

"I thought the sleep would do you good."

"Where's the kid?"

"I think he's gone off to the woods. Fred?"

"Yeah?"

"Would you do somethin' for me?"

His face brightened a little. "Anythin' you want."

"Don't call Robbie 'kid.'"

He swallowed. "I didn't meant nothin' by it."

"I know you didn't. It's just that it upsets me somehow."

"Why didn't you say so before."

"I wanted to but I—well, I just never got around to it."

"When you want somethin' from me . . . if I do somethin' ain't right, you tell me."

"All right."

"I don't know much but I kin learn."

"All right."

"I promise you I'll never get drunk like that again. You kin count on it." He hesitated, then leaned over and kissed her quickly on the cheek and went out.

She sat at the table looking after him. She'd been frightened half to death last night. It was the sheerest kind of good fortune that he had passed out but the desperation in his voice this morning had told her much and the look on his face when he realized that their marriage was still not consummated, had told her a great deal more. She thanked God she had acted as she did. It would have been a great mistake to let him know how afraid she had been or to humiliate him further by treating him with anger or scorn. He was a child really. If she handled him properly it would all work out fine.

In the barn, Fred milked the cows and poured some of the milk into a smaller bucket for the calf. He forked some hay in to the mare's stall and began cleaning up. He worked furiously and even though it was quite cold, he began to sweat. His headache disappeared. He felt replete and grateful. Twice he had almost ruined everything and twice he had been saved by a miracle. He would make sure that he didn't make any more mistakes.

After an hour had passed, Robbie came into the barn. He stood watching Fred with grave, unsmiling eyes. So quietly had he entered that for some minutes Fred was not aware of the boy's presence. Then he began to get an uncomfortable feeling that he was being watched. He turned and saw Robbie. He leaned the fork against a stall and straightened up.

"Come here, Robbie." Robbie came forward, slowly. Fred wiped his hand across his mouth and then he said, "I ain't had much experience in bein' a father, but I'll do what I can, see?" Robbie didn't say anything and his silence made Fred uncomfortable. "Your maw says you was jealous of me." Robbie felt a sting of resentment. His mother shouldn't have told Fred. It was something just between them. "Now you got no reason for that," Fred continued, awkwardly. "Your maw loves you an' I figger she wants us to get along. You want somethin', you ask me, see? If I can get it, I will. Soon's the snow's here I'll git you a rifle and you can go huntin' with me and help set the traps."

Robbie's face got sullen. "I don't want a rifle." It was on the tip of his tongue to say he didn't want to go hunting or trapping either, but something warned him to keep silent.

Fred's face got darker and then he shrugged. He said, "Okay, I can't do no more than try. We got along all right before, I don't see that there's much difference now."

Robbie dropped his eyes and kicked at the side of the stall but he still didn't say anything. Finally, he said, "Is it all right if I go now?"

Fred shrugged again. "Nobody's holdin' you."

Robbie went out. His behavior had taken the edge off Fred's good spirits, but Fred was not a man to worry about trifles. Sooner or later the kid would get used to the idea and

181

then everything would be all right. He ought to get him a present, maybe. When he'd been a kid, he'd always wanted a pony. He made up his mind that the next time he was in town, he'd ask Campbell if he knew anyone who had a pony they wanted to sell. After that, he put the incident out of his mind.

Robbie came into the house and sat down at the kitchen table. He watched his mother stirring the great pot on the stove and the room was rich with the smell of grape jelly. She turned and smiled at him, then she saw the look on his face and she put down the spoon. She said, "Robbie, what's the matter?"

He avoided her eyes, as he had Fred's, and ran his thumbnail around a knot in the pinewood table. She waited and when he didn't say anything she reached across and took his chin in her hands as she had done the previous night outside the hall. She pulled his head up. "Tell me. Are you still upset about my marryin' Fred?"

Robbie's eyes were accusatory. "You told Fred I was jealous."

She sighed. She saw that until Robbie accepted the situation it was bound to entail one crisis after another. And Robbie was acting like a spoiled brat. He'd never carried on like this before. It was ridiculous and pathetic and annoying all at the same time. His lower lip was thrust out in a pout and his eyes were full of self-pity.

She said, "Now you listen to me, young man. I did my best to understand you last night. And I went walkin' with you when I should have been with your father."

"He's *not* my father!"

She took a deep breath, holding back her anger, then she said firmly, "He is. You might as well understand that once and for all, Robbie. For better or for worse that's the way it is and I'll not have you carryin' on like a baby now that there's no chance of changin' it. I asked you before I did this was it what you wanted and you said yes. It may not be easy for either of us for a while but we've got to make the best of it. It won't be easy for Fred, either, until we get to know each other better. We've all got to help. You included. And I'll not have you mopin' about here like you'd lost your best friend when there's no reason for it a-tall. Fred's been good to you. He took you to the fair and he insisted against my will that you be allowed anything you wanted. He's put up with your pesterin' and your questionin' when many another would have boxed your ears and I'll not have you settin' yourself against him without him havin' done a thing to deserve it. Do you understand that now?"

Robbie nodded. His mother hadn't spoken to him like that in years. It only confirmed his suspicion that his place in his mother's affections was being usurped. She was taking Fred's side against him. It made him dislike Fred even more but from now on he would have to hide it.

16

Half an hour before dawn the stag with the strange white mark on its forehead was already close to exhaustion. It had been two hours since it had heard the first wolf howl and seen the first gray shadows racing toward it through the trees. After that, the battle had been fought in deadly silence. Twice the wolf pack had trapped the deer and twice, with a courage born of desperation, it had fought free of the deadly circle of fangs. But the escapes had been costly. The deer's flanks were bleeding from half a dozen slashes where the wolves had tried to cut the vulnerable back tendons and bring it down hamstrung and helpless. Now it pounded through the snowy woods, lungs at the bursting point, and every muscle quivering with strain. Around it in a tightening circle the wolves kept pace. They no longer attacked. They knew the stag was nearly finished. They were deliberately running it into the ground. When it fell, they would be on it in a snarling fury of fur and fang. The stag knew it, too. Its eyes were starting from its head, its nostrils dilated and ringed with foam. As it ran it flung bright red blotches on the snow. The scent of the blood set the pack to slavering.

And then in the throes of terror, a half-forgotten recollection stirred in the buck's fevered brain . . . a fragment of a memory that somewhere—once—there had been a refuge. It stopped, wheeled, and lowered its antlers. The closest wolf caught unawares felt the horns tear into his entrails and was thrown twenty feet to one side. In the same instant, the buck had broken the ring and was plunging off at right angles to its original trail. Minutes later, the pack at its heels, it exploded out of the trees and pounded across the frozen clearing toward the Sharron farm. The wolves saw the hated buildings of the man thing and redoubled their efforts to bring down their quarry. But hope had given the deer a final surge of strength. It kept ahead of the leaders of the pack and cleared the split rails of the potato field in one soaring leap. The wolves lost precious time floundering through the soft drifts piled against the fence. While they struggled, the buck neared a heavy rail and wire enclosure abutting the lower end of the Sharron barn. With the last of its waning strength, the stag cleared the seven-foot fence and turned.

The leader of the wolf pack was a gray blur racing across the snow. He leaped for the barrier. It was a magnificent leap. His two front paws reached the top rail. He levered himself up like a dog and crouched precariously, hackles quivering, slavering mouth agape. Then he leaped for the deer's throat. The deer caught him in mid-air and flung him clear of the pen. He struck the side of the barn and the impact broke his back. A second gray killer sprang for the top bar and missed. As he slid back down, he was pinioned through the wire. One front paw caught and he hung helplessly, still slashing at the antlers, as he died. Two more wolves were gored trying to surmount the barrier, then, licking their wounds and snarling in frustration, they slunk off in search of another victim. The stag stood quivering, waiting for them to return for a good ten minutes, then it sank down in exhaustion. After an hour, it struggled to its feet. Only then did it discover it was trapped. It had cleared the top rail by a good foot when it raced in from the fields, but the pen had been built to hold a fawn. It gave the full-grown stag barely room to turn. Had it been fresh it might have been able to clear the seven feet from a standing position, but the chase and the loss of blood had weakened it. It tried twice, but its leaps were over a foot short and each time it fell back heavily. The sun began to clear the treetops. The deer lowered his antlers and lunged at the barrier. The ancient rails groaned and splintered but the heavy wire held them fast. Again and again the deer hurled himself at the walls of his trap, but the pen had been built by Tom Sharron for a fawn Robbie had called Lightning. Tom had never built anything in his life that did not have a look of permanence about it.

In the house, Fred Carter sat up in bed. Mary awakened by his sudden movement looked at him. "What is it, Fred?"

"Listen!"

From outside came a screeching sound as if taut rusty wires were being ground against each other. The sound was punctuated by shuddering thuds. Occasionally, there was a noise like that which is heard an instant before a tree topples when its last few fibers crack and splinter.

"What on earth can be makin' a racket like that?"

"I'll see."

He flung back the covers and pulled on his boots and overalls. He ran to the back of the house, pulled open the back door, and stopped dead in astonishment. In the unused pen was a live, terrified, full-grown buck. The whole story was clear at a glance. The buck had leaped into the pen to escape the wolves and then been unable to get out. One wolf hung from the wire gored almost beyond recognition and the snow inside the pen was spotted with blood. Fred hurried off the porch for a closer look. As he neared the enclosure, he heard a sound to his right. He spun. In the snow next to the barn was a wolf. The baleful yellow eyes glared at him murderously and the lips curled back from the long fangs in a snarl of defiance. From the strange rigidity of the body it was obvious the back was broken. Fred estimated the distance from the pen to where the wolf lay. The distance was a good thirty-five feet and there were no tracks in the snow where the wolf

186

might have crawled. He felt a tingle of admiration for the buck. It had thrown that wolf over a seven-foot fence to its present position and there was no doubt as to who had gored the one which hung in the wire. The stag's magnificent antlers were sheathed in frozen blood. Also, there were blood spots in the snow where the rest of the pack had run off. It had been a mighty battle and the deer, its vulnerable flanks protected by the barn, had won. The deer had frozen into immobility as the man appeared, but now as Fred walked toward him, the spell broke. He redoubled his efforts to get out of the pen. Fred watched in amazement. The stag's antlers were enormous and he had a strange mark on his forehead like a streak of lightning. The head would probably be worth some money. Fred would have loved to have left the whole scene just as it was to show Jed Clawson but he saw that the pen was about to give way under the deer's frantic butting. The center rails on both sides were split clean in two from the battering and only the heavy wire fencing held them together. He hurried into the barn for his rifle.

At the same instant, Robbie came out on the back porch with his parka pulled over his boots and trousers. Like Fred, he stopped short in astonishment, realizing instantly what had happened. He was stunned by the wonder of it. Then he saw the mark on the deer's forehead. Lightning! It was his deer. The one he had nursed back to health when he found it starving in the forest. He had it for almost a year before letting it go. And here it was! It had remembered and come home when it was in danger. He gave a glad cry and started down the steps of the porch. Fred emerged from the barn carrying his rifle. The realization of what Fred intended to do, following so swiftly on his own elation, paralyzed Robbie. His face got whiter than the flannel of his nightshirt. He wanted to cry out but he couldn't make any sound. His throat closed up and the sweat broke out on his palms. Watching him, you would have thought it was he who was going to be shot. Fred levered a shell into the breach of the gun and leveled it. Inside Robbie's head he screamed but nothing came out of his throat.

Fred hesitated a second. The hesitation was not caused by any doubt as to whether or not to kill the deer. Venison was hard to come by in the winter months and this was too good an opportunity to miss. But Fred admired courage in men and animals more than any other virtue and his hesitation was a kind of unconscious tribute to the stag's spirit . . . a moment in which Fred could fix the scene in his mind before it ended. He put the gun to his shoulder. He sighted carefully. The hard smash of the high-calibered weapon shattered the morning stillness. The deer staggered at the impact of the bullet. It sank to its knees, it tried valiantly to lift its head and then collapsed. Fred walked over to the pen and looked down in satisfaction. After a second, he turned and noticed Robbie.

He said, "Robbie, bring me my dressing knife!"

He walked around to the front of the pen and examined the wolf caught in the wire. He shook his head again. The wolf had died snarling and his lips had frozen away from his teeth in a frightful grimace. Its ears would bring a bounty come spring. He turned, expecting to see Robbie coming with his knife. The boy stood exactly where he had been before. He hadn't moved an inch. Fred frowned.

"Robbie!" The sharpness of the voice made Robbie start. "What's the matter with you? I told you to get my knife!"

Robbie turned slowly and started back into the house.

Fred spat in exasperation. "Not there! In the barn!" Robbie kept on moving up the steps. "*Robbie!*" The voice was a lash of anger. It caught Robbie and held him. He turned slowly and moved back down the steps toward the barn. He moved as if only his legs were alive. Fred watched him for a moment and then shrugged, shot the second wolf, and turned his attention to the pen. It had been battered out of shape when the deer lunged violently, so that the door was sprung. It took all of Fred's strength to force it. When he got it open finally he found Robbie standing beside him, holding the knife. He took it from the boy's nerveless fingers. He did not notice his face. He went into the pen. Robbie turned away, slowly.

Fred said over his shoulder, "Wait a minute, Robbie. Now's as good a time as any fer you to learn to dress out a deer."

Robbie stopped dead in his tracks again. It was a ghastly dream. The waves of dizziness began to sweep over him. He swallowed to prevent himself from being sick.

"Come here!" The words bit through his consciousness as if from a great distance. "What in hell's got into you this morning? I ain't gonna tell you again, come here!"

Robbie turned. He went back. He stood beside his stepfather. He heard Fred say, "Now watch." With a swift expert movement, he drove the razor sharp knife into the body of the deer that had once been Robbie's pet. The hot red blood flowed out onto Fred's hands and stained the snow. In the icy air a thick steam rose from the wound. Robbie was going to faint. Sweat broke out all over his body. His stomach writhed in nausea. "That's where you start, then you open him along here." He drew the knife along the carcass. More blood flowed and the skin writhed back from the red gash. Fred looked up to see if Robbie understood. He saw Robbie's face. The knife stopped in mid-stroke. Fred's hand began to tremble. He had seen that look of craven horror on a human face once before. It had destroyed a dream and burnt his wife alive. He dropped the knife in the open wound. He said in a half-strangled voice, "You do it."

Robbie shook his head. If he opened his mouth he would be sick.

"You pick up that knife! You hear me? Pick it up!" The

189

voice had lost all semblance of control. It was hoarse with fury. *"You pick up that goddam knife or I'll break every bone in your body!"*

"NO!!!" It was a scream of anguish and terror.

Fred's fury broke. All he could see was his brother's face, his wife burning. His iron fingers found the back of Robbie's neck. He drove the boy's face toward the bloody wound in the deer's belly. Robbie vomited. Every nerve in his body shrieked in alarm. Mad with fear, he struggled with the strength of a maniac. But he was pitted against a man to whom something equally terrible was happening. With vicious force, Fred drove the boy's face down until it was touching the deer's body.

"There it is! Do you see it?!"

With a sudden wrench, he plunged the boy's face into the open wound. Robbie felt the hot wet blood touch his face. He tried to get his breath and the thick redness sucked into his mouth and nostrils. Searing red hot snakes of excruciating fire cork-screwed through his mind. With one reflex of super-human strength, he arched his body away from the bloody crater and fainted.

Fred stood looking down at him, his breath coming in shuddering gasps. A muscle was jumping wildly in his face and his whole body was trembling. Without a word he turned and walked away, leaving the boy lying unconscious in the snow.

A few minutes later, Mary, dressed, hurried out to the yard. There was no sign of Fred except a set of footprints leading away from the pen. She found Robbie, his face and body covered with blood, lying unconscious next to the body of the deer. She was close to complete hysteria herself before she got him to bed. She cleaned him and found no sign of a wound, but not knowing what had happened made her frantic. She went out to the back porch and called for Fred until she was hoarse. No one responded.

190

17

Fred sat on the edge of the steel cot in the harness room and stared ahead of him into nothingness. The room was icy cold and he had no coat but he didn't notice. Now that the initial violence of his reaction was over he felt little of anything except a paralyzing numbness. It made him incapable of thought—oblivious to emotion. Twice he heard her calling him and once she came and pounded on the locked door of the room. He didn't answer and the frantic appeal in the voice touched only the outer fringes of his mind. Some time later the numbness began to leave him. It went slowly leaving a void of nausea in its place. He took down a bottle from its hiding place. As usual the cheap liquor burnt his throat and stomach but it sent waves of warmth radiating along the taut nerves. He drank steadily until the bottle was empty but the emotions generated in those dreadful moments over the body of the deer could not be burnt out so easily.

He was thoroughly drunk when she came to pound on the door a second time. He let her pound for perhaps a minute, then got up and opened it. Her face was white and her eyes frantic. For some reason this gave him acute pleasure. It helped to have somebody else suffer. It took the edge off his own bitterness.

She saw at once he was drunk. She said, unsteadily, "We've got to have a doctor."

He stood without moving—without saying anything, his eyes burning at her. She bit her lip and tried to keep her voice level. "Fred, listen to me, Robbie's still unconscious. He's got to have a doctor."

"He's fakin'," he said brutally.

"What?"

"I tell you he's fakin'! He don't need no doctor." His voice was shaking with anger. Mary stared and his voice rose half an octave. "What are you lookin' at me for? I tell you he don't need no doctor. I know what's wrong with him. He's a yellow stinkin' little coward!"

She hit him with every bit of strength in her body, the force of the slap snapped his head back against the doorjamb. She should have known better. He was still half out of his head and he was drunk besides. He knocked her down with one back-handed swipe then dragged her to her feet and shook her until her teeth rattled and her hair fell loose. His fingers almost met driving into the flesh of her shoulder blades. She was sobbing brokenly when he flung her down in the straw of one of the stalls and stormed back into the harness room slamming the door.

She dragged herself to her feet, her head reeling. In the house she found the Very cartridge which was to be used only in case of acute emergency. Her hands were still shaking as she fitted it into the stubby gun. She had never fired a rocket before but Tom had shown her how the gun worked. She went out to the back porch. She held the gun above her head with both hands and pulled the trigger. The rocket burst high above her head. There was very little breeze and the scarlet mushroom hung in the quiet air like a blotch of blood against the pale winter sky.

Sergeant Miller of The Royal Canadian Mounted Police slid his arms into the sleeves of his parka and turned to Mary. His face wore a frown of concern. The neighbors had all gone back to their homes and in a few minutes the doctor, too, would be leaving. She'd be alone again. He didn't like it but there was nothing he could do unless she made a complaint. Presumably she had told the doctor what had happened. She had refused to tell him or the neighbors anything. But something had taken place. That much was certain. Something more than just the fact of the boy being sick. The bruise on her left cheek and the tiny cut at the corner of her mouth had been made by an open hand. A fist would have brought a larger swelling and there would have been more broken blood vessels beneath the skin. Carter had hit her then. Had he also hit the child? And if so, what for? What peculiar combination of circumstances could lead a man—even Carter—to hit a lovely woman like this? The Sergeant would have given a lot to know and he made a mental note that if his path ever crossed Carter's in the line of duty he'd make sure the man got what was coming to him.

It was a queer situation all round; a distraught woman, an unconscious child, a drunken husband lurking in the barn and refusing to come out even when half the countryside converged on the farm. At one time there had been five dog sleds in the yard. The rocket had caused more excitement than he had seen in some time. Then there was that half-gutted deer frozen in the pen and the bodies of the wolves. Obviously they were tied up with this, too. There were signs of a scuffle in the snow beside the carcass. A boy and a man. It seemed pretty clear that Fred had started to dress out the deer and something had intervened. He couldn't have been drunk at that time because the incision in the deer's belly had been made by a steady hand. A sharp clean cut. The drunkenness must have come afterwards but again, why? If she knew she wouldn't say. She'd said only that the boy was sick. She'd been afraid to leave him for the hours it would take to get to the doctor and back. If this were true why hadn't she sent her husband? There were too many unanswered questions. A lot too many. Years of work up here had given him an instinct for trouble and right now the instinct was kicking up an unholy fuss. He picked up his gauntlets. He said, "You're sure you wouldn't like me to stay over? I have a sleeping bag in my sled." There was the faintest hesitation before she answered.

"No, thank you, Sergeant. You've been more than kind. It's sorry I am to have brought you all this way for nothin'. It's the doctor I really wanted."

"It's been no trouble, Mrs. Sharron, . . . I mean Mrs. Carter." He drew on the gauntlets and put a hand on the door and then swung back. "I've left you some more Very lights. I know you've been told not to use them except in the most acute emergency but if any time you feel . . ." he paused realizing he was getting into deep water, ". . . well . . . just don't be afraid to use them."

"I'll not forget. Thank you."

He touched his glove to his forehead in an informal salute and went out. A second later she heard the dogs snarling as he roused them, then the crack of his whip followed by the sound of sleigh runners in the snow. She turned back into the living room. The doctor was still with Robbie. She paced the room, then came out to the kitchen and made a cup of tea. She was on the second cup before the doctor emerged.

He was a little man with a pair of snapping blue eyes, a sharply urgent manner, a habit of playing with his pince-nez. When he was upset he had a pattern of speech that was like the rattle of a machine gun. He called everyone within a radius of a hundred miles by their first name. He shook his head almost irritably. "I don't understand it. The boy's in shock or rather he was."

"He's out of it now?"

"Yes. I gave him a strong sedative. He'll sleep for several hours."

194

"Then there's no danger?"

"No, he'll be all right."

"Thank God. I was that worried I thought I'd go out of my mind!"

"Are you sure you can't tell me any more about what happened?"

She wrung her hands helplessly. "I've told you all I know. He can't stand to see anything die and the sight of blood upsets him something terrible. You remember what he was like when Tom shot that deer two years back."

"Yes, I remember."

"My husband must know what happened but he won't say anything. He's been like a crazy man."

The doctor tapped his lower teeth with the edge of his pince-nez impatiently. He said, "Then your guess is that Robbie fainted when Fred started dressing the deer and Fred is angry because he thinks the boy's a coward."

"I don't know what else to think a-tall."

The doctor shook his head. "I suppose it could have happened that way but I'd stake my reputation that something more than the mere sight of blood was the cause of this. Dammit, woman, children are resilient! Even sensitive ones like Robbie. They get sick at their stomachs, they cry, sometimes they run fevers, but hell and fury they don't go into shock!"

"Are you sure he'll be all right?"

"Positive. Just make sure he doesn't overdo for the next few days." Mary nodded.

"I'd like to talk to your husband. Where is he?"

"I think he's out in the barn. I'll go and see."

"You'll do nothing of the kind. I'll find him myself."

He started away and Mary said, "Doctor McLeod?"

He turned. "Yes?"

"Be careful. He's drunk and he's in that wild a mood there's no tellin' what he'll do if you rouse him."

The doctor raised one eyebrow quizzically. "Oh," he said and went out.

Mary was wrong about one thing. Fred was no longer drunk. The bottle he had emptied had been all there was and he was now getting the letdown both from the liquor and the violent release of his emotions. He stood leaning against a stall, twisting knots in a piece of heavy rope and pulling them so tight that the veins stood out on his wrists and forearms. When he saw the doctor coming he didn't look up. He made another loop in the rope, slid the end through and snapped it taut.

"What do you want?"

The doctor pursed his lips. He was not over five feet six. The top of his head barely came level with Fred's shoulder and he couldn't have weighed more than one hundred and twenty pounds but he was the kind of a man who could lead an assault on hell with a roman candle. When he liked people his sharp blue eyes had a warm twinkle in them. When he didn't like people or found them difficult his eyes were apt to be like twin rapiers. They were like rapiers now. They bored right through Fred. He wasted no time on formalities.

"What did you do to that boy in there?"

Fred looked up belligerently. "What do you mean?"

The staccato voice snapped back almost before Fred had the words out of his mouth. "Carter, whenever a man says to me 'What do you mean' after I've asked him a simple question I know he's got a guilty conscience."

Fred drew his lips back tautly against his teeth. "I didn't do nothin' to him."

"Look, Carter. That boy's in shock. Somehow or other you frightened him half out of his senses. There's no guarantee that this may not affect his mind." Doctor McLeod didn't really believe this, but it had the desired effect.

Fred's face turned a shade whiter. He ran his tongue over his lips. "You mean he'll be loony?"

"He might be."

"Jesus!"

"Jesus is right!"

"I didn't mean him no harm."

"That's what people say when they've killed somebody with a gun that wasn't loaded."

"I told you I didn't mean him no harm!"

"Then you *did* do something to him?" The question was rapped out so suddenly that Fred had no time to think. He saw he was being forced into a corner and tried to bluster his way out.

"Look, I don't have to stand here and answer your damn fool questions. If there's somethin' wrong with the kid fix him up. That's what you're here for. If there ain't then what are we kickin' up all this fuss about?"

"Fred, you and I both know if anything happens to that boy you are responsible."

"The hell I am!"

"The hell you're not!"

"I tell you I didn't hurt him. What ever happened he had comin' to him."

"Did he? What have you got against the boy?"

There was an infinitesimal hesitation, then Fred's face twisted. "If you must know he's a miserable stinkin' little coward just like my brother Billy. I ain't havin' another one like that around me. I'll kill him first!"

The concentration of bitterness and defiance in the voice took the doctor unawares. Knowing Fred he had been prepared for belligerence but this was something far beyond a mere explosion of anger. His mind raced back over a span of twelve years and stopped dead. He gave a mental whistle of surprise.

He said curtly, "Who told you the boy was like Billy?"

"Nobody had to tell me. I seen it with my own eyes."

"I don't believe you!" The taunt stung like a whiplash. The muscles tightened into hard knots under the fabric of Fred's shirt. His face got red.

"If you'd seen him when I stuck the knife in that deer you'd know. He was scared witless when he seen the blood."

"What blood?"

"The blood from the deer."

"And that made you mad?"

"You're goddam right it made me mad!"

"How mad?"

"Mad enough to break his lousy little neck."

"And mad as you were, you didn't do anything, eh?" The voice was goading, rhythmic, excited, "You didn't lay a hand on him?"

Fred didn't see what was happening. Didn't realize that the taunting rhythm of the questions was having exactly the effect the doctor wanted. There was a white line around Fred's mouth and the cords stood out on his neck. "You're goddam right I did something. I did plenty!"

The doctor threw the last question viciously. Drove it home like the point of a rapier. "Well, what did you do?"

"I grabbed the little bastard by the back of his skinny neck and I rammed his face down in the deer's guts that's what I did! And I'd damn well do it again! I'll teach him to be afraid."

The doctor watched the working of the face as the memory of the scene washed over it; saw the big hands opening and closing convulsively. Fred came out of it slowly. He saw the doctor staring at him and he knew immediately he'd been tricked. He stiffened. Before he could move the doctor said sharply, "Don't do it, Fred! *Don't do it!*"

They stood toe to toe, their eyes locked. Beads of sweat broke out on Fred's forehead and suddenly, though there was no outward evidence of it, he broke. The doctor continued to hold his eyes but inwardly he breathed a deep shuddering sigh. That had been much too close for comfort. A few seconds later, Fred said hoarsely, "You son of a bitch, get off my land."

The doctor didn't flinch. The crisis was over now and he held the upper hand.

"Don't be a fool, Carter! You're going to kill somebody someday if you don't learn to control that temper of yours. Now you listen to me. I'm going to drive some sense into you if it's possible. In the first place, what you did to Robbie is strictly between you and me. The damage is done now and it won't do any good to tell anyone. It might do a lot of harm."

"I ain't ashamed of what I done."

"Right now that's not important one way or the other. What is important is that what you did to that boy, you did because you think he's a coward like your brother Billy. You think so because he got sick when he saw a little blood." There was no answer. The doctor hesitated, then went on. "You've got nothing to say? All right, then listen. I saw a man who had been awarded the Victoria Cross go into hysterics when he was bitten by a snake. I knew a heavyweight boxer who was scared to death to pick up a live bird. I treated a parachute jumper who fainted every time I gave him a hypodermic. Does that mean anything to you?"

"A man's afraid or he ain't. Nobody can tell me different."

The doctor sighed. He said, "Fred, every man is afraid of something. Even you."

"I never been afraid of nothin' in my life."

199

The doctor shook his head. "Tomorrow is another day," he said quietly. He turned and went out.

Fred watched the doctor go. He was suddenly struck by the fact that he was alone again. He had hurt the boy, he had beaten the woman. More than likely he had turned the whole countryside against him. It wouldn't matter that he had been within his rights. That the kid and the woman, too, had only got what was coming to them. They'd go back to hating him again. For one fleeting second he felt a flash of tired helplessness, then he straightened his shoulders and set his jaw. Let them hate him. Let them do their worst. To hell with them. To hell with them all. He hadn't needed them before. He didn't need them now. He dragged a couple of horse blankets off the wall and started toward the tack room. He'd never felt so tired in his life.

18

Mary never knew the precise moment when Robbie awakened. Sometime after midnight she fell asleep in the chair beside his bed. She woke to find him lying quite still with his eyes fixed on the ceiling. She caught her breath in relief and, as she spoke his name, he turned his head slowly to look at her. The big dark eyes rested on her steadily and the face in the lamplight was deathly pale. She drew his head against her breast, and cradled him, crooning softly. There was no response. His body was stiff and unbending. His arms didn't go around her neck and over her shoulder, his eyes were still wide. She said, "Oh darlin'."

He didn't say anything. She pushed him back to arm's length and looked at the pale pinched face. She did her best to keep her voice level. "Are you all right?" He nodded. She felt alarmed and helpless. She heard herself talking to cover her own anxiety. "You gave us a terrible scare. The doctor's been here and the neighbors and even Sergeant Miller. Robbie, what happened?" He turned his face to the wall. "Robbie!" She moved to the edge of the bed and pulled him back till she could see his face. Not a muscle had moved. There was no sign of tears. Only that cold unwavering glare. It was a look that didn't belong on the face of a child. It shut her out as effectively as if she had been in another world. She tried again desperately. "Robbie, please tell me. What happened?"

"Where's Fred?"

"Why I don't know. I'm thinkin' he's in the barn. You didn't answer my question."

He looked at her—through her. His eyes and his thoughts were outside the room. After a moment he said so softly she could barely hear him. "He shot my deer."

"Your deer?"

"It was Lightning."

"Lightning?" He was delirious, of course, but even as she thought this her mind fled back to the scene in the pen. She had been so distraught she hadn't noticed but now, remembering, she saw the deer again. She saw the blaze on its forehead. It *had* been his deer. The one he had found in the forest and kept as a pet for almost a year. She felt a lump forming in her throat. It could hardly have been worse. She said brokenly, "Oh, Robbie, I'm sorry."

"He likes to hurt things. He's a bad man."

"Robbie, you mustn't say things like that."

"I hate him. I'll hurt him. Someday I'll hurt *him*. You'll see. I'll hurt him bad."

"Robbie!"

He pulled away from her, turning his face to the wall again and when she tried to pull him back he wrenched his shoulder from her grasp and refused to be moved. Then she buried her face in her hands. Some time later she pulled herself to her feet. She looked drained of every ounce of energy. She made her way back to the bedroom and lay there in the bed, wide-eyed. It can't have happened, she thought. Not any of it. It's all a bad dream. I'll wake up tomorrow and find everything as it was forty-eight hours ago. She kept thinking it over and over as if the repetition might make it true.

She was wide awake when Fred came into the room. How dare he come here, she thought. How did he have the gall to be beside her after what had happened. She pulled herself as close to the wall as she could so that not even by accident would he touch her. Fred felt her withdrawal and set his jaw grimly. Well, let her. He didn't need her. He didn't need anybody—least of all that sniveling kid. He kept thinking it over and over as if the repetition might make it true.

It was a dismal breakfast. Fred and Mary ate in stony silence avoiding each other's eyes. Once when she had her head bent Fred looked up and saw a pale purple splotch on her cheek and the tiny cut in the corner of her mouth. Perversely the sight made him furious. She had deserved it, hadn't she? She had had no right to hit him. He'd only told her the truth about her kid. He searched for some way to get her to look at him. He ate as badly as he could, making loud noises with the coffee, swabbing his plate with a huge piece of bread. She took no notice. It was as if he didn't exist. He deliberately knocked over the remainder of his coffee. She ignored it. He pointed to the sopping mess on the table. "Clean it up!"

She got up obediently and mopped the table with a rag. She didn't look at him. She poured him another cup of coffee in silence. He tasted it, then banged the cup down. The coffee spilled again. "It's lousy!"

She got up quietly, "I'll make some more."

As she passed him moving toward the stove he jumped up and seized her. He heard himself saying brokenly, "Listen to me. I didn't mean it. I didn't want to hurt you. I didn't know what I was doin'!"

She raised her head and met his eyes. "Let go of me, please."

He shook his head like a hurt dog. "You got no right to treat me like this. You hear me?" He found himself shaking her. She made no resistance. Suddenly Robbie appeared in the door of the kitchen. Fred stopped and looked up. He met his stepson's eyes. It was as if a small fist had struck him full in the face. He dropped his hands from Mary's shoulders. For one moment the anger held him, then he crumpled visibly. He turned and went out.

203

Mary said, quietly, "Your breakfast is ready, Robbie."

He came to the table and sat down. He ate very little. Twice she tried to draw him out but it was useless. He answered in monosyllables. She gave up. Time she told herself. It's too soon. Give him time. It will all work out. Everything does. It just takes a little time. If only she knew what had really happened! That was the worst. Not knowing.

Fred had always had two outlets for emotion; liquor and work. This morning the liquor was gone. He hurled himself into his work with a fury that left no time for thought. He waded steadily through all the regular chores and then turned his attention to the partition at the end of the barn. It had needed rebuilding for a long time. He took the sledge and hit it a massive blow springing half the timbers loose from one end. A few more strokes would have demolished it completely but he tossed the sledge aside and began ripping the cross-nailed timbers out of their sockets by brute force. He worked with silent furious concentration. The rusty nails screeched, twisted and snapped; the boards bowed and splintered. The sweat was streaming off him. He stopped long enough to discard the heavy coat and went back to work. Once he gashed his hand on a nail but he scarcely noted. It was some time before he realized he was being watched. He straightened, breathing heavily. Robbie stood at the door of the barn with his black eyes fixed unwaveringly on the man. He didn't move as Fred turned and again Fred had the sensation as he met the child's glance that he was being struck. He set his teeth and went back to work. The eyes never left him. He could feel them boring into his back following his every move. He began to think about what the doctor had said. Maybe the kid was really loony. The thought unnerved him. He straightened and flung one of the timbers halfway across the barn.

"Get out of here! You hear me. Get out!"

Robbie stood there letting the fury of the voice wash over

him, then turned slowly and walked away. Not until the boy had disappeared did Fred return to his work.

Outside the barn Robbie stopped and looked back. He waited for some time to be sure Fred wasn't going to follow, then he walked quietly around the building until he came to the small utility door on the opposite side away from Fred's line of sight. He opened the door, slid through it and stood listening. He could not see his stepfather now but he could hear the noises made as he labored at the stall. A few feet to Robbie's left was a ladder leading to the loft. He closed the door, stepped away from it to the foot of the ladder. He began to climb. Almost at the top of the ladder he paused. From this position he could look over the stalls and down through the length of the barn to the opposite end where Fred was still absorbed.

Robbie felt his heart beat quickening and the roof of his mouth went dry. He thrust one arm through the ladder so that he could hold on more easily. Below, Midnight caught Robbie's scent, swung her head, whinnied, and thumped the stall with her hooves. Fred turned and looked toward the door of the barn. Robbie held his breath. After a second Fred spat and went back to his job. Robbie began to climb again. It was awkward going for his hands were numb now with the cold and the bulky fur jacket impeded him. He squeezed himself through the trap at the top of the ladder and stood up. It was a half loft covering the north portion of the barn. This late in the year most of the hay had been fed to the stock but there was still a heap of it piled against the far wall. The floor was covered with an inch or two of broken chaff. Robbie moved across it with the soundless skill and caution he had learned in the forest. It took him a good ten minutes to get to a spot close to the pile of hay and almost directly above the place where Fred was working. He leaned forward craning his neck. He could see the top of his stepfather's head, the

205

back of his neck and shoulders. His mouth was totally dry now and his heart thundering so loud he was afraid for a second that the man could hear it. He stepped back and put out his hand. His fingers closed around the shaft of a pitchfork thrust into the pile of hay. He drew the fork out inch by inch until the needle-pointed tines were free. Below Fred was bent double straining at the foundation beam of the stall. A film of dust sifted down on the back of his neck and then a small bit of chaff floated down just head of him. He straightened and looked up. The boy was standing on the edge of the loft, the pitchfork raised, its blades pointed straight at Fred's chest. For a second they stood frozen that way. Then a look of contempt crossed Fred's face.

He said, "Well, what the hell are you waitin' for? Throw it! Show me you got that much guts!" He stood stock-still waiting. Robbie's knuckles whitened around the handle of the fork. The taunting voice rang in his ears, "I'll make a bargain with you. I won't move. All you got to do is throw it! *Come on you gutless wonder!*" In Robbie's hands the fork began to tremble. He wanted to do this more than he had ever wanted to do anything. He tried to will himself to let it go but his hands were frozen to the shaft. The tears began to well into his eyes. The strength ran out of his arms. The point of the fork dropped suddenly caught the edge of the loft. The wrench pulled it out of Robbie's hand. It turned end over end in mid-air. It plummeted toward Fred's face. Robbie screamed. Fred caught the fork with one hand and flung it away. He stood staring upwards for a moment then spat disgustedly and turned his back. Robbie felt a thickening in his throat. He stepped away from the edge of the loft and flung himself down on the pile of straw. He sobbed as if his heart would break.

Sometime later he became aware that Fred was gone. He lay there in the cold while wave after wave of shame drenched him. Nothing he ever did was right! If it was summer he'd go away. He'd go as far away as he could. He'd live by himself in the forest where no one would ever know how different he was. Someday when he'd grown big he'd come back. And when he did he'd make his stepfather pay. He'd show him whether he was afraid or not when he was big. He'd thrash him till he pleaded for mercy. He'd make him get down on his knees and beg like a dog. And afterwards—only afterwards —he'd kill him. The vision made him feel a little better.

19

The black waters broke the unbreakable grip of ice. The blue-berry bushes shed their canopies of frozen crystal; a million trilliums burst the steaming peat and thrust blanched fingers toward the canopy of pines. Everywhere the fragile ferns unfolded delicate green tongues in the shadow of the rocks. The does walked awkwardly, their bellies drum-taut with life and the bear cubs wrestled playfully in the tender grass. The world was a welter of color and a madness of song. Not for another twelve months would it be as fresh, as clean, as richly alive.

And in the midst of this land where every square inch of the earth was celebrating the end of winter an island of winter bleakness survived. Around the Sharron farm the loveliness of the season came unnoticed. A pall of bitterness brooded over the sunless house. It seeped out to the barn and amid the green glory of the season, it hung limp and flaccid in the air like some loathsome sickness.

Fred kept telling himself it didn't matter but his appearance belied his thoughts. There were hollows in his cheeks and a tight grim line around his mouth. In the months before the episode with the deer, something had happened to him. He had been touched, if only briefly, by something he had never known—a sense of belonging. He had become accustomed to laughter, to gentleness, and to small but important kindnesses. Outwardly there had been little sign of the change, but inwardly the hard shell of defiance he had carried as a shield had been ruptured almost insensibly. Now, with all of the old wounds reopened there was no retreat from their pain.

He had expected so little of life, that what he had received; the companionship of a woman who did not love him and the responsibility of a child he had never fully understood, had been enough to draw him into the net of near happiness. He mourned that happiness with a sick longing which corroded his nerves and left him sleepless and exhausted.

It was doubly frustrating because their attitude left him helpless even to strike back. There was no open rebellion. His authority was not questioned but he was an alien in his own house, a stranger under his own roof. Every gesture he made went unnoticed or was misconstrued. When he spoke his words were greeted with stony silence. When he asked direct questions he was answered in monosyllables. In his presence they looked through him as if he did not exist, and on the rare occasions when he met their eyes he felt as if he had been scalded. His food was prepared and set before him in silence, his clothes washed and laid out when he was not present. In the bedroom she offered no resistance but she made it so apparent she didn't want him near her that he came to feel that making love to her was an act of violation. He would not give in. The more they slighted him the more he tried to fight back. The very realization that Mary detested him made him continue to share her bed when he would have been glad to sleep elsewhere. His pride and his stubbornness made him deliberately subject himself to humiliation long after a lesser man would have had enough. But the hollows in his cheeks grew deeper and the wild helpless resentment in his eyes increased.

He tried everything he knew to get them to notice him. For two days he swore viciously at the table. Her face got red and she sent the child away but she made no protest. He demanded ridiculous and unnecessary service. She provided it in cold silence that was a thousand times worse than defiance. Once in an explosion of sheer fury he had swept the dishes off the table and stood up staring at them in such anger that Robbie ran to his mother's arms. In that moment Fred had been ready to kill them both and afterwards in the barn for the first time in his life he had cried. Deep shuddering sobs that wracked him to the core of his being. That same day he had tried to make amends. He couldn't bring himself to face her after that first morning but he had gone out to the woods and collected an armful of flowers and ferns. He had arranged them in an awkward bouquet and laid them on the cutting board in the kitchen. They were still there, the petals of the flowers brown and withered, the ferns shriveled and dead. She had not touched them and he was too proud to take them away.

He sat at the breakfast table now, watching them—his eyes hot and feverish. They had their heads bent over their plates communicating with each other by a look or a gesture, for since his outburst they no longer spoke in his presence. They were shutting him out as effectively as if he were in another world. He swallowed painfully and pushed aside his untouched breakfast. He wanted to scream out loud—to seize them and shake them till sounds tumbled out of their mouths. He tried to tell himself as he had so often before, that it was actually better this way. He was fed and looked after and he didn't have that sniveling kid dogging his footsteps everywhere he went. He didn't have to put himself out to be nice to the woman. He could eat the way he pleased, go without shaving, curse and swear if he felt like it. The thought no longer helped.

There was a sound in the driveway. Mary's face brightened. She caught her son's eyes. They both got up from the table and went outside. He heard their voices raised in greeting. He heard Jed Clawson's voice and then Bedelia's. A second later Mary laughed. The sound made Fred crazy. He smashed his chair back and flung himself out the back door. He stood on the back porch, his face white, the cords standing out in his neck. All of them looked up at him. Bedelia put her hand to her mouth. Fred came down the steps slowly. When he was a few feet away, he said, "Get out! Get out of here! Get off this land, both of you! You come back here and I'll kill you." Bedelia gasped and backed against the wagon. Jed got pale. He was not a coward but he was not a fool either.

He said quietly, "Get in, Bedelia."

Bedelia scrambled back into the rig and Jed followed. From the seat, he said, "Good-by, Mary . . . I'm sorry." Mary bit her lip. "Good-by, Jed . . . Bedelia." They drove off. Mary turned to Robbie, "Come, dear." She didn't look at Fred. She made no mention of the incident. If his behavior had had the slightest effect on her there was no sign. Without another word she turned and led Robbie back into the house. Fred stood watching them go, his mouth working.

Inside Robbie looked back through the screen door. He said, hoarsely, "I hate him. I hate him!"

Mary pulled him away from the door. "Hush, darlin'. It's all right. Why don't you go out the front and down to the beaver dam. I'll ring the triangle when lunch is ready."

He shook his head sullenly. He never went to the forest any more and the change in him was almost more than she could bear. He seldom smiled. She couldn't interest him in anything. He was dull and listless at his lessons and the books he had read with such eagerness before no longer absorbed him. When she suggested that he read he would pick up a book obediently but his eyes did not see the print. She was never to know what had happened in the barn. Robbie was too ashamed to tell her and to Fred's credit he never mentioned the incident, but she had finally gotten from Robbie the true story of what had happened the morning she had found him unconscious by the body of the deer. It was this that had driven from her every bit of the respect she had once had for her husband. She could have forgiven him for what he had done to her in the barn, but as a mother, she could never forgive him for the change he had wrought in her child. Not only had Robbie lost the bright sheen of wonder, the happy interest in everything about him but particularly since the episode in the barn, he clung to her almost desperately, refusing to let her out of his sight as if she were the only stable thing in his universe.

In the beginning their attitude toward Fred had not been planned. It had just happened. It was impossible to avoid him and equally impossible to act toward him as if nothing had occurred. The only alternative was to try to ignore him. His reaction had been unexpected and had at first given her a bitter satisfaction. If it hurt him, so much the better, but the satisfaction was rapidly being overlaid by fear. He was becoming more and more violent. With the first realization of danger she had considered taking Robbie away but in addition to the fact that she had very little money there was no place she could go. She had no relatives in Canada and the best she could do to provide for them was to get some unskilled job or go back to teaching school. This would necessitate their living in a city and she felt instinctively that such an environment would only make Robbie more insecure and push him farther back into the morass of fear and self-doubt. He loved the forest and while he seldom went there now, she was sure that eventually he would go back to it and she hoped it would act as a counteragent against the corrosion of his home. Furthermore, if they were to run away it would be tantamount to giving Fred the farm which Tom Sharron had worked so hard to build and this she could never bring herself to do.

For a while she had hoped Fred would leave of his own accord when he saw that he wasn't wanted but she knew now that this hope was futile. He had the tenacity of a boa constrictor. No amount of misery or humiliation could break him.

Once when he had brought the flowers she had felt an unexpected start of contrition. For one brief second she had hesitated. Then Robbie had come into the room. She had looked at the pale pinched face, the dark circles beneath the eyes, and she had thought, I'm insane! He might have killed my son! Am I going to accept the overtures of a man who missed being a murderer by sheer accident? She had swept the flowers to one side and not touched them since. It was the last flicker of sympathy she had felt. She had loaded a shotgun and hid it in the back of the broom closet. She had made up her mind about one thing: if he ever laid a hand on Robbie again she would kill him!

She sent Robbie to his room and then bent down to get an apron full of potatoes from the bin under the cutting board and suddenly found her head swimming. She broke out in a cold sweat and clutched for the edge of the board to support herself. After a moment the dizziness went. She stood there breathing a little heavily.

It's the strain, she thought. I'm worrying too much about this. She poured herself a glass of water and began to peel the potatoes.

20

Fred drove the buggy into Pineville. He'd met two rigs coming out of town and forced them both into the ditch. It hadn't made him feel perceptibly better. There was no particular reason for him to be in town today but after that scene with the Clawsons this morning he'd had to get away. He pulled the lathered horse into the hitching rack and got down. The silence which had fallen on the short main street when he drove in, deepened. He felt the impact of half a dozen pairs of eyes. No one knew exactly what had happened on the Sharron farm the day the Very light went up but there was no doubt in anyone's mind that Fred Carter had been responsible. It had been the first time he had been in town since. He strode up on the porch toward the general store. Three men who had been sitting there talking, got up and walked away. Lilly Cartwright came out of the store, stared at him icily and swept past him without a word. There were four or five people inside. Everyone pretended not to see him.

He clenched his fists. At the counter a French Canadian homesteader was ordering from Mr. Campbell. Fred said, "Gimme a package of tobacco." He flung a half dollar on the counter. In the silence the coin rang on the wood and then spun, vibrating like an air hammer before it settled.

Mr. Campbell looked up quietly. His craggy Scotch face was grim. He said, "You'll wait yur turn."

Somebody snickered. Fred spun around looking for the author of the sound. He saw for the first time that Dr. McLeod was in the room. The doctor was looking at him thoughtfully.

All the other faces were turned away. He heard Mr. Campbell say, "Will that be all then, Henri?" The Frenchman pursed his lips in exaggerated thought. "I am not sure, m'sieu." It was obvious he wanted nothing else. Campbell had already added the bill but the Frenchman's temper had been roused. He looked directly at Fred. He said again, "No, I am not sure. Perhaps. . . ."

He never finished the sentence. Fred shoved him roughly out of the way. "Gimme that tobacco!" Henri staggered back and brought up against a table of oil lamps. One of them crashed to the floor. Suddenly there was a knife in Henri's hand. Fred turned to face him. He saw the knife and something that might have been a gleam of relief crossed his face. He said, hoarsely, "Come on, Frenchy."

Dr. McLeod stood up and put a hand on the Frenchman's arm. Henri shook the arm off angrily but the doctor seized his shoulder and spoke quickly in the man's ear. When he straightened up, the Frenchman stared at Fred and put the knife away slowly. He went to the door. He seemed about to go on out and then he stopped. He turned back. He spat contemptuously at Fred's feet. Without waiting to see the result of the action, he turned on his heel and started out. It was a mistake. Fred covered the distance to the door in two huge strides. He seized the man by the back of the neck and the belt and hurled him bodily off the steps into the street. The Frenchman fell heavily. He was half stunned. He tried to get to his feet but before he could do more than get to one knee Fred was upon him. He hit him across the face with a back-handed swipe that started the blood spurting from the man's nose and knocked him flat in the dust. Fred said, "Get up! You want trouble, you're gonna get it!"

A curt voice said, "Not from you, he isn't. You're going to be out of circulation for a while." Fred turned. Sergeant Miller stood in the roadway. He said, "Are you going to come quietly or are you going to give me the satisfaction of dragging you in."

Fred wet his lips in anticipation. "You try and take me, Mountie!"

The mountie was two inches shorter than Fred but still well over six feet. He would have liked to teach this "woman beater" a lesson with his fists but Headquarters took a very dim view of constables who engaged in brawls. He slipped his gun out of his holster. He said, "Let's go, Carter."

The sight of the gun broke the last barrier of Fred's control. He lunged forward. The policeman side-stepped neatly and brought the barrel of the gun down on Fred's skull. Blood spurted and Fred staggered. He went down on one knee but he didn't stay there. He lurched to his feet like a wounded bull coming up out of a wallow. His eyes were glazed. The mountie let the gun hang by its lanyard. He stepped in and hit Fred twice cleanly on the chin. The blows would have felled an ox. Fred shook his head and tried to wipe the blood out of his eyes. The mountie measured him again and hit him with everything he had right behind the ear. Fred swayed for a moment then his knees buckled. He went down. The mountie put the gun back in its holster and felt his knuckles. Both hands were numb. It wouldn't have surprised him in the least if they were broken.

Dr. McLeod came down the steps from the store and looked down at the body. He said, "Very neat."

The Sergeant rubbed his knuckles ruefully. "For a moment there I thought I'd bitten off more than I could chew. Never saw a man stand up after I'd laid a forty-five across his skull."

The doctor grunted. "This is no ordinary man."

"So I've been told," there was an edge of sarcasm in the voice. "You better look at that cut before I take him in."

The doctor nodded. "Bring him over to the office." He turned searching the onlookers with his eyes and spotted the

216

Frenchman Fred had struck. "Henri, let me look at that nose."

The Frenchman came over, scowling. The doctor seized the nose between thumb and forefinger and felt it none too gently. "It's not broken. You want me to patch it up?"

The Frenchman shook his head, wiped the blood away with his forearm and turned to the Sergeant. "What you do with him, eh?"

"Take him to Brownsville and lock him up. You want to file a complaint for assault and battery?"

"No, m'sieu. When you are finish with heem then maybe it will be my turn."

The Sergeant hitched his belt. "You'll have a long wait if I have anything to do with it."

The Frenchman gave a Gallic shrug which seemed to indicate that how long he had to wait was of no particular importance.

A few minutes later in the dispensary Fred was still unconscious. The doctor finished the bandage on his head and straightened up. "There, that ought to hold him." He crossed to the washbasin and began soaping his hands while the Sergeant slipped a pair of manacles on Fred's wrists. The doctor rinsed his hands and reached for a towel. He said, "What are you going to charge him with?"

The policeman took out a cigarette and tamped it crisply against his thumbnail. "Everything I can find in the book. I've been waiting to hang one on this bozo ever since that day out at the farm."

The doctor tossed the towel away with a gesture that was elaborately casual. "You know what happened out there, of course."

Miller frowned and blew out a haze of smoke. "I know one thing. He hit her."

The doctor nodded thoughtfully. "Yes, I think he did."

"Any man would hit a woman like Mary Sharron ought to be horsewhipped."

"I suppose you're right."

The Sergeant's eyes narrowed. "What do you mean you *suppose* I'm right?"

"Just what I said. I suppose you're right. I suppose it has no real significance that she hit him first."

"What?"

The doctor's surprise was elaborate. "You mean you didn't know?"

"I don't believe it!"

"Did you see him?"

"No. The bastard wouldn't come out of the barn long as I was there. But I wouldn't believe what he said if he swore on a stack of Bibles."

"He had the marks of her fingers on his face. From the size of the welts it was no love pat."

The Sergeant scowled. "Well, she must have been provoked to the point where she didn't know what she was doing. I can't see her hitting anybody. She's just too . . . too . . ."

"Too much of a lady?"

"Exactly."

The doctor waved his pince-nez. "Well, as I said before you may be right. Anyway, that's all past now. Will you have a nip?"

"You know I can't. I'm on duty." He was scowling at the doctor.

"You don't mind if I do?"

"Go ahead."

The doctor took a bottle of brandy from a desk drawer and poured a finger or two into a porcelain cup silently. He said, "Cheers" and took a swallow. The Sergeant ground out his cigarette irritably. The doctor didn't appear to notice. He smacked his lips and then shook his head. "Not very good brandy. Sister sent it to me. A frugal woman. Very frugal. Can't ever make her see I'd much sooner have a small bottle of good brandy than the large economy size."

The Sergeant snorted. He knew damn well he was being led up the garden path and he had an unpleasant suspicion that when he got to the end he wasn't going to like the view. He said, "All right, out with it."

The doctor raised his eyebrows. "Out with what?"

"Don't give me that stuff. I've known you for six years."

"Well, there is a little something that sticks in my head about all this."

"I knew it. But if you're going to try to tell me that Fred Carter is a fine upstanding citizen and that I must give him a pat on the back for smacking his wife around and knocking people into the street you might as well save your breath."

The doctor sucked in his lower lip as if in the throes of making an important decision. "You're right," he said finally, "I'd better not say anything."

The Sergeant swore. He got up and paced the room. "The man's a menace, I don't care what you say!"

"I haven't said anything."

"But you'd like to, wouldn't you?"

"I could be wrong."

"Somehow or other you never seem to be."

"Well, let's put it this way. I don't think I am this time."

The Sergeant sat down. He lit another cigarette. He crossed his legs and then uncrossed them. "All right. Shoot."

The doctor cracked the faintest suspicion of a smile. "Let's go into the other room first. I'll lock this up so's he'll be safe if he comes to." He carried his cup of brandy into the outer office and sat down behind the desk. The Sergeant dropped into a worn leather armchair. The doctor took off his pince-nez and polished them. "Now then," he said. "Do you know anything about what happened that day?"

"No. She wouldn't talk to me."

"Uh hmm. Well, she talked to me and what she didn't say I think I can fill in. The three of them woke up in the morning and found the deer trapped in the pen. Fred shot the deer and started to dress it out. Somehow or other the boy was nearby. Fred looked up and saw something on the boy's face that made him so wild that he took the kid by the back of the neck and shoved his head into the deer's entrails."

"The bastard!"

"Hold on now."

The Sergeant's jaw was set. "Go ahead."

"The boy went into shock. Fred left him in the snow, locked himself in the barn and proceeded to get roaring drunk. The boy didn't get better and the mother went to ask Fred to go for a doctor. I'm guessing at this part, mind you, but I think it's pretty straight. Fred refused. She hit him and he hit her back. She fired the Very light and the rest you know."

"So far you've only succeeded in making me want to beat him to a bloody pulp. How could any man in his right mind do that to a helpless child?"

"Exactly."

Miller's head snapped up. "What do you mean?"

"I mean Fred was not in his right mind and he didn't know what he was doing."

"You've lost me."

The doctor leaned forward across the desk and his voice became curiously intense. "Then try to follow this. You know Fred Carter's history. You know that he once lay in a barnyard with both legs broken, a rib sticking through the wall of his chest and a fire roaring down on him. His wife was in the house along with his brother whom he'd taken care of since he was a kid. Fred was incapable of saving himself or his wife. Only the brother could do that. But the brother took one look at the blood pumping out of Fred's chest and went berserk."

"I thought it was the fire that spooked him."

"Maybe it was. Nobody will ever know that. But I treated Fred here in this room before they took him out to the county hospital and the thing that stuck in *his* mind . . . the thing he kept babbling about in delirium was the fear he read on the boy's face when the boy saw the blood. Because of that fear, Fred had to lie there and face what he must have thought was certain death and he had to watch his wife burn in front of his eyes. That boy's face was engraved in Fred's memory along with the most terrible connotation it is possible for the human mind to hold. He came back from the hospital a changed man. He'd always been taciturn and humorless but now he was carrying a resentment that you could almost feel.

"Now let's go to the boy. The boy practically grew up in the woods. Dubois says the kid is untouchable as a woodsman and he has an absolutely uncanny feeling for animals. They like him and trust him. The boy, possessed of this exaggerated love of wild creatures, goes hunting with his father one day. He leads the father to a deer which the father shoots. The boy is too young to realize what he has done, of course, until he watches the deer die. Then suddenly the whole meaning of death, the utter finality of it and the terror, is brought home to him in one blinding instant. For a highly sensitive child it's too much. He throws up. He runs away. The Sharrons had a suspicion that he even tried to drown himself. It takes days for him to get over the experience. But children are resilient. They bounce back. Robbie like Fred recovers externally but inside he still has the fear probably coupled with a sense of shame and guilt."

"Now the stage is set. We have a rough, uneducated, physical man who has a violent unreasoning feeling about cowardice tied up with the sight of a boy in the presence of blood.

And we have a child who has an equally violent and equally unreasoned allergy to killing and the sight of blood. By the greatest chance of the century they are brought together above the newly blooded carcass of a deer. What happens? The boy loses his head and the man is kicked back ten or twelve years to the point where his brother defected. He may even have seen his brother's face in that moment. Only this time he's not crippled. This time he can do something about it. What he does you already know."

The Sergeant shifted his weight and stubbed out his cigarette. He pulled at his ear lobes uncomfortably and then he said, "Look, I don't want to be rude but aren't you a little out of your field?"

"Of course I am. I don't pretend to be a professional head shrinker, but it doesn't take a hell of a lot of knowledge or experience to figger out what happened when you know the history of the people involved. Most emotional problems are complicated by the fact that we don't know what caused the trouble. In this case we do."

"You *think* we do!"

"All right. I may be reaching a little. But it's a reasonable assumption. If there's any possibility that I'm right, wouldn't it be sensible to give Carter the benefit of the doubt?"

The Sergeant blew out a long breath, then got up and paced the room. Finally, he said, "You really believe that's what happened out there?"

"I'm certain of it."

"Why did Carter get drunk then?"

"Because he always gets drunk when he's upset. It's a release. He's strong willed, impulsive, stubborn, but he's not nearly as tough emotionally as he thinks. When he calmed down he must have realized what he had done. He started drinking because he couldn't face himself."

"Well, if he was so damned conscience-stricken why didn't

he go in and ask her forgiveness instead of beating her? Why didn't he go for a doctor when she asked him?"

"Well, there you have the interesting point. My guess is that he knew what he'd done to the boy but he didn't know *why*. He had to have a reason for his behavior or admit to himself that he was an absolute monster."

"I'll go along with that last part!"

"Shut up and listen. He told himself the boy deserved it; that he'd done it to teach the kid a lesson. Because he was a 'stinking yellow little coward' as he put it to me later. He transferred all of his brother's weaknesses and cowardice to Robbie and the transfer made him feel partly justified."

The Sergeant shook his head uncertainly. "I don't know."

"If you don't buy it how do you explain what happened today?"

"That's easy. The man's a bully pure and simple."

"Is he? Up to the time of the incident on the farm how long had he been around—ten years—twelve?"

"So?"

"In all that time did he ever give any trouble? As far as you know did he ever push anybody around?"

"What are you suggesting?"

"I'm suggesting that you are falling into the trap that everyone falls into. You are judging Fred by what he seems to be and Mary Carter for what she seems to be and neither judgment is completely right. In the eyes of this community Mary Sharron is a beautiful, charming, and for this country, a highly educated woman. People not only look up to her, they consider her sort of a saint in homespun. On the other hand, Fred is an ignorant man. He doesn't know how to be charming and worst of all he's surly and aloof. People naturally distrust a man like this. They find it's easy to see the worst in him."

"That's an exaggeration."

223

"Is it? Let me ask you something. Tom Sharron was everyone's friend and rightly so. He was a fine man. Now just supposing when you answered that Very light you'd found Mary Sharron with a bruise on her face and a split lip and she was still married to Tom. Would you have wanted to throw the book at him? Would you have decided if you ever got the chance to make *him* pay for what he'd done, as you did with Fred?"

The Sergeant scrubbed the back of his neck with his knuckles. He said, ruefully, "I knew damn well I shouldn't have listened to you."

"You see the point, don't you? That bruise on Mary's cheek gave you the chance to work up a good head of steam against that 'surly brute' Carter. It's all too easy to resent him. I do myself sometimes."

"What's your explanation for today?"

The doctor wound the ribbon of his pince-nez around his finger. "He came to town looking for trouble. I was at Campbell's when it happened. He was at the point where he had to explode or crack up."

"Why? The whole mess started almost three months ago."

"I think something's eating on him. He's in worse shape now than he was the day I talked to him in the barn. Somehow or other he's being made to pay for what he did to Robbie. It may be just his conscience but I have a suspicion that his conscience is getting a very able assist from outside."

"If you mean that it's all Mary Sharron's fault—"

"She's black Irish, Miller. She loves fiercely. I imagine she can hate the same way. I don't like to shatter any illusions you may have about her but nobody is all black or all white. I think she's crucifying Fred for what he did to Robbie. In one way she's got a bigger problem than he has. She's a little bit of a snob, and as far as Fred is concerned, she can't see the forest for the trees. She's so concerned with the fact that he's crude and sometimes brutal that she can't see that basically he's not a bad piece of work."

"You honestly believe that about him?"

The doctor's voice contained a trace of impatience. "The man spent half his life taking care of a no-good brother. He married a prostitute and held his head up afterwards. He was a hell of a lot more tolerant toward the people who condemned him than you or I would ever have been. When Tom was killed he went out to the Sharron farm without being asked, to help her run it. He didn't owe her anything and yet he even refused to let her pay him the big salary he was in a position to demand. He saved both their lives in a blizzard. He bought them presents he could ill afford. What more can you ask of a man?"

"Well, when you put it that way."

"What other way is there to put it?" He hesitated, then decided since he had gone this far, he might as well shoot the works. "At the risk of being proved a complete idiot, I'll tell you something else. The impulse of a psychopathic personality would have been to kill the boy that day over the carcass of the deer. Remember, Fred was so badly shaken that he acted instinctively. His instinct was not to harm the boy but to jam his face into the deer's entrails. In other words, to make him face the thing he feared. He said to me afterwards, 'I'll teach him to be afraid.' It was brutal but far from homicidal."

"Are you trying to tell me he's not dangerous?"

"Of course not. He's extremely dangerous. Now more than ever. I don't think he'd kill anybody deliberately but he has an ungovernable temper. He might easily have killed you there in the street, or Henri. He's a powerful man and he's no more responsible now than he was when this all started."

"Then what do you want of me? You can't expect me to let him go after what you've told me."

"I don't want you to let him go."

"Then what do you want?"

"The whole world is against him now. Or so it must seem to him. It isn't going to help if the police climb on the band wagon. Lock him up and charge him with whatever is necessary but don't throw the book at him. I'll write a note to the circuit judge. And whatever you do, try not to let him see how you feel. Don't treat him like a mad dog. If you do, you may push him too far and find yourself indirectly responsible for murder."

"It's that serious?"

"It could be. He's at a crucial point right now. He can go one way or the other."

"Why don't you tell him all this?"

"Because I don't think I could make him understand. He's not stupid but he doesn't have the capacity for abstract thought particularly now. Mary might be the solution. I'd give a lot to know exactly what has gone on out there during the past two months."

"I still find it hard to believe that she could have done this deliberately."

The doctor smiled. "I rather thought you would."

"What the hell do you mean by that?"

"She's an extremely attractive young woman. It's just possible you are something more than objectively concerned with her welfare."

The Sergeant picked up a book and slammed it down on the table. "Now you cut that out!"

The doctor laughed.

21

Doctor McLeod had intended to get out to the Sharron farm the same day, but a logger came in with a multiple fracture and his visit was forestalled. It wasn't until the next afternoon that he drove into the Sharron barnyard and met Mary as she came down the back steps to greet him. Her face was a trifle pale but she was smiling broadly and the casual observer could never have known she had received news that morning that her husband was in jail.

She said, "Dr. McLeod! What a nice surprise!"

He took her hand. "How are you, Mary?"

"We'll talk about that later. Come inside and I'll put the kettle on."

He let himself be led into the house but he balked at entering the living room.

"No, no, no. Let's just sit here in the kitchen."

"Fine, I like it better myself." She took down the kettle and found the teapot. "And to what do we owe the honor of this visit?"

"I had to make a call at the Clawsons' and I thought I'd come by and see how Robbie was gettin' on."

She frowned. "He's not himself a-tall, Doctor. I'm glad you dropped by. I'd like you to have a look at him."

"I'd better have a look at you, too. Your color's not too good."

She put down the spoon she'd been holding. "It's strange you should say that. I've been thinkin' about comin' in to see you."

"Oh?"

"It's silly, I know. I've not been sick a day in my life but I haven't felt a-tall well lately. I don't seem to have any appetite and I . . . I . . ."

"Yes?"

"Well, I've been lightheaded like. I thought perhaps I needed a tonic."

"Then it's a good thing I came by. Let's have a look at you."

"There's not all that hurry now."

"It'll take a few minutes for the kettle to boil. Off with you."

She went into the bedroom. Sometime later he took the stethoscope from his ears and straightened up. "You can get dressed now." He folded the instrument, put it in his bag, and walked to the window. His face was thoughtful. Behind him he could hear the rustle of her clothes as she dressed. After a moment she said with slightly forced gaiety, "From the looks of you I'm not long for this world."

He grunted. "If all my patients were as healthy as you I wouldn't have a practice. You're strong as an ox."

"But what about the dizziness then?"

He turned back and the keen blue eyes fixed themselves on her appraisingly. "You mean to tell me you really don't know what's wrong with you?"

She felt a sudden wrench of misgiving. She swallowed. "What is it?"

"It's very simple. You're pregnant."

He saw the color drain out of her face. She swayed as if she had been struck. The long tapered fingers dug themselves into the coverlet of the bed. When she spoke her voice was hoarse and bitter. "It's impossible!"

He snapped the fasteners on his bag with an air of finality. "And why is it impossible?"

"Well because . . . because I'm still flowing for one thing."

"It happens sometimes. Once in every two or three hundred pregnancies."

"You're sure?"

"I'm sure."

She put her fist to her mouth and set her teeth against the knuckles. Unbelievingly he watched her bite down till the blood flowed. He unsnapped the fasteners of his bag again. It had all seemed so simple in the office when he talked to the Sergeant. All he had to do was tell her Fred's side of the problem. Try and tell her now, he thought grimly. The best laid plans of mice and men. . . .

The tea was bitter in her mouth. She pushed the cup away and sat staring stonily at the table. The doctor had been gone for over an hour. He'd looked at Robbie and found nothing wrong with him. If only he had found nothing wrong with her! Pregnant! She still couldn't believe it. Robbie was nine. Seven of those years she was married to Tom and she had wanted another child desperately. It hadn't come. How then could she have conceived with Fred? It had never occurred to her that he might get her with child. How could it? She had responded to Tom's ardor with every fiber of her being wanting him, desiring him, praying she could give him another child. If ever she should have conceived it should have been then. But she hadn't. And now after lying with a man she detested, she had conceived. It was wrong. It was almost evil.

Why hadn't she been careful? Why had she let him make love to her at all? The answer was not easy to face. She had wanted to hurt and humiliate him. To punish him. If she had tried to refuse to sleep with him there would have been a scene. A violent scene and in the end she would have been forced to do what he wanted. The more she fought the greater his victory would have been in the end. So she had let him come to her but she had given him nothing. She had been icy and unresponsive. She had lain quiescent, motionless, under his most ardent caresses. She had taken a vicious satisfaction from what it had done to him. It had made him feel, she knew, like the animal he was. She had let him see her contempt and disgust. And when in his brutal insistency he had refused to leave her alone she had almost been glad. The frustrations and the humiliation she had been able to subject him to had been almost as gratifying as sleeping alone. And all the while she had been setting the stage for her own destruction. Now the victory would be his. What satisfaction he would take from the knowledge that he had gotten her with child in spite of what she had done to him!

And there was an even greater problem to face. Something that up to now she hadn't even thought about. Robbie. When she began to show he would know, too. Perhaps even sooner than Fred. Having grown up on a farm and in the forest the mating of animals was a commonplace to him. He had known the process by which life was created since he was old enough to understand. But she and Tom had taught him that the sex act was an impulse of love. How could that be reconciled with the fact that she was going to have Fred's child? He would feel betrayed in the very moment when he most needed assurance and understanding. She put her head in her hands and suddenly her whole body began to tremble violently. She pushed herself erect and over to the sink. She stood there gasping while her forehead beaded with cold sweat and tears forced themselves out of her tightly shut eyes.

The doctor drove his rig back to town slowly. He had gone out to the Sharron farm for the specific purpose of talking to Mary about Fred. Her reaction to the fact that she was pregnant had made that impossible. He shook his head remembering the way she had looked. That beautiful face twisted with disbelief, her voice hoarse and unsteady as she tried to make him admit he could be wrong. He had been close to the mark when he told the Sergeant she could hate as fiercely as she loved. At one point he was sure she had been about to ask him to help her get rid of the child. But she had thought the better of it. He had no fear that she would actually attempt it. She was too fine a woman for that but in her state of mind she might very easily miscarry anyway and a miscarriage out in this wilderness was no casual matter. The boy was a problem too. His mind was chuck full of the same corrosions that had made his mother blanch at the thought of pregnancy. No wonder Fred had had to get out. Having to face these two across a dinner table every day was more than even a normal man could stand. The trouble was it was nobody's fault really.

Mary had a grievance. A very strong grievance. There was no doubt that the boy had altered. He was silent and preoccupied, almost sullen. You could hardly blame a mother for hating a man who had been responsible for the change in him. He doubted if either of them could be made to forgive Fred even if they were brought to understand his problems. There was nothing physically wrong with any of them, of course, but they were bent on destroying each other as surely as if they were deliberately consuming arsenic.

He looked around him. The fields were thick with wild flowers and the air so heavy with their scent it was difficult to breathe. If you listened very closely you could hear the steady hum of bees beneath the shrill piping of the birds. The sun was bright but not yet so hot as to be uncomfortable. In the deep shadow of the pines a man could still find himself taken by a slight shiver. A bright clean beautiful day and in Brownsville Fred Carter would be sitting in a jail cell hating the world and everything in it because he thought it hated him and at the Sharron farm Robbie and Mary were grimly nursing their grievances regardless of the effect it had upon the lives of all of them.

231

22

Fred was the only prisoner in the R.C.M.P. cell block in Brownsville. For two days he paced his cell like a wounded leopard, whirling at the sound of every footstep and wondering how long he was going to be penned up. He was a man accustomed to wide open spaces and violent activity and the enforced idleness gnawed on his already ragged nerves. He was in a particularly vicious mood when Sergeant Miller stepped into his cell on the third morning.

Miller didn't seem to notice the malevolent gleam in the prisoner's eye. He thrust his hand into the pocket of his uniform and brought out a package of cigarettes. He said, "It's all right, Carter. There are no strings attached." There was a frozen moment when Miller's eyes held Fred's levelly, and, in the outstretched hand, the package was as steady as a rock.

Fred let the breath out of his lungs slowly then reached out and took the cigarettes without taking his eyes off the policeman. He began searching his pockets for a match. Miller snapped a lighter and held it. Again there was the tiny hesitation from Fred before he leaned forward and lit the tobacco. His eyes were acutely suspicious. He inhaled deeply, blew the smoke out through his nostrils and extended the package.

Miller shook his head. "Keep 'em. I'll see that the constable brings you some matches." He pointed to the corner of the room. "That can is for butts. Don't grind 'em out on the floor."

Fred put the cigarettes into his shirt pocket while Miller set a polished boot on the edge of the bunk. He said, "Look,

Carter, you may not be in any mood to listen but there are some things you ought to be told. First of all, you've been charged with disturbing the peace and resisting arrest. I'm sorry about the last part. It may make your sentence a little heavier but I had to clout you and that calls for a full report. I want you to know there was nothing personal in it. I would have taken exactly the same action with anybody under the same circumstances."

A look of surprise replaced the bewilderment on Fred's face. He took a deep drag on the cigarette and then turned away toward the window. He said shortly, "I had it comin'."

Miller was taken aback. This he hadn't expected. For a brief moment he debated telling Fred what Doctor McLeod had said, but he thought the better of it. He said instead, "I came to tell you that you'll be here for ten days. You've got to go before a judge and the circuit court won't be here for at least a week. When your case comes up, I'll do what I can to get your sentence suspended."

Fred swung back from the window belligerently. "Why? Why are you doin' this for me?"

The Sergeant ran a hand over his freshly shaven chin, then he said, "Well, I'll tell you, Carter. As I see it, you've had a lot of trouble since you came into this territory and this is the first time you've ever had a run in with the law. I think every man is entitled to one mistake."

Fred stared for so long that the stub of his cigarette burnt his fingers. He stared, dropped it and ground it out beneath his shoe. He said almost inaudibly; "Thanks."

The Sergeant straightened up. "If there's anything you want within reason, let the constable know."

Fred nodded and the Sergeant went to the cell door and rattled it. A constable came and let him out. As the door closed Fred came over to the bars. "There is one thing."

"Yes."

"They don't know where I am or when I'll be back."

"I've already sent word to your wife."

Fred watched them go out through the door at the end of the cell block then, put up a hand and touched the outline of the package of cigarettes in his shirt pocket as if to reassure himself. He paced to the window and stood staring silently at the empty parade ground. He found it difficult to believe what had happened. Ever since the day when the Sergeant had gun-whipped him, he had been waiting for a chance to get even. This morning, when Miller stepped into his cell, he had had that chance and he had lost it. Not only had he lost it, but he had found himself accepting a cigarette and admitting that the whole thing had been his fault. The strangest part of the whole situation was that he no longer resented the Sergeant.

The desire to get even was gone. Why? Well, the first reason was that Miller had caught him off guard. He had expected the man to come swaggering around sneering and gloating because he had managed to get Fred behind bars. Instead he had strolled into the cell as if nothing had happened. And although Fred had started the trouble, Miller had apologized for hitting him and had acted, in a kind of a way, as if he were to blame instead of Fred. You couldn't hit a man who acted like that. There wasn't anything you could do if you were a man but admit the truth . . . that whatever you got you had coming. So there was a lesson here someplace. Maybe fighting wasn't always the way out. Maybe it wasn't even the best way.

There had been a moment, before Miller held out the cigarettes, when Fred had felt the anger boiling in him but for once it hadn't spilled over. And because it hadn't, he might get his sentence suspended and he had one less enemy. It wasn't a big thing but Fred had a feeling it was important. All his life he had fought and all his life he had made enemies. Before he came to the Sharron farm, he couldn't remember ever being liked by anyone except Millie. He was not sure that even Billy had liked him. The only time he had sensed a change in people's attitude toward him had been in the months before he shot the deer. Like the time he'd brought her the phonograph and stopped in Pineville on the way home. There had been something in the people's eyes that afternoon that had embarrassed him and yet warmed him at the same time. And when she'd seen the phonograph the look on her face had turned his insides to water. He had not had to fight anyone from the moment he came to the farm until now and it had been the best time of his whole life.

Love was a word that didn't come easily to him, but he knew now that he loved her with a force so strong that everything else in life paled by comparison. The fact that she had set a barrier of silence and icy contempt against him filled him with a sick helplessness that not even anger had been able to quench. Each time he had blundered against it, it had grown higher and stronger. The more he fought, the more hopeless his cause had become. And yet he had never admitted it was hopeless. There had to be a way to reach her and the Sergeant's visit this morning had given him the first glimmer of hope. It had shown him that sometimes more could be accomplished by keeping your temper in your pocket. It was a momentous conclusion for a man whose approach to every problem had always been a headlong attack. In the past, those he couldn't solve by brute strength he had worn down by sheer stubborn persistence and he had seldom counted the cost to his own or other people's feelings.

Now for the first time he faced a problem which would not yield to muscle or blind aggressiveness and one from which he could not retreat because he was bound to the heart of it by bonds stronger than he had ever believed possible. He had to get her back and he saw, now, that it would never be by force. If there was something in him that made him lash out against everything he did not like or understand, then he would have to change what he was. He would have to learn from what had happened this morning. Most of all he would have to keep a tight rein on his temper. He cringed every time he remembered how he had struck her there in the barn. It was anger that had done that. It was anger that had made him shove the kid's face into the body of the deer. Not that he wasn't justified. The kid was a sniveling little coward and he deserved a lot more than that.

When it came right down to it, the kid had been the cause of all the trouble between them. The night they were married she'd gone off for a walk because the kid begged her. Because of that he'd gotten drunk waiting for her to come back. Only a miracle had saved him that night but if it had been ruined, it would have been the kid's fault. And then just when everything had been going fine, it had been the kid again. Damn his whining little soul, sneaking into the loft with a pitchfork and then not even having the guts to throw it! There was no place in the world for cowards big or little. Sooner or later they'd ruin everything just like Billy had done. A man who couldn't look danger in the eye was better off dead. Fred had never met a situation in his life that could make him flinch. It was not that he had never known fear but he had never known a fear he couldn't master and blind horror or panic was something he couldn't even imagine. He had seen it take possession of men before that night Billy had left him to die and it had always made him see red. No, the boy had only got what he deserved.

And as a matter of fact, he, Fred, wasn't to blame for what had happened out there in the deer pen, any more than the Sergeant was to blame for what happened in the street. He had been ready to kill the Mountie for that but when Miller had come in to the cell and practically admitted it had been his fault, Fred's anger had disappeared. Wasn't it possible the same thing could happen with Mary? If he went to her and admitted he'd been wrong. . . . If he accepted the blame for everything that had happened . . . if he let her see how sorry he was and how much he wanted to make amends . . . wouldn't she have to forgive him? The more he considered it, the more certain it seemed that he had found the solution. All he had to do was keep his temper. He mustn't get angry no matter what she said or did. He must be meek . . . kind of . . . and he must talk softly. . . .

If he promised her faithfully that it would never ever happen again, she had to forgive him. What else could she do? She was generous and warm and kind. She'd made him see many times when they talked together how something he was about to do would hurt someone else. Like that time his apples had been so much better than Jed Clawson's and she wouldn't let him take them to market the same day as Jed. He'd wanted to take them so folks could see Carter had grown the best apples in the whole county but she'd said no. Jed was a good neighbor. If Fred took his apples Jed would get less money for his crop. He might even have trouble selling them and his feelings would be hurt having all his friends see that Fred was a better farmer. They'd lost some money because of it for there'd been rain and he'd been late getting the crop to market but he'd let her have her way and it had turned out right 'cause Jed and everybody else had admired the crop anyway and he'd still got a fair price. No, she didn't like to hurt anybody and all he had to do was make her see he knew he'd been wrong.

He felt a kind of wonder singing inside him. He visualized her face as he talked to her. How first it would be dark and angry with that black fire burning in her eyes and then gradually the anger would go away as he talked until finally she reached up and touched his cheek like she used to do before,

237

and she looked at him with that funny soft smile he could never quite explain and she'd say as if he were a little boy, "It's all right, Fred." And it would be all right. It was all so simple when you looked at it the right way. He could hardly wait to get out to put his thoughts into action.

23

He was fined fifty dollars and given thirty days but the sentence was suspended. He didn't lose his temper once during the hearing and he bought the Sergeant a carton of cigarettes and shook hands with him before he left. He couldn't wait to get back to the farm because now he knew at last that there was a way to make it work. She was going to take him back because there was nothing else she could do. Now that he had seen that his attitude had been the whole trouble all he had to do was change. He would get along with the boy somehow. It wouldn't be easy, but if he kept out of the kid's way it could be managed. It had to be. He was a new man.

When the MP's truck dropped him at Pineville he refused to let himself get upset by the attitude of the townspeople. He even managed to smile at one or two of them when they passed. He went to the livery stable and got the horse and rig and paid the liveryman. Then as he came out of the stable leading the horse, he saw the people clustered at the end of the lane looking at him. For a second he didn't understand and then he saw the Frenchman he had pushed that day in Campbell's store leaning against the side of the building waiting for him to reach the street. He felt the sudden rush of anger that always seized him at the prospect of a fight. His fists balled themselves and his heart began to thump against his ribs. He let go the horse's bridle and started down the street and suddenly he realized what he was doing. He stopped dead. After a moment he sprung his fists and let the hands hang quietly at his side. Slowly that thudding of his heart receded. He turned and went back to the rig. He climbed in and started down the street.

At the entrance to the alley the Frenchman caught the horse's bridle. He said, "One moment, m'sieu. You and I 'ave something to settle." Fred took a deep breath and let it out slowly. He tried to move the horse and the Frenchman reached up and cut the reins with his knife. Fred got down off the wagon carefully. In front of him, Henri balanced cat-like on the balls of his feet waiting; the knife, not gripped in his fist, but cradled in his palm with the fingers uppermost in the manner of all experienced knife fighters. Fred took a step forward and the knife moved in a tight menacing little circle. Fred said, "I don't recall usin' a knife on you, Henri." The Frenchman grinned unabashed. "There is some difference in our size, m'sieu." He moved the knife so that it gleamed wickedly. "This will make me taller."

Fred swallowed. This was not easy but he was going through with it. "Before you start usin' that thing I want you to know I'm sorry for what I done. I don't blame you for wantin' to get even."

Surprise froze the smile on the Frenchman's face for a second, then the smile disappeared. He said, "If you think this will save your skin, m'sieu, you are mistaken. No one makes bleed the nose of Henri Laplante and goes free to boast about it."

"I ain't boastin'. I ain't gonna let you put that pig sticker under my skin neither but I figger you got a beef. Put that knife away and I'll let you swing on me."

The point of the knife dropped a fraction and the French-man frowned. Behind him he heard a low murmur in the crowd. He had an unpleasant suspicion that he was beginning to look like a fool. He said, "Enough of this. Fight!" He lunged. The knife sliced through the side of Fred's shirt as he dodged. His face went grim and he circled, cautiously. The

240

Frenchman feinted and lunged again. The knife grazed Fred's arm bringing a thin line of blood. Fred's eyes got narrower. His heart began to thunder again.

The Frenchman wet his lips. Somehow the desire to fight had gone out of him but he was committed now and there was nothing he could do. He lunged again and Fred's mammoth hand flicked out catching the knife arm behind the wrist. The Frenchman cursed and twisted but he was like a child in Fred's grip. Fred pulled him in tight, then bent the arm till the knife dropped from the fingers. Henri's whole hand was shock white from the pressure on his wrist. Fred kicked the knife away. He was breathing heavily. He thrust Henry back without releasing him. The Frenchman's face was twisting with pain despite his efforts not to show it.

Fred said, "I told you before I wasn't goin' to let you put that knife in me but you still got a swing comin' if you want it." He let the arm go. The Frenchman looked thoroughly bewildered—at the very least he had expected a broken arm. He massaged the bruise without taking his eyes off Fred. After a moment, Fred said, "Well, come on. I ain't got all day."

The Frenchman scowled. "I do not understand, m'sieu. You want me to hit you?"

"That's what *you* want ain't it?"

"You will not defend yourself?"

"That's the idea."

The Frenchman shook his head and then quite suddenly he grinned. He reached up and slapped Fred very lightly with his open hand. "Very well, m'sieu, I 'ave 'ad my 'swing' as you put it. The honor of Laplante is satisfied." He held out his hand. For a moment, Fred was too surprised to move, then awkwardly he took the proffered hand. He felt himself relaxing and a fountain of exultation exploded in him. It had worked! It had been an effort but he had held his temper and now he was shaking the hand of the man who a few minutes before had been his enemy. It was a more satisfying feeling than any victory he had ever known. Out of the corner of his eye he could see the townspeople staring at him in stunned surprise. He heard Henri say, "You 'ad better come in the store and we will put somesing on that cut though I assure you, m'sieu, I keep my steel very clean."

Fred shook his head. "Thanks I ain't got time. There's somethin' I got to do."

He knotted the severed reins, climbed back into the rig and started the horse at a brisk trot. At the edge of town he turned and looked back. The whole town was staring after him, and the Frenchman waved.

On the way back he kept the horse going at a steady pace. He met no one on the road. Perhaps because the sky in the northwest was darkening rapidly. There was a storm coming, but he paid no particular attention. Storms were not uncommon at this time of year and were generally soon over. Moreover, this morning he had more important things on his mind.

As he broke out into the clearing he saw Robbie at the pump. The boy looked up, saw the approaching rig, and ran into the house. A few seconds later, he came back out and cut across the field into the bush. Fred drove on into the barnyard. He stabled the horse hurriedly, the sense of sustained elation he had found in Pineville still with him. Coming across the barnyard toward the house he had to hold himself back to keep from running up the steps to the kitchen. He opened the screen door. It squeaked a little and even with his preoccupation he made a mental note to oil it. She was standing at the flour board making bread. She had on a pink cotton dress with little white flowers on it and a white apron that made her hair look almost blue. She had a smudge of flour on her cheek but she looked spotlessly fresh and clean as she always did. He glanced down self-consciously at his own clothes rumpled from ten days in jail, then ran a hand through his stiff blond hair. They'd let him shower and shave at the jailhouse but there'd been nothing to slick down his hair and he'd had to shave with one of those little safety razors and had cut himself twice. He probably didn't look very presentable but he'd done the best he could. He'd even got most of the dirt out from under his fingernails with a pine splinter.

She didn't look up at him when he came in and her face in profile didn't change expression. Now that he was face to face with the moment, his mouth had gone dry and he didn't know how to begin. All the phrases he had memorized had gone clean out of his head. He stood shifting his weight uncomfortably and trying to work some saliva into his mouth so he could speak. He cracked his knuckles once, then he said, "I . . . I been in jail. I don't know if you knew." The words dropped into the silence flatly, hollowly, and she gave no sign that she had heard. He stumbled on awkwardly. "They said they'd tell you. I . . . I don't know if they did."

"They told me." The reply was cold, disinterested. She hadn't looked up and she kept kneading the bread silently.

In spite of his resolution, he felt a flush of the old anger and stubbornly fought it down. He wet his lips and took a breath. "I been thinkin' since I been in jail . . . and . . . well, . . . I . . . I got to talk to you." It came out haltingly and the sound of it rang dismally in his ears. It didn't sound a bit like he'd meant it to be. Something was all wrong.

She still hadn't looked at him and the steady kneading of the bread was getting on his nerves. He felt the pressure building inside him again. Why? *Why must he always get mad?* It was the very thing he'd promised himself he wouldn't do. If only she would look at him maybe it would be easier. Impulsively he stepped forward and took her by the shoulders. His voice was thick and unsteady, "Listen to me . . . please I got to talk to you."

She didn't resist when he pulled her upright away from the board. Her head came up and her black eyes met his with icy contempt. "What is it, Fred?"

He hesitated, then flung out an arm helplessly. "This is no good! I didn't mean it to be like this. I just want you to listen for a minute." She stood silent, motionless, waiting. He swallowed again. "Look, I know what I done was wrong. I know it. An' I'm sorry, see? I wasn't myself when I hit you. I won't never touch you again. It was all right for you to hit me." The next was very hard, but he set his jaw and blundered on. "I shouldn't of said to you what I did about the kid. I mean the boy . . . Robbie. An' I'm sorry for what I done since. The swearin' and well you know the rest. The Clawsons can come whenever they want. And I just want you to know that no matter what I . . . (why was it so hard to say this when he felt it so deeply?) well, I . . . I love you and I don't want to hurt you no more—ever." His voice was trembling with sincerity. He waited for something of understanding in her face, some flicker that might show him that some day, if not now, it might be all right again. None came.

She said, "Is that all?"

It was there still. That thing he couldn't fight. . . . Couldn't see. He shook his head like a wounded bull. "What else can I say? What can I do to make you understand?"

She stared at him and then she said, "It's of no interest to me at all what you do or don't do. My only desire is to have as little contact with you as humanly possible."

He could no longer fight the anger. "But we can't go on like this forever!"

For the first time her eyes burned with black fire, and her voice rose, "Can we not then? Can we not? Have you seen my son? Before you came to this farm he was the happiest child alive. He doesn't smile any more. He doesn't laugh. He doesn't play. He's full of hate and fear and you did that to him. *I'll never forgive you for that as long as I live!*"

He heard himself shouting, "*I can't help it if the kid's a coward! Do you hear me? I can't help it!*" Too late he tried to stop the words.

"Get out," she said. "Get out of my house. Don't come near me. Don't touch me. I've a gun in my bedroom. If you try to come near me I'll kill you!"

24

He was drunk now. Almost as drunk as he could get but not quite drunk enough. He could still think. He would keep on drinking until he could stop thinking or until the liquor he had brought back from the village ran out. This time he was going to drink himself into unconsciousness. He'd tried before without success. He'd drunk before until he couldn't stand, couldn't see, and didn't care what he was doing. But he always knew. There was always some fragment of his mind that clung grimly to the edge of consciousness and oblivion was always just a hair's breadth away. He loved the taste of liquor. He loved the way it burned his throat and the explosions of warmth it made when it reached his stomach. It made his head reel and numbed his thinking but it had never done for him what it did for other men. It never dropped him into oblivion when he wanted it to because some part of him kept remembering Tiger Lane and the human derelicts in the cages with him, their blotched faces purpled with ruptured blood vessels, their trousers stinking of excrement and soaked with urine where they had voided themselves in their stupor. There was something inside Fred Carter which recoiled from these remembrances so that even when he awoke with gummed lips and throbbing temples he could not touch more alcohol to relieve his agony. He had tried and his stomach promptly hurled it back where it came from. Sometimes it would be weeks before he could look at liquor again. Today he drank savagely. Maybe today he would be successful.

Robbie sat at the edge of the beaver dam, his back propped

against a fallen log. He didn't quite know why his mother had sent him away as Fred was driving up but he was glad. He hadn't wanted to face his stepfather. The sight of him coming had brought back the sickness he had begun to lose while the man was away. Why hadn't they kept him in jail? Didn't they know he was a bad man? Didn't they know he had struck Robbie's mother? She had never admitted it but he had seen the bruise on her cheek and the cut on her lip and once when she hadn't known he was watching he'd seen her at the kitchen mirror daubing iodine on the inside of her mouth. Some day Robbie would make Fred pay for that. Some day when he was big he'd cut the man to ribbons. He took out his small stag-handled knife and drove it to the hilt in the black mulch. "There!" he said. "Take that, and that and that!" He twisted the knife in the wound; he envisioned it slicing into Fred's flesh and then the wound gushed bright gouts of blood and the old familiar nausea swept over him. He pulled the knife out of the dirt and sagged weakly back against the log. After a while he put the knife away and rolled over on his stomach.

Almost on a level with his eyes there was a bright extrusion of gum on the bole of a tree and he remembered how he had sat here one morning so long ago and stuck a sliver into a bubble just like this and watched the bright gold liquid squeeze itself out of the tiny tear and drop down to a curl of bark. It had been the same morning he had swum. The first and last time he had ever gone in the water so early. How long ago that had been and how different everything had been then! His father had been alive and there had been nothing in the whole world to worry about. Now everything had changed. Everything. His mother never smiled any more. She never sang in that sweet soft voice that he could hear from his bed as she and his father sat out on the front porch. No one sat there any more. No one did anything any more. Everything was different. Everything except this bubble of gum. It might even be the same bubble he had pricked that morning. All healed now so you couldn't see the wound. It had probably been there since before he was born and maybe some day another little boy would come and lie here where he was lying and look at it and touch it and maybe break it and watch the golden tear fall onto a curl of birchbark.

It was funny how the bubble of gum didn't care. Nothing cared really. Somehow you sort of felt that everything in the world ought to know how unhappy you were. You sort of expected that the animals would be different. When you got up in the morning it seemed strange to see the sun shining and hear the birds singing as if the whole world was exactly the same as it had been before. It was a lonesome thing to know you could feel so wretched inside and still nothing cared. Nothing even knew. The otters still frolicked like idiot children . . . the minnows fled as you approached and came back to cruise around your legs and you couldn't tell if they were the same minnows you had seen when the world was bright and wonderful or if they were different minnows and just acted the same. It was scary, too, to think that when you were dead and buried in the ground and maybe there was nothing left of you but just some dust and a lot of hair—because everybody knew that hair never disappeared—that those same minnows would still be flitting about over the sand bar as if the world hadn't changed one single bit. He loved them as he loved everything in the forest but they didn't know Robbie Sharron. It made no difference to them that he was unhappy. It wouldn't make any difference to them even if he died right now. They'd keep right on filling the sunlit shallows and flashing away at the slightest sound.

He'd never thought of all this before and it made him feel sadder, emptier, lonelier, than he had ever felt before. After a while he stretched out by the log. He picked a flower and

248

pulled the petals off it gravely, then let it fall from his fingers. The sun turned slowly and crept up the bank until it touched him with warmth where he lay in the shadows. He shivered a little as the cold dampness fled away and then he fell asleep. Had he not been so preoccupied with the strangeness of life and the inevitability of death he might have been aware that there was a very subtle difference in the forest today. A difference that only someone as acutely attuned to it as Robbie would have caught. As it was, he never became aware that the whole of life around him was a little subdued. It had been over an hour after he appeared before the beaver had come out to work and then they had come only in twos or threes. The birds twittered but there was a kind of uncertainty in their talk. On the game trail a red fox downwind of a rabbit came upon him unawares. It should have been certain death but the fox hesitated and the rabbit bolted. A she-bear turned over a log literally crawling with grubs. She licked up a mouthful and then tossed her head restlessly and turned away. The two cubs cocked their head in ludicrous astonishment. High up a hawk circled, not in smooth, effortless parabolas, but in short unsettled arcs. After a while it left the sky.

As Robbie slept, a cloud slid across the sun. The beavers slithered silently back into the water. A doe shepherded her fawn into a dense thicket. A hush came over the conversation of the birds. The drone of the bees in the meadow stopped suddenly as if on a cue. The silence was deafening. A porcupine rustled once in the underbrush and then the whole forest was deathly still.

In the kitchen, Mary slid the freshly baked bread out of the oven and straightened up. It had been over two hours since the scene with Fred and she still felt a little sick. She had felt sick ever since she arose this morning and part of yesterday, too, but the quarrel had made it worse. It was strange because if the doctor was right she should be over the unpleasant part of her pregnancy by now. She set the bread on the window sill to cool and sank down at the table. She felt her insides quivering and a tiny film of cold sweat began to bead her forehead. "This is ridiculous," she told herself. "You've never gone through anything like this before." She bit her lower lip and put her head down. "I mustn't faint now," she told herself. "I can't!" After a moment she felt a little less dizzy but the cold, clammy feel of her skin did not disappear. I've been working too hard, she thought. Much too hard for a pregnant woman but what else could I do? I've got to rest now though. I feel strange. Not sick exactly, just strange. Maybe it's something to do with the weather. It's close today. Terribly close. The sun disappeared half an hour ago and it's getting dark. I suppose there's going to be a storm. Maybe I need some fresh air. She took a deep breath and pulled herself to her feet. It was amazing how much effort it took. It was as if her body didn't want to move. She steadied herself against the table and started towards the back porch. Gracious, it was dark. . . .

She pushed open the screen door and went out on the small stoop. The air was still. Still as death and it was getting darker by the second. Directly above her, the sky was a sick milky blue but to the northwest the whole horizon was purple black and impenetrable. Up out of the blackness gigantic greenish-gray clouds were boiling into the heavens devouring the remnants of light and sky. And still there was no sound. It was as if the earth were holding its breath for the onslaught. Then faintly she heard the steady rumble of thunder more ominous because there was no sign of lightning. The flashes must be inside the storm itself but the clouds were so dense they were not visible. The vanguard of the storm could not be more than a few miles away now and the sound of the thunder increased in volume till the ground began to tremble.

Suddenly, she was seized by panic. Robbie! He was out there in the forest! He'd be caught! And even as she thought, the straw of the barnyard stirred. She felt a slight wind sucking away from her toward the storm and then abruptly the full force of it caught at her skirts nearly dragging her from the porch. The dust and debris of the barnyard sluiced away as if it were being whirled into the maw of a monstrous vacuum cleaner. There was a hollow roaring in the wind set against the steady barrage of thunder. She clutched at the porch railing and screamed, "Robbie! Robbie!" The words sucked out of her mouth and the heavens closed over.

She took a step forward, bracing against the wind, and as she did so there was a slight pain somewhere. Her legs felt hot and wet. She looked down. The little porch was flooded with blood. She stared at it, unbelievingly. The color began to drain from her face. "Oh, my God! Oh dear merciful God! The baby! Oh God, oh God, oh God! Fred! Please!"

Then she felt the strength rushing out of her. She sank down on the porch. "Robbie! Fred! *Fred!*" The rain smote her like a mighty fist mingling with the blood that was now running down the stairs. It drowned the last of the light. It was like a tidal wave. She felt consciousness leaving her. She opened her mouth for air and the rain drove in choking her. I'm dying, she thought. "Mary, Mother of God, I'm dying here in my own blood, and I've lost my baby! Oh, Blessed Virgin, forgive me. I *did* want it! I did! I did!" She lay there on the porch as the rain swept in in flat sheets drenching her clothes and matting her hair.

At the first sound of thunder, Fred lurched out of the tack room to the door of the barn. He watched the approach of the storm with drunken concentration, steadying himself against the same beam where he had seen her that night she agreed to marry him. A long time ago. A long, long time! The updraft came sucking the chaff out of the barn behind him and half choking him with dust. He coughed and rubbed his eyes and brushed his rumpled clothes ineffectually. Then he heard her calling the kid. He couldn't see her 'cause the main door of the barn faced the forest and the back porch was opposite the far end but he snorted. "The kid again! Always that kid! Didn't know 'nough to come in out of the storm." She called again and the panic in her voice caught at him. He ought to go and help her but she didn't want him. She'd only married him 'cause of the neighbors and the kid. She thought he was stupid and said she'd shoot him if he came near her again. Well, let her. He didn't care if she shot him or not. He didn't care what anybody did any more. People were all right but people didn't understan'. Nobody unnerstood. He didn't un-derstan' himself. Funny how that Frenchy had shaken hands when he wouldn't fight. Why wouldn't she do the same thing? Didn't want to hurt her. Only wanted to protect her. Love her. Now she wouldn't let him near her. To hell with her . . . hell with all of 'em. Didn't need 'em. Didn't need anybody.

At first he thought he imagined it, but then it came again. Or did it? It was hard to tell with the thunder and the wind. He strained his ears. She was calling him and something about the sound sent him lurching out of the barn. The rain hit him the very second he moved. Driven by a full gale it smashed him flat against the barn and left him gasping. It drove at him with such force he could scarcely breathe, but it cleared his head a little. He fought his way along the side of the barn. It was impossible to see. The force of the storm knocked him off his feet twice before he reached the porch. He clung to the railing, head bent, and the first thing he saw was the water flowing down the steps and over his boots. But the water was red. His eyes followed it gravely up the steps and stopped at her figure. The pelting rain was driving a fine red mist out of her skirts. All the water on the top of the steps was red. Red water. Very strange. Red water. *Blood!* In that instant his mind went dead cold sober. He lurched up the remaining steps and knelt. She was still conscious. In the half light her face was ghastly gray.

"Fred. Fred!"

"What happened?"

"The baby! I've lost the baby!" Her voice was weak, only half audible over the flooding noise of the rain and wind.

He stared numbly, then swept her up in his arms. He staggered inside. There was a wild churning in his head. She'd said *baby!* He set her down on the couch. His arm and the right side of his sodden shirt was red. The red ran off her skirts with the water, staining the couch. He shook his head helplessly. "What'll I do?"

She bit her lip. She was going to faint now and she couldn't stop it. She said, "Stop bleeding . . . ice . . . get ice . . . doctor." Her head fell back. He grabbed for her pulse and put a hand on her breast. The heart was still beating. He stood up and looked around wildly, then from somewhere came a fragment of control. He ran into the kitchen and grabbed the tea towels off the rack. He came back to her, took the hem of her skirt and tore it open to the waist. Her underthings were a sodden mass of blood. Unless he could stop this she was going to die. He thrust the towels against her groin. In a second they were soaked. He shook his head again, then set his jaw and ripped her underthings away. He'd never seen so much blood. He wrenched off his belt and buckled it around her waist. He ran first to the icebox—slivered the ice frantically with a pick, then to the linen closet and got two heavy towels. He folded one, packed it with the ice, and thrust it against her, then took the other and folded it lengthwise. He thrust one end under the belt in back, brought it through her legs to hold the ice pack in place and cinched it under the belt across her stomach. The padded towel reddened ominously but at least the blood stopped drenching her thighs.

He was breathing heavily. The doctor! He tore open the

cabinet where the Very gun was kept. He fitted the rocket and ran out to the back porch. He fired the rocket. It exploded perhaps five hundred feet up and he could barely see it. The rain washed the red mushroom out of the sky before it had time to form. He flung the gun away and narrowing his eyes against the rain stared at the barnyard. It was flooded. Well, the hell with it. Flood or no flood, he had to get her to the doctor. He ran down the steps and began slipping and sliding across the barnyard. Just before he reached the door there was a tremendous crash of thunder as a tree at the edge of the forest half a mile away literally exploded. Even in the rain you could see the flash. The front of the barn buckled inward like the side of a paper carton and the mare was screaming and kicking in terror.

He had no time for niceties. He hit her a blow on the side of the head that numbed his hand and staggered the horse, then backed her out of the stall. Fingers trembling, he got her in harness and led her out. She balked again at the door and he had to lash her with the whip to get her to move. She came out into the rain and he led her to the porch and tied the reins securely. He went into the house. The blood had not yet seeped through the bandage. Pray God it had stopped! He took the big tarpaulin from back of the kitchen door and lashed it over the back of the cart, then ran into the house and wrenched sheets and mattress off the bed. He went back outside and slid the mattress on the floor of the cart. It left about two feet of air space beneath the tarp. Inside again, he wrapped her in a blanket and carried her out and slid her onto the mattress. He adjusted the sheets and tied them across her body so she was held securely, then untied the reins and vaulted into the wagon seat.

The rain was so heavy he could see only the outlines of the horse. He snapped the reins and called out. The horse wouldn't move except to dance nervously in place. He took the whip and lashed her across the flanks. She reared and started off, fetlocks splashing as she strained against the mud and wind. Out the gate she tried to halt and pull back. He set his teeth and lashed her again. Every mile he made now was worth two when the rain had been on the ground long enough to soak in. Then the roads would be a foot deep in mud and impassable. The mare tried bravely to run. She actually got the cart moving at a kind of half gallop. He didn't like cutting her up but there was no choice. He leaned forward and slashed her again. She screamed as the whip brought blood to her flanks. She'd never been lashed before and terror put strength in her legs. The cart lurched and slithered wildly.

In the back, the bed sheets kept Mary's body from being thrown against the sides but the bone-shattering jars started the bleeding again. For a time it seemed fortune was with them. The cart suddenly acted as if it had taken wings. They came to the part of the road that ran beneath the trees. It had been raining less than twenty minutes. The road was soaked but nowhere near as much rain had reached it as in the open. Beneath the top wetness it was hard as ever. The mare tore along, her flanks bleeding, her mouth flecked with foam. The rain drove down but here it came in blasting gusts and above their heads the trees bent almost double with the force of wind and water. Twice lightning crashed near them but the horse was more frightened of the human terror behind her now than by anything else. They slewed wildly around a corner, the back right wheel went into the ditch, smashed over a rotten log, jounced off a granite outcropping and ran smoothly once more.

Almost immediately after that Fred hauled the gasping horse to a stop. In front of them a huge windfall blocked the road. There was no way around. The forest walled them in on either side—the great trees shrieking and bending to the weight of the storm. He lifted the seat of the wagon and took out a

255

double-bladed ax. He waded into the tangle of wet wood and slashed at the broken branches. In less than a minute the massive trunk was clean for a width that was slightly broader than the width of the wagon. He unhitched the horse and dragged her up to the barrier. The horse shied and tried to get away. He climbed up on the log and dragged at the reins. She braced her feet. With nothing to hang onto he was pulled off the tree and flat into the mud. When he got up his mouth was bleeding. He looked to the right. Just off the road the underbrush was piled four feet deep. He pulled the horse around so it was facing the brush, then went behind it and whacked it on the lacerated rump. The animal leaped forward crashing down on the brush. Fred hit it again and it floundered through. He plunged after it as it stood trembling and rolling its eyes under the big trunks beyond. He led it around the broken trunk and back onto the road beyond the windfall. He tied it to the tree, then climbed over it and dragged the wagon up until the tongues projected over the log and the front wheels almost touched.

He went back and took Mary out. He carried her over the log and laid her by the side of the road. She was getting drenched now, but he couldn't help that.

He went back to the wagon. He set his shoulders under the front seat, braced his legs and began to straighten. The wheels came up slowly ten times heavier than normal with their weight of mud. He set his teeth and lifted. The wheel passed the top of the log. He strained forward. The back wheels moved a quarter of a turn—half a turn—three quarters. Then the front wheels rested on the log, the harness tongues pointing at the sky. Shaking with effort he got off and went behind the cart. He set his back against the tail gate and shoved. The front wheels rolled forward off the log and came down with a splintering crash on the opposite side. The wagon was now straddling the log which came within a few inches of the black mud welded to its bottom. Fred shoved it forward until the back wheels touched the bark of the tree, then went behind it again. He set his palm under the tailboard and lifted. His legs quivered with the effort. The veins popped into terrible relief on his arms and forehead. After a second, blood gushed from his fingernails. The wheels came up but not high enough. His lungs were like molten fire, the pain in his arms excruciating. He closed his eyes, pulled his lips flat against his teeth and heaved. The wagon went up and forward. The wheel missed the log entirely and the tailboard crashed down on the far edge ripping off a great chunk of bark.

Fred sank forward on one knee gasping. There were silver flashes in front of his eyes and his head was ringing. He lurched to his feet, scrambled over the log and hitched the horse. His heart was thundering and his breathing, harsh and unsteady.

When the horse was harnessed he went over to Mary. Her face was whiter than chalk and the blood had begun to seep through the blanket he had wrapped her in. Cold fear gripped him. How much blood could a person lose and still be alive? He bent his head to her chest but with the roaring of wind and rain he couldn't tell whether her heart was still beating or not. He picked her up and slid her under the tarpaulin once more and tied her down. How much time had he wasted here? Half an hour? An hour? He had no way of knowing. He got back into the cart and lashed the horse again. Once more they went careening down the narrow road. Once a tree thundered to earth behind them and twice more lightning smashed into the forest close by. The rain slashed at them and bits of branch and pine cones pummeled horse and driver alike, but they passed the road to the Clawson farm without having to stop. The horse was weakening rapidly now. Not even the whip could make her move faster. Fred could see her chest heaving like a huge bellows. But there were only five miles

257

to go—two to the bridge. Beyond the bridge the road was oiled.

The bridge was out. He knew it even before he got there. Not only out but washed away. The quiet creek now was raging white water. No power on earth would get an exhausted horse and cart across that fury. It had overflowed the banks and the road on each side so that not even the stumps of the bridge supports were visible. For a moment Fred felt beaten, helpless, but something stronger than his exhaustion drove him out of the cart. He unhitched the tarpaulin and wrapped her in it. He couldn't tell if there was any more blood. He didn't even know if she was alive. Now it was only a question of going on—on till he couldn't go any more. He swung the limp body over his shoulder and began to fight his way through the trees along the edge of the stream. A hundred yards from the bridge there had been a giant spruce whose branches spanned the creek in dry weather. If it was still there. . . .

His head was throbbing so it was hard to keep his eyes open. The rain beat against the back of his head and sluiced down his back. Once a good-sized branch tore loose just behind him and knocked both of them to the ground. He didn't feel either the shock of the blow or the pain of it. He twisted as he fell, keeping his body between her and the ground and he never released his grip.

The big spruce was down, its roots washed out, but it had fallen diagonally across the creek. The white waters were foaming through its branches. There was a good five feet of water between the new shoreline and the roots. He stepped into the current cautiously. It pulled at his ankles threatening to drag his feet from under him. He went back to the ground and walked up stream a few feet and tried again. It was as if a huge hand beneath the water was gripping his legs trying to pull them from under him. He edged forward trying not to lift his feet but as he moved each foot the current dragged it sideways and he had to fight to keep it on the bottom. He tried forcing his feet upstream against the water but it was useless. He was almost within reach of the roots now but the water was up to his thighs. He knew if he moved his feet an inch more they would go out from under him. He could go neither forward nor back, for even as he struggled the water had gained a foot up the bank.

Out of the corner of his eyes, he saw the jagged stump hurtle around the bend in the river. He flung the woman ahead of him and fell forward. His fingers caught at the muddy root. His body swept down stream. She was jammed safely between his outstretched arm and the root maze. The stump rocketed past where his body had been a split second earlier and the root section raked over his torso. The water flowing from Mary toward him was tinged with red. He dragged himself forward. Her clothes had caught on the roots and that helped him a little. He got onto the log. About a foot of the trunk was still out of the water. He hauled himself up and dragged her after him, losing the tarpaulin in the process. At the last instant the shoulder of her dress caught on a jagged stick and a part of it was torn away.

He put her across his back and inch by inch worked his way across the torrent holding onto the branches which thrust out of the water like supplicating arms. He got to the other side. He didn't look back. He made his way downstream. When his feet felt a hard slippery surface free of mud and the wet tangle of brush, he knew he was on the road. He took a deep sobbing breath. Three more miles, he told himself. Just three more miles.

25

Ian and Fern Campbell who ran the Pineville general store had made it a habit to spend their evenings during times of emergency in Dr. McLeod's home. Fern had had some hospital experience before she came to Pineville and eighteen years under the doctor's eye had turned her into a fairly efficient nursing assistant. In acute emergencies even Ian could give a reasonably professional account of himself. Neither would accept any money for their services. They were aware that while the doctor's practice was large, the remuneration he received was often negligible. On numerous occasions like the time of the fire which took Tom Sharron's life, the doctor worked for days without sleep and without any financial recompense whatsoever.

Thus the afternoon of the storm they had closed the store early. They had been sitting in the doctor's small living room since just after four o'clock, but there had been no emergencies. It was now a little after nine. It was dark outside but there was little perceptible difference between the darkness of night and the blackness which had accompanied the storm. The wind had been dying for the past half hour but the rain still came down in a solid wall. Thunder still crashed and ragged spears of lightning tore the fabric of darkness every few minutes. None of them could remember a storm of such intensity. Fortunately, it was almost impossible to flood a countryside so full of natural water basins. The lake levels would rise with the storm, the streams would overflow for a day or so and then the land would emerge rain—bright and shining.

The only reminders of the storm would be a couple of bridges washed out, half a dozen windfalls along the road, and masses of debris piled along the banks of the creek. There would be some damage to crops and property, of course, but there was little likelihood of human casualty.

There had been a protracted lull in the conversation when Ian put down his coffee cup, drew his shaggy gray brows together and stared at the doctor. "And what's the matter now, John? Have ye somethin' particular on your mind that you're so far away?"

The doctor started. "What? Oh, oh, no—sorry, Ian." He smiled. "I was only thinking about what you'd told me."

"Ye mean about the fight?"

"Yes."

Ian nodded gravely. "Aye, it's somethin' to make a man think all right. I tell ye the dust from the MP's car had not yet settled when Laplante stepped out of the forge. He must have been waitin' there for them to bring Carter back. The moment I saw him I said to meself I said, 'Ian Campbell, ye can bet all the silver you've got in your till there'll be blood in the streets this mornin'.' And then would ye look how it turned out? The two o' them shakin' hands like they were long lost brothers."

"You sound disappointed?"

"Ach, it's not that. It's only that ye canna figger that man Carter atall. One day he's pickin' a fight with a body who's given him no insult whatsoever and the next he's acting like Christ himself in the garden of Gethsemane."

Fern said, "Ian!"

Ian colored. "Well, ye know what I mean. Now, if he'd acted like he was afeared it'd be different but he had the best of Laplante and still offered to give him a hit for free. For free, mind. Do ye figger that now?"

The doctor sucked his lips against his teeth thoughtfully. "It's interesting all right."

Ian shook his head again doggedly. "I never knew ten days in jail to make that much change in a man. Do ye suppose it could be that he's not got over the blow the Sergeant gave him with his gun?"

The doctor smiled. "I hardly think it's that." He pushed himself up from the chair and strolled over to the window. It was impossible to see out, of course, but occasionally a flash of lightning would illuminate the picket fence and the gravel walk leading to the front door. You saw the vista hazily through the blur of water coursing down the panes and the pelting curtain of rain. He took out his pince-nez and tapped them against his teeth. He was sorry he had missed the fight this morning. It was hard to imagine Fred the way Ian and Fern had described him, but the fact remained that he had refused to whip Laplante when he had the opportunity and he had even turned the other cheek. It was interesting. Damned interesting. It didn't seem possible that the suspension of Fred's sentence and the treatment he'd received in jail could have worked such a radical change in him and yet something had affected him.

The doctor felt restless and impatient. He wanted to talk to Sergeant Miller. He was dying to know now what had happened during Fred's incarceration. He would also have given a lot to be present when Fred got back to the farm. If he had really decided to turn over a new leaf, the way Mary reacted to his homecoming could have an acute bearing on both their futures. He had meant to get down to Brownsville while Fred was locked up, but there had been two imminent pregnancies and an acute appendix. There just hadn't been time. Oh, well, it was out of his hands now. Best not worry about it.

He put his glasses away and was about to turn back into the room when a particularly brilliant flash of lightning lit up the window. It was followed almost instantly by a clap of thunder that shook the house. The doctor blinked. It had been only a split second but in that moment he could have sworn he saw a movement on the pathway. Impossible, of course. No one would be abroad in this. A trick of the light probably. He rubbed his eyes and fumbled for a cigarette. There was a muffled thump at the front door. He dropped the package of cigarettes and ran for the hallway. He turned the knob and the door crashed inwards hurling him against the wall and at the same instant a massive figure stumbled past him into the living room. Fern screamed. Ian leaped to his feet. The doctor slammed the door and ran in.

Fred had brought up forcibly against the heavy oak table. He stood there now half bent over and breathing like an animal. One dripping sleeve had been ripped off the shoulder of his shirt and hung like a bloodstained rag from the buttoned wrist. The other sleeve was gone entirely and the rest of the shirt was in tatters. His bare torso had been sluiced down by the rain but now a dozen cuts, scratches and abrasions were beginning to show blood. One shoe was missing; the other was like a huge club foot packed into a great lump of black mud. His blond hair was matted with grime and leaves and there was a two-inch, blood-soaked gash over his left ear. The water ran off him making a muddy red pool at his feet, as he stood desperately gripping the limp body of his wife.

The tarpaulin which had once covered her was gone, and the sodden, bloodstained blanket was torn half through and hanging loose. One end of it had been dragging in the mud and only the once white towels with which he had tried to staunch the flow of blood covered the lower half of her body. The chalk white limbs were bruised and lacerated where he had dragged her out of the tree roots and even her blouse and brassière had been half torn from her by the frenzied clutch of his fingers. He had her now under the knees and shoulders.

Her hips sank deeply between his arms while her head lolled back over his forearm as if the neck were broken. The water ran in a steady stream from her tangled hair onto the polished table top and her face had that faintly greenish hue of a corpse. The whole picture was something out of a nightmare.

After that first scream, Fern had stood frozen. The doctor turned on her almost savagely. "Intravenous. Five per cent glucose and saline 1000 CC's. Move!" The whiplash tone startled Fern out of her stupor. She blinked and then sped away without a word. The doctor dug his fingers into Ian's arm. "Come on, man, get a hold of yourself. Help me get her into the other room." Ian nodded numbly and stepped forward. Together they tried to lift Mary out of Fred's arms. It was like trying to get her out of a vice. The doctor swore. Ian wet his lips. "What is it?"

"Muscular catalepsy. He's carried her for so long he can't let loose. Look at his eyes. He doesn't even know where he is. Fred!" The word had no effect. He reached up and slapped Fred hard. The eyes didn't waver and the grip didn't relax. "Fern, drop that intravenous and bring me a needle of pentathol. Quick!" He turned to Ian. "Now when I give him this shot, hang on to him. He's got enough wrong with him now without having him bust a cheekbone on the floor."

Ian nodded, still shaken. "What's the matter with her?"

"She's had a miscarriage."

"She looks dead."

"She may be. *Fern, where's that needle!*"

Fern ran in. "Here." The doctor snatched the hypodermic, rammed it into Fred's upper arm and sunk the plunger.

"Watch him. He may go all of a sudden!"

Fred did. Within seconds he quivered and went limp. The doctor wrenched Mary out of his arms and Ian and Fern barely managed to keep Fred from plunging face down on the rug. They started to drag him to a couch and the doctor

264

snapped, "Leave him! He'll be all right." He carried Mary into the small operating room and laid her on the table. He tore the towels away from the uterus as Fern brought in the intravenous equipment. She set it up swiftly. Ian took his hand off Mary's wrist and shook his head. "I canna' get a pulse," he said hoarsely.

The doctor put a stethoscope to his ears and bent over her. He moved the cup twice, listening carefully, then he straightened up. "She's alive. Just." He bit his lip and glanced at the intravenous equipment. "Is that feeding?"

Fern nodded. She looked shakier than the doctor had ever seen her. Mary Sharron was one of her closest friends. He said, "Look, Fern. Don't fall apart on me now. The next fifteen minutes are going to decide whether she lives or dies."

Fern swallowed. "I'll be all right. It was just the shock, the way he came in and . . . the way they looked . . ."

"Good girl. Now I want adrenalin and caffeine fast."

"Intravenous?"

"Yes. She's going to need at least five transfusions, maybe more. I think she's blood type A but Ian, you'd better check. You'll find it in the files. I've run blood checks on everybody around at one time or another. Dig out those that match and can be reached and get 'em over here as quick as you can. I want at least one donor here in fifteen minutes."

Ian went out on a dead run. The doctor took a scalpel and cut off the remnants of dress and brassière. He worked swiftly and efficiently, cleaning her and treating the multiple scratches with antiseptic. Before he had finished Fern had arranged the intravenous sedation. She said, shakily, "Will she live?"

"I don't know. She's lost an awful lot of blood. If we can get her out of shock she may have a chance."

"We'll have to do a curettement. You'd better prepare her for surgery. We'll give her the transfusions at the same time."

"Direct?"

He nodded.

"What about cross checking the blood?"

"No time. We'll just have to pray it works. Don't take your eye off those injection tubes. I'll go and see what we can do about Goliath."

He went out and Fern put a hand on Mary's forehead. The skin was still unnaturally cold and clammy.

26

Head hanging, chest heaving, the mare stood where Fred had left her at the edge of the rising stream. Before Fred had completed the crossing the water washed over her hooves and splashed her fetlocks. Instinctively she shied back. The wagon had slewed to the left when Fred hauled it to a stop and now, as the mare moved, the left rear wheel went off the road and onto the shoulder where the run off from the crown had made the mud deep and thick. The mare didn't notice. Now that her feet were out of the water she let her head hang again trying to suck strength back into her lungs. The wheel settled deeper with most of the wagon's weight resting on it. By the time the water reached the mare again the wheel had sunk almost to the hubcap. The mare started again, driving the rim deeper and still the water reached her. She backed frantically but her hooves slipped in the mud and the wagon refused to budge. She wasted precious energy straining against the immovable shafts and too late tried to pull round to her right. The wheel gave an inch—two inches and then stuck fast. In panic the horse flung herself against the traces, lunging sideways, to free herself. It was useless. The water crept up slowly covering her fetlocks and her knees. It took half an hour before the water reached her belly. By then the wagon was half floating but she had no strength left to pull it loose.

Robbie awakened as the preliminary updraft of the approaching storm stirred the trees. He sat up just in time to feel the full fury of the first wind and watch the trees snap their tops toward the onrushing clouds. The glade was already in half darkness and the patch of sky he could see through the opening above the pond had the bilious look of an ugly bruise. He struggled to his feet and dove for the underbrush as the wall of water rushed across the pond toward him. Driven by the full force of the storm's wind the rain hit the trees with the solid smash of a tidal wave, driving through the trunks and drenching him even as he ran. There was an earsplitting crash as the tips of a dozen evergreens were ripped loose from the trunks in that blinding instant when the wind shifted direction one hundred and eighty degrees. The rain beat against the branches with a hollow roaring that muffled all but the loudest crashes of thunder. Robbie flung himself flat, his heart hammering with excitement. It took him a moment to realize what that first crash had been and then he saw the headless trees thrashing against the sky and he knew what had happened. After a moment he crawled cautiously back to the edge of the clearing. He held his forearm above his eyes and squinted against the wind, keeping his face close to the ground.

Every twig, every flower, every blade of grass around the pond had been beaten flat in that first massive onslaught and now the water lay like a thick film of oil on the sloping mat of vegetation. It wanted to run down hill into the pond but the force of the wind and rain beat it back forming it into long wavering lines so that it crawled slowly up the bank and then ran down again in quivering confusion like a thing alive. The surface of the pond was a sheet of foam wanting to rise to the wind and being pounded flat by the rain. Three hundred yards away a blinding spear of lightning hit the top of a pine. There was a rending explosion and the tree split from cone to root in a welter of blue white sparks. The shock wave of thunder buffeted Robbie like a giant hand and the sound almost burst his eardrums. The rain was icy cold and yet where it drummed on his naked arms and shoulders it stung like the touch of fire. And still he could not move. He was numb with the wonder of it—lanced through with a dreadful fascination. Every once in a while a branch would tear loose and hurtle through his field of vision and once a dead limb, thicker than a man's thigh, smashed into the undergrowth within ten feet of him. Still he was immune to fear—lifted on a plane of trembling exhilaration.

Beneath the fierce cacophony of the storm there came another sound; a low ominous rumbling steadily increasing in intensity. It came from upstream to his left. He twisted to look and a wall of water swept around the bend in the stream. Its four-foot forward slope was a foaming jungle of tree stumps, branches, marsh weed and splintered boards. An irresistible battering ram, it thrashed down the narrow flume smothering underbrush, uprooting saplings and drowning the banks in a seething maelstrom. It catapulted into the pond dumping thousands of gallons of water and tons of debris into the tiny basin. The pond exploded. The water foamed up to within inches of Robbie's position, then the beaver dam ripped loose and the juggernaut rolled on, still rumbling like a volcano. The backwash overran Robbie's elbows. He dragged himself upright, clinging to the thrumming trunk of a fir. The water rose above his ankles. He stepped backward, clutching for support. He knew he should go home—his mother would be frantic—but he couldn't tear himself away.

The bore had cut itself a channel down the middle of the pond and the hump of it ran a good foot above the level of the surrounding water. It was impossible but there it was—a raised river dragging the backwater into a sea of whirlpools where stumps and weeds and bits of newly splintered boards spun dizzily like passengers on a wild merry-go-round. At the far side of the pond there was a young sapling whose roots had been caught in one of the vortexes. The tree stood straight up out of the water like a flagpole spinning crazily on its axis. Robbie decided he would wait until the sapling fell before he went home.

It was a good hour before he stumbled up the porch stairs into an empty house. There was a trail of blood across the kitchen floor and the living room. The couch was splattered and sodden with it. He felt the hot dizzy nausea gripping him again, but he forced himself to look in the bedrooms. The mattress and sheets were gone from his mother's bed. He went out to the back porch and clung to the supports letting the rain and wind beat against his face. After a while the nausea disappeared. He fought his way to the barn. The horse was gone and the wagon. Both of the barn doors had been blown away and the whole side facing the wind was caved in. The timbers still groaned and screeched in agony. He made his way back to the house. He couldn't go in and face the blood again. He crawled in under the porch. The ground was inches deep in water but the stairs broke the wind and kept the rain off him. What could have happened? Maybe his mother had been hurt in the storm and then came the more terrible thought. Maybe Fred had hit her again! He'd hurt her badly this time. He might even have killed her. The possibility pushed Robbie into motion. He crawled out from under the porch and began to run toward the gate.

Half an hour later he found the windfall across the road, saw where the branches had been hacked away and the bark torn loose from the tree where the tailgate had struck. He found the river swirling where the bridge had been and he made his way along the bank to where the giant spruce had arched over the stream bed. The spruce was down but the rising water had put it out of reach. Between him and the muddy maze of roots there was a fifteen-foot torrent. He struggled back to the road. The shock of finding the empty blood-drenched house and the ceaseless battering of the rain and wind had made him thickheaded. He felt oddly detached from himself and his surroundings and he didn't seem to be able to think clearly. Had they gone across the bridge before it went out? He knew somehow they hadn't. How did he know? And then he remembered the splintered timbers the wall of water had disgorged into the beaver pond as he lay watching from higher ground. Those had been the fragments of the bridge.

But if they hadn't got across where was the wagon and the horse? Maybe they'd left before the storm started. He'd been asleep. He didn't think he'd slept long but there was no sun to tell him how much time had passed. If they had gotten across they must be in Pineville by now. Somehow he had to get there and find out. Maybe below him there was a spot where the water had piled enough refuse in the narrows to make a crossing possible. He started downstream. A quarter of a mile below the road there was something wedged in the fork of a fallen tree. It didn't really surprise him or shock him. Somehow he had already known he would see it. It was the body of the mare half submerged, shiny black from the water and still imprisoned in the harness tongues. On the far bank a few yards farther down, part of the wagon had been hurled upside down in the brush. The water was reaching for it again breaking over the shattered tail gate and spinning an undamaged wheel.

They must have been on the bridge when it went out, he thought. Something at the water's edge caught Robbie's eye. He reached down into the water a few inches from his feet and detached a torn piece of cloth from a branch. It was pink with small white flowers on it. The dress his mother had been wearing. He felt neither frightened nor surprised. He stood there for some time, then he put the piece of cloth inside his shirt and began following the bank of the stream, looking. He searched until it was pitch black. He found a tarpaulin he

271

recognized as one which used to hang behind the kitchen door but that was all. They might have been washed down into the lake, he thought. Tomorrow I'll go into Pineville and tell the doctor and Mr. Campbell. They'll know what to do.

The wind was beginning to die now, but the rain came down as heavily as ever. He couldn't face that long journey back to the farm and he didn't want to sleep in that house anyway. He walked away from the stream. The level ground was calf deep in water and the hollows were up to his thighs. He sloshed through them oblivious to the rain and the moaning in the trees. Near the top of a small hill there was a granite cave he'd found when he was five. A fox had raised its young there one year and in winter it was a hibernation place for bears.

Robbie struggled up to the mouth of the cave and stood panting against the rock. From inside there came a low, ominous rumbling. He turned his head. In the darkness he could see nothing. It's a bear, he thought idly. A big old he-bear. If it was a she there'd be cubs and she wouldn't growl, she'd charge. He pushed himself off the wall and stepped into the cave. The ill-tempered rumbling increased. Robbie sank down on the ground. He didn't care at all whether the bear attacked him or not. His body ached in every muscle. His flesh was raw from the exposure to the pelting rain and the lashing of the branches. It was dry inside the cave and the granite was still warm from the midday sun. He put his head on his arm. He went to sleep.

The rumbling in the cave ceased abruptly. There was a restless snuffling, an energetic grunt, then a resounding thump as the bear collapsed.

After a few seconds, the cave reverberated to the strange sounds of a child's exhausted breathing punctuated by the deep sonorous snores of a giant bear.

27

Fred opened his eyes and stared at an unfamiliar ceiling. His head ached. Every muscle in his body was stiff and sore. He tried to struggle upright and a hand restrained him gently. Somebody said, "Easy does it." He turned his head. Dr. McLeod was standing by the bed.

The doctor said, "How do you feel?"

Fred stared, frowned, and then remembrance flowed through him. He started up, thrusting the doctor's hands aside.

"It's all right, Fred, *it's all right!*"

Fred stopped struggling. "She's not dead?"

"No she's all right. It was a fine thing you did."

The tensions flowed out of Fred's muscles. He sank back slowly until his head touched the pillow. He wet his lips. He said, "Was it . . . was it . . . what she thought?"

The doctor nodded gently. "I'm afraid it was . . . she had a miscarriage."

Fred closed his eyes. A tremor ran over his face and he flung an arm across his forehead. After a second his lips moved. "My baby. She didn't tell me . . . it was my baby . . . I never even knew." Again the tremor shook him.

The doctor felt a surge of helpless sympathy. He said, quietly, "She can have more children, Fred."

Fred took his arm away from his forehead and opened his eyes. There was anguish and desolation written in his face. He said, emptily. "No. She don't want no more of me. She won't never let me near her again. I shoulda knowed from the beginning it wouldn't work. I gotta git out. I gotta git away from here."

There was sharp snap from the doctor's fingers. He looked down. He'd broken his pince-nez. He flung the one glass away irritably. He paced over to the window and looked out. Keep your mouth shut, he told himself. The man's right. The whole thing is impossible. She'll never accept him and he'll never accept the boy—it's an unholy mess—and you'll only prolong the agony if you start meddling—let him go—let him cut it clean, no matter how it hurts—but still he turned back.

"What happened yesterday *might* have changed things, you know."

Fred looked up. The nightgown and the stiff blond hair standing up out of the bandage on his head gave him a boyish, appealing look. There was no bitterness in his voice when he spoke—only a kind of hollow finality. "Sure," he said, "like the time they got caught in the blizzard. It'll pass. And what's the good of it? It ain't right anyway. I only done what any man woulda done. I made it cause I happen to be a little stronger'n most. That's nothin' to build on. There ain't gonna be a blizzard or a hurricane every time she gets to comparin' me to Tom Sharron or thinkin' what I did to her kid."

"Fred, about the boy—"

Fred shook his head. "I know what you're gonna say. If I could make up to the kid it'd be all right . . . Well, I can't. It ain't I don't want to, but I know myself. I spent ten days in jail thinkin' about it. Every time I see his face I get mad all over again."

"He's only nine—children change."

"Not this kind. I grew up with Billy."

"The boy is not Billy," the doctor snapped. "He's not responsible for what Billy did or failed to do."

"I ain't *makin'* him responsible! I just can't swallow him.

274

After what I done to him he tried to kill me. Climbed up in the loft and got a pitchfork. If he'd throwed it I might a had some respect for him. But all he did was drop the fork and bust out bawlin'. When the fork fell and he thought it was gonna hit me he screamed."

"I told you before that every man is afraid of something. Now don't get that 'shut up' look. Listen to me. Every man feels fear unless he's an idiot. It just happens that some men are stronger than others. They have more resistance to panic. But every man has a weakness—pray on that weakness long enough and every man has a breaking point. By accident you discovered Robbie's. Because you've had a terrible experience that you can lay at the doorstep of that particular frailty you've decided the boy is all coward. I'm not saying that's not possible but it isn't likely."

"Why isn't it?"

"Well, for one thing, he has no fear of animals. I've seen him pet a half wild husky that you or I wouldn't dare touch."

"I seen it, too. But the dogs don't go after him. What's there to be afraid of if they're gentle?"

"All right then, how do you account for that night in the blizzard when he came to get you?"

"You ain't tryin' to tell me that's courage? He ran home cause he'd a froze to death if he hadn't. He got home all right but left his mother in the snow."

"Only because he couldn't lift her."

"Maybe so, maybe not. I'll tell you again; a man's afraid or he ain't and that goes for kids, too. I watched Billy all his life an' I know. I seen it other places. I seen men when a log jamb broke push their best friends into certain death all because they was rotten with fear. It makes me sick to my stomach. You say every man's got a fear. All right. What's mine?"

The doctor took a breath. "I'll make a guess, if you like."

"Make it."

"As far as I know you're not afraid of anything where you can strike back. Sheer physical strain is a catharsis for you."

"A what?"

"You run off fear like you'd run the cream off a pitcher of milk—by plunging into danger and lashing out at it. I'll be willing to wager that if you were ever put in a situation where anger and muscle wouldn't help, you'd crack."

Fred shrugged. "Maybe you're right, but I still don't believe it. Where's my clothes?"

"There in that closet. You shouldn't get out of bed today."

Fred swung his feet to the floor and stood. He lurched dizzily, then steadied himself against the bed.

The doctor said, "I told you."

"I'll be all right in a minute." He straightened and crossed to the cupboard. He opened the door. "These ain't mine. They're new."

"Ian Campbell brought them over this morning. There wasn't much left of the others."

Fred took the clothes out of the closet and flung them on the bed. "Tell him I'll pay him soon's I git back to town."

"I don't think he'll take any money for them. You're kind of a hero around Pineville this morning."

"I ain't no hero and I'll pay for the clothes."

"Suit yourself. The shoes and socks are under the bed."

Fred drew the nightshirt over his head and dropped it on a chair. He looked down at his body. His whole torso was daubed with antiseptic and there were seven pieces of adhesive neatly crisscrossing his chest and abdomen.

He looked up startled and anxious. "Was she cut up like this?"

"Not as bad as you are. Part of the time you must have had her covered with a blanket. She had her share of bruises."

"What time'd we get here?"

"About nine o'clock last night."

"I been sleepin' ever since?"

"I gave you a sedative."

He drew on a sock. "I don't remember gettin' here."

"What do you remember?"

"Everything I guess up to the time I got back on the road after crossin' the creek."

"The bridge was out?"

"Yeah." He paused, thinking back. "We got across on a tree that was down in the water. I don't remember much after that except thinkin' I only had three more miles to go."

"You carried her three miles without stopping?"

Fred tightened the laces on a shoe. "Don't know whether I stopped or not. I thought she was still alive when I left the river. After that I didn't know."

"You just made it. We gave her five transfusions. Half the village was up giving blood last night."

"She must be real sick."

"No. They bounce back as soon as you replace the lost blood. She'll be good as new after a few days' rest. She wants to see you."

Fred stopped buttoning his shirt and looked up. "What for?"

"Well, I think it's about the boy."

Fred dropped his eyes and returned to the shirt buttons. "Yeah, it would be."

"He wasn't with you when you arrived last night. I told her you'd probably left him at the farm."

"I didn't see him."

"You mean he wasn't there when you left?"

"Last I seen him was just after lunch yesterday. He ran off to the woods when he saw me comin'."

"He didn't come back?"

"Not as far as I know."

277

"Then he must have been out in the woods when the storm hit?"

"I guess so. What time is it?"

"Eleven o'clock. Are you going to talk to her?"

Fred hesitated for just a second, then shook his head. When he spoke his voice was unsteady. "It's better I don't. Tell her—I'm glad she's all right and tell her . . . oh hell, tell her I'll try and find the kid for her before I leave."

"You're going back to the farm now?"

"Yeah."

"The river's still in flood."

"I'll git across somehow. It can't be no worse than it was last night." He pulled the door open and started out.

The doctor said, "You're sure you won't change your mind? She's just next door."

Fred stopped in the doorway, his back to the doctor. Suddenly his shoulders slumped and his whole body seemed to go slack. The tremor that had seized him earlier shook him again. He turned back slowly. His eyes were swimming and his voice was thick and unsteady. He said, "Why did she have to kill my kid? He never did nothin' to her." He turned and went out before the doctor recovered from his surprise.

28

The doctor pressed his thumb and forefinger against his eyes and let out a long breath. He'd been up all night and what had happened this morning hadn't made him feel any better. Fern came into the room and he looked up. "Any news about the boy yet?"

She shook her head. "Not yet. Ian just came back. The stream's still floodin'. They're gettin' some men together to try to get a rope across so they can make a temporary bridge. They did talk to Jed Clawson, though, across the water. He's goin' up to the Sharron place, but he's on foot. The road won't be passable for at least a couple of days. It'll be dark before he can get back down to the river."

"Have you told Mary?"

"Not yet, I'll tell her now."

"Never mind, I have to look in on her anyway."

She looked at the bed where Fred had been. "Where's Carter?"

"He's gone back to the farm."

"In his condition?"

"Do you know any way of stopping him when he's made up his mind about something?"

"Did he talk to her?"

"No."

"I cannot understand it. After what he did last night he goes off this mornin' without even sayin' a word to her. Does it make sense to you now?"

The doctor let out a sigh. "It's a lot more complicated than it seems. Go to bed, Fern."

"You'll send somebody round if you need me?"

"I will."

Fern went off. The doctor took a breath and pushed open the door to Mary's room. She was sitting up in bed, her face taut and anxious.

"Is there any news?"

The doctor shut the door. "Not yet. Jed Clawson's on his way out to the farm but we won't know if Robbie's there till almost dark."

"But why?"

"The roads are impassable. The bridge is out. It's close to ten miles from the river to your place. He has to do it on foot both ways."

She wrung her hands. "Oh, God, if anythin's happened to Robbie, I don't know what I'd do." She broke off as she saw the doctor turn away. "What's the matter? . . . You're keeping somethin' from me, aren't you? . . . He's hurt. . . ."

He hesitated for an instant and then turned back. The usually sharp blue eyes were tired and angry. "No, I'm not keeping anything from you."

"Then why did you turn away like that?"

"Fred Carter risked his life to save you last night. You have yet to ask me how he is."

She frowned and caught her lip between her teeth. "I suppose that was ungrateful of me, but I've been so worried about Robbie."

"Surely." It was only one word but he could not conceal the acid edge in it.

The blood mounted to her face. "You don't know all the facts, Doctor."

He felt the pressure building inside him. He ought to get out now—get out of the room before he said something he'd regret, but he was too tired to stem his indignation. He said, "I know a few you don't even suspect."

Anger boiled openly into her eyes. "I'd be obliged to you, Doctor McLeod, if you'd be kind enough to explain that remark."

"Do you know for example that your son tried to kill Fred Carter with a pitchfork?"

For a second she looked stunned, then a white line formed around her mouth. "I don't believe it."

"No! You've a great facility for seeing nothing but virtues in those you love and nothing but faults in those you don't."

"That's not true." Her voice shook.

He went on ignoring her denial. "Last night your husband brought you thirteen miles through the worst storm this country has ever seen. You were unconscious, helpless, a dead weight. Yet he still got you across a flooded river when the bridge was out and then carried you in his arms almost three miles through wind, rain, mud, and God knows what all else. There's not one man in ten thousand could have done it and not one in a million who would even have tried. Do you realize what a man must feel for a woman to do what he did?"

"If he feels so much for me how could he do what he did to my son? But then, perhaps you don't know about that, do you?" she said, furiously.

"I do know. I also know he had a very good reason for what he did. A reason you're intelligent enough to have seen if you hadn't been so ready to find a reason to condemn him."

"Ready to condemn him? Can you imagine any decent man doing what he did. Can you imagine Tom Sharron doing it?"

The doctor took a deep breath. "Look, Mary, Tom Sharron is dead. There may not be another like him but that's no excuse for destroying a man who's done his level best to be as good a husband as he knows how."

"How do you know what kind of a husband he's been? I

refuse to overlook everything he's done just because he saved my life."

"You also refuse to give him credit for doing his level best from the moment he married you to measure up to the impossible standards you set for him."

"It's out of your mind, you are."

"Is it? Since the day he married you I've never seen him unshaven or without a haircut. He's even struggled manfully to improve his table manners. He ran the farm so well that there isn't a more profitable one in the country and on top of all this he risked his life to save you when he believed you aborted his child."

"What?!!"

"That surprises you, doesn't it? Well, it did me, too. But after the way you've treated him, what did you *expect* him to believe? I told you ten days ago you were pregnant. Why didn't you tell your husband?"

She was chalk white as she stared at him but the anger still burned. "Because we weren't speaking to each other, that's why."

"You don't believe that any more than I do. You forget I watched you bite into your knuckles till the blood ran the day I told you why you were having dizzy spells. And something else. That child was conceived *after* the incident with the deer. It makes me a little ill to think how far you must have gone to hurt him. Is it any wonder he believes you killed his child?"

"He has no right to believe that of me."

"No right? *No right!* You have the right to believe whatever you please of him but your motives must be above suspicion!"

"He almost killed my baby!"

"Your *baby* is nine years old and, in any case, Fred was not responsible for what he did to Robbie."

"What do you mean he wasn't responsible?"

"How could you miss it? You know Fred Carter's history. You know he saw his wife burn because of his brother's horror of blood. What do you imagine happened when he saw the same look on your son's face? He didn't see Robbie that day. He saw his brother Billy. You've crucified him ever since without asking yourself if there might be a reason. You've used his love for you as a weapon to punish him. You'll forgive me if my sympathy is with your husband."

"Would you mind leavin' me alone."

"I'll be glad to." He opened the door, then turned back. "Oh, one more thing," he said. "Fred told me to tell you he's glad you're all right and that he'll try to find your son for you before he leaves." He went out and closed the door.

29

The bear awakened slowly, pushed himself up to a sitting position and yawned prodigiously. He had slept all night with the boy's scent about him so that now for the moment he was unaware of it. He swung his head lazily and saw the boy lying just inside the mouth of the cave with the sunlight glancing off his tousled hair. The bear sat stock-still and looked very puzzled. He put his head on one side and then on the other. After a moment, he gave a sort of half-hearted growl. The boy stirred, sighed, and went on sleeping. The bear stuck his tongue out and licked his nose. He scratched desultorily at a flea with his left hind foot along the under side of his belly. He was an old bear, large and somewhat ludicrous as bears can sometimes be, and most of the hair was rubbed off a patch on his left shoulder where he had been scratching against a tree. He yawned again, then got to his feet and shambled up to the boy. He bent his head and sniffed at the boy's clothes. He didn't like the man-smell but he had seen this particular man-thing before. It never carried the stick that made noise and its smell never had the hot sting in his nostrils that the man-things sometimes left behind them when they ran away or before they made noises with the sticks. He raised his head again and looked out of the cave. Not far from the entrance there was a blueberry bush. The berries were almost ripe. The bear opened his mouth and a drop of saliva fell on the dust of the cave an inch from Robbie's face. The bear raised his paw and stepped over the boy's figure delicately, moving his huge bulk like a ballet dancer. Once outside the cave he didn't look back.

Robbie awoke an hour later. He sat up slowly and looked about him. Fifty feet away a large bear was browsing lazily among the berry bushes. Robbie turned his head and looked back into the cave. It was empty. He pulled himself to his feet. The bear stopped feeding long enough to give a short disinterested glance, then returned to his breakfast.

Robbie came out of the cave. The morning dazzled him. The sky was blue traced with long tenuous streamers of white cloud and the air was crystal clear. The pines burnt deep, lustrous greens into the pattern of sunshine shimmering as if each needle had its own shining coat of polish. Around the cave the granite potholes were brim full of amber rain and below, through the maze of trunks, Robbie could see an ebony glint where the lees of the storm still stood, black and silent, in the hollows. By mid afternoon the thirsty peat would have drunk the last of them but the ground would be spongy and wet for days to come. From where he stood he could not see the stream but he could hear it . . . still rushing down its swollen channel toward the lake and filling the quiet morning with the faint memory of thunder. By morning it, too, would have receded. The only symbols of the storm would be the masses of debris piled along its ruptured banks and the headless trees that marked the passage of the wind.

He reached into his shirt and took out the piece of cloth he had taken from the half submerged branch the night before. He stared at it feeling a thickening in his throat and he had to clench his fists to keep the pain from spilling into his eyes. After a while he folded the cloth carefully and slid it back inside his shirt, then made his way slowly down off the granite hummock and into the trees. For a while he walked aimlessly but always out of sight of the stream and away from the lake. He didn't want to go near the lake. He didn't want to see what might be floating there at the edge of the water or entangled in the mass of rubble the river would have vomited into the basin. The same feeling kept him away from the banks of the stream.

It was possible that in the rain and darkness last night he might have missed what he knew had to be there, somewhere, between the bridge and the deep black waters of the lake. How he wished now he had had the courage to throw the pitchfork that morning in the barn! They would have taken him off to prison maybe but it wouldn't have mattered. He'd have saved his mother from whatever Fred had done to her. And now she was gone. Both of them were gone. The man he hated and the woman he loved. There had been so much blood at the house. Maybe she'd been dead before they reached the river. He almost hoped it was true remembering how he had felt that day as he sank deep down into the black water and saw the sunlight growing dim on the surface far above him. It was a terrible way to die. He pushed the thought away from him and began moving slowly toward the stream. He'd be at the road in a few minutes and he'd see if it was possible to get across now on that tree that had fallen into the water. He had to tell them in town what had happened. And when he'd done it he'd go away. He'd go into the woods and live by himself and he wouldn't care about anybody ever again.

Fred reached the river and found it flooded as the doctor had predicted. It was still moving with deadly swiftness but except for the places along the edge where it foamed through drowned branches and boiled around the boles of trees it ran smoothly now—a deceptive smoothness that was marked by small, vicious whirlpools and oily, deep-running slicks. It looked more fearsome now than it had in the fury of the previous night even though it had fallen several feet. Fred made his way upstream to the tree trunk on which he had crossed

286

but it was no longer in the same position. The tangled top of the tree which had been touching the Pineville shore had been lifted by the rising water and pushed downstream about twenty feet. It was still within easy reach but the change in position had caused the tree to pivot on its axis bringing the roots farther away from the opposite shore. A good twelve feet of treacherous current now separated roots and solid ground. Fred didn't like the look of it. Twelve feet was less than twice his own height. A man could jump it easily with a running start but there could be no running start here. Once in that water there was nothing to hang onto. Nothing to keep your feet from being swept from under you.

He walked upstream and down half a mile in either direction but there was no place which offered a better chance of crossing. He came back to the tree. He looked at the water again, then set his jaw and began to edge out along its length. The tree was slippery now and he had to squeeze his way through a maze of branches and jagged broken limbs. Once the tree rolled treacherously and only a convenient handhold saved him from being hurled into the current. He got to the end of the trunk and wormed his way to the outermost solid root. The water foamed at his feet and splashed over his boot tops. He turned around and began to let himself down into the water. It was like trying to hold his feet on a moving platform. By the time he was in as far as his waist his body was streaming away from the log like a limp rag. He began to haul himself back out and realized with a start how weak he was. His muscles trembled with the effort. Still he knew he could get back on the root if he wanted. The question was, did he want to? He'd come to cross the stream. He'd said he'd get across. There was no other way to do it. He either let go now and hoped he could make it to the opposite bank or he went back to Pineville and admitted he had failed to get across the stream or find the boy like he had promised. He let go.

A black hand came out of the bed of the stream and seized him by the waist. It dragged him down several feet, then flung him to the surface. He saw the shoreline rushing by him in a green blur and caught part of a breath before he was dragged under again and tumbled helplessly end over end in a cold well of darkness. He struck out blindly. His hand collided with something that numbed his arm to the elbow. He came to the surface again, his lungs bursting, and was instantly spun round and round in a tight dizzy circle. His vision was blurred and his head ringing. The whirlpool spat him out and he went under again still trying to fight his way across the current. His body brought up against something smooth buffeted, and scraped free. He knew he had not much strength left. He broke the surface for a third time and saw he was bearing down on a windfall. He ducked his head and flung out an arm. His fingers scraped over slimy wood and then dug into a projection. He hung on grimly, half drowned, the water still washing over him. He pulled himself back slowly against the current, resisting the impulse to breathe till his mouth was free of the water. Hand over hand, he fought his way along the slender trunk till he got to the shore. He lay there motionless beneath a huge pile of brush. He didn't move for three or four minutes, then as his strength began to flow back he got to his knees and started to push himself erect.

Eighty-seven pounds of clawing fury landed full on his neck and shoulders. The impact knocked his breath out and half collapsed him in the mud. He fought to get his head up and was met by a rain of vicious stinging blows and raking scratches. He rolled and the thing left him only to leap at his throat. He held one arm across his face to fend off the attack and thrust out the other arm. His fingers closed on flesh. He got to his feet and held the thrashing boy at arm's length. Robbie was crying with fury. He struggled maniacally in his stepfather's grasp. "You killed her!" he screamed, "you killed my mother!"

Fred dug his fingers deeper into the boy's shoulder and tried to shake him into submission. "You're crazy!" he gasped hoarsely. Robbie bent his head and sunk his teeth into Fred's forearm. Fred cursed and let go. The boy tore loose and ran up the bank. At the edge of the trees he turned back, his face working with an equal mixture of hate and anguish. "You killed her," he said again. "You killed her!" He turned and ran into the trees. Fred stumbled up the bank. "Come back here, you crazy fool! You don't know what you're talking about."

Ahead of him he caught a brief glimpse of the boy before the trees swallowed him. He began to run, splashing through the pools and stumbling through the sodden undergrowth in pursuit. He ran two or three hundred yards calling the boy's name, then stopped. The boy had disappeared. Fred walked unsteadily to a log and sat down on it. He put a hand to his face and rubbed it across his eyes. The kid had said, "You killed her! You killed my mother!" Where the hell had he got that idea? He shook his head and sighed. It would be impossible to find him. The only thing he could do was go on to the farm and get his things and get out. At least he could tell her that the kid was alive and unhurt. Strong, too. He put a hand up and touched his eye ruefully where one little fist had landed. It wouldn't surprise him in the least if the boy had given him a shiner. Now there was a strange thing! He'd never have believed the kid would have the guts to tackle him like that but then he'd been half crazy thinking his mother was dead. Wild little bastard! He shook his head again. He decided he would rest for a few minutes and then cut through the woods to the farm.

Robbie had been on his way to the bridge when he'd seen something stir down by the water half hidden by undergrowth. He'd gone down to look and seen the body of his stepfather lying in the mud. Obviously, the man had been there all night hidden by the brush and Robbie had missed him in the rain and darkness. So he had survived after all and his mother had been the one who had drowned. As Fred started to rise, Robbie's attack had been instinctive. He had struck in blind fury before the man had been able to fend him off. Now he stood stock-still, listening as the thrashing in the brush behind him stopped. He began to circle back cautiously guiding himself by the sounds of Fred's heavy breathing which could be heard a hundred yards away in the damp air. He moved up slowly on the man's flank and stood among the trees watching the hated back and shoulders. If only he had a gun now—or even a bow and arrow—he could kill him easily. And yet to kill him so quickly, even if he had the weapons, would be nothing. He ought to be made to suffer as he had made them suffer. And then the idea came to him. It filled him with a terrible elation.

If it worked, no one but Robbie would ever know what a dreadful revenge he had taken. He would hold the secret all his life and then maybe on his deathbed he would tell those who were gathered around him what he had done and they would turn pale with awe and fear at the frightful justice he had meted out. The only problem was how to get Fred to follow him. He'd lost him so easily just now that perhaps the man wouldn't chase him again even if he showed himself. How then? What did the partridge do when she wanted to lead you away from her nest? She dragged one wing in a pitiful imitation of a wounded bird and the first time you saw it you followed her thinking she would be easy to catch. And she always managed to stay just a step or two out of reach until she'd got you where she wanted you, then she suddenly snapped the "broken" wing into flying position and flew away.

The trick had fooled a lot of hunters. There was no reason why it shouldn't fool one more.

Robbie felt a deadly excitement. He moved out of concealment and stepped forward until he was only a few paces behind Fred. Then he deliberately stepped on a sodden stick. The stick broke with very little sound—(it was not wise to be too obvious)—but it was enough to spin Fred around. He saw the boy standing a few feet away. He lunged. The boy dodged away and began to run across the glade. Fred started to follow and then realized the hopelessness of it. The boy ran like a deer and he himself was dead tired. He had started to sit again when the boy tripped on a piece of branch and went sprawling. He was still too far away from Fred to reach. But he got up slowly and when he did he was limping. Fred straightened. The boy was trying to run but he was favoring one leg and moving painfully. Triumphantly Fred lunged forward again.

The boy might be able to outdistance him now but when that ankle began to swell he'd have to slow down. All Fred had to do was keep him in sight and wait for nature to take its course. He'd bring the boy back to her after all with nothing more wrong with him than a sprained ankle. Then his promise would be fulfilled and he could get out. He ran steadily, not extending himself any more than he had to. The boy was already having difficulty. Once he fell again and this time Fred came within inches of reaching him before he got away. They ran like this for several minutes then the underbrush began to thin and the sound of the stream grew fainter. They were coming into an area of forest that Fred had never seen before.

The trees were larger here and immensely tall, so that they shut out the sun almost completely and the man and boy ran below their branches in a vault of thin green silence. The air was difficult to breathe—heavy with the scent of resin and decay. Thick moss grew halfway up the mottled trunks and rolled away underfoot, softening the outlines of granite upthrusts and the eerie shapes of ancient windfalls. Giant fern grew lush in the hollows and scarlet and ocher fungus made bright blotches of color at the bases of the trees. The ground was soggy wet so that their feet made ugly squelching sounds as they ran. Fred scarcely noticed. He was too intent on watching Robbie and noting that the boy was obviously weakening, even though the lack of underbrush made the running easier. Fred saw he was gaining. Ahead of him the way came to a slightly open area with a low moss covered slope beyond. The boy skirted the open and struggled painfully up the slope at one side of the clearing. At the top he stopped and looked back. Fred had not yet reached the clearing itself. The boy lurched on his sprained ankle and seemed to panic. He turned one way and then the other, then ran across the top of the slope. Fred grinned. This time the kid had made a mistake! Had he turned to his right into the trees Fred would have had to follow his path up the side of the hill but since the boy had turned left all Fred had to do was to run straight across that open glade and up the gentle slope and he'd cut the boy off. He caught a breath of relief and increased his pace.

He ran six full steps into the quagmire before he realized he'd been tricked. He tried to turn immediately but the mire thinned by the heavy rains was already over his knees and rising rapidly. His legs were caught in a vice and a frightful stench rose from the ooze where the mossy covering had broken. He flung about, looking for something to give him purchase. Nearby there was the outline of a moss-covered branch. He strained toward it, feeling his body sinking deeper with each movement. His fingers touched the branch. He pulled. The wood crumbled to wet pulp in his fingers. He looked up. The boy was standing on the bank above him, watching, as an old and sadistic cat might watch a wounded mouse struggling beneath her paws. There was no sign of an injured ankle now. In spite of his predicament, Fred felt a flash of grudging admiration. His first thought had been that the boy had tricked him into the mire when he saw he couldn't escape, but now he saw that he'd been led there deliberately. The kid was smart. Damned smart. He said, "Look, kid, I didn't hurt your mother. She's in the doctor's office. She's all right."

Robbie's face didn't change. He reached up and pressed his hand almost unconsciously against the piece of his mother's dress folded beneath his shirt. He knew where his mother was and he knew who had put her there. Fred's lies wouldn't save him this time.

Fred saw that talking wasn't going to do any good. If he was going to get out he had to get out himself. He cast his eyes around. There was nothing within reach. Above his head a tree arched out from the bank just below where the boy was standing. But its branches were far out of reach. The ooze had touched his hip bones and it was still rising. He flung himself back. The movement lost him a good inch and for the first time in his life a flash of cold horror lanced through him. It was only an instant but in that instant he broke into a cold sweat, his throat convulsed and he almost cried out. He cursed violently, his anger mounting. Damn that stinking brat! The mire was nearly up to his waist. "Damn you, kid, get me out of this!" Robbie stood motionless, watching, waiting. Fred turned his head helplessly. He pushed down with his feet. It was the wrong thing to do. There was nothing to push against. He dug his fingers into the moss. It ripped like rotten cloth, dropping his fingers into the black slime. Christ! Christ almighty! He looked up at the tree. It was farther away than ever. "Robbie!" The name was ragged and uneven on his lips and it echoed away mockingly in the forest. "Robbie—Robbie—Robbie."

Robbie wet his lips, but he didn't reply.

A numbness began to grip Fred's legs. The slime was icy cold deep down and the pressure of it was cutting off the circulation. He couldn't move the muscles in his legs. His mouth began to get dry and he felt his chest constricting involuntarily. He heard the doctor's words ringing in his ears. "I'll wager that if you were ever put in a situation where anger and muscle wouldn't help, you'd crack!" I won't! he thought. I won't! But the thought had no strength behind it. It swam away from him. There was something building in him. An agonizing pressure that he couldn't resist. It choked his throat and thundered against his eardrums. It was a bubble of horror in his chest. The ooze touched his rib cage and the bubble burst. Blind panic flooded him. He screamed. The sweat ran into his eyes and he thrashed like a lunatic, splashing the black slime on his face and clothes. He screamed and screamed and screamed. And then it was over and he was still and trembling.

The violence had left him but the trapped helpless look didn't leave his face. His eyes were bright with horror, but he was rational again and he knew now what Billy Carter had felt the night of the fire—what Robbie Sharron had felt that morning by the body of the deer. He even knew what all of those men had felt when they pushed their friends to death in log jambs. Now he knew what it was like and what the doctor had meant when he said every man was afraid of something. Yes, now he knew. Only now it was too late. Now he was going to die here in this mire that was almost up to his armpits. And he was afraid of this death—afraid of the stench of it and the cold finality of it—the remorseless inevitability of it. His body drowned in a pit of slime where it could never be recovered, where it would remain forever until part of the stench in his nostrils now was the stench of his own rotted flesh melted, jellied, curdled into a part of this clotted ooze. He raised his head unsteadily. He said, "I'm sorry, kid, I'm sorry for what I done to you."

Robbie scarcely heard the words. During Fred's frantic screams and struggles he had stood drinking the scene with cold satisfaction, but now that the man was calm he saw the eyes. They weren't the eyes of Fred Carter, the man he hated. They were the eyes of an animal—helpless and terrified. They were the eyes of all the things he loved that feared to die and suffered such agony in death. They were the eyes of the deer his father had shot and the rabbit expiring under the fangs of the fox, and the bear that had struggled so pitifully in this same mire two summers ago. And suddenly, his victory was hollow and empty and sickening because it didn't matter what the man was or what he had done, he couldn't die like this.

There was a mossy windfall. He wrenched at it and it crumbled in his fingers. There was nothing he could use to make a safe path to the man. No reeds or rushes, no dry branches. Nothing but fragile ferns and lumps of useless fungus. He had no knife with which to cut pine boughs and there was no time to gather enough green twigs to make a dry platform. His mind raced swiftly, discarding each useless idea, almost before it formed.

Then his eye fell on the tree growing out of the bank below him. One of its branches grew over the mire. It was the one Fred had looked at so longingly a few minutes ago. The branch was about eight feet above the man's head but it would sag with Robbie's weight on it. He shinned up the trunk and inched his way along the branch. The mud was almost at Fred's armpits. The man's face was white, his eyes closed. Robbie could hear his hoarse, frightened breathing. The branch gave beneath Robbie's weight. If he hung by his hands now, Fred could reach his feet. But what would happen when he had to support Fred's weight. His fingers wouldn't hold. They'd both be pulled down into the quagmire. He bit his lip and stripped off the braided rawhide belt his father had made him for his sixth birthday. Feverishly, he slid the belt under the tree limb, put the tongue through the buckle and pulled it tight, making a loop around the branch, then he looped the remainder of the belt around his ankles twice and sunk the tongue of the steel buckle into the last hole. It was impossible now for his feet to pull loose from the tree limb. The limb might break or the belt and drop him headfirst into the mire but he tried not to think about that.

Below him, Fred opened his eyes and looked up in mingled hope and apprehension. Robbie swallowed once and then let himself down. Fred caught the outstretched arms and they locked wrist to palm like circus aerialists. Their eyes locked at the same moment. There was fear in both but it was fear controlled. The color came back into Fred's face. He said, quietly, "Listen to me, son. Whatever happens I want you to know I didn't hurt your mother. She's safe in Pineville like I told you. She had an accident, but she's all right. I love her as much as you do. I'm sorry for what I did to you. See, I ain't very bright and I . . . I didn't understand."

Robbie bit his lip. The belt was cutting into his ankles. He said, "Hurry."

Fred took a firmer grip on the skinny arms. He began to pull slowly. His body came up an inch at a time. Robbie's face twisted in agony. His arms were pulling out of their sockets and he felt the blood on his legs where the rawhide had cut through the flesh. Fred stopped pulling. He said, hollowly, "We'll never make it, Robbie. Thanks for the try." He started to release his grip and Robbie dug his fingers into Fred's huge forearms frantically. "No, don't let go! It's all right!" Fred hesitated. He looked down at the black mud and swallowed. Robbie bit his lip. "Hurry, please!"

Fred tightened his grip and pulled again as gently as he could. Tears forced themselves out of Robbie's tight shut eyes. Fred shut his own eyes. He couldn't bear to look at the twisted little face. He pulled again and the boy cried out. Once again he stopped pulling and again the boy's fingers bit into his arms. He heard Robbie's hoarse whisper. "Pull." He strained once more, shifting his grip to the boy's upper arm. The branch creaked. He held his breath and slid his left hand to Robbie's shoulder. His body came out of the slime as far as the hips. Robbie moaned with relief as the strain was transferred to his body. Gasping and straining, Fred clawed his way up the boy's body. His head came level with Robbie's chest. Another inch or two and he could reach the branch. He looked up. The overalls had slipped down from the boy's ankles and blood was oozing from beneath the rawhide cutting into the flesh. Fred closed his eyes and wriggled higher. All but his legs were loose now. He stretched upwards and his fingers touched the branch. He transferred his weight to the wood and dragged himself free. He got an elbow over the trunk. He drew himself up. He anchored a knee around a fork and bent down. He said, "Can you bend?" Robbie strained upwards from the waist and caught the outstretched hand. Fred drew him up. With shaking fingers he unbuckled the belt and guided the boy back along the branch to the trunk and lowered him to the ground.

Robbie fainted. Fred leaped down beside him. He took a handkerchief, dipped it in a pool of clean water and bathed the boy's ankles. He smoothed the shock of unruly black hair back from the forehead and cleansed the white drawn face. The closed eyelids had the faint bluish cast that she had and the curve of his cheek was like hers, too. After a moment, he picked the boy up. Through the thin fabric of the shirt he could feel the heart beating. He moved him slightly so that Robbie's head lay on his shoulder. He could feel the breath

297

against his skin. He held him gently, as one might hold something infinitely precious. He started off through the woods. He was covered with mud from head to foot. The bandage the doctor had put on his head was bloodstained and filthy. The stench of the quagmire was still in his nostrils. He should have been exhausted but the ache was gone from his muscles and the boy was a feather in his arms. He walked lightly like a man in a dream.

When he got to the road, the men had lashed some logs together and made a temporary bridge. He let them help him across the stream and into Ian Campbell's buggy but he wouldn't let them take the boy from his arms.

30

Ian Campbell came into the bathroom and laid a complete set of new clothing on the chair. He stared at Fred, naked except for a bath towel wrapped around his waist, and said dourly, "The shirt may be a wee bit too small but I've no got an unlimited supply of mammoth sizes. I've yet to see a man had a way with clothes like you have."

Fred wiped the last of the lather off his face and grinned. "I'll fix it up with you later."

"You'll fix nothin' but I'll be obliged to ye if you can make these last till I can order some more."

Fred pointed at a huge black ring around the bathtub. "There was nothin' to wash the tub with."

"Aye, well, we'll not worry about that either. It's a miracle you got yourself clean. We could smell ye half an hour before ye came in view. We had to burn everything ye had on. What happened?"

Fred reached for an undershirt. "That's kind of a secret between me an' Robbie. I'll tell you one thing. That kid's got more guts than most men."

"Ye mean ye didn't know that before today?"

Fred slid one leg into the levis thoughtfully. He said, "There's a lot of things I didn't know before today. Where is he now?"

"The doctor's tapin' up his ankles. I suppose you're not prepared to tell us how that happened either."

Fred shook his head. "You'd better ask him."

Ian drew his grizzled eyebrows together and scowled. "I

already have. I got nothin' out of him either. The both of you are about as communicative as a pair of clams. It's a mighty strange situation all 'round if you ask me."

Fred ran a comb through his stiff blond hair without any visible effect. "Can I see him now?"

"I suppose so."

They went out into the living room and Dr. McLeod fixed Fred with a baleful stare. He said, "You can find more trouble in half an hour than the average man can find in a lifetime."

Fred laughed. A rich base rumble that shook the room. The doctor and Ian stared at one another in astonishment. The doctor recovered first. He said, "Sit down and I'll change that bandage."

Fred sat obediently facing Robbie on the couch. "Have you seen your mother?"

Robbie shook his head. "Not yet, sir."

"But she knows you're back?"

"Yes, sir. Mr. Campbell told her."

Fred glanced at the boy's taped ankles and winced as the doctor unwound the last strip of bandage. He said, "We're pretty much of a mess, ain't we?"

The doctor snorted and Robbie grinned. "Yes, sir."

The doctor began wrapping Fred's head and squinted at his left eye. "Where did you get that shiner?"

Fred reached up and touched the eye gingerly. He winked at Robbie. "I ran into a windmill."

Robbie dropped his eyes and blushed.

The doctor glanced from one to the other. "What in tarnation is goin' on here?"

Fred spread his big hands eloquently. "I don't know what he means. Do you, Robbie?"

Robbie's blush deepened. Even his ears got red but there

300

was a delicious excitement in his eyes. He said, "No, sir. I don't know a-tall."

Fred said. "You see? We don't know what you mean—'a-tall.' "

The doctor grunted. "I see," he said, testily, "Well, you can go along now, Robbie, and see your mother if you want to."

Robbie bounced up. "You come, too." He was looking at Fred.

Fred frowned. He said. "Well—I—uh—I—got some things to do. You go along."

"But you'll come later."

"Sure. Sure. I'll come later."

Robbie smiled and got to his feet. He winced.

Fred said, "Maybe I better carry you."

"No, sir. It's all right, I can walk myself."

"You're sure?"

"Yes, sir. Don't forget." He went out limping a little.

Fred watched him go. He turned to the doctor. "Is it all right for him to be walkin'?"

The doctor nodded. "It won't do him any harm."

Fred turned back and looked at the door where Robbie had disappeared. "Them ankles *hurt*," he said, proudly.

The doctor glanced at Ian. Ian spread his hands and shrugged to indicate it was beyond him, too. The doctor sighed and tapped Fred on the shoulder. "You're finished. And try to stay out of trouble till it heals up, will you? I just finished taking the stitches out of the crevice Sergeant Miller gave you. Your head's beginning to look like an old baseball."

Fred touched the bandage. He said, "What are you complainin' about? If it wasn't for me you'd have nothin' to do most of the time."

The doctor scowled. "Thanks to you, I haven't had any sleep since yesterday morning. You come back here covered

301

with slime and stinking to high heaven and acting like you've just swallowed a cage full of canaries. You don't say a word about what happened or where or how you found the boy and you expect me to be delighted with you."

Fred chuckled. "Okay. I'll git along so you can git your rest." He stood up and started for the door.

The doctor said, "Fred?"

Fred turned. "Yeah?"

"Are you still figurin' on leaving?"

The light went out of Fred's eyes suddenly. "Yeah," he said, "I'm still goin'."

"What about Robbie?"

"What about him?"

"Well, he needs somebody to look after him. His mother won't be able to get out of bed for about a week."

Fred took his hand off the door and frowned. "I never thought of that."

" 'Course the Clawsons did offer to take him."

"The Clawsons?"

"Why not?"

"Why you know them Clawson kids ain't worth the powder to blow 'em up!"

The doctor kept a straight face with an effort. "What's wrong with 'em, Fred?"

"Why them kids tie cats up and then shoot at 'em with BB guns!"

"Well, you know boys will be boys."

Fred glowered fiercely. "You ever see Robbie do anythin' like that?"

"No. No. Can't say as I did."

" 'Course you ain't. You won't neither. That boy's . . . well . . . he's sensitive. He don't like to see things hurt. I don't want no son of mine bein' subjected to no influence like them Clawsons."

302

"Then you'll stay . . . just till she gets back, I mean?"

"Goddam right, I'll stay."

"Well, I'll tell the Clawsons then."

"You do that. Only . . . uh . . ."

"Only what?"

"You better not tell 'em what I said. I mean they probably think their kids is all right."

"I'll remember."

"I'll go an' git me a horse. Robbie says the mare got drowned an' I can't do much out there without a animal."

"What about Mary? You promised the boy you'd see her."

The old pain flickered in Fred's eyes. He said, "You . . . you got to git me out of that."

"How?"

"Well, can't you tell the kid . . . I mean Robbie—that she's not strong enough to have no visitors?"

"You don't want to see her?"

He balled his fists and pressed them together in front of him. "No, I can't go through that no more. I jist can't."

"All right, Fred."

"Thanks." He turned and went out.

Ian stared at the doctor in astonishment. "He's leavin'?"

The doctor sank into a chair and ran a hand over his eyes. "You heard him."

"But what for, man?"

"He's got his reasons."

"But he was so . . . so different just now. I've never heard him laugh before. And why, mon, he even made a joke. I tell ye the whole thing doesnae make sense. Look how he's suddenly taken to the lad—"

"I know. I know. Once that was the biggest hurdle of all but now . . ."

"Well, what is it then? Was it somethin' to do with the miscarriage?"

"Somethin'," the doctor said grimly. "He thinks she aborted his child."

"What are you saying, man?"

"I'm saying what Fred thinks."

"But Mary Sharron could never do a thing like that!"

"He thinks she could and he has good reasons for it."

"What reasons?"

"I can't go into that."

"But why did ye not tell him he was wrong. He *is* wrong?"

"Of course he is. And I don't quite know why I didn't tell him except that I've a suspicion I've meddled too much in this already. I think if it's to work out . . . ever . . . it has to be worked out between them. I've told her what Fred believes. If she wants him to know differently . . . if she's woman enough to sit on her pride and admit that she gave him plenty of cause for what he believes . . . then she'll tell him. If not . . . well, then, the marriage is not worth saving anyway."

Ian shook his head, heavily. "I knew they'd had a quarrel the day she fired the rocket but I'd no idea . . . no idea a-tall. Ye think it's for good then?"

"I don't know, but I know I'm all through butting in. I haven't the temperament to play psychologist. I get my emotions all mixed up with those of the patient. I love Mary Carter dearly and yet this morning I lost my temper completely and said a lot of things I regret. I hurt her, I hurt myself and I doubt if I succeeded in doing anything but make her hate her husband even more."

Ian threw up his hands. "Thank God I'm just a storekeeper. It's more peaceful that way!"

31

Fred picked Robbie up under the armpits and hurled him bodily into a pile of hay. Robbie spat out a mouthful of chaff and dove for his father's legs. Fred tried to run and Robbie tripped him. He went sprawling on the floor of the barn. Robbie was on him instantly, pummeling away mercilessly. Fred groaned. He held up his arms in dismay.

"I give in!"

Robbie seized his arms and pinioned them on his chest. "You're sure?"

"I'm sure."

"You'll not be attackin' me now when my back is turned?"

Fred shook his head.

"Cross your heart then and spit."

"You gotta let me go first."

Robbie's eyes were dancing. He released one of Fred's hands with elaborate caution, every muscle alert. "Now don't you be tryin' anythin'. I'm ready for you!"

Fred shook his head again solemnly. He moved his hand slowly up to his heart and began to cross it, then suddenly jammed his fingers under Robbie's armpit and tickled him ferociously. Robbie screeched with laughter and leaped away.

"You cheated," he crowed. "I'll get you now. You'll just see if I don't." He flung himself on Fred again and they rolled in a stifling cloud of dust. Fred suddenly went stiff. Robbie sat up scornfully. "It's no use playin' possum now. It won't save you a-tall." Fred was staring over his shoulder at the doorway of the barn. Robbie swung round and followed his glance. He leaped up and raced for the doorway. "Mother! They'd said you'd not be comin' home till tomorrow." He hugged her fiercely. "We were goin' to town to meet you."

She embraced him with a small tight smile but her eyes were on Fred. He got up slowly, dusted himself a little, and disappeared into the tack room. He shut the door quietly behind him. She bit her lip and looked down at Robbie. His face was streaked with dust and his hair full of straw but he looked wonderfully happy. He said, "I'm the champion wrestler of all."

"Are you now?"

"I am that. I beat him all the time." He turned round looking for Fred and his face fell. "Fred! Fred!" He pulled away from his mother and started for the door of the tack room.

Mary said, "Robbie!"

"Yes, ma'am."

"I wouldn't bother him now if I were you."

"Why not? It's all right."

"I'm sure it 'tis but I think maybe he wants to give us a few moments alone."

He looked from her to the door and back again. He said unbelievingly, "You said it would be all right."

She worried her lower lip with her teeth unhappily. "Well, I hoped it would, lad. I truly hoped it would . . . for all our sakes."

"But he said he loved you. He said he loved you as much as me."

"I know, darling, you told me."

"But don't you love him at all?"

He saw the tears come into her eyes. She pulled her against him fiercely. "Oh, Robbie!"

"Don't you want him to stay with us?"

"Yes, darlin', I want him to stay."

306

"Then why don't you go and tell him. He'd stay, I know he would!"

"Robbie, I can't do that."

"But why?"

"Because it wouldn't do any good. There are some things between a man and a woman can't be settled just by words and wishing. Come along to the house now and I'll make some supper."

"I'm not very hungry, ma'am."

"Well, come along anyway. I'll need your help."

"Yes, ma'am." He came slowly glancing back at the closed door of the tack room.

Fred snapped the fasteners on the suitcase. One of them didn't work and he found a piece of cord and tied it through the handle to hold the bag closed. He dug some money out of the mattress and shoved it in his pocket. He looked around. She'd come here once to change the bandage on his arm. She'd sat there on that very chair. There'd been a tiny frown of concentration on her face as she bent her head and the lamplight had made soft shadows on the milky skin. Her hair had been blue black and shining. Her lashes longer than any he had ever seen. He remembered her fingers, how gentle and soft they'd been, and she'd looked up anxiously to see if she'd hurt him and caught him staring at her. And his heart had thudded in embarrassment and he'd turned away half angrily feeling the blood rush to his face. And he'd lain on that iron cot getting stinking drunk, thinking about raping her. His palms still sweated when he thought of that moment. He must have been insane. He'd flung a bottle through that window the night she refused to marry him and split his knuckles on the door. He didn't think he could ever do anything like that again. Something had gone out of him now and he didn't know whether he was glad or sorry. And it was all over. He hadn't been ready for it and probably he never

307

would be. He didn't regret very much now except the kids, the one living and the one dead. Somehow it had never occurred to him that he could ever be a father. A real father . . . well, it was just something else that couldn't be helped or changed. He had deserved the rest probably, but she might have spared him that. And yet he couldn't hate her. The thought of her still filled him with a kind of wonder which shouldn't have gone with the ache in his loins and the dryness in his throat but did just the same.

He picked up the suitcase and went out closing the door. He thought about taking the rig she'd brought out from town. It was still in the barnyard where she had left it. But he couldn't take it without asking her and he didn't want to do that. He ought to say good-by to the boy, at least, but he couldn't face up to that either. Better to cut it clean. They wouldn't notice him leave. They'd be all wrapped up in each other. He started across the barnyard. He passed the porch and the back steps. He was almost at the drive. One more step and he'd be out of sight till he reached the road. The screen door banged.

"And just where do you think you're goin', Mr. Carter?"

He stopped with a sticky, panicky feeling in his chest. He turned slowly, the red creeping into his face. "Why I . . . guess I . . . I'm leavin'."

"In that condition?"

He looked down at his clothes and brushed uneasily at the straw still clinging to his trousers. "It don't matter," he mumbled self-consciously.

"Does it not indeed? I'll have no husband of mine goin' off lookin' like a hobo."

"But . . ."

"You march right back in this house and take a bath."

He stared at her, his mouth half open. "A bath?"

"You heard me—a bath. Did I not find you and Robbie

grubbin' in the dust of the barn a few minutes since? I'll not be disgraced by havin' you go off like that."

"But I . . . I . . ."

"Don't stand there scuffin' the dust, man. You'll be trackin' it into my kitchen and I've just this moment finished cleanin' it. Now come along before I lose my patience altogether."

He came back slowly and up the steps.

She said, "Leave that suitcase out here. You'll not be needin' it inside."

He came into the kitchen awkwardly, all hands and feet. Robbie was sitting at the table, watching him gravely. Fred tried unsuccessfully to smile. He half raised his hand and let it fall. He said, "Hi, Robbie."

Robbie nodded. "Good evenin' to you, sir."

Fred stood wiping the palms of his hands on his trousers, while Mary pushed past him efficiently. He said, "Your maw . . . that is, your mother—she thinks we ought to take a bath."

"I already took one."

"Oh, yeah. I didn't notice."

Mary came back. "I suppose neither of you thought of takin' a bath while I was away?"

Fred's eyes met Robbie's.

"I thought as much," Mary said. "And what do I find when I come home but the two of you up to your ears in dirt." She thrust a pair of enormous white towels at Fred. "Here. You'll find the water hot and waitin'."

Fred took the towels. "Yes, ma'am." He went off to the bathroom. The moment the door closed, Mary looked at Robbie. "And what are you sittin' there for when there's things to be done?"

He bounced off the chair. "Yes, ma'am."

"And hurry!"

"Yes, ma'am."

As he went out of the kitchen Mary turned to the sink and

309

leaned against it. She bent her head and pressed her finger-tips against her eyes. "Holy Virgin," she whispered aloud, "I don't deserve it, but please help me. I've got to have time and this is the only way I know. He's got to believe I didn't take his child. *He's got to!* If he goes believin' what he does, he'll carry the black shadow of it to his grave. Help me, Mother. Show me the way to tell him without admittin' that I know what he thinks. That's something else that mustn't ever trouble him waking or sleeping as long as he lives."

The splashing from the bathroom eased and she straightened up. She took a deep breath and pushed herself away from the sink. She waited a minute or so and then went to knock on the bathroom door. "Are you finished in there?"

His voice came through the door partly muffled. "Yes, ma'am."

"Well, put a towel around you then. Your clothes are laid out in the bedroom."

There was a moment's pause and he opened the door. He had one of the big white towels wrapped around his waist. She gasped inwardly as she saw his torso. He had ripped off most of the adhesive but his whole chest and the part of his stomach she could see was a mass of partly healed cuts and gashes. The doctor's words rang in her ears. "Not one in a thousand could have made it—not one in a million would even have tried." She bent her head quickly so he would not see her eyes. Less than a hour since he'd been wrestling with Robbie in the barn. It must have been terribly painful and yet he would not have said anything. She realized abruptly that in all the time she had known him she had never heard him complain. She pushed past him into the room and began picking up his clothes. She said, "Well, that's a bit better. Now go and get dressed before you catch your death."

She felt him leave silently and turned to watch him go. His back, too, looked as if it had been raked with barbed wire.

And yet even the lacerations could not detract from the hard beauty of his body. The long sculptured muscles, the massive corded shoulders, and the slender waist. The big blunt honest hands. She called out, "I've laid out a razor and all the rest."

He went on into the bedroom without answering. His neck was still red but whether from anger or embarrassment or only the heat of the bath, she couldn't tell.

Robbie popped into the kitchen. "All ready?"

"All ready. Can you do it now?"

"I can. But will it be dark enough?"

She glanced out the window. "It will be by the time he's finished shavin' and all. Now hurry."

"I will." He dodged away and she hurried into Robbie's room.

In the master bedroom, Fred stood staring down at the clothes she had laid out for him. He had never worn such clothes in his life. There was a pair of gray trousers, beautifully tailored, but without any buttons for suspenders. Instead there was a narrow black belt run through the loops. Beside the trousers was an open-throated shirt of soft green and gray plaid. On the floor were black shoes without tops and light gray hand-knitted socks with small green diamond clocks. Even the undershorts were new. He reached out and touched the shirt. It was the softest wool he had ever felt. He lifted the trousers. They weighed almost nothing. He half turned toward the door to go back for the stained levis he had left in the bathroom but then he remembered she had taken them. He turned back and sat on the edge of the bed. He was bewildered and nervous. It would almost have been better if she'd been angry or silent like she had been before. He knew now how to cope with that. He didn't understand her this way. Why couldn't she just have let him go and be done with it? Seeing her again had brought back all the old hunger. He supposed it would never leave him. He shook his head and crossed to the mirror. The water in the pitcher was hot. When he had shaved he dried his face and sat again on the edge of the bed. In spite of everything, the bath had relaxed him. He didn't feel now like facing the thirteen miles into town. And how could he walk into Pineville wearing these fancy clothes? Damn, he should have pretended he didn't hear when she called to him. Now he was tired and hungry and miserable. He had thirteen miles to walk in the dark and he had to go out and face the both of them looking like a fancy Dan. He squeezed his fists together and swore silently. Well, it didn't matter really. He'd looked like a fool a good many times before. It wouldn't hurt once more. He put on the clothes. He was surprised to find that they felt good. Warm and yet unexpectedly light but they were bound to look ridiculous.

Apprehensively he moved over to the mirror. He stared at himself. His eyes widened. He frowned. He turned away impatiently but the mirror drew him back like a magnet. He shook his head. In his whole life he had never looked in a mirror without a certain distaste. His face was too big and his nose had been broken and his clothes had never fit. His collars always wrinkled. His hair wouldn't stay down and he could scrub for hours and somehow he always looked like a bum. He could hardly believe the man in the mirror was Fred Carter. The face hadn't changed or the hair but the clothes made him look different. How could they make such a difference and why hadn't he ever thought of buying clothes like this before? He pulled up his trousers. The green in his socks matched his shirt. He let the trousers fall again and then went to the door. He took a deep breath and opened it.

The room was candlelit and in the soft light of the tiny flames fresh linen gleamed on the circular table and glasses and silver sparkled on the cloth. She was arranging the silver with her back to him. Her dress was cut off the shoulders and

312

her skin shone like white marble in the candlelight. She turned. He stood in stunned astonishment, his throat thickening. Her eyes were blacker than jet, her hair swept back from her forehead and caught with a silver band. Her face was a clean lovely oval in the shadows. He had never seen the dress before. It was a kind of deep blue and it caught rich highlights along the curve of her breast and the slender length of her waist. She looked at him carefully and there was pride and pleasure in her eyes.

She said softly, "I don't wonder you're surprised but Robbie and I decided that just once before you leave we should have a proper dinner."

Robbie appeared from the shadows at the far corner of the room. He stared at his father and said, "You look grand, Fred."

Fred turned his head to look at Robbie but he couldn't speak. Mary came forward and took his arm. She led him to the table. "You sit here."

He allowed himself to be seated, his head swimming and his eyes followed her around the table. "Robbie, you sit here." Robbie sat, his eyes unnaturally bright in the candlelight, turning from his mother to Fred and back again. Mary sat opposite Fred. "Now then, Fred. Would you say grace." She folded her hands. "Fred!"

He started and her words sounded again in his inner ear. He bent his head but his tongue was thick and his mouth dry. He swallowed painfully, then he said, "For what we are about to receive may the Lord make us grateful." Mary and Robbie echoed an "Amen."

She smiled across the table. "Thank you, Fred."

He looked at her and at Robbie and suddenly pushed himself erect. He said, "I got to get out of here!"

She gave a little cry and came round to him as he started away. She caught his arm. "Fred, please!" He didn't dare look at her. He stared straight ahead. His jaw set, the muscles in his face pulled into hard lines. "Fred, listen to me. We've all been terribly wrong about a lot of things. Me most of all. You want to leave and I don't blame you for that. But don't go like this. Is it too much to ask of you to share a meal with us before you go? I'll not ask anything more of you, I promise. *Please!*" He turned to look at her. He saw that she wasn't fooling with him like she'd been about the bath. She wasn't trying to humiliate him. She meant it. He turned and came slowly back to the table. They ate in silence. He scarcely touched his food. Try as he would, he could not tear his eyes away from her.

When the meal was over Robbie excused himself and disappeared. Mary sat with her head bowed, her hands in her lap. Fred watched her, the frown still on his face. Finally he waved a hand at the table. He said, "Why did you do this?"

She raised her head. Her eyes were a trifle red. She said emptily, "Does it matter now?"

He cleared his throat. "I thought first you were tryin' to make a fool of me."

"Fred . . ."

"I know now you wasn't but, Mary, it ain't no good. I can't never be the kind of man you want." He looked down at his clothes. "You can dress me up any way you like but it don't change what I am."

"You can't forgive me, is that it?"

He shook his head helplessly. "It ain't I can't forgive. I ain't foolin' myself. I can't stop lovin' you no more'n I can stop breathing. I won't never be able to forget the way you look right now but . . . I don't know the words . . . I can't explain nothin'. I just know I got to git away."

Oh Holy Mary, she thought, help me now, please! Another minute and he'll be gone and no way to get him back. She bit her lip. She said, "Robbie will be heartbroken."

He squeezed his fists together on the tablecloth. He said huskily, "I was all wrong about him. He's a good kid. I mean . . . a good boy. I wonder you didn't shoot me for what I done."

The chord sang inside of her. She said quickly, "I wanted to—I thought about it. For a while—I even thought I didn't want your child." She bent her head quickly so that she wouldn't see his face but she felt him freeze. She didn't dare look up again. She twisted her hands in her lap. Her palms were damp. She said, "The doctor told me I was pregnant the day after they arrested you. I was all mixed up. Confused and frightened and I thought I hated you so much that I even thought . . . God forgive me . . . of doing something to get rid of the child." Her voice was low now but the words thundered against his ears. "I think it must have been God's punishment on me when I lost it. I know it must have been terrible for you but it was worse for me. I've wanted another baby ever since Robbie was born."

She sat with her head bowed, waiting. An eternity later he said hoarsely, "*You wanted my baby?*"

She brought her head up. Her eyes were wet again but they were clear and unafraid. She met his glance squarely. She said, "I wanted it."

The silence fell again but the thunder had gone out of it. He looked down at the tablecloth and toyed with a fork. He said finally, "I was thinkin' . . ."

"Yes?"

"Well, it's gettin' kind of late and I was thinkin' maybe . . . that is—if you didn't mind. I might stay over till mornin'."

"I think that'd be very nice, Fred."

"I'll take my stuff back to the barn."

She looked across the table at him. His head was bent and his neck, as usual, was flaming red. She bit her lip, then got up and came around the table. She stood beside him and put

315

her hand under his chin and raised his face. She said, softly, "And is it the barn that you'd like to be sleepin' this night? Am I so old then, and so ugly, that I can't bring your manhood upon you? Can you not . . ."

She never finished. He was out of the chair, his mouth buried on hers, crushing her to him. The breath went out of her and she strained against him, her eyes brimming. When he released her she clung to him fiercely while he buried his face in her hair and kissed the hollow in her neck. He felt a wild singing under his heart.

He said, huskily, "The doctor told me you could have another baby." She leaned away from him and the tender mockery that had not been in her eyes for years bubbled deep and soundless. She said, "He said more than that to me. He said with a little effort we might be havin' several. I gather from the way you've been carryin' on you'd not be adverse to the effort."

The smile started at his eyes.